INTO THE SUNSHINE

◆

MARK RITTER

◆ A NOVEL ◆

GMH
PUBLISHING

Published by GMH Publishing LLC

First Edition: January 2020

Scripture quotations are taken from the *Holy Bible*, King James Version.

The publisher is not responsible for websites, or their content, that are not owned by the publisher.

Cover Design and Book Design by Mark Ritter
Cover © 2020 by Mark Ritter. All rights reserved.
Cover Photograph taken by Mark Ritter. © 2020 by Mark Ritter. All rights reserved.
Author Photograph self-taken by Mark Ritter

ISBN 978-0-578-55632-1 (paperback)

Also available in e-book format.

*Dedicated to my Mom and Dad
for their endless love and support.*

Connect With the Author

To stay updated on the status of my upcoming books, to read insightful posts, or to simply see pictures from whatever hiking trip I've recently taken...follow me on Twitter at:
www.twitter.com/MarkRitterBooks
Or search for my Twitter username: **@MarkRitterBooks**

After arriving on my Twitter page, click the "Follow" button to be sure to see all of my posts!

Contact for Fundraiser Opportunities

If you'd like to learn more on how this book could potentially be used as a fundraiser at the church you lead or attend, please email the publisher to find out if there are currently any promotions running: **gmhpublishing@outlook.com**

Acknowledgements

First and foremost...thanks be to God for giving me the gift and motivation to write. It's my hope that this book contains a strong and uplifting Christian message that is pleasing to Him.

Second, my parents...my Mom for being the best and most caring mother you could ever imagine; for using her skills as a teacher to teach me how to be a good writer at a very early age; and for fully proofreading this book. And my Dad for always thinking of us before himself, and for enduring a very demanding job for many years to provide for us.

Third, since I haven't found the girl of my dreams yet, and also have no siblings, I'll move on to mentioning three of my best friends who've shaped who I am today. I don't know who to mention first, so I'll go in alphabetical order. Joel, for always being an encouraging and dependable friend and never letting me forget the humorous side of life. Paul, for also being an encouraging and dependable friend to relate to as we've had such similar life experiences. And Ryan, for becoming a supportive and valued friend, all from what began as a mere church acquaintance.

Fourth, my Aunt Marilyn for being a wonderful aunt, and for generously contributing to the editing process of this book by doing a comprehensive proofread before it was published.

Beyond that, I want to thank anyone and everyone who I've ever called a friend or girlfriend at different times in my life. I've learned that God places different people in our lives at different times, for different purposes. That's generally a good thing and helps us develop more as people. But on the sad side of that, it means that sometimes people can drift away simply because situations change...we don't go to school anymore, we don't work together anymore, or we don't live in the same apartment complex or neighborhood anymore. But to all of you, I'm very grateful for the time we've shared together, and you are not forgotten!

Finally, I want to thank *you* for choosing to read this book! I truly hope you enjoy it!

INTO THE SUNSHINE

◆ 1 ◆

Friday, April 16th
Hotel Room in Nashville, TN
3:16 p.m. (Central Time)

As I sat next to Megan on that sad spring day many years ago, I remember how I was trying my hardest to hold back my tears. I couldn't remember the last time I had cried, and I didn't want this to be the next. It wasn't because I was embarrassed or because I felt compelled to prove my masculinity. It was rather because I knew staying strong—or at least appearing to—was the best thing I could do for Megan at that point.

That wasn't easy, though, sitting next to her in my college dorm room that morning as she cried harder than I'd ever seen her cry. From when we first met during our freshman year, all the way to this point in our senior year, this was by far the most daunting thing we'd ever faced for that whole time we'd been a couple. Honestly, it was really hard right then to understand why God was letting all of this happen.

She then looked at me with her tear-filled eyes, as we sat next to each other on the edge of my bed. She sniffled and then spoke in a broken voice. "I can't believe this is happening, Kevin."

I inhaled nervously, not knowing quite what to say as I held her a little tighter with my arm that was already around her. "I know," I finally said, exhaling and still trying my hardest to hold back my tears.

As I looked at her, she held tissues to her eyes as she kept crying. Her light brown hair was tied back in a ponytail that morning. She wore light tan shorts, and also wore a dark brown t-shirt, which used to be mine.

I remember how Megan liked the way that t-shirt complimented my dark brown hair when I'd wear it. But after a few washes, it shrank just enough that it was too tight across my shoulders. Thanks to my somewhat broad shoulders and trim waist, I still have that problem with shirts, even today. So I gave her the shirt, and she ended up wearing it quite often back then. With her skinny and petite figure, it was big on her, but she always looked pretty cute in it, in my opinion.

In fact, that was the shirt she wore just a week before that when we went for one of our afternoon hiking trips to take advantage of a warm spring day. We went to our usual hiking place—a state park not too far from campus. We had a good time that day—as we always did—and neither of us would've ever imagined we'd be sitting next to each other facing what we were facing just a week later. But we were.

Other than the sound of her crying, I remember how my dorm room was completely silent that morning. It was barely 9:00 a.m. and I remember how the usual morning sunshine was pouring in through the window. But from the time Megan had come over to my room that morning, the silhouette of bright light it created on the floor had already inched closer to the window as the sun was getting higher in the sky. Ironically, it promised to be a nice day outside with blue skies and summer-like warmth—quite nice for early May in northern Indiana.

After a few minutes passed, I remember how it seemed Megan was able to gather herself some. She then looked over at me, still sniffling some and wiping her eyes. "I'm sorry for all of this crying."

I turned toward her, feeling overwhelming sympathy. "It's fine," I said in a gentle voice while still trying not to cry.

She then wrapped both of her arms around me as we sat there holding each other for several quiet minutes. It was in those moments I fully realized the magnitude of this situation. There was no question that our lives would soon look a lot different because of this...in more ways than I even knew at that point.

~ ~ ~

Now, as I sit here this afternoon in this hotel room in Nashville, it's been almost eight years since that day. Considering the reason that's brought me here to Nashville right now, it's no surprise my thoughts keep going back to that day...and my time in college. I suppose that would explain why I decided to take out my laptop from my suitcase and do something I haven't done for a while—journal.

There's a big and quite elegant-looking maple desk next to the window in this room, so here I sit, typing. With the window open, the light breeze from this 74-degree April day feels very nice right now. The window also gives me a nice third floor view of a well-landscaped boulevard just a few hundred feet away. Even though it's approaching 3:30 p.m. on a Friday, rush hour traffic doesn't seem to have started yet. But as I watch some occasional cars pass by, it serves as one more reminder that time never stops.

I seem to realize that a little more with each passing year. From the time I became an airline pilot, the years of my life have gone unbelievably fast. Looking back, it's obvious my career has progressed nicely. Even though I had to work my way up through the ranks by enduring some lower-level pilot jobs, the job I have now—flying full-size aircraft—is undoubtedly my dream job. But other than my career, I have to admit I'm disappointed I'm still single.

It's reflective moments like these when I wonder how I got to be twenty-nine years old already—with thirty not that far away. But what's probably more unbelievable is that I've been out of college for almost eight years already. When I think back to all the memories I have from college, they don't seem nearly that long ago.

Unfortunately, of all of those memories, the ones I've been thinking about the most right now are obviously from that sad spring day when I sat with Megan crying beside me in my dorm room—and, of course, from everything that transpired after that. However, I can't forget there were many good times that Megan and I shared together before that. Some even felt like a dream...a very good dream.

Like the day we first met—that's still my favorite memory of our time together. It's safe to say that none of the great times Megan and I shared together would've ever happened if things hadn't worked out exactly the way they did on that late-summer day, early in our freshman year when our paths crossed for the very first time.

~ ~ ~

That day was August 23rd, to be exact, and it was the day I went away to college. It's hard to believe—and accept—that almost eleven and a half years have passed since that day now. But I still remember it as clear as ever. That morning began with my parents and little sister helping me move into my freshman dorm room at the college I'd chosen in Indiana.

I remember moving wasn't a pleasant task that day since Indiana—along with the entire Midwest—was in the middle of a late-summer heat wave right then. But thankfully, the moving process didn't take nearly as much time as I thought. Soon enough, it was time for the inevitably sad goodbye before my parents and sister headed back home.

Not much later, I met my roommate, Scott, when he arrived with his parents and began moving in. He seemed nice, but it still felt weird that I'd be sharing a room with someone whom I barely knew. After he finished moving in, he and his parents left to go buy some last minute things he needed for the dorm room. So since my parents and sister were already on their way back home to the Chicago suburbs, I decided to head to the campus bookstore to buy the textbooks I needed. Little did I know what would happen in the moments to follow.

It was mid-afternoon by that point and I remember how the sun was beating down as I walked across the campus. I looked around as I tried to acquaint myself with my new surroundings. I remember that some of the older brick buildings looked very rich in history—and architecture—as they'd probably seen many students just like me come and go every four years throughout the past decades.

I also remember the exact navy blue polo shirt and khaki shorts I wore that day. They were a going-away present that my parents and sister had given me that morning. I had a feeling I'd be wearing that outfit a lot in the coming weeks. Every time I thought about how nice of a gift it was, it reminded me how much I already missed them, which almost brought tears to my eyes as I walked.

~   ~   ~

A few minutes later, I found the campus bookstore and as I walked up to the entrance, I saw someone walking behind me out of the corner of my eye. When I got to the door, I thought I'd be polite and open it for them.

When I did, I turned around and saw it was a girl with long light brown hair, wearing sunglasses, which she took off as she approached the door. She smiled and thanked me as I held the door for her. Her cute smile and the quick glimpse I got of her charming brown eyes all made a lasting impression on me.

Like me, she was certainly dressed for summer. She wore a bright pink t-shirt with tan shorts and flip-flops, and I noticed she had a slight suntan.

When we got inside, she took a plastic shopping basket from the stack they had inside the door and handed it to me.

"This is for opening the door for me," she said, smiling, as she then took one for herself.

"Thanks," I said.

We proceeded to hunt down the textbooks we needed in the store, and unfortunately, we disappeared from each other among the many tall aisles of books. I quickly became regretful that I didn't start more of a conversation because from the very short impression I got from her, she seemed like a nice person.

Thankfully, God didn't let us go too far from each other. Just a few minutes later, with each of us having quite a few heavy books in our baskets, we found ourselves in the same aisle.

I looked over at her. "Are you following me?" I joked.

She smiled. "No, I'm trying to find the History book I need."

After we established we were both freshmen, both needed the same book, and would be in the same History class together, I took one from the shelf and set it in her basket that she was now holding with both hands. Then I took another for myself and held it up and examined it for a few seconds.

"Wow, we're going to build a lot of muscle carrying this thing around all semester," I said.

She giggled. "I know. This thing is like half my body weight."

I laughed, thinking she might almost be right since she looked to be around 5'4" with a slender build.

"I'm Kevin, by the way," I said, reaching out to shake her hand.

She set her basket down and shook my hand. "I'm Megan. It's nice to meet you," she said with a smile.

Since that was the last textbook we both needed, we then walked to the checkout line together. The line wasn't too long, but I was glad to see there were still about four people ahead of us, which would give us a chance to talk some more.

We both set our baskets down on the floor as we stood and waited. Then I curiously looked down at hers. "How is it you have almost twice as many books as I have?" I asked.

She smiled. "That's probably because I'm an English Literature major and the whole subject is based on books."

I nodded. "That makes sense. So what do you want to do with that major?" I asked.

"After I graduate, I want to get my master's degree and then my Ph.D. so I can become a professor and teach English...but hopefully literature too."

"Hmm, that's neat," I said. "What made you want to do that?"

"Well, ever since I was a little girl, I've always loved reading. It's always amazed me how a really good story or poem has such great power to touch so many people in so many ways."

I nodded. "You're right," I said, realizing how passionate she is about literature. "It definitely sounds like you picked the right major."

"Yeah, it wasn't a hard choice," she said. "So what's your major?" she asked curiously.

"Aeronautical Engineering," I said. "Ultimately, I want to become a commercial airline pilot, but my parents wanted me to get a degree first, so I decided to learn how to design planes before I learn how to fly them."

"That's a neat way to go about it. What made you want to be a pilot?" she asked, tilting her head a little as she looked at me.

"Well, from the first time I got on a plane when I was a kid, I remember how I was so amazed that flying was even possible. I was glued to the window for the whole flight. And I remember how we climbed through the clouds, into the sunshine, and it felt like we'd entered a different world. It was so dreary on the ground that day, but in the sky, the clouds were bright white and it was as sunny as you could ever imagine."

She smiled. "Well, it sounds like *you* picked the right major too."

The line moved a little, so we both shoved our baskets forward with our feet.

"So where are you from?" I asked.

"Columbus, Ohio," she said. "What about you?"

"Chicago...but technically about thirty miles west of the downtown area...in the suburbs."

"Do you like it there?" she asked.

"Pretty much," I said. "But I don't have much to compare

it to because I've lived there my whole life...even in the same house...until today, of course."

She nodded with understanding. "I've actually lived in the same house my whole life too. I think it's going to feel really weird being away like this and only seeing my parents and little brother every six weeks or so. I'm really going to miss them...and my church too."

"Yeah, I'm definitely going to miss my parents and sister...and my church," I said. "But they have a church on campus here that's supposed to be pretty good."

"Can I help who's next, please?" the cashier shouted.

We both looked at each other and Megan signaled me to go ahead, but I insisted she go first. As she walked up to the counter, I was disappointed I didn't get a chance to ask her to the student union to have ice cream, which was the plan I'd been formulating in my mind as we'd been talking. But then I remembered she'd be in my History class, so this wouldn't be my only chance. Nevertheless, I still really hoped that she'd wait for me after she checked out.

Thankfully, she did, and I actually helped her carry all of her books back to her dorm room after that. Her roommate hadn't moved in yet, but Megan still had her side of the room mostly unpacked and situated. What I noticed most was how many books she had stacked up high on the shelves above her desk. She explained that those were for recreational reading, which she obviously did a lot of. After we set down the textbooks we'd just bought, I finally asked her if she wanted to go get ice cream, and she eagerly said yes.

~   ~   ~

We ended up staying at the student union and talking until long after we finished our ice cream. It was about two hours, but it barely felt like thirty minutes as we both clearly enjoyed each other's company. Then later that same day, we met up again for dinner and ended up talking even longer. It was obvious that our personalities were very magnetic and we enjoyed every second we spent together.

As I walked her back to her dorm that night, it was around 8:30 p.m. and it was mostly dark. I remember as we casually walked across campus, I felt more and more butterflies in my stomach as we got closer to her dorm. I wanted so badly to reach out and hold her hand, and even more, I wanted to kiss her before this night was over. Finally, I was able to carry out the easier one of those and I reached for her hand. Before I knew it, our hands joined effortlessly and she turned to me and smiled as we walked.

By the time we arrived at the front door of her building, my heart was racing because I knew if I was going to kiss her, it would have to be now. But instead, we stood and looked at each other for a few seconds, and I'll never forget how the traces of light from the building illuminated her face on that warm night—she was absolutely beautiful.

She looked up into my eyes. "I don't know if I've ever seen anyone with your color eyes before. They're like this pretty combination of blue and gray."

I smiled. "People tell me they change colors depending on what color I'm wearing."

She giggled. "Seriously? Or are you just messing with me?"

"No, I'm serious," I said. "Tomorrow, if I wear a gray shirt, I'm sure they'll look more gray than blue."

"Will I see you tomorrow?" she asked.

"I hope so," I said.

She smiled. "Me too."

At that moment, I was finally able to gather the courage to

kiss her. As soon as our lips met, I knew I'd remember that moment for the rest of my life. After that, we set plans to meet up for lunch the next day. Then we kissed again and finally said goodnight before I headed back to my dorm.

When I went to bed that night, I remember lying awake in the dark for several hours while Scott was sound asleep in his bed across the room from me. It really hit me right then how much my life had changed that day. I was living in a different place, sleeping in a different bed, and many miles away from my parents and sister.

But what filled my mind the most was how ecstatic I was about having met Megan. I knew starting a relationship with her would probably bring the biggest change to my life of them all, and I couldn't have been more excited about that.

I said a long prayer that night thinking of Ecclesiastes 3:1, "To every thing there is a season, and a time to every purpose under the heaven…"[1] I asked God to guide me through this new season of my life called college that He had bestowed upon me. I also thanked Him for introducing me to Megan and asked Him to do His will, hoping so much that this new season would be the beginning of Megan and me becoming a big part of each other's lives.

~   ~   ~

In the weeks to follow, we *did* become a big part of each other's lives and it didn't take long before we were seeing each other virtually every day. Back then, a typical day for us included going to our classes throughout the day, sometimes meeting up for a quick lunch, but definitely meeting up for dinner each night at the student union. After we'd eat there, we'd go downstairs and play pool or go bowling, and then later on we'd usually end up in the quiet study area sharing a couch, fully immersed in our schoolwork.

After that, we'd usually drop off our backpacks at our dorm rooms and take a leisurely nighttime walk around the campus. We'd hold hands and simply enjoy the beauty of whatever season it happened to be—unless it was bitterly cold, of course.

Many times, those walks would bring us to a place on campus that we referred to as "our spot." It was a quiet and secluded place behind the science building that overlooked an open area of campus that had grass blanketing the rolling hills and a few evergreen trees in the distance. We'd usually lie down in the grass, hold hands and look up at the sprawling Indiana sky. On clear nights it held many stars, and sometimes, a very bright moon. Some of our deepest conversations happened right there...and, of course, we did our share of kissing there as well.

Even though that's how many nights looked for us, we still found a good variety of other things to do...many times, with our mutual friends. We all went to quite a few basketball and football games on campus, and also went to the campus recreation center to swim fairly often—even though none of us were elite swimmers by any means.

But no matter what we did, every day Megan and I would make time to read the Bible together and then join hands and pray. We also went to the campus church service every Sunday. Needless to say, our faith was always a big element of our relationship. That's probably why, early on, we decided to save ourselves for marriage.

It was also our faith that taught us to accept and love each other for who we were. When the "fairy-tale" stage of our relationship began to wear off after the first few months, we discovered each other's flaws and realized we didn't always agree on everything. But despite all of that, we learned to love each other anyway and our love only grew stronger as our relationship progressed.

As our time in college pressed forward, I don't think there was much doubt in either of our minds that we'd get married someday. But sadly, that never happened, and that's when these memories start to bring a heaviness to my heart again as I sit here typing this.

~ ~ ~

Now, many years have passed since our time in college...and since that sad spring day at the end of our senior year when everything as we knew it fell apart for us. After that, it was no surprise that I felt a lot of loneliness and sadness from not having Megan in my life anymore. I'm quite certain she felt the same at that point. But what surprised me was just how different my life felt without her. We'd become such a huge part of each other's lives, and then, all of a sudden, we weren't.

But as time passed, I thought about her less and less, and we proceeded to go all of these years without seeing each other or talking. But that'll change today because we'll soon come face to face at a rehearsal for our friends' wedding—the very wedding that's brought me here to Nashville for this weekend.

I remember when I officially found out about this wedding; it was about ten months ago. I got a call from Scott—the same Scott who was my college roommate—and he was eager to tell me that he and his girlfriend, Rachel, had just gotten engaged. Not surprisingly, he proceeded to ask me to be his best man. Obviously, I quickly said yes, given that we've been best friends since all the way back to our freshman year of college.

Since then, we've been like brothers, and ironically we've even been mistaken as brothers more than a few times. We're both about 5'10", have short dark brown hair, and have a fairly athletic build. However, I'd say we only share a slight facial resemblance, if any. Either way, I've always referred to him as the brother I never had, and I'm honored to be his best man.

As for the maid of honor, Rachel chose Megan because their friendship originated in much the same way as it did for Scott and me. They were also paired up as roommates for their freshman year, but unlike Scott and me, they weren't mistaken as siblings very often, if ever.

Rachel is several inches taller than Megan and she's a brunette, which is a noticeable contrast to Megan's 5'4" stature and light brown hair. But in the beginning, they also had some differences in lifestyle, which led to a rough start to their friendship. However, they eventually became very close and have remained best friends ever since.

Beyond all of that, there's actually a much bigger reason that I'm the best man and Megan is the maid of honor. It's safe to say, Scott and Rachel may have never met—or ever cared to meet—if it wasn't for Megan and me.

Simply put, Scott and Rachel were quite different from each other back in the early part of our freshman year. Scott, like me, was very strong in his faith and wouldn't miss church for anything. On the other hand, Rachel had strayed from her faith pretty quickly after beginning college.

Even though she was one of the top players on the college soccer team—even as a freshman—she didn't make the best choices off the field. She and several of her teammates went to quite a few drinking parties back then, and they weren't even able to remember much of it the next day. Unfortunately, she didn't find her way to church much at all at that point.

But one Sunday in October of our freshman year, Megan

was somehow able to convince Rachel to join us for our weekly tradition of going to church. Soon after that, Megan and Rachel's friendship began to grow, as did Rachel's faith. A few weeks later, Scott joined us for church one Sunday, even though he usually attended an earlier service. It was at that point he and Rachel met for the first time, and they surprisingly hit it off. As they say, the rest was history.

But I never thought it would've taken them eleven and a half years to get married from that point. But since Rachel had grown so strong in her faith, she felt called to go on a long-term mission trip overseas after they graduated. So while Scott accepted a job and moved here to Nashville, Rachel was across the world on a mission trip that ended up lasting longer than either of them had expected. They tried to stay together while she was gone, but they eventually broke up, only to get back together when she returned home a few years ago. In the end, I'm glad it all worked out for them.

~   ~   ~

I'm also glad to be a part of their wedding. That would certainly explain the excitement—along with some nervousness—I felt this morning as I caught a flight from Chicago down here to Nashville. Considering Scott didn't want a bachelor party, the groomsmen and I took him to lunch at his favorite restaurant shortly after I got here. We actually ate outside and the sunny, 74-degree day made it very comfortable. After lunch, we went to the tuxedo shop to do our final try-on.

Actually, I'm still thinking about something that happened there. After we were all handed our freshly pressed tuxedos wrapped in plastic, we headed to the dressing rooms. Only a few seconds after all of our dressing room doors closed, I heard

Scott's phone ring through the soft rustling of all of us unwrapping our tuxedos.

"Hey Rachel," he quickly answered. "Yep, we're here right now trying them on." After a few more seconds, he spoke again. "I don't know. I don't have it on yet. But I'm sure it'll look fine."

Even though there were several dressing rooms between him and me, I could still hear every word of his call.

"How's everything going on your end?" he then asked her.

He paused for a few seconds. "Oh, you went with Megan? How's she feeling now?"

After several seconds, he eventually replied with a disappointing tone. "Hmm. Well, we should be thankful that she's at least well enough to be here at the wedding. A few months ago, it didn't look like she'd be able to do this."

I had no clue what he was talking about, but it didn't sound good. Either way, I felt some sympathy for Megan when I heard that.

Then he continued. "Okay, yeah. I should go too. I still have to try this on. I love you, too. Bye."

He didn't say anything about it after we were done trying on our tuxedos—nor did I ask him about it. I figured if it was something he wanted to tell me, he probably would've by now. After all, since college, every so often he's filled me in on what Megan is up to—from what he hears from Rachel.

In fact, a while back, during the planning stages of this wedding, he shared with me that she had a boyfriend and she'd be bringing him to this wedding. Even though it was the first I'd heard of that, he said they'd already been together for "a while." I was happy for her when I heard that.

After we were done at the tuxedo shop, Scott had to finish a few things before the rehearsal. But he insisted he didn't need me or the groomsmen to help him with anything. So he encouraged us to go out and enjoy the nice weather...or go back to the hotel and relax until the rehearsal at 5:00 p.m.

The groomsmen chose the latter so they could spend some time with their wives. Since I don't have a wife—or a girlfriend—and since I just had plenty of time in the sun during a layover a few days ago in Miami, I chose to come back to my hotel room. I took a nap and then I began typing this journal entry.

Now, it's time to bring this to an end, since I still need to change clothes before I leave for the rehearsal. I have to say, I'm still thinking about what I overheard Scott saying on the phone earlier about Megan. I can't help but wonder what to expect when I see her now. Will she be sick? Will she be injured? I really don't know, but I hope it's nothing serious.

Aside from all of that concern swirling in my mind right now, I'm also feeling plenty of nervousness. No matter what, it's going to feel weird seeing her again, given that we haven't seen each other since college. It'll also be weird meeting her boyfriend. It's not because of jealousy, but rather because I know situations like that have a way of feeling awkward...at least for me. But beyond all of that, it still seems sort of surreal that in less than a half hour from now, I'll be standing face to face with her after all of these years.

◆ 2 ◆

It's safe to say my nervousness was in full force earlier today when I drove up to the church where the rehearsal was being held. After I parked, I saw it was 4:48 p.m., which meant I was twelve minutes early. As I nervously sat there in my rental car, the late-afternoon sun from this pleasant spring day was shining in the side window.

In that moment, I knew I was just a few minutes away from seeing Megan, and that was certainly part of why I was so nervous. But something else was making this moment difficult for me—something that I asked Scott about earlier today, and he hesitantly told me.

He said I'd be the only person in the wedding party who wouldn't be bringing a significant other. So obviously, that meant I'd be the only person who was single at this rehearsal. He explained that most of the groomsmen and bridesmaids are married, and for the few who aren't—according to their RSVP— they'll still be bringing someone, which I knew included Megan.

But as I continued sitting in the car, I kept trying to remind myself that since I've become an airline pilot, being single and having this "never-at-home" lifestyle has mostly been the preferred way of life for me. Nevertheless, as I finally got out of the car, it was impossible to ignore the loneliness I felt as I began walking up to the church, completely alone.

~ ~ ~

When I nervously treaded up the front steps and opened the door, I instantly found myself in a loud and crowded lobby area. It wasn't a huge space but it still held several tall fig trees that sat in each corner with couches sitting next to them. I was still early, but based on the amount of people who were already congregating there, I was one of the last ones to arrive.

I scanned the room and I was glad to see that the khaki pants and pale blue dress shirt I wore seemed to fit in just fine with the "business casual" dress code. As I continued looking around, I saw some glimpses of old friends I hadn't seen since college.

Then fairly quickly, I saw Scott and Rachel standing across the room talking with Megan. Since they hadn't seen me yet, I began to politely work my way through the crowd to get over to them, and by that point, my heart was racing.

As I got closer, I saw Megan was definitely well-dressed. She was wearing a navy blue knee-length dress with high heels and her light brown hair was just as long as I remembered it to be in college. So far, I didn't notice anything to be wrong with her. I also didn't notice anyone around her who looked to be her boyfriend.

When I finally approached them, Scott looked up and greeted me. "Hey! There he is!"

I smiled as Megan and Rachel then turned around to greet me as well. First, Scott and I shook hands, then Rachel hugged me, and lastly Megan hugged me. Her hug felt very familiar, yet anything but ordinary, since it had been almost eight years since we'd last seen each other.

Before we had a chance to start any conversation, I noticed the pastor had made his way over to us.

Rachel quickly looked over at him. "Is it time already?" she asked him.

"Yeah," he said, looking down at his watch. "It should only take a few minutes," he said.

Scott turned to Megan and me. "Sorry to cut out but we just have to run through a few things before the rehearsal starts."

So that left Megan and me standing there looking at each other—both of us quite nervous and neither of us knowing what to say.

Thankfully, before much silence could set in, she spoke. "It's good to see you again."

"Yeah, it's good to see you, too," I quickly replied as I moved closer to her to let some people get through behind me.

She studied me for a second. "You look...just like you did in college," she said, pushing back some strands of her hair behind her ear.

"Thanks," I said. For the most part, I suppose she was right. I still weigh about the same and have somehow maintained an athletic physique, despite only sporadic workouts—mostly during layovers at hotel fitness centers.

"You look good too," I said, seeming fairly certain she'd lost a little weight. She was always thin in college, but she looked even thinner now. That was the only indication—and a rather subtle one, for that matter—that anything might be wrong with her. Her complexion was slightly pale, but that was no different from college—except of course, during the summers when she'd acquire a slight suntan.

Beyond all of that, she looked more grown up now. Yet the cute and youthful appearance she had in college was far from lost. She could still easily pass for mid-twenties, even though, like me, she's nearing thirty.

After a few more silent seconds passed, just as I was going to speak, she beat me to it again. "So Scott and Rachel told me you started a new pilot job a while back."

"That's right," I said. "About a year ago I got a job with a bigger airline and I'm flying full-size aircraft now. Before that, they probably mentioned that I flew small regional planes for an airline in Atlanta. But with this new job, I've moved back to the Chicago suburbs now and found a nice apartment there."

"I'm happy for you," she said genuinely with a smile. "So do you ever fly international flights or is it just domestic?"

"For me, I only fly domestic flights," I said.

"Well, that's probably good that you can stay closer to home...at least sort of close," she said. She then looked at me inquisitively. "I have to say, I'm curious to know how you have a suntan in April when you live in Chicago."

I smiled. "It's from all of the vacations I take on my days off, which are usually to somewhere warm with a beach. Since it's pretty cheap to fly when you're a pilot, and since I'm single, there aren't many days I spend at home."

"I see," she said. "It sounds like you're happy...I'm glad to see that."

"Yeah, I am," I said. "So tell me what you've been up to...Scott said you're living in Cincinnati now?"

"Yep, I moved there from Columbus about two years ago because I found a better technical writer job there. But more recently, I've started a different job, but it's still in Cincinnati and I'm still a technical writer."

"So being a technical writer means you write technical stuff?" I asked lightheartedly.

She smiled. "Well, basically, yeah. I write instructions and user guides for software programs," she said. "It's not exactly the job I thought I'd be doing at this point, but after I finished my master's degree in English, I felt a little burned out from being in school for so long. So I decided to take a break for a year or two and find a job of some sort and save up some money for my Ph.D. But now, after I've been in technical writing for almost six years, it's sort of become my career."

"So I assume you still want to be a professor?" I asked.

Her face quickly showed disappointment and I immediately became regretful that I asked.

"Well, I do," she said, "but it isn't going to be any time soon since I haven't even started my Ph.D. yet." She frowned and paused for a quick second before she spoke again. "Life has thrown me a few surprises recently."

That was obviously what Scott was talking about with Rachel during his phone call I overheard earlier. But I still had no idea what she was dealing with, and this didn't feel like the time or place to ask.

"Well, you still have plenty of time to get your Ph.D.," I said, trying to encourage her.

She nodded but didn't seem very convinced.

At that point, we both saw the pastor come out into the lobby again, looking like he was ready to make an announcement. "Okay, if everyone could make their way into the church, we're ready to get started now," he said.

As we all began walking into the church, Megan and I walked in together, since we'd been standing next to each other. By this point, it was pretty clear to me that her boyfriend wouldn't be attending this rehearsal. I figured maybe he'd be arriving tomorrow for the actual ceremony, even though all of the significant others of the bridal party had already arrived and were there at the rehearsal. In any case, since Megan and I were both alone, we ended up sitting down next to each other in one of the empty pews.

~   ~   ~

For the next hour, we all went through several dry runs of the ceremony—walking up to the front, standing in the right places, and exiting the church in the right order—to make sure everyone knew what they were doing for the ceremony tomorrow.

After that, it was time for the rehearsal dinner, which they had at an Italian restaurant. We had a small private room, which felt comfortably rustic with real wood paneling on the walls and several lanterns mounted on them. They had two long tables set up for us, each with maroon table cloths. The groomsmen seemed to gravitate toward one table and the bridesmaids toward the other table.

Fairly soon after we all sat down, they brought the meal out and it was one of the best Italian meals I've had in a while. It was nice to catch up with the other groomsmen too—many of them being my friends from college. Even though our lives look a lot different now, in many ways, it felt like we'd never been apart because we joked around with each other just like we did in college.

After the meal, we saw there was a dessert table in the front of the room. Since Scott was immersed in a conversation with his future father-in-law, I, along with a few of the groomsmen, decided to make our way over to the table to see what they had.

When we got in line, I noticed Rachel was a few places ahead of us and she was standing with a well-dressed blonde girl who I recognized to be Lindsay, one of the bridesmaids.

"Where did Megan go?" I heard Lindsay ask Rachel.

"She's sitting down over there talking to my mom," Rachel said, pointing across the room.

Lindsay looked over. "Oh, now I see her. How is she feeling these days?"

"Well, a little better, I guess," Rachel said. "But she still couldn't drive here from Cincinnati. Luckily, it was on the way for Susan, so she got a ride from her."

Lindsay shook her head with sympathy. "I just feel so sorry for her right now," she said.

"I know. She's been through a lot," Rachel said, "but I'm so glad she was able to come to the wedding. It means so much to me that she's here."

They then moved forward and took plates from the table to get their dessert. It wasn't my intention to have eavesdropped, but they weren't that far away and I couldn't help but hear what they were saying. Right then, it became clear to me that whatever Megan is dealing with, it seems big enough that quite a few people know about it.

It's also big enough that she wasn't able to drive herself from Cincinnati to Nashville. The fact that she rode here with another bridesmaid also implied that her boyfriend wouldn't be attending this wedding at all.

That was a little confusing to me, but as I thought about it, I realized it had already been several months ago when Scott had told me she had a boyfriend and something could've changed since then. As we moved forward in line, I tried to focus back on the conversation the groomsmen were having, but it was hard to forget what I'd just heard about Megan.

Before long, the rehearsal dinner began winding down and people were starting to leave. Several of the bridesmaids left—including Megan—but not before they said a quick goodbye to us groomsmen. Right after that, the groomsmen and I decided to take Scott out for another lunch tomorrow, since the wedding doesn't start until 2:00 p.m. So just before I left, I told Scott what we'd planned and he seemed appreciative of it. After that, I left and came back here to my hotel room and, of course, started typing this journal.

~ ~ ~

Now, it's time to wrap this up and head to bed. Tomorrow will be a big day for all of us, but especially for Scott and Rachel. It could very well be the biggest day of their lives, and I want so much for everything to go well for them. I think it will, considering we all went through the procession several times at the rehearsal today.

And as far as my best man duties are concerned, I'm all set. Their rings—which they gave me earlier—are sitting safely on top of my wallet over on the dresser, and I've had my speech written and memorized since before the rehearsal today. So other than feeling some expected anxiousness now on the night before, I don't think there's much reason to be concerned.

I wish I could say the same after seeing Megan today. With her, I can't help but be concerned right now. Everything I've heard from her—and from other people—doesn't sound good, even though I'm still in the dark on what's wrong with her.

Regardless, I really hope things get better for her. I'll definitely say a prayer for her tonight because it sounds like she needs it. I hate to see anyone go through difficulties, but especially when it's the girl who I once loved very much.

◆ **3** ◆

Sunday, April 18th
My apartment
8:07 p.m. (Central Time)

I'm happy to say the wedding went very well yesterday, but my concern for Megan has only grown stronger because she wasn't feeling well for much of the reception. Other than that, it was amazing how fast the day and evening went yesterday. We all showed up at the church, and before I knew it, we were all saying our goodbyes last night at the banquet hall after the reception ended. That's how fast it all went.

Then this morning, I caught an 11:20 a.m. flight back to Chicago—as a passenger, of course. I then made the forty-minute drive from the airport to the western suburbs before arriving back here at this two-bedroom apartment that I call home.

I proceeded to spend the better part of this afternoon carrying out the familiar routine of unpacking, doing laundry, and then repacking, since I go back to work tomorrow to begin a three-day flying trip. Now, as I have some spare time on this Sunday night, I decided to sit down at my dining room table and continue writing in this journal before I head to bed.

~ ~ ~

Even though yesterday went really fast, when I think back to it now, it sort of already feels like ages ago. It's hard to believe that it was just yesterday morning when I was waking up in the hotel room and had the wedding—and all of the day's activities—still ahead of me. I was able to sleep until 8:30 a.m. that morning before I went for a workout at the hotel fitness center.

Then I met Scott and the groomsmen for the lunch that we'd decided upon last night. It was much like our lunch the previous day, except we went to a different restaurant and Scott was way more nervous. But that was understandable since it was only about an hour until the wedding at that point.

After lunch, we began the short drive over to the church. As the sun was shining and the temperature was rising, it was obvious we were in store for yet another sunny day in the mid-70's—absolutely perfect weather for a wedding.

When we arrived at the church, Scott and all of us groomsmen changed into our tuxedos in a surprisingly spacious walk-in coat closet. Before long, it was approaching 2:00 p.m., so we headed out to the lobby where the bridesmaids had just emerged from the fellowship room. We then began lining up together to make our grand entrance. As I lined up next to Megan, it was the first time I'd seen her for the day and she looked very nice.

Her light blue bridesmaid dress was very flattering on her, and her hair—which she wore down—was curled flawlessly. She was also wearing a wrist corsage, as all of the bridesmaids were. And for someone who usually didn't wear much makeup, hers was done perfectly today.

Just as she looked stunning, she also looked quite nervous, as we all were. So I tried to lighten the mood.

"You know, you clean up pretty nice," I said, looking over at her.

She smiled, yet her nervousness was still apparent when she spoke. "Thanks. You too."

Before we could say anything else, we were cued to walk into the church. So Megan and I quickly joined arms, tried to take our steps in unison with each other, and made sure we didn't walk too fast down the aisle as the rest of the wedding party followed us.

After we all took our places at the front, Rachel appeared in the doorway at the back of the church with her father standing next to her. When the organist began playing, everyone in the congregation turned around to see her.

She looked beautiful in her white wedding dress. Her long dark hair flowed down elegantly with her veil and she held a big bouquet of white roses in front of her. Then she and her father began walking slowly up to the front. I glanced over at Scott, standing next to me in his black tuxedo, watching his bride walk up the aisle. From the look on his face, I think it's safe to say that was the most joyful moment of his life so far.

When Rachel and her father reached the front, the ceremony began, and cameras were flashing more than at some sporting events I've attended. They exchanged their vows, the pastor gave a condensed sermon, we sang some songs, and before I knew it, the ceremony was ending and Megan and I were arm-in-arm, walking in procession out of the church.

It was then time for pictures—and many of them, for that matter. The photographer moved very quickly, shuffling us all around to take every possible combination and pose. By the time we were done, I was seeing spots everywhere I looked from all the flashes.

We then headed over to the reception hall where Scott and Rachel, their parents, and all of us in the wedding party formed a receiving line outside the ballroom. After being there for a while and greeting all of the guests as they arrived, we—the wedding party—began our formal procession into the ballroom. Scott and Rachel went first, Megan and I followed, and the rest of the wedding party then followed us.

After we sat down at the head table, I finally had a chance to notice how nice everything looked—numerous ornate chandeliers hanging down from the ceiling, flowers everywhere, and of course, several hundred people sitting at dozens of round tables applauding Scott and Rachel.

Barely a minute later, Scott's father took the microphone and gave a short speech and then ended with a prayer. When he was done, he handed me the microphone and I knew it was time for my big moment...the best man speech.

Despite the flash of nervousness I felt when I took the microphone, I proceeded to give a good speech. I briefly told the story of how Scott and Rachel met eleven and a half years ago, and how for a while after that, they were living on separate sides of the world. I explained that even though the strength of their love was tested during that time, in the end, their love for each other prevailed—similar to how God's perfect love for us will always prevail. Everyone applauded when I finished, and when I sat down, the servers quickly began serving the meal. I glanced at my watch and I couldn't believe it was already after 6:00 p.m.

~ ~ ~

As the evening progressed, everyone became well-dispersed from their assigned tables as they mingled with other guests. Scott and Rachel made their way around the room to talk to all of the guests and I noticed Megan went off to talk to Rachel's parents. After I'd been around Megan much of the day, it was clear she was attending this wedding alone, for whatever reason. That's certainly what I had assumed after I heard at the rehearsal how she had to get a ride from Ohio with another bridesmaid.

Just as everyone else was mingling, I did the same by finding some old friends from college. As we talked, the time passed effortlessly and the daylight that once filled the ballroom through the many picture windows had turned to night.

A good way into that conversation, I happened to glance across the room and I saw Megan was now sitting at a table by herself, staring down at her phone. I know her very well, and although she can sometimes be quiet and reserved, I knew it wasn't like her to withdraw like that—especially at something like a wedding reception. So I excused myself from the conversation and weaved my way around the abundance of round tables—and people—to get over to her.

She heard me approach and looked up from her phone. "Hi."

I instantly knew by the look on her face that she didn't feel well.

"Are you okay?" I asked as I sat down next to her.

"Well...yeah, but my stomach is bothering me right now," she said.

"Are you sick?" I asked.

"Not really," she said. "My stomach has just been problematic lately. But I'm trying to lay low right now because I don't want Scott and Rachel to get worried about me. This is their night and they deserve to enjoy it."

"Can I do anything for you?" I asked.

She subtly shook her head no, but I could tell she had something on her mind.

"If you don't tell me, I'm going to keep asking until you do," I said.

She looked at me. "Well...I was looking for some bread before, but they took everything from the tables now. I was thinking it might help my stomach."

I stood up. "Let me find you some."

She looked up at me. "No, you don't have to do this, Kevin."

"Don't worry about it," I assured her.

I walked over toward the kitchen and found a server, and fairly quickly, she came back with a basket of bread, complete with a cloth napkin, some foil-wrapped squares of butter, and even some crackers thrown in too. I handed her a tip and then made my way back to Megan's table.

I set the basket down in front of her and then sat down next to her again.

She looked at me with an appreciative smile. "Thanks for getting all of this. You really didn't have to do this."

"It's fine. I hope you feel better after you eat this," I said.

"Actually, this might sound weird," she said, "but I think it might help if I go outside for a few minutes."

"Okay," I said. "You just need some fresh air?"

"Yeah, I think that would help," she said.

"You still want the bread?" I asked.

"Definitely."

"You want some company?" I asked.

"You really don't have to go with me," she said. "I don't want to see you miss the reception just because I'm not feeling well."

"It's fine," I said, getting up with her.

She carried the basket of bread and we walked together as we made our way through the crowd. Just before we left the ballroom, I noticed they had a giant punch bowl sitting on the dessert table filled with ice. It held numerous bottles of water and soda, so I quickly grabbed two bottles of water for us.

We walked across the expansive tile floor in the deserted lobby and then I saw some glass double doors that looked like they went out to a terrace in the back. So we went outside and the nighttime air felt refreshingly cool, but certainly not cold by any means. As soon as the door closed behind us, the sounds of the reception became nothing more than soft and muddled background noise to an otherwise quiet evening outside. We wandered across the terrace and sat down on two lounge chairs that faced away from the building.

"I got you a bottle of water, since I know you don't like soda...unless that's changed," I said, handing her the bottle.

She smiled. "No, that hasn't changed...and thank you," she said, setting the bottle down beside her chair.

"So you don't need to go to the doctor or anything now?" I asked. "You just have an upset stomach, right?"

"Yeah," she said. "I'll be okay...eventually."

She then took some bread and started eating and then passed the basket to me. "You want some? It's pretty good, actually."

"Sure," I said, ripping off a piece. "It was a good dinner, but there's always room for bread, right?"

She smiled. "Yeah, it looked good, but I didn't eat much." She turned to me. "Like I said, you really don't have to stay out here with me. I hate to see you miss the reception."

"No it's fine, "I said. "I just hope you feel better."

"I should in a little while," she said.

"Do you have this problem a lot?" I asked.

She looked down before she spoke. "Um, sort of."

The way she said it, I could sense that was all she wanted to tell me. I clearly wasn't getting the whole story, but I knew it really wasn't my business.

Some silence set in as we sat there snacking on the bread and I figured this was probably a good time to change the subject. "So how are your parents and brother doing these days?"

"Good," she said. "They all still live in Columbus. My parents are still working and Matt's twenty-six now and a financial analyst and lives not too far from them." She then turned to me. "How are your parents and sister?"

"Well, my parents retired and moved to Florida... Tallahassee, to be exact. And Katie finished college last year and moved back in with them for now while she looks for a job."

"Jobs can be hard to find these days," she said.

"Yeah, that's what I hear," I said. Then I turned to her again. "So do you go back to Columbus a lot? It's only a two-hour drive from Cincinnati, isn't it?"

"Yeah, it is," she hesitated. "But lately my family has been visiting me more than I've been visiting them."

Some more silence set in as we both took a drink from our water bottles.

Finally, she spoke. "So I have to say I'm a little surprised you're at this wedding by yourself and haven't found Miss Right by now."

"Well, I guess I'm a little surprised at that too," I said.

She turned to me with a half-smile. "Don't worry. I'm sure you'll meet someone when the time is right."

"Thanks," I said. "I was a little surprised to see you here by yourself too."

"Well, I was in a relationship up until recently," she said, "but we're not together anymore."

I turned to her with sympathy. "Sorry to hear that."

"Thanks," she said, leaning her head back on the chair and looking up at the sky. She took a deep breath and then seemed eager to change the subject. "You can actually see a lot of stars tonight...but there's only a crescent moon."

"Yep," I said, looking up.

"This sort of reminds me of our spot," she said. "Remember that?"

"Yeah, I do," I said, thinking how it would be absolutely impossible to forget that.

~   ~   ~

After we were lulled into some comfortable silence, she pointed up to the sky. "I can see a plane way up there...or at least its small blinking lights."

I looked up. "Yeah, I see it."

"Where do you think it's going?" she asked.

"Somewhere east, but it's definitely not landing here in Nashville because it's flying too high for that," I said.

"How high do you think it's flying?" she asked.

"Well, I'm pretty sure it's at cruising altitude, so probably around 35,000 feet," I said.

"Hmm," she said. "So this might be a dumb question, but why don't planes have headlights? They just have the small little blinking lights on the wings?"

"Well, they have landing lights, which are basically like headlights, but we only turn those on when we're below 10,000 feet."

"I never knew that," she said as we both watched the strobe

lights of the aircraft gracefully advance across the sky while hearing the distant whisper of its jet engines. After a few seconds of silence, she spoke again. "It never seems like they're going very fast when you see them up in the sky like that," she said.

"Yeah, but they are," I said.

She turned to me. "How fast do they actually go?"

"Well, it depends on the speed and direction of the wind, but generally at cruising speed, the aircraft I fly go about 450 knots, which is just over 500 miles per hour."

"Wow, I didn't know they went that fast," she said. "I'm getting a whole flight lesson right now."

I smiled. "Yeah, I guess you are."

Then she turned to me again. "By the way, I'm really proud of you that you became a pilot."

"Thanks," I said. "And I hope you know that you can still become a professor someday. Even if things haven't gone the way you've hoped or thought, it can still happen. I don't want to see you give up. You're really smart and I think you'd make a good professor."

"Thanks," she said with a small smile.

I turned to her. "So after talking about planes, I have to know...are you still afraid to fly?"

"Is the sky still blue?" she asked sarcastically.

"Well, actually, it's not," I said. "It's dark right now."

She threw me a playful smile. "You know what I mean."

"So I take it you've still never flown?" I asked.

She shook her head. "Nope."

I didn't know quite what to say after that, but before I could think of anything, we were both startled as we heard the door to the building open abruptly.

Lindsay, one of the bridesmaids, stepped one foot outside and then froze as she looked at us. "We were panicking!" she shouted to us. "We've been looking all over for both of you. We're about to do the cake-cutting ceremony and we need you guys inside for that."

I looked at Megan. "Are you okay with going back in?" I asked softly.

She nodded.

"Okay, we'll be right in," I called out to Lindsay. I turned back to Megan. "I think we just got in trouble."

She laughed as we got up out of our chairs, gathered up our water bottles and the basket of bread, and went back inside.

~ ~ ~

Not long after the cake-cutting ceremony, 10:00 p.m. approached quickly and it became time for Scott and Rachel's final "send off." For that, everyone first lined up on either sides of the lobby leading out to the front door. Then we all clapped as the two of them walked through the passageway that we'd formed to the limo waiting for them out front. It was the last we'd see of them for this weekend because they were leaving first thing in the morning to take a cruise for their honeymoon.

After they left in the limo, that pretty much capped off the reception. As the guests left, the ballroom began looking pretty empty. Then Rachel's mom told all of us in the wedding party to go around and collect the flowers from the tables because she was going to take them to a nursing home in the morning.

After we did that, everyone in the wedding party was getting ready to leave, but I found Megan again. "It looks like you're feeling better," I said, noticing that from the look on her face.

"I am," she said. "Thanks for going outside with me before…and for getting the bread."

"Sure, no problem," I said as the moment then became a little awkward. "So we probably won't see each other tomorrow, so I guess this is goodbye."

"Yeah, I guess it is," she said.

"But we can keep in touch, if you want," I suggested.

"Yeah," she said, getting out her phone. As we exchanged numbers and email addresses, I kept wondering in my mind if she was simply being polite by doing this or if she genuinely wanted to keep in touch. I knew her very well back in college, but somehow I just couldn't read her in this moment.

After that, we walked to the front door together where a few of the bridesmaids were waiting for her since they drove together. Then she and I both reached our arms out to hug almost simultaneously and then embraced for a few seconds.

"It was good to see you again," she said, gently patting my back.

"Yeah, it was good to see you, too," I said.

After we let go, she and the bridesmaids left and then I said some final goodbyes to some of my college friends who were also leaving. Then I left, realizing it was probably an "early" night compared to some other weddings. I arrived back at the hotel around 10:45 p.m. On the short elevator ride up to my room, I found myself wondering if the goodbye that Megan and I just had was a "goodbye for now," or a "goodbye for good."

~ ~ ~

Now, a day later, as I sit here in my apartment finishing up this journal entry tonight, I'm still wondering the same thing. Until I found out about this wedding a while back, I thought I'd never see her again. I'm sure she thought the same.

So I'm not sure if this wedding was God's way of introducing us back into each other's lives, or if it was simply a chance for us to briefly reunite, so now our last memory of seeing each other will be a much more pleasant one. One thing I *do* know is when I think back to that final goodbye we had during our senior year of college, it still breaks my heart.

◆ 4 ◆

As it turned out, my workday was cut short today, which has given me some unexpected time to finally confront those not-so-pleasant memories from the latter part of college that this past weekend has seemed to rekindle. Despite my day ending unexpectedly early, it began about as routinely as anyone could ask.

The first flight on my schedule today—which began this three-day flying trip—was from Chicago to St. Louis, where we arrived a few minutes early. After that, the next flight was to Fort Lauderdale, Florida. For that one, I was the pilot flying, since the captain flew the previous flight. We flew over a mess of thunderstorms on our way there, but it was nothing but clear skies after we entered Florida and touched down a few minutes early again.

Then the last flight of our trip—and for our workday—was a flight to Atlanta. But that whole area was being plagued by the same mess of thunderstorms we'd just flown over. So obviously, that flight was delayed but they hadn't canceled it. After the captain and I waited for over an hour, our airline dismissed us from the flight because we'd soon become "illegal" to fly, since we'd been on active pilot duty since early in the morning.

That flight would've continued with another crew, but I saw it eventually got canceled as apparently no flights were getting in or out of Atlanta for much of the afternoon. For me, the result was some unexpected beach time here in Fort Lauderdale today. And now, as I'm back at my hotel room after dinner, I'm sitting out on the balcony with my laptop to enjoy the end of this sunny, 83-degree day.

In a little while, I'll need to get to bed to prepare for an early flight tomorrow morning. As it's planned now, my schedule will put me in Minneapolis for tomorrow night, where I know it won't be 83 degrees.

But for now, I can enjoy this nice weather and use this time to journal because I have a lot on my mind. Ever since the wedding this past weekend, I've found myself thinking back again to everything that happened toward the end of my senior year of college with Megan. I'd love to say I've come to peace with all of it, but I don't think I have. I honestly still don't understand why we had to face everything we faced back then. But the bigger thing that bothers me is that I still question some of the choices I made during that tumultuous time.

~ ~ ~

I remember when the month of May began that year, Megan and I had no idea the challenges that we'd soon be facing. Instead, we were focused on finishing up our last few weeks of classes and getting ready to carry out the plans that we'd developed for after we'd graduate.

Since we'd been together for all four years of college and we were quite certain we'd be together forever, it was no surprise that our plans first included us moving to the same town—Columbus, Ohio. That's where I'd begin flight school to hopefully become a pilot, and Megan would begin grad school to hopefully become an English professor.

Obviously, Megan had lived in Columbus for her whole life up until college, but there was a much bigger reason we chose to move there. Even though she was accepted at several other schools—including two in the Chicago area—the school in Columbus was, by far, the most affordable. Since her mom worked on campus as a secretary in the admissions office, Megan was eligible for a tuition discount. She wouldn't even have to take out any student loans and she'd also be able to save money by living at home with her parents.

She actually almost went to that school for her undergrad degree, but when she qualified for an academic scholarship at the college where we both ended up attending, she decided to go "away" to college, even though Indiana is only the next state over from Ohio.

For me, our plan of moving to Columbus worked fine because they had several flight schools in the area, and I was confident I could find some sort of basic part-time job to help me pay for my schooling. The only tricky part was how I'd afford my own apartment there since I wasn't going to move in with Megan and her parents, nor were Megan and I going to live together before we were married.

My parents offered to help some, but I don't think they intended on paying for all of my living expenses. Megan felt very bad about that, but I assured her many times that my moving there was the best option we had to allow us to live close to each other.

As for our relationship, Megan and I were thinking we'd get engaged a year after graduation and then get married in

another year after that. By that point, she'd be done with her
master's degree and I'd hopefully be getting my first real pilot
job. That was the plan we believed we'd carry out until God
threw us a big surprise only a week and a half before
graduation.

~   ~   ~

It was almost mid-May by that point, and that's when I
received a phone call I was never expecting. I remember how
the loud ring startled me as I was sitting quietly in my dorm
room studying for final exams. When I answered, I quickly
found out that it was regarding a job opportunity at a private
jet business.

During the call, I realized I had sent them my resume a
while back during that previous year when I was looking for a
summer job. I remember thinking that it sounded like a neat
company because they operated a fleet of small private jets for
charter flights, mainly flying corporate CEOs and executives to
out-of-state meetings.

I knew I obviously wasn't qualified to fly for them back
then, but I thought they might have a non-flying job available
for that summer. It certainly would've been convenient, given
that they operated out of a small executive airport fairly close
to my parents' house in the Chicago suburbs. But I never heard
back from them at that point. However, they had apparently
held on to my resume and now they were eager to interview me
for a Business Coordinator position.

So with encouragement from Megan, I made the drive from
Indiana to the Chicago suburbs on a day between my final
exams for the interview. I met with the owner and the
Managing Captain and it was a pretty relaxed interview. I
quickly learned that many years ago the owner had attended

the same college as I had and majored in Aeronautical Engineering, just as I was doing. After that, it made more sense why they were so interested in me.

They said the job would include taking reservations, scheduling flights, coordinating the pilots' work schedules, and handling the billing. They also said they'd be willing to work around my plans of attending flight school and said that after I got my ATP (airline transport pilot) certificate in a few years, I'd probably be able to begin flying for them as a copilot, which I was very happy to hear.

Finally, they stepped out of the room for less than a minute and came back and offered me the job right there, on the spot. I thanked them, but told them I would need a few days to decide. There was no doubt it sounded like the perfect opportunity to begin my career, but I knew this would interfere with the plans that Megan and I already had.

When I got back to campus that day, Megan was quick to tell me that she'd gladly attend one of the schools in the Chicago area where she was accepted, so I could take the job. But I didn't like that idea because she'd have to take out student loans to attend one of those schools and I wasn't sure if either of them would reaccept her, since she had officially declined them a while back. I also didn't know how she'd afford an apartment on her own while she'd be in school full time.

Because of those things, I was seriously considering turning down the job offer from the private jet business and moving to Ohio with Megan, which was after all, our original plan. But Megan quickly said I'd be foolish to turn down such a rare opportunity and said she was convinced the job offer was simply God's way of telling us He wanted us both to live in the Chicago area.

I remember before we went off to study for finals that night, we said a long prayer together asking God for guidance and clarity. We both knew we had a lot to figure out yet, but we also knew we didn't have a lot of time since the private jet business was expecting a decision in a few days.

~   ~   ~

After we both finished our finals the next day, Megan was eager to tell me about a new idea she had. It first included me accepting the job offer in the Chicago area, but much to my surprise, it also included us getting married in a few months.

She said, after we were married, we could get an apartment together and she'd postpone grad school for a few years and find a job instead. She believed that between my modest salary from the private jet business and whatever job she could find, we'd make enough to live off of for a few years until I got a real pilot job. After that, she'd consider going to grad school.

That definitely caught me off guard and the words "married" and "few months" resonated in my mind. We weren't even engaged yet, but we were going to throw together a wedding in a few months? And I definitely wasn't keen on her postponing grad school for a few years. To me, that sounded like the first step of her giving up on becoming a professor.

When I told her I wasn't ready to get married yet, I could see her excitement turn to disappointment almost instantly. When I asked her what she thought about having a long-distance relationship until she finished school, she didn't like that idea at all. She candidly, yet politely, said that living six hours away from each other for the next two years sounded like nothing more than a slow and painful process of breaking up. Deep down, I mostly agreed, but it was the only option we had, since neither of us wanted to see each other give up the good opportunities we had.

After we talked about it more, it was clear we weren't going to figure things out right then. So we finally agreed to take the rest of that day and think about everything on our own.

~   ~   ~

What happened from that point forward certainly wasn't what either of us expected. Even after all these years, it still surprises me how everything panned out. But I know one thing was for sure, God was definitely at work, even though I still wonder if I misinterpreted what He was trying to do.

When I got back to my dorm room that day, the first thing I did was grab my Bible and sit down. After I scoured through the index looking for verses about decisions, direction, and God's guidance, I'd found several. But the one that resonated the most was Proverbs 3:5, "Trust in the Lord with all [your] heart; and lean not [toward your] own understanding."[1]

At first, I read that thinking Megan and I should trust that God has a plan for us to stay together, even though I didn't understand yet how we would. But then as I sat there reflecting on it more, that's when my thoughts began to take an unexpected turn.

As I read that same verse a second time, it suddenly had a completely different meaning to me. I began to wonder if His plan was actually for Megan and me to go our separate ways and we should trust in that plan, even though we certainly couldn't see or understand why He wouldn't want us to stay together.

I remember how I immediately tried to push those thoughts out of my mind and convince myself that God still wanted Megan and me to be together. But as I sat there that day, still holding my Bible, I realized trying to force our relationship to work wasn't the right answer. It would only delay our heartbreak if, in fact, His ultimate plan for us was to go our separate ways. As I felt more unrest building each second, I finally said a long prayer right then and asked Him to give me the clarity that I needed, but I was afraid He may have just done that.

~   ~   ~

I remember the next day all too well. It was May 19th and graduation was only a few days away. When I woke up that morning, it sure felt as though the clarity I had prayed for had been given to me. But in no way were things leaning in the direction I'd hoped they would.

Before I even got out of bed, the unfortunate facts were as clear as day to me. I knew I wasn't ready to get married, I knew neither Megan nor I wanted a long-distance relationship, and I knew neither of us wanted to see each other give up the opportunities we had. So at that moment, I became convinced that God's answer to this was for Megan and me to go our separate ways.

As I immediately began to think about my life without Megan, it was a devastating thought that put knots in my stomach. But despite that, I truly believed that breaking up would be the best thing for both of us.

After I got dressed that morning, Megan called and quickly offered to come over to my dorm room because we both knew we had a lot to talk about. It was barely 9:00 a.m. when we sat down next to each other on my bed as the morning sun was shining in through the windows.

As soon as I broke the news to her, tears instantly began filling her eyes. "Please don't break up with me, Kevin," she said, looking down and shaking her head. "Please don't do this."

"I'm sorry, Megan. But don't you think if God wanted us to stay together He would've made it easier for us...where one of us wouldn't have to make a huge sacrifice?"

"No!" she said as she quickly faced me. "That's what love is about...making sacrifices for each other. I don't want to think about my life without you, Kevin. And I've told you so many times that I'll give up going to grad school for now if that's what I have to do."

I shook my head. "I love you too much to let you do that. That's just not fair," I said. "I know this isn't the way either of us wants it to end, but it just doesn't seem like we're meant to stay together."

Still sniffling, she then stood up and grabbed tissues from my desk. She then looked at me with tears still running down her face. "I want you to think about your life without me, and if you're okay with that, then I'll just have to get over you. But if it breaks your heart like it breaks mine, then we need to find a way to make this work, because I can't bear to think that we're breaking up when we're still in love."

She nervously took a deep breath, then sat down next to me again as she kept wiping tears from her eyes. All the while, I was trying my hardest not to cry.

I spoke softly. "I'm sorry, but I really think this is what's best," I said.

She then looked down and put her hands to her face. She proceeded to cry the hardest I'd ever seen her cry. It was a terrible feeling to watch her cry and it took everything I had not to cry myself at that point.

After several minutes, she spoke with tear-filled eyes and a broken voice. "I can't believe this is happening, Kevin."

I held her a little tighter with my arm and inhaled nervously, not knowing what to say. "I know," I finally said, exhaling and still trying to not cry. I felt absolutely awful for breaking her heart. I also felt overwhelming sympathy for how she felt because I felt the same heartbreak she did.

After we both held each other for several minutes as we sat on my bed, she eventually got up and left. That's when I sat down at my desk and tears quickly began flowing from my eyes. Still to this day, there's been nothing that's broken my heart as much as that did. In that moment, I had just lost the one I loved...forever.

In the days after we broke up, I painfully yet decisively accepted the job at the private jet business, moved out of my dorm room, and officially graduated. I remember just minutes after the commencement ceremony had ended—just as we'd planned—Megan and I met up one last time to say our final goodbye. That was a very sad moment because we both thought that would probably be the last time we'd ever see each other for the rest of our lives.

~ ~ ~

Even though I was convinced back then that it wasn't God's plan for Megan and me to stay together, I've questioned that several times through these years—especially now, after the wedding this past weekend. When I think about if we would've stayed together, it breaks my heart to think that we'd likely be married by now, and probably have kids too.

However, as I've become even stronger in my faith at this point in my life, I'm realizing—as I'm typing this—that if God wanted all of that to happen, it would've happened. That thought certainly eases some of the heartbreak.

I suppose the bigger question that still remains right now

is why He had us cross paths again after all these years. And also, why it comes at a time when she happens to be dealing with some seemingly significant health problems.

But before I think about any of that, there's still the very basic question that's still unanswered. Does she even want to keep in touch now? It makes me sad to think that she may not, but should that make me sad?

Up until a few seconds ago, I had absolutely no answer for any of that. But when I glanced at my phone just now, I noticed I had a text message. Surprisingly, it's from Megan, and she just sent it about fifteen minutes ago.

Hey Kevin! How was your trip back to Chicago? Where are you flying next? Anywhere interesting? Going back to work today wasn't fun for me, but I suppose those boring user guides don't write themselves! Hope you're having a good night!! :)

That's certainly a text message I wasn't expecting right now. But it answers my question, and I'm obviously glad she wants to keep in touch. Even though I'll soon be heading to bed now, I'll definitely text her back before that to keep this communication going. I have to say, as this day comes to a close, her message has brought me a certain type of joy right now—a type I haven't felt for quite a while.

◆ 5 ◆

Sunday, May 9th (Mother's Day)
Hotel room in San Diego, CA
9:02 p.m. (Pacific Time)

I didn't realize it, but it's been about three weeks since I last wrote in this journal and there's definitely a lot to catch up on since then, especially involving Megan. But right now after a full day of flying, my schedule has brought me here to San Diego for tonight.

My shift began this morning with an 8:20 a.m. flight out of Chicago to Dallas. After landing there, I was actually glad to have a break from flying in the form of a seventy-minute layover. Even though I love flying, I was far from thrilled that I had to work today. First, this was yet another Sunday morning where I was flying and, therefore, unable to attend church. But today was also Mother's Day, and obviously, due to my flying schedule, I wasn't able to spend any time with my mom—or any of my family, for that matter.

However, my layover in Dallas gave me plenty of time to call her. Not only did I talk to my mom, but also my dad, and even my sister, Katie, since she's living with them now. My mom was certainly happy to hear from me, even though I'm sure she was expecting my call. She said the three of them had gone out to a Mother's Day brunch earlier, which was obviously Katie's idea. Then she thanked me for the flowers I sent yesterday.

It doesn't seem like flowers and a phone call are enough to express my gratitude for her as a mother and for everything she's done for me throughout my life. I have so many memories from my childhood when she selflessly cared for my sister and me, and there's no question that I wouldn't be where I am today without all that she's done for me.

Before long, my dad got on the phone too, and they were eager to tell me how nice the weather has been down there in Tallahassee lately. They said it's been in the mid-80's and sunny every day for the past seven or eight days in a row.

There's no question they enjoy being retired and living in Florida now. Sometimes it's still hard for me to believe that they're actually retired. Even though my dad is sporting a little more gray hair now, they just don't look like they should be retired. It's easy to forget they're in their late 50's because they both stay pretty active.

Of course, that's much easier to do now that they live in the Sunshine State. My dad goes golfing quite a bit and my mom is content spending time working in her garden, which has impressively become the source of most of the vegetables they eat now.

Even though they were both born and raised in the Midwest, neither of them have ever liked cold weather very much. So it's no mystery why as soon as they retired a few years ago—while Katie was in college—they moved out of the Chicago area and down to Florida.

As our conversation progressed, they asked me where I've flown lately. They always seem to enjoy hearing about the places I visit, even though none of my trips are all that exotic, since I only fly domestically. So I briefly told them about some layover time I'd spent in San Francisco, Omaha, and Memphis throughout this past week.

Then my mom told me more about how her garden is doing so well.

"You wouldn't believe how good this zucchini is this year," she said. "Even your sister likes it."

Toward the end of our conversation, they asked when I was going to visit them next, as they always do.

"Hopefully soon," I told them.

Unfortunately, it's not very easy for me to get down there because Tallahassee's airport is fairly small and there aren't a lot of commercial flights that go in and out of there every day. Furthermore, of the few flights there are, they tend to fill up very fast. So usually I end up flying to Jacksonville and then making the two and a half hour drive over to Tallahassee from there. Either way, despite the difficulties I have getting there, I usually try to visit them every six weeks or so.

After I said goodbye to my parents, the phone call wasn't quite over. They handed the phone to Katie and then walked away, leaving just the two of us—brother and sister—to talk to each other. Ever since Katie moved back in with them after she finished college last year, my parents do this every time I call. I guess I see their reasoning because these forced phone conversations are essentially the only interaction Katie and I have with each other nowadays.

As soon as it was just two of us on the phone, I spoke first. "So how's your job search going?"

"Well, I still haven't found anything," she said.

"Do you think you're sending out enough resumes?" I asked.

She paused for a few seconds. "I'm doing the best I can, Kevin."

"I know. But like I've told you before, you can't always just apply to jobs that are posted. It helps to send your resume to companies, even if you don't know if they're hiring. That's exactly how I got my first job with the private jet business."

"I know," she said. "I was around when that happened and you've still told me that story over and over. But you have to understand that not everyone can just fall backwards into great jobs like you have."

That comment certainly irritated me. "You know, Katie, just because I've been blessed with some good opportunities doesn't mean I've fallen backwards into all of them. I've worked really hard to get to this point and I've worked up through the ranks just like anyone else would have to do. Do you know how many hours I spent studying for my certification exams? Do you remember how busy I was with working for my entire time through flight school? Do you know how many times I was stuck with all the bad flying schedules back when I was a regional pilot?"

"Okay, fine. I'm sorry," she said casually.

I took a deep breath and did my best to push my aggravation aside. I then decided to change the subject and inquire about her boyfriend. "So how's Todd?"

"He's fine."

"That's it?" I asked.

"Well, what else do you want to know?" she asked defensively.

"I don't know," I said woefully.

After some silence, she finally spoke with a hint of an apologetic tone. "So where are you flying next?"

"Well, I'm in Dallas right now, and I'm flying to San Diego in about forty minutes, which is where I'll spend tonight. Then tomorrow I fly to Denver and then Tampa."

"That sounds like a decent schedule," she said.

"Yeah, it should be."

"Well, you probably want time to get ready for your next flight now," she said.

"Okay, I guess I'll talk to you later then," I said, knowing it would be the last time we talk until the next time I call my parents.

"Be careful," she said. She always says that at the end of our conversations, and I'd like to think that's her way of saying she loves me, without actually saying it. Either way, it's proof she still cares about me, even though we've clearly drifted apart in recent years.

~ ~ ~

I'm still a little baffled how she and I have come to this point where it seems like we don't have anything in common anymore. The facts remain that she's almost seven years younger than me and her carefree, "live for today" personality is quite different from mine. But when we were younger, those differences certainly didn't stop us from getting along pretty well, which was nice, considering she's my only sibling.

I remember the day like it was yesterday when I first found out I was going to have a sibling. I was six years old and my parents invited me to sit down at the kitchen table to talk one evening. They told me the news, and I remember the great excitement I felt. Finally, I'd have a sibling! I later found out that my parents had tried for several years to have a second child, and just when they had all but given up, my mom became pregnant with Katie.

After Katie was born, I was obviously seven years old already, and I remember how I loved just holding her in my arms, cradling her to sleep. As we both got older, since both of our parents worked full time, I basically served as her baby-sitter when we had the summers off from school. But neither of us minded the arrangement—at least for most of the days.

Now, she's twenty-three, graduated from college last May with a Business degree, and almost a year later she still doesn't have a job. Given that my parents moved to Florida after she went away to college, she also found herself moving to Florida after she graduated to move back in with them. She certainly wasn't thrilled about that, but it was pretty much her only option since she had no job and no income.

Since then, she's met Todd. But my parents aren't too keen on him—nor am I. For some reason, she hasn't always picked the best guys to date, but it's not because she hasn't had many to choose from. Since the time she entered high school, guys have always been interested in her. She's pretty outgoing, easy to talk to, and has a decent sense of humor. But also her long straight blonde hair, bright blue eyes, and slender 5'6" physique certainly don't hurt either.

Even though she found a boyfriend soon after she moved to Florida, she obviously still hasn't found a job. I feel sorry for her, yet sometimes I wonder how hard she's looking because it seems like Business should be a practical degree that employers would want.

But she's never been very excited about the business field. It was simply the major she happened to choose when she was still undecided after she finished her first year of college. However, my parents were happy with that choice because they thought that degree would land her a job soon after she graduated, but it obviously didn't. Nevertheless, I hope she finds a job pretty soon or at least finds some sort of direction in her life, because it makes me sad to see her floundering like this.

~   ~   ~

Shortly after that phone call, I departed from Dallas for my last flight of the day, which brought me here to San Diego where it was sunny and 74 degrees when I landed this afternoon. I then rented a car, checked into my hotel, changed into shorts and a t-shirt, and made the relatively short drive to the beach.

Even though I have to leave here tomorrow morning to begin another day of flying, that was no excuse not to enjoy the time I had here tonight. So I found a beach-side café and had a nice dinner there.

After that, I took my shoes off and walked onto the beach, and the familiar feel of sand under my feet instantly made me feel like I was on vacation. By that time, the beachgoers were thinning out as the sun was sinking lower in the west sky over the waters of the Pacific. There was still a little time before sunset, but I've found that a sunset can attract a crowd of its own on these West Coast beaches. As soon as I sat down on the sand, I decided to call Megan before it got any later.

That first text message she sent me a few weeks ago was actually the beginning of us keeping in touch on a regular basis now. We've been texting every day and talking on the phone at least every other day. In fact, I'm flying out to Cincinnati for my two days off to visit her on this coming Friday and Saturday, which will be the first time we've seen each other since the wedding a few weeks ago.

I've already booked a hotel room and reserved a spot on a flight out there, so I don't have to fly standby like I normally do. She's taking Friday off from work, and—like many people—she has weekends off, so that means we'll have two full days together.

Having just sat down on the sand, I was ready to call her, but I decided to text her first. Even though it was 7:00 p.m. here in San Diego, it was actually 10:00 p.m. in Cincinnati.

Hey! I made it to San Diego now. If you're still up, I have some time to talk.

She texted back right away. *Sure! I'd love to talk!!*

~ ~ ~

So I gave her a call. After not even two full rings, she answered, "Hey!" obviously knowing it was me. "So how's San Diego?"

"It's good," I said, stretching my legs out on the sand in front of me. "I'm on the beach right now."

"That sounds nice," she said.

"Yeah it's neat because the sun is getting lower, but it's still pretty bright, so it's reflecting off the ocean right now," I said. "But enough about that. How was the time with your family today?" I asked, remembering how she mentioned before that her parents and brother would be visiting her for the day.

"It was good," she said. "We went out for a Mother's Day brunch and then just sort of hung out for a while."

"That sounds like a nice day," I said, sensing from her voice she wasn't content about something. "So why don't you sound happier?"

"Well, they've left now, the weekend is over, and I just know how stressful work is going to be this week." she said. "They want the first draft of the user guide for one of the modules done by Tuesday, and I'm barely halfway done with it," she said. "Then they want the one for the next module done by Thursday. I'm so tired of them putting so much stress on me to make these unrealistic deadlines...especially since this is only a temporary job."

"Well, just relax," I said, leaning forward in the sand. "You can only get so much done in the time they're giving you, and they'll have to accept that."

"I guess," she said. "I'm sorry to complain like this."

"It's okay," I said. "I know you're going through a tough time right now."

From talking with her over these past few weeks, I found out that she was laid off from her permanent technical writer job back in January. That job was the very reason she made the 110-mile move from Columbus to Cincinnati about two years ago in the first place.

So after she was laid off, she looked for another job for a few months in both Cincinnati and Columbus. The best she could find was this temporary job she has now—still in Cincinnati—but it's only a twelve-month position. She started in mid-March and they hired her specifically to write all of the user guides and documentation for a software package they'll soon be rolling out. After that's done—in about ten months from now—her job will end and she'll be unemployed again.

"I try not to think about my career situation too much right now," she said, "because when I do, it just gets me down. I mean, this whole technical writer thing was only supposed to be for a year or two while I took a break from school. And then after I got laid off five and a half years into it, I thought that would finally be a good time to start my Ph.D. but then life got in the way of that. And now it just feels like it would be such a difficult endeavor to go back to school."

I still didn't know exactly what she meant when she said "life got in the way," except that she's dealing with some sort of stomach problems that I still know very little about. Whenever I've gently inquired about it during our past phone conversations, she's assured me that she'll tell me more when I visit.

Despite not knowing the full story, I still tried to reassure her. "Well, a lot of people would tell you their career hasn't been a straight path to get to where they want, but they eventually get there—or at least wherever God wants them to be," I said. "And for me, even though I've had a fairly straight path to my dream job, it's still taken some time to get to this point, and I've still been faced my share of difficulties and discouraging times along the way too."

"Really?" she asked. "You know, with all that we've caught up on during these past few weeks, we actually haven't talked much about your career. All I know is what you briefly told me at the wedding and the few things that Scott and Rachel told me through the years. But it seems like they only told me the good parts because they never mentioned any difficulties."

"Well, don't get me wrong, God has definitely blessed me with some good opportunities," I said. "But even with good opportunities, things can still be very challenging. I found that out pretty quickly after college when I started at the private jet business."

"Yeah," she said eagerly. "I've always wanted to know how everything went with that."

"Well, it turned out to be a lot different than I thought," I said. "I started out in the desk job and little did I know how busy and chaotic that would be. Basically, on my first day, I was thrown into managing every administrative function of that business...all while I was attending flight school. There was just way too much work to do with that job and not nearly enough time to do it, which made it really stressful. I remember there were many times I wondered what in the world I got myself into."

"That sort of sounds like my job," she said.

"Yeah, but also like your job, I knew it would only be temporary," I said. So maybe it'll give you some hope to hear that there was a better job waiting for me around the corner. After a few years, when I earned all of the certificates and licenses I needed to fly, they moved me out of the desk job and into a full-time copilot job. That's when I realized again how much I love flying, even though I was still just flying the small private jets."

"That's neat," she said. "And then after that is when you moved to Atlanta? Because I remember that Scott and Rachel told me that you moved."

"That's right," I said as I leaned back watching the sun fade to a deep orange as it kept sinking down closer to the horizon. "After I'd spent a few years flying private jets, I decided it was time to break into the airline industry. So that's when I found a job with a regional airline, flying a little bigger aircraft than before, but they were still pretty tiny. But that job turned out to be a big wake-up call for me."

"What do you mean?" she asked.

"Well, the schedules were challenging, the pay was surprisingly low, and then because the airline was really struggling, I was even put on furlough, which is basically like getting laid off."

"Wow. I didn't know you were laid off," she said.

"Yeah, that was probably the toughest time in my career because of the uncertainty," I said. "I didn't know how long I'd be off from work and all the while, I didn't have a paycheck. In the meantime, I was applying at other airlines, but I wasn't hearing anything back. I remember I started to think that my days as a pilot might be over at that point. And given the difficulties I had in that job, I began wondering if God wanted me to do something else with my life...but I had no idea what."

"I can relate to some of that," she said. "That must've been tough."

"It was," I said, grabbing a handful of sand and watching it flow down through my fingers. "But the good thing about a furlough is that there's a chance you'll eventually get called back to your job...and thankfully, I was after six months and then I was able to get back to flying."

"That's good," she said.

"Yeah, even though that wasn't a glamorous job, I'd never been so happy to return to it," I said. "But then it wasn't too much longer before I got my current job about a year ago and upgraded to flying full-size aircraft and moved back to the Chicago area."

"So are you a captain now too?" she asked. "Because I remember from back in college how you were talking about wanting to be a captain."

"Actually, I was a captain at the regional airline before I left there," I said. "But now at this airline, I'm only a copilot...or First Officer, as they call it. That's the way it works with airlines...even though I have a lower title now, I'm making a lot more money because I'm flying bigger aircraft. But hopefully someday I'll have enough seniority to become a captain of these big aircraft too."

"Well, either way it's impressive and I'm really happy that it ended up well for you," she said. "It must be so neat to have your dream job now."

"Yeah, it is," I said. "And I'm really humbled that I've come this far. But I have to be honest, sometimes it doesn't feel like a dream job."

"Really? What do you mean?" she asked.

"Well, imagine getting up at 2:00 a.m. for an early flight, and then being in two or three different time zones in a day. And I definitely have some hotel stories. Many of them involve loud parties, and others involve various types of bugs...even bed bugs."

"Eww. I don't do well with bugs," she said.

"Then you wouldn't have liked some of the hotel rooms I've walked into," I said. "It doesn't happen a lot, but every so often I'll walk into a room, start to settle in, then see a few too many bugs crawling around the room or even see bed bugs crawling on the white sheets in the bed. In those cases, I walk right back out and end up sleeping in my rental car instead."

"I would *not* like that," she said.

"It's not fun," I said. "But actually, that's *not* my least favorite thing about being a pilot."

"Do I even dare ask what's worse than bed bugs crawling all over the place?"

"Well, it's nothing gross," I said. "It's actually the issue of working on Sunday mornings. It just seems that there are so many weeks where my schedule includes a flight on a Sunday morning, which prevents me from going to church. But that's all part of being a relatively new pilot. I don't have enough seniority to get the more desirable shifts, so I'm stuck with what's left. Like a few weeks ago for Easter, I couldn't even set foot inside a church that day because I had to fly."

"That would be tough," she said.

"It is, but it doesn't stop me from reading the Bible and listening to sermons on my phone throughout the week. And for the weeks I have Sunday morning off, I'll usually find a church in whatever city I'm in and go. But it's hard to attend my church at home very often. So I'm obviously not part of a small group or any other social aspect of my church...so I feel sort of isolated sometimes. But ironically, it's common to feel isolated when you're a pilot. Even though you're around people all the time, many of them you'll never see again in your entire life and the only constant is yourself."

"So do you get lonely?" she asked.

"Sometimes," I said as I watched the very last part of the glowing orange sun disappear under the horizon. "But it seems the worst when I'm at home," I said. "So that's probably why I make it a point not to be at home very much and why I take so many vacations on my days off."

"Hmm," she said with a sympathetic tone.

I continued. "So I guess the lesson is that no one's life is perfect and even though you're in a tough spot right now, you're not alone with having struggles in your career. But I really doubt things will stay this difficult for you. Hopefully my career is proof that even though you have to go through tough jobs and tough situations, things can still turn out pretty well in the end. But nothing will ever be perfect."

"Yeah, that's true," she said.

"Have you read Romans 12:12?" I asked.

"I'm sure I have at some point," she said. "But I don't particularly remember what it's about."

"Well, it says how we should be, 'Rejoicing in hope; [and] patient in tribulation...'[1] So even when we face tough times, we should still stay hopeful and wait patiently for God to carry out His plan," I said. "You have to remember that this is only a small portion of your life. Things are going to get better and I'm sure God still has a lot of good things planned for you."

"I know," she said. "But that's so easy to forget sometimes when I get caught up in the day-to-day struggles with everything and when I have these busy and stressful weeks at work."

"Yeah, but just think, for this week you only have to work four days, and then I'll be out there on Friday and Saturday and you can show me around your stomping ground," I said.

"Yeah," she said brightly. "I'm looking forward to that. I'll look for stuff to do, but I might not be the best tour guide because I don't get out much. Since I live and work in the suburbs, I've only been to the downtown area a few times when my parents and brother have visited."

"Well, that's okay," I said. "I'm sure we'll find stuff to do."

"Are those sea gulls that I hear?" she asked.

"Yeah, they just started swarming all around because some people sat down not too far from me and started tossing pieces of bread at them."

"Don't people know, they're not supposed to feed them?" she asked.

"I don't know. It's probably some tourists," I said.

After barely a minute, even more of them started showing up—some circling while they squawked and others walking aggressively across the sand toward the people with the bread. So I decided to get away from the feeding frenzy and got up and walked further down the beach. By now, the sun had obviously set, and there was only a residual yellowish glow radiating from the west sky.

"You want to know something about sea gulls?" I asked as I walked along the beach, carrying my shoes in one hand and holding my phone to my ear with the other.

"Sure," she said.

"Did you know they live for over twenty years?"

"No they don't!" she said. "You're messing with me, aren't you?"

"No, it's true, they live a long time, and they're really intelligent too."

"Smarter than us?" she asked.

I laughed. "Well, they can fly without needing years of training like me, so maybe."

"Hmm...twenty years? That seems long for a sea gull," she said.

"It's true," I said. "Look it up on the internet."

"Well, I guess I believe you, but I just remember how much of a jokester you were with me back in college."

"Well, you did your share of joking around with me too," I said.

"Not *me*," she said sheepishly.

"Yes *you*," I said as we both laughed.

"I can't believe I'm laughing right now," she said. "You always had a way of making me feel better."

"Well, I'm glad I could cheer you up," I said.

By that point, it was getting late for her—being on Eastern time—so we said goodnight and ended our call. I left the beach shortly after that, and as I made the short drive back here to my hotel, I really hoped her week at work wouldn't be as bad as she's expecting it to be.

~   ~   ~

Now, after I've easily gotten lost in this journal for the past hour, I think it's time to bring this entry to a close, since I have to get up early for work tomorrow to continue this flying trip. I must say, I'm looking forward to getting this flying trip done and getting to Cincinnati to visit Megan.

I'm not sure if the fact that I'm visiting her means that we're trending toward getting back together or if we've just discovered an unexpected friendship with each other at this point in our lives. Right now, I'm not sure how a relationship would work with us living in separate states and with me flying so much. But either way, it'll be good to see her again because I know one thing is for sure—I still enjoy her company.

◆ 6 ◆

Friday, May 14th
Hotel room in Cincinnati, OH
9:10 p.m. (Eastern Time)

Today was the first day of my two-day trip to Cincinnati to visit Megan, and now I finally have a clearer picture of everything she's been going through during these past several months. Needless to say, my heart grew heavy with sympathy for her as she told me about everything. But despite all of that, we still ended up having a pretty good time today.

We just said goodnight a short while ago and then I came back here to my hotel room. Even though the sun has mostly set now, the residual warmth from the day is still noticeable from the light breeze coming in through the window. It was in the low 80's and sunny all day, so shorts and a t-shirt were the only attire I needed.

From traveling to all the different cities where my job takes me, I can easily conclude that the Midwest states have seen a lot of warm weather so far this spring. Today, it certainly allowed Megan and me to spend a lot of time outside once I got here.

Since the last flight of my shift yesterday didn't get into

Chicago until 9:40 p.m., there weren't any more flights to Cincinnati for the night. So since I didn't need to go back to my apartment for anything, I spent last night in Chicago at a hotel near the airport. Then this morning, I flew out at 9:15 a.m. to Cincinnati—as a passenger, of course. After jumping over to the next time zone, it put me here at 11:30 a.m. Then I rented a car and started the thirty-mile drive from the airport to Megan's apartment.

Back when we first planned this visit, she told me it probably wouldn't be good with her condition to drive to the airport to pick me up, and she apologized several times for that. I wasn't mad because I know she's normally very kind and generous in nature, but it still left me confused. However, after what I learned today, it certainly makes more sense now.

Either way, my drive went fairly quickly and took about forty-five minutes as I made my way northeast to get to the far northern suburbs of Cincinnati where she lives. The landscape became increasingly more open with some gentle hills, yet there were still some strip malls and stores that sporadically lined the divided highway I was traveling on.

After I was almost convinced that I'd driven right past her apartment complex without knowing it, I finally saw the main entrance. I turned in and then headed down the narrow road that weaved through it. There were numerous older-looking, three-story apartment buildings on each side—all with reddish brown brick and flat roofs. There was also a small clubhouse and a small, bright blue swimming pool behind it. They had some nice landscaping near the pool, and being mid-May in southwest Ohio, everything was green and in full bloom already.

After I found her building, I parked in front of it and I

noticed it was almost 1:00 p.m. Thankfully, I had grabbed a quick snack in the airport before I rented the car, so I wasn't starved. As I closed the windows and turned off the engine, I felt excited—and a little nervous—that I was now only a few moments away from seeing Megan.

~ ~ ~

After I made my way up to the second floor of her building, I headed down the narrow hallway, found her door, and knocked.

A few seconds later, she opened it and smiled. "Hey Kevin! It's so good to see you again." She stepped out into the hallway and we hugged. She was wearing a stylish light blue t-shirt and tan shorts, and I noticed she had a little more makeup on than I remember her wearing in college, but still not a lot by any means. As I remembered how she looked at the wedding a few weeks ago, I quickly observed again how she looks skinnier than she did in college.

After she invited me in, my eyes gazed around her apartment for a few moments to take in everything. Remembering how clean and organized her dorm room was in college, it was no surprise to see that her apartment was the same way. It wasn't heavily decorated and even seemed a little bare, but not surprisingly, she had several big bookshelves in her living room packed full with all of her books. It was obvious books were still her passion and her collection had clearly grown even bigger since college.

"Not a bad place to call home," I said.

"Thanks," she said. "As you can see, it's not the most modern place because almost everything is original from twenty-some years ago when it was built. But it serves its purpose." She then looked at me. "So from your text message, it doesn't sound like you're starved right now, but I have plenty to eat if you want anything."

"Thanks, but I think I'll just take some water right now," I said.

We stepped into her kitchen and she got two glasses out of her cabinet and began filling them with ice. Then she turned to me. "Oh, I don't know if you've talked to Scott since the wedding, but Rachel said they had a great time on the cruise for their honeymoon."

"Yeah, that's what he said when I talked to him last week. I'm really happy for them."

"Me too," she said, filling the two glasses with tap water. She then handed me a glass and we walked into the living room and sat down on her couch, both sitting sideways so we faced each other.

"Thanks for the water," I said, before taking a sip.

"Sure."

As I made myself comfortable, I was then surprised by something I saw. Sitting on the arm of her couch was a stuffed toy raccoon that instantly brought fond memories back to my mind from our college days.

"Wow! It's been a long time since I've seen our mischievous little friend," I said, picking him up and realizing that every detail looked exactly as I remembered from college—his charcoal-colored fur, his black markings around his eyes, his pointed nose with white whiskers, and his ringed tail.

She smiled. "Yep, I got him out yesterday. I thought he'd be a good conversation piece for us."

"I can't believe you kept him all this time," I said.

"Well, yeah...I did," she said.

There was no question that we had a lot of memories tied

to that stuffed raccoon. It all originated from an October night during our freshman year when we casually showed up at our spot behind the science building—only to find a raccoon there. As soon as we saw him, Megan screamed and clenched my arm. She quickly started backing away from him, and I could tell by the look on her face she was terrified.

He, on the other hand, didn't seem too scared as he kept eating a banana peel that he must have found in the garbage somewhere. But after he realized we weren't leaving, he eventually galloped away peacefully with the banana peel still in his mouth.

Because of the way Megan reacted, I asked if she'd had some sort of bad experience with raccoons in the past. But as I suspected, that wasn't the case; she was simply scared of them. By that point in our relationship, I was beginning to realize that she was scared of a lot of things for no direct reason. But despite her numerous fears, I still loved her.

A few days later, when I was shopping for a few things for my dorm room, I accidentally wandered down the toy aisle and the stuffed toy raccoon caught my eye. As soon as I saw it, I thought it would be a funny gift for Megan, so I bought it. When I gave it to her, I told her she could cuddle with it to help her overcome her fear of raccoons. She thought it was funny, but she also thought it was sweet because it was the first gift I'd given her in our relationship.

Eventually, it became the token of a game we had between us where we'd both try hiding it in drawers, backpacks, or anywhere imaginable to scare each other. I must add that she's the one who started that game, and it's safe to say we both succeeded at scaring each other more than a few times.

"I'm surprised you didn't try to hide him somewhere to scare me," I said, "but maybe we've outgrown that now."

"Maybe. Maybe not," she smirked.

I smiled at her. "You seem happier now than when we talked on the phone a few days ago," I said. "I'm glad to see that."

"I *am* happier," she said. "Somehow today, everything I've been dealing with during these past several months feels a little closer to being behind me now, even though I'm not sure that's true."

"So other than the layoff, and now being in this stressful job, what else have you been dealing with, if you don't mind me asking?"

"I don't mind. I was going to tell you anyway when you visited now," she said. "There's actually been a lot that's happened, so I might as well start at the beginning."

My heart sank as I knew whatever she was about to tell me wasn't going to be good.

She took a deep breath before she began. "I suppose the middle of January is when it all started. It was like dominos. One fell, then another, and then another. But I don't want to get ahead of myself. About a year and a half ago, I met this guy, Brian, at the company where I previously worked. He worked in a different department, but we kept passing each other in the office and that's how we started talking. He seemed really nice, and we seemed to have some things in common, so we started dating. After we dated for about a year, things had gotten pretty serious. So he proposed, and I said yes. He said that we could set a date for the wedding later on."

I nodded as she continued talking.

"Then a month after we got engaged, his parents got divorced after they'd been married for thirty-six years. At first, he was shocked because they never let the problems with their marriage show through to anyone else. After the shock wore off, he was devastated. I felt so bad for him because he was such a sweet guy and he always treated me really well, but it seemed like everything he thought he knew about love had suddenly been shattered. Even before that, he was a little nervous about marriage, even though he still proposed. But seeing his parents get divorced made it much worse for him, and I could tell our engagement was scaring him more by the minute. I think you can probably guess what happened next."

She took a sip of water and continued talking.

"It was a Saturday in the middle of January and he texted me and said we needed to talk. An hour later, we met at a coffee shop and he said he was just too scared to get married. He said he didn't know if he'd ever be ready, and he didn't want me to wait indefinitely. So he broke up with me. I gave him the ring back right there in the coffee shop. He then kept apologizing, probably because I was crying, even though I was trying not to. Then we finally hugged and went our separate ways. So I went from being engaged to being completely single all in about ten minutes."

I saw tears starting to well in her eyes.

"I'm sorry to hear that," was all I could think of saying, as I felt so bad for her. "Do you still love him?" I asked.

"Well, it's been four months, so I'm getting over him," she said, wiping a tear from her cheek.

She took another sip of water. "And then a week after he broke up with me was when I got laid off. They eliminated hundreds of jobs, including mine, which was the very job I moved to Cincinnati for in the first place."

She paused for a moment and looked down as more tears began filling her eyes.

I slid down to her end of the couch and put my arm around her. "I'm sorry you had to go through all of that. We all have tough seasons sometimes, but things always have a way of getting better."

She looked up, wiped her tears, and took a deep breath. "I know. You're right. I need to be strong," she said as she seemed to have restored her composure. "So as if all of that wasn't enough," she continued, "I've been having these stomach problems. But it's really more of an anxiety problem. Do you remember in college how I'd get really nervous sometimes, like before a big exam or something?"

"Yeah, I remember that."

"Well, after college it got worse and sort of turned into an anxiety problem," she said. "I was battling it off and on, and eventually I got it under control pretty well. But when Brian broke up with me, and then when I got laid off a week later, all of that just sent me over the edge."

"Yeah, that's a lot to deal with," I said. As I reflected on what she'd just told me, I wasn't entirely surprised to hear about her struggles with anxiety. With the rather long list of things she was scared of back in college—including raccoons and flying, to name a few—she clearly showed some tendencies toward this. But it never seemed severe enough for me to be concerned. I simply wrote it off to her being the nervous type.

Nevertheless, I had no idea that all of this had been going on with her during these past several months. It quickly occurred to me that Scott most likely knew all of this, since Rachel and Megan are best friends. For a split second, I wondered why he didn't tell me at some point, but I figured that he probably wanted to respect Megan's privacy.

She continued. "It got to where I was having panic attacks several times a day, and with each one of them, it would usually include me throwing up. I couldn't even go out some days because I was just too nervous and the only place I wanted to be was at home. I was afraid to go anywhere because I kept having this constant fear that something really bad was going to happen with whatever I did. If I drove over a bridge, I was afraid it would collapse. If I went in an elevator, I was afraid I'd get trapped. You get the idea."

I nodded as I looked at her, feeling my sympathy grow.

"So with all of the anxiety and panic attacks, it started to affect my stomach," she said. "It felt upset almost all of the time and it became hard to eat because every time I'd eat anything, I'd feel really, really full. Then sometimes I'd get pains in my stomach, and other times I couldn't keep anything down. So for a while, all I ate were bread and crackers, and not very much of them, for that matter. Then that led to a bunch of other problems with malnutrition. Luckily I was laid off then because there's no way I would've been able to work at that point."

"I'm sorry to hear all of that," I said. "That sounds really tough."

"Thanks, but I'm getting a little better now, and I'm trying to eat a more balanced diet. But I'm still not eating normal amounts yet because I get full so quickly. So that's why I'm so skinny now. I guess I could gain a little weight, but I don't know of any girl who likes to gain weight. And this is probably way more than you needed to know."

"No, it's fine," I assured her. "I'm sorry you had to go through all of that." As her words continued settling in my mind, her comment about not wanting to gain weight left me concerned and made me wonder if she may have an eating disorder as well, but it didn't seem appropriate to ask.

Instead, I tried to reassure her. "From what you said, it already seems like you're a lot better than you were. So that's good," I said, optimistically.

"Yeah," she said. "I found a good therapist who specialized in anxiety, and the sessions helped. But I maxed out the number of sessions that insurance will pay for, so I haven't gone for a while. Some days like today, I feel fairly decent, but I still have other days where I'm so weighed down with anxiety it's hard to leave my apartment. That's made the situation with my job even worse. And because of that, my regular doctor just wanted to shove pills at me, but I don't want to take any pills."

"So you're not taking any medication?" I asked.

"No, I hate that idea," she said with a spirited tone. "I don't want to just be numb to everything. Life isn't always happy times, but God is always with me and will help me through this. I'm sorry, but I shouldn't have to alter the chemicals in my brain to get through the hard times in my life. Everyone fights me on this...especially my parents...but I just don't want to be on medication."

"Well, in a few months from now, this will all be a distant memory," I said calmly. "You'll have a better job, and I'm sure your anxiety and stomach problems will be better too."

"Well, thanks," she said with a small smile. "I wish that were true, but I think it'll take more than a few months. My therapist said I'll have tendencies toward anxiety for the rest of my life. It doesn't mean that I'll have panic attacks all the time, but I'm never going to be completely free from it."

"Well, if that's true," I said, "then I suppose it's a lot better than some of the other health issues you could have."

"Yeah, you're right," she said, lightly nodding, seemingly contemplating what I'd just said. Then she quickly stood up from the couch. "Well, you didn't come here to listen to me go on about all of my problems. I want to do something fun now and get out of this apartment. I was thinking that we could go mini-golfing, if you want."

"That sounds good to me," I said.

As we got ready to go, my mind was still processing everything she'd just told me. It was then when I fully realized the magnitude of everything she'd been through. I also realized she might have been right when she said it'll take more than a few months for her to be normal again—or at least whatever normal may look like for someone dealing with anxiety.

~ ~ ~

After we left and had driven just a few miles from her apartment, Megan pointed out her church as we drove by it.

"I go every Sunday," she said. "I like it there. It's non-denominational and I found a small group and they've definitely helped me through all of this stuff I'm dealing with now."

"That's good to have a group like that," I said.

After a few minutes, we arrived at the miniature golf course, and as we began our game, the mid-afternoon sun felt pretty hot. As Megan lined up her first shot, I looked around and realized it was a nice place as there were several waterfalls and streams flowing throughout the course. It was also impossible not to notice the giant silly animal figures placed on many of the holes.

One of those caused us an issue on the fourteenth hole. We were supposed to hit the ball into a hippopotamus' mouth and then it was supposed to come out of his right ear, which was the only way to get to the putting green. When I hit my ball, it went right into his mouth, but it never came out. So I walked up to it and leaned over to look inside, but I couldn't see much. So I got down on my knees and elbows and reached into his mouth trying to feel around for my ball.

I heard Megan laughing behind me. "I'm sorry I'm laughing, but this just looks really funny right now. This would make a really good picture."

"You better not take my picture," I said lightheartedly, still feeling around for my ball.

"Too late!" she called out. "And I'm posting it as we speak."

"Yeah right," I said. "I can tell you're bluffing."

She sighed. "You're right...I'm too nice."

Just then I was able to fling my ball out through his ear, but it went flying right over the putting green and plopped into one of the many streams on the course.

"Oh no!" Megan called out as she tried not to laugh too much. "It just went in the water. I guess that hippo really doesn't like you."

I got up and turned to her. "I'm glad I'm entertaining you here," I said sarcastically.

"Me too," she said, giggling as she followed me over to the stream. Even though I could see my ball clearly through the water, when I tried to fish it out with my putter, I wasn't having much luck. Then Megan tried to help me but she accidentally dropped her club into the water. Before we could grab it, the current had already taken it to the waterfall and then it went flailing down the eight foot drop before splashing into the stream at the bottom of it.

The people who were playing on the hole down there quickly looked up at us.

"Sorry," Megan shouted down.

They gave a friendly wave back but they were probably still wondering how in the world a putter would end up flying down the waterfall.

Megan turned back to me with her eyes big, looking very

embarrassed, yet still having a hint of a smile. "Okay, can I just curl up in a corner somewhere now?"

I smiled. "I know. We've put on quite a spectacle for everyone."

Then we both began laughing—quite a lot—and I noticed the people playing behind us were also laughing. We then decided to finish the last four holes with one club and one ball and just switch off.

After we finished, we told the girl working behind the window what happened. After she eventually believed us, she also laughed a little. Thankfully, she didn't charge us for a putter and said they'd fish it out with a skimmer net after they close.

As we walked back to the car, Megan turned to me. "Well, this definitely gives us a funny story to tell."

"Yes, it does," I said, smiling.

"I still had fun, though," she said, looking at me with her brown eyes and a cute smile. "This might sound weird, but that was probably the most fun I've had in these past few months."

"Me too," I said, looking in her eyes as we walked.

When we arrived back at the car, it was barely 4:00 p.m. but I was getting pretty hungry. So we went for an early dinner at an old diner in town that she suggested. It looked pretty authentic inside with a long counter and spinning stools attached to the floor in front of it. They also had plenty of booths—which is where we sat—and barely fifteen minutes after we ordered, we had our food.

But before we began eating, we both intuitively bowed our heads and said a short prayer together before we ate—just as we did before every meal in college. The food was good, even though Megan only ate about a third of her meal. However, from what she told me earlier, I guess eating part of a chicken sandwich and some fruit is a decent step in the right direction for her.

Just after they cleared our plates, I looked over at her. "So is there anything you want to do now?"

Her eyes lit up. "Actually, I have an idea," she said. "There's this park I go to sometimes and they have some trails to walk on, and after that I like to sit next to the lake and watch the ducks. It's really peaceful."

"Okay, that sounds like a plan," I said.

~   ~   ~

After we left the restaurant, we headed to the park. We drove only a few miles before the suburban landscape had quickly evolved into a winding two-lane road that was surrounded by thick foliage on both sides. Before long, we saw the park entrance and turned in on a narrow road that looked like it led straight into more forest. A short ways in, we came upon a large paved parking lot with a few cars parked in it and some people around. Some were sitting at the picnic tables and others were sitting down by the lake.

By now, it was just after 5:00 p.m. and the sun was shining at a lower angle, but sunset was still several hours away. When we got out of the car, we had a good view of the surprisingly big lake. It was surrounded by dense woods on every side except for the side we were on which was, of course, the picnic area. Also, just as Megan said, the lake had a lot of ducks swimming in it.

She then led me to a trail that hugged the edge of the lake, which gave us some good views as we walked. After we ended up walking for about a mile, she suggested we turn around and head back.

When we arrived back at the picnic area where we started, she looked at me. "So are you up for sitting by the lake and watching the ducks now?"

"Sure," I said.

She got a blanket out of her car and then we walked over to a spot at the edge of the lake that was only about fifty feet from the parking lot. "This is where I usually sit," she said, starting to unfold the blanket for us to sit on. We spread it out on the ground and sat down next to each other. There were probably over a hundred ducks swimming around and some of them were softly quacking while others kept dipping their heads in the water.

"So do you know all of these ducks by name?" I joked.

"Most of them," she said, smiling at me.

"Do you ever feed them?" I asked.

She quickly turned to me. "No! I don't feed them. Don't you see the signs everywhere saying not to feed them? I've actually seen some people get citations for that."

"Wow, they must be serious about that," I said.

"Well, they're wild animals and they can find plenty of natural food on their own, as long people don't condition them to be fed every day," she said. "I know this sounds funny, but that's actually a big part of what I like about coming here. When I watch the ducks, it gives me a different perspective on life. They don't know where their next meal is coming from, but they somehow have the knowledge and peace that they'll always find enough food to eat. Looking at them, they're not worried about anything; they're just living in the moment, floating around on the lake."

I turned to her. "You know, that reminds me of Matthew 6:26. It says basically what you just said...how the birds in the wild don't plan out where their meals will come from, yet God feeds them. And don't we mean more to God than the birds?"[1]

She nodded as I paused for a second.

I then continued talking. "So basically, we should learn from the birds on how to live a more carefree life."

She stared out over the water. "I wish I could live like that," she said softly. "I can't imagine how different my life would be if I could just relax and not worry about anything."

"Well, changing your mindset on life doesn't happen overnight," I said. "But over time, I'm sure you'll get better with that. I think we all need to get better with that to some degree."

She nodded as she kept staring at the lake.

After we both quietly reflected on that for a few moments, I finally spoke. "So tell me why all of these ducks keep burying their heads in the water, so all you see is their tail and their feet flapping. Is that how they find food?"

"I think so," she said. "I think they eat plants and bugs they find in the water."

"Sounds tasty," I said.

She smiled. "Not really."

After we sat there for a while longer watching the ducks and enjoying the scenery, we decided to leave. We then stopped for ice cream, and I was glad to see she ate almost all of her cone. After that, we ended up back at her apartment and I noticed she was beginning to look pretty tired.

Despite that, she quickly suggested that we could relax and watch some TV together. So we sat down next to each other on her couch and eventually found a show to watch that looked pretty funny. After we watched that show and another one after that, she was yawning quite a bit, even though it was barely 8:30 p.m.

"You look like you're going to fall asleep," I said, looking over at her.

"I know," she said. "I get tired pretty easily now because of everything I've been dealing with."

"Well, I should probably leave anyway," I said, "and then we can meet up tomorrow morning before I fly out later in the day."

So we got up and she walked with me over to her front door.

"So what time do you want me to come over tomorrow?" I asked.

"Nine o'clock?" she asked, before she yawned again.

"That works," I said.

"So I'll see you then," she said as she looked at me and smiled as we stood barely a foot from each other. I got the feeling if I would've kissed her right then, she certainly wouldn't have minded, and it almost seemed like that's what she wanted.

"Well, goodnight," I said, turning away to open the door.

"Goodnight," she said with a hint of disappointment in her voice. But a few seconds later she spoke brightly. "Sleep tight. Don't let the bed bugs bite."

I laughed. "That has a different meaning now after the experiences I've had."

She laughed. "I know. That's why I said it."

I smiled back at her just after I stepped out into the hallway. "Goodnight."

"Goodnight, Kevin," she said warmly before closing her door.

~ ~ ~

Now, as I sit here in this quiet hotel room finishing up this journal entry—and just minutes away from going to bed—I realize today has left me with a lot to think about. First, I'm still wrapping my mind around everything Megan's been dealing with—and still is. But on a brighter note, we both had a great time today and it's clear we still enjoy each other's company.

Based on how she acted when we said goodnight, I'm sensing that she'd really like to begin dating again. Part of me would really like that too, but another part of me wonders how or if this will work between us.

It's hard to ignore the fact that we live over three hundred miles from each other. Then the fact that I usually have only one full weekend off each month would make a relationship with her even more difficult. I suppose I could visit her on the weekdays that I have off, but she'd be working for the better part of those days.

Consequently, this could end up being a relationship where we only see each other once a month, which is exactly what we didn't want after college—and ultimately one of the big reasons we broke up. Additionally, I don't know if starting a new relationship is the best thing for her right now considering she just had a broken engagement four months ago.

Either way, I think it's time to end this journal entry and head to bed before I let my worries convince me that getting back together with her is a bad idea.

But whether this is unnecessary worry or legitimate concern that we should both pay attention to remains to be seen. Either way, I'm going to pray about it tonight, and I'm thinking now that Megan and I should definitely have a serious conversation about all of this tomorrow morning.

• 7 •

Saturday, May 15ᵗʰ
My apartment
8:19 p.m. (Central Time)

I woke up around 8:00 a.m. this morning in my hotel room in Cincinnati, and little did I know I'd soon be in for quite a scare. The morning started out normal enough, despite the fact that I was a little nervous about the conversation I'd soon be initiating with Megan.

I flipped on the TV and the weather forecast promised another warm, summer-like day. Appropriately, I threw on a pair of shorts and a t-shirt and then finished packing my clothes from yesterday in my suitcase. Before long, I was ready to head down to the lobby to check out and then head over to Megan's apartment.

But before I could leave the room, my phone rang. As I quickly reached for it in the pocket of my shorts, I thought it might have been Megan, but I didn't know why she'd be calling. When I looked at it, I saw it was my sister and panic immediately shot through my body. I knew something had to be wrong because she never calls me like that, let alone before 9:00 a.m. She's rarely even awake at that time in the morning.

I quickly answered. "Katie? What's the matter?"

"Hey Kev. Why does something have to be wrong? I can't call my brother to say hi?"

Just from hearing the tone of her voice, I could tell at least nothing really bad had happened. But I was still concerned why she was calling and found myself pacing back and forth in the room as I talked to her.

"I just panicked there for a second because...well, you never call me like this and I thought something was wrong," I said.

"No, nothing's wrong," she said.

"Okay..." I said, still baffled why she was calling me.

"So where are you flying today?" she asked with a pleasant tone.

I had to quickly catch myself because I realized I hadn't told her or my parents about how Megan and I are back in touch again—let alone that I was in Ohio visiting her.

"Well, I have a few days off, so I decided to take a trip to Cincinnati," I said.

"Cincinnati?" she quickly inquired. "Why didn't you go somewhere with a beach like you normally do?"

"Well, I hadn't been to Cincinnati for a while, so I decided it would be neat to go," I said.

"Hmm," she said, almost as though she knew I was omitting something. "Well anyway, I don't know how to bring this up, so I'll just ask you. I was wondering if I can move in with you...just until I find a job."

"Oh, now I see why you're calling," I said as I stopped pacing and found myself standing in front of the window.

"Well, how was I supposed to ask you? Come on Kev, you have to understand Mom and Dad are driving me crazy. They're treating me like I'm still a little kid. You know how it was when you still lived at home."

"I know, I know."

"So can I move in with you or not?" she asked.

"Yeah, you can move in," I said. "I'm not home very much, so yeah."

"So you're saying you're glad you won't have to be around me very much?" she asked, seeming slightly offended.

"No, I didn't mean it that way," I said as I turned away from the window. "I just meant that you'll have the place to yourself most of the time, and it seems like that's what you'd want."

She paused, seemingly letting any anger she had pass. "It'll just be until I find a job. Besides, you have a second bedroom, so it's not like you don't have room for me."

"Yeah, you're right, but I don't have a second bed, so are you planning on bringing your bed?" I asked.

"No, I'm not renting a moving truck just to move my bed up there," she said. "It's really old and it's not very comfortable anymore, and I'm going to tell Mom and Dad to throw it out after I leave."

"Well, then I guess you could sleep on the air mattress I have," I said, turning back toward the window.

"So you're telling me even when you're not at home and your bed is just sitting there empty, I'll still have to sleep on the air mattress?" she asked.

"Well, I guess not," I said, realizing I should choose my battles wisely, knowing she'd most likely sleep in my bed when I'm gone whether I agreed to it or not. "But promise me that my bedroom isn't going to look like what *your* bedroom looked like when we were growing up."

"Well, I'll try," she said, "but you should know by now that I'm never going to be as neat and organized as you are," she paused for a second. "You're not going to charge me rent, are you?"

"No, I won't charge you rent. But you'll have to be genuinely looking for a job."

"Okay, but I hope you know that it might take some time," she said.

"Yeah, it might," I said, "but on the other hand, you might find one quicker than you think because there should be a lot more jobs for you around the Chicago area."

"We'll see," she said.

"And another thing..." I said decisively, "I want you to come to church with me whenever I'm home on a Sunday."

"Church?" she asked. "You're starting to sound like Mom and Dad."

"You need to go to church, Katie."

"I don't know what you mean by that...or if I should be offended...but I guess I'll go if that's what you want," she said.

"Good."

"So when can I move in?" she asked.

"Well, I guess whenever you're ready," I said before I paused. "Wait a minute. What about Todd? How is this going to work with you living in Chicago and him living in Tallahassee? And please don't tell me he's moving to Chicago too."

"No, he's not," she said. "He broke up with me two days ago."

"Really?" I asked. "What happened?"

"Well, I don't really know," she said. "He just sent me a text message and said we shouldn't see each other anymore."

"A text message?" I asked. "Weren't you guys together for almost a year?"

"Yep, we met right after I moved here."

"That's really rude he couldn't even sit down and talk to

you about it," I said. "Sorry you had to go through that. Are you okay?"

"I'm fine," she said. The tone of her voice sounded like she had no feeling or emotion about it at all, but she's always been good at hiding her emotions.

"I bet Mom and Dad were happy," I said.

"Oh yeah, they were really happy because, as you know, he definitely wasn't their favorite person," she said.

"Well, I think there's someone much better out there for you than Todd," I said.

"Yeah, probably," she said.

"So now I get it," I said, turning away from the window. "You're not with Todd anymore, so you have nothing keeping you in Florida."

"Not only that," she said, "but I still have some friends from high school in the Chicago area, so maybe now I'll at least have some sort of social life again."

"So do you think you'll miss Florida at all?" I asked, standing next to the bed, studying the painting on the wall.

"Well, when it'll be snowing and frigidly cold in Chicago, I'll definitely miss the sunny and 70-degree winters they have here," she said. "But living here never felt like home to me. I always felt like I was just visiting Mom and Dad who happened to be living in a different house...and a different state, which felt really weird. So now it's like I really don't know where *home* is for me anymore."

"Well, maybe you'll feel more at home living in my apartment, since it's only a few miles from our old house," I said.

"Yeah," she said eagerly, "have you driven by it lately?"

"Actually twice since I moved back here," I said. "The

people who bought it didn't make many changes because it looked pretty much the same. The subdivision did too."

"Hmm," she said. "It'll still be interesting to see it and drive down those streets again."

"Yeah, we have a lot of memories from there," I said as I reflected on how it seemed like just yesterday that I was teaching her how to ride a bike on those quiet, tree-shaded streets of our neighborhood. Once she learned, I remember spending many days that summer riding around every square inch of our subdivision with her. It was one of only a few neighborhoods around that somehow felt really tucked away from the busy suburban streets that—even back then—were lined with numerous retail stores and restaurant chains.

I walked over to the window again and quickly focused back on our conversation. "So are you thinking you'll stay in Chicago for good?" I asked.

"I don't know...maybe," she said.

"So I'm just guessing you probably haven't told Mom and Dad about this yet, have you?" I asked.

She snickered. "Nope, I have a feeling they're going to freak out because now they won't be able to keep tabs on me anymore. So I'm not telling them until a day or two before I move out."

"Well, that's your decision, I guess. I should probably get going now," I said, turning around and looking at the clock next to the bed, knowing Megan was probably starting to wonder where I was. "Let me know when you're ready to move in, and we'll plan for a day when I'm at home."

"I will," she said. "In the meantime, I'll start quietly packing. I don't have a lot of stuff, so I'll probably be ready pretty soon." She then paused for second. "Be careful flying."

"I will," I replied.

As soon as we hung up, I sent Megan a quick text message letting her know my sister had called and I'd be a few minutes late. Then I stuffed my phone back into my pocket, grabbed my suitcase, and left. Even though the phone call with Katie left me with a lot to think about, I knew the more immediate matter for the day was obviously the conversation that I'd soon be carrying out with Megan.

~   ~   ~

When I pulled into a parking spot outside of Megan's building, it was about 9:15 a.m. I quickly walked inside and made my way up the stairs, and then down the hallway to her door. Even though I had a little more clarity than I had last night regarding what I'd say, I still felt a twinge of nervousness run through me as I knocked on her door.

Within seconds she opened it. "Hey Kevin!" she said as we greeted each other with a hug again. She was wearing a pale pink t-shirt and jean shorts today.

I closed the door behind me and we walked into her living room. "Sorry I'm late," I said.

"That's okay," she said. "Why did your sister call?"

"Well, she's going to move in with me." I proceeded to explain a few more of the details as we stood across from each other next to her coffee table.

"Well, that'll be different for you...at least when you're at home," she said.

"Yeah, it will," I said. "We've definitely grown apart through these past several years, so it'll be interesting," I said with an uneasy tone.

"Hmm. Well, maybe this is her way of trying to get closer to you again," she said encouragingly.

"Well, maybe," I said, not entirely convinced of that.

"Or maybe it's *God's* way," she said. "I can tell you from experience that having a sibling that you're close to is a really great thing," she said. "Nobody knows you as well as they do, and the friendship and bond that my brother and I have means a lot to both of us."

"Yeah, you're right," I said, reflecting on her words for a few seconds before I nervously took a deep breath. "Anyway, I was thinking we should probably sit down and talk now."

She gave me a curious look. "Okay," she said tentatively.

We both sat down on each end of her couch, sitting sideways again so we faced each other.

"So I'll get right to the point," I said decisively. "I think we're both probably thinking about the possibility of starting a relationship again. Am I right?"

"Well, the thought has definitely crossed my mind," she said. "What about you?"

I nodded. "Yeah, I've thought about too, but I think we need to talk about it."

I could see her concern quickly grow as she looked at me intently with her brown eyes.

I continued. "We really need to make sure that this is what we both want and that we're both ready for something like this. I mean, you just had a broken engagement four months ago, and I don't know if you're ready to get back to dating yet."

"I feel like I'm ready," she said, looking straight at me without hesitation. "I mean, I still think about Brian, but I know I'm getting over him."

"Well...okay," I said, as her response seemed fairly convincing. "Obviously the next issue is that we live over three hundred miles from each other."

She frowned as she looked down to the floor.

I spoke candidly. "I don't know if you know this, but I

usually can only get about one weekend off each month. I wish it was more, but it's the way it is since I'm pretty low in seniority. The rest of my days off are usually weekdays. So in reality, this could end up where we'd only see each other once a month. And given that neither of us wanted this type of long-distance arrangement after college, I don't know what to say about it now."

She inhaled nervously. "Well, I think we might be able to handle the long-distance better than we would've right after college. It wouldn't be as big of an adjustment because it's not like we've been seeing each other every day up until this point like we were back then. And we're not twenty-two years old anymore, so we'd probably have more realistic expectations. But either way, if things worked out between us and we stayed together, we'd eventually move closer to each other anyway and we wouldn't have to wait two years for me to finish grad school this time."

"I agree with all of that," I said, "but I just want you to know that I'm not exactly in a position where I'm able to move right now. Even though a lot of pilots can commute, my job isn't eligible for that. So I have to live in, or at least live close to, the city I'm based out of, which is obviously Chicago. I could try to get a job at a different airline and maybe somehow I could be based out of Cincinnati, or at least be allowed to commute from Cincinnati, but I don't know how likely that would be...or how quickly that would happen."

She quickly spoke. "I wouldn't expect you to leave your job. And I absolutely wouldn't want you to move to Cincinnati, considering that I don't know if I'm staying here or not. But for now, I have to stay. I don't think I told you but I had to renew my apartment lease back in March, so I still have another ten months left unless I want to come up with a huge amount of money to pay my way out of it. But regardless of that, I also still have ten months left to this job and I promised them I'd stay until the end of this project. I feel like I owe that to them because even though it's really stressful for me, it would really leave them in a bad situation if I quit right now."

"Well, I wouldn't expect you to leave your job either," I said. "So basically with your job, your apartment lease, and me not being able to move in the near future, we'd have at least ten months of a long-distance relationship."

She looked at me curiously from across the couch. "So what do you think about that?"

"Well, there'd be some challenges," I said. "But I know we'd definitely enjoy whatever time we spent together, even if it was just one weekend every month."

She nodded as I saw some hope in her eyes.

I quickly asked. "What are *your* thoughts?"

"Well, I sort of feel like God is bringing us back together," she said. "But there's no way to know for sure...that is, until we try."

I nodded.

She took a deep breath. "If it was anyone else, I probably wouldn't even want to try this long-distance thing. But we're so good together. And when we walked away from each other after graduation that day..." she paused as she held back some tears, "I never thought we'd have a second chance, and I didn't even know if we'd ever see each other again, and that really broke my heart. But now we have that chance, and I don't think we should throw it away. I don't know how all of this will work, but life is way too short to not find out...right?"

I nodded. "Yeah, you're right. We shouldn't give up before we even try."

"That's right," she said. "If God wants us together, then we have to believe that He already has everything figured out with this, even if we don't see it yet. Like it says in 2 Corinthians 5:7, we should '...walk by faith, not by sight...'[1]"

When she spoke those words, I finally felt at peace about getting back together with her and a smile came to my face as I looked up at her.

She smiled back at me. "So are you thinking what I'm thinking?"

"Well, if you're thinking that we should get back together, then yeah."

She kept smiling as I slid down to her end of the couch. I put my arm around her and she leaned her head on my shoulder.

After a few seconds, she turned to me. "So I guess this means we're officially boyfriend and girlfriend now, right?"

I smiled again. "Not without a kiss." I then turned and kissed her. When our lips met, it felt a lot like our very first kiss at the beginning of our freshman year—except this time it felt comfortably familiar. Either way, I know it's another moment in our lives that neither of us will forget, regardless of what the future will hold for us.

~ ~ ~

Even though I had to leave for the airport at 4:00 p.m. today, we still enjoyed the remaining hours we had together. We first went for a leisurely walk on a path that wound through the neighborhood next to her apartment complex. We walked close and held hands under the bright sunshine and it seemed almost surreal—and exciting—that we're back together after all these years. We then went to a local sandwich shop for lunch where she ate about half of her sandwich.

After that, we decided to go back to the park where we were

yesterday and go for a longer "hike." We went on the same path as yesterday that wrapped around the lake, but we went much further today. We held hands for some of the way, at least when we weren't dodging tree roots or keeping our balance on the sloped, unpaved trail. Then we finally arrived at a point where we found a cleared spot at the water's edge and sat down.

"I bet people sit here and fish," I said as I looked over at her.

"Yeah, it seems like a good spot for that," she said. She turned to me and smiled. "Listen to what you hear right now."

I paused and listened. "I don't hear anything, except for some birds chirping."

"Exactly," she said. "Doesn't it feel like we're hundreds of miles away from everything?"

"Yeah, it does," I said, wrapping my arm around her as she leaned her head on my shoulder.

Even though we were on the opposite side of the lake from where we sat yesterday, we still saw quite a few ducks swimming around.

After a few peaceful minutes passed, she finally spoke. "You know how when we were talking before and I said how much it broke my heart when we went our separate ways after college?"

"Yeah..."

"Well, I hope you didn't take that the wrong way," she said. "Back then, I really thought it was a big mistake to break up, and it *did* break my heart. I remember in that following year there were so many times I thought that we should've stayed together, even if it would've been long-distance, and even when I didn't think I wanted a long-distance relationship."

"I wondered that myself sometimes, too" I said. "But ultimately I've concluded that if God wanted us to stay together, we would've stayed together."

She nodded. "You're right. I eventually came to that realization too. When I started grad school, I was really busy, and I figured you were busy too with having a job and being in flight school. I realized how hard it would've been for us to carry on a relationship at that point in our lives. We probably would've had some pretty unrealistic expectations for it too. And also, I realized that it really wasn't the right time for us to get married right after we graduated, like I wanted. So even though it broke my heart and it didn't make sense when we broke up, God was at work and it all makes sense now."

I smiled at her as it felt good that we'd both come to peace with that, considering that it once caused us a lot of heartbreak in the past.

She turned to me and smiled. "But I'm really glad to have a second chance now."

"Me too," I said as I leaned in and kissed her.

After some more kissing, we got up and continued our hike and turned onto a trail that led us away from the lake and even deeper into the forest. Even though it was a sunny day, the thick foliage blocked most of the sunshine, except for a few thinner spots where the sun created a speckled pattern on the ground. After a while, we turned around and headed back the same way we came because Megan explained lightheartedly how the rest of that trail continues through half of Ohio.

When we got back to the parking lot, it was almost 3:30 p.m. and we figured we had hiked about four miles. Even though I was thirsty and little tired from the hike, I could tell from Megan's face that she probably felt much worse than me.

She said she was tired and also admitted that her stomach was bothering her. So because of that—and because I had to leave for the airport at 4:00 p.m.—we headed back to her apartment.

~ ~ ~

As we stood in her kitchen drinking water and eating a few crackers, I was glad to see that she began to feel better. But I'm certain she still felt the same sadness I felt because the time we spent together during these past two days was regrettably coming to an end.

A few minutes later, we found ourselves standing in her foyer, trying to say goodbye.

"This is the part I don't like," she said, standing before me with her eyes getting watery. "I wish you had tomorrow off too, especially since it's Sunday. You could come to church with me...I really think you'd like it."

"I'm sure I would, but maybe next time," I said, feeling the same disappointment she felt.

She frowned a little. "I can walk out with you," she said.

We walked down her hallway and then down the stairs, holding hands the whole way. When we got outside and stood next to my rental car, I saw some tears running down her cheeks.

We looked in each other's eyes and then we kissed.

"Thanks for coming out here," she said, sniffling and wiping the tears from her cheeks. "These were the best two days I've had in a long time."

"Me too," I said as I realized that even though I've been to some pretty neat places, it still doesn't compare to spending time with someone you care about.

She smiled. "So do you know when you'll be able to come out here next?" she asked.

"Not yet," I said. "I'll let you know as soon as I get my schedule."

"I'm sorry I can't drive up to see you at all...or fly," she said.

"It's okay," I said. "But you're getting better and the day will come when you'll be able to do that," I said.

"Well, maybe driving, but I don't know if I'll ever be able to get on a plane," she said.

"That's okay," I said as I hugged her.

She smiled. "Thanks for understanding."

"Sure. Let's pray before I leave," I said.

We stood close and said a quick prayer asking God to bless us in our renewed relationship and to reveal His plan for us, whatever that is, when the time is right.

After that, I looked at her and she looked especially cute standing there looking at me with her pretty brown eyes and with her hair blowing in the breeze as it looked almost blondish in the bright sunshine. It's a picture I won't soon forget—the day we got back together.

"Why do you keep staring at me?" she asked playfully.

I laughed. "Because you look especially cute and kissable right now."

She giggled as she rested her arms on my shoulders and kissed me.

It was a long kiss, as we both knew it would be a few weeks before we'd see each other again.

Finally, she drew back. "Okay, I don't want to make you late for your flight, so you better go because otherwise I'm going to keep kissing you."

I laughed. "And that's supposed to make me want to leave?"

She giggled before kissing me once more.

Finally, I opened the car door.

"Be careful," she said, looking at me with tears beginning to fill her eyes again. "Every time you fly, just promise me you'll be careful."

"I will," I said, still not fully understanding why she—along with my sister—worry so much about me flying. "You know it's statistically the safest way to travel, right?"

"I guess, but I can't help it," she said. "I just worry about you."

"I promise I'll be careful," I said.

We kissed one more time and then I left. The forty-five-minute drive to the airport went smoothly, but it had a somber feel as I knew that each mile I drove was taking me further from Megan—for now at least. The flight to Chicago went fast and arrived a few minutes early.

And now I'm back "home," sitting in my apartment on this quiet Saturday night. I'll definitely need to go to bed soon, since I have to get up early tomorrow for work to begin another flying trip. As I bring this entry to a close, I know Megan and I have only officially been back together for barely twelve hours now, but I'm already missing her...and already feeling the challenges this long-distance relationship will bring.

◆ 8 ◆

Thursday, May 20th
My apartment
9:57 p.m. (Central Time)

This was an eventful day, to say the least. It was the day my sister moved in with me, but I'll also remember this day by the startling phone call I later received from Megan. But before I get too far ahead of myself, I'll start from the beginning.

Even though the four days leading up to today were nothing but routine for me as I proceeded through my schedule of assigned flights for my flying trip, things weren't nearly that calm for my sister and our parents during that time. After Katie finally broke the news to them a few days ago that she was moving in with me, it created quite a stir in their household.

My parents immediately told her they wouldn't allow her to move out, but Katie insisted she was moving out anyway. From what I understand, after they had a few days of some raised voices—and some tears—my parents reluctantly accepted the news, on one condition. My dad insisted he'd drive up here with her because he didn't want her driving the almost 1,000 miles from Florida to Chicago by herself. My mom also wanted to come up here for this, but since there wouldn't be much room left in Katie's car with all of her stuff packed in it, my mom flew here.

She arrived this morning, and thankfully, the thick cloud cover we had earlier didn't bring any rain, and her flight was on time. She was rather easy to spot in the crowd of people waiting for rides when I picked her up at the airport. She was dressed like she was still in Florida, wearing white shorts and a bright turquoise t-shirt with sandals and sunglasses nestled in her curly brown hair.

After that, it wasn't even twenty minutes after we got back to my apartment when Katie and my dad arrived. They'd spent the night in Indianapolis, then drove the last two hundred miles this morning to complete their two-and-a-half-day road trip up here.

They too were dressed like they were still in Florida, wearing shorts, t-shirts, and sandals. It seemed my dad's hair was probably a tiny bit grayer than the last time I'd seen him weeks ago, but his commanding and fit 6'2" stature still makes it hard to believe he's in his late 50's.

When they walked in, of course, my mom and dad hugged each other right away while Katie hugged me. It was pretty clear Katie had been spending her share of time outside lately— probably at the pool in my parents' subdivision—because she had more of a tan now compared to the last time I saw her. Also, her already-blonde hair looked even lighter now.

After we'd all exchanged hugs, Katie then slowly walked into my living room. She looked around and I could tell she was quite wowed with my apartment. It was the same reaction she had when she and my parents visited me shortly after I moved in last year, which was the only other time she'd seen it until now.

My reaction was much the same back when I toured it for the first time before I signed the lease. The contemporary architecture with vaulted ceilings, hardwood floors, dark maple kitchen cabinets, and granite countertops all got my attention. But the town house design with attached garages and the lavish clubhouse including both outdoor and indoor swimming pools left me with only one thought...*where do I sign?*

Then I turned to her. "You want to see your room?"

"Okay," she said with some noticeable eagerness.

I led her down the hallway to my second bedroom as my parents followed us. As we walked into the room, she started looking around. It was pretty bare, which was exactly how it's been since I've moved in. It was nothing more than four walls, a window, and an old desk I rarely use. My parents followed us in and looked around as well, almost as though they were inspecting it.

My dad eventually turned to me. "Were you going to get a bed for this room?"

"Um, probably not," I said.

My dad didn't look too happy with that response.

I quickly continued. "But we sort of agreed earlier that she can sleep in my bed when I'm not home." Then I turned to Katie. "But when I'm home, I'm still sleeping in my bed, and you're sleeping on the air mattress."

"Fine," she said with a dismissive tone.

Even though she agreed, that didn't provide much comfort. I was still fairly convinced that she'd be taking over my bedroom before I knew it. Images of her bedroom while we were growing up flashed through my mind right then. I remember her clothes were scattered all over the place, all of her makeup was spread out on top of her dresser, and her many pairs of shoes were thrown everywhere. But I quickly reminded myself that I'd only be home for a handful of days each month.

After my second bedroom apparently passed "inspection" for Katie, we all decided our next order of business would be lunch, since we were all hungry. So we decided to go to a sandwich shop down the street for a quick meal.

~   ~   ~

When we got back from lunch, it was obviously time to start the moving and unpacking process. So we began by unloading Katie's car. I quickly concluded that she had lied when she told me she didn't have a lot of stuff. Her car was packed as tight as it could be, which eventually translated to boxes and gym bags piled up in her bedroom...and in my living room.

It appeared that she'd brought almost all of her stuff, which made it clear she was probably planning on staying in the Chicago area for a while. Either way, it left me wondering how all of it was going to fit in her room.

In the midst of the four of us unpacking and trying to find a place for everything, my phone rang and I saw it was Megan. "I have to answer this," I announced. "I'll be back in a few minutes."

I quickly stepped outside. "Hey Megan!" I answered.

I could immediately tell she was crying. "I'm so sorry to call you like this because I know your sister is moving in today," she said.

I could immediately tell something bad had happened. "It's okay. What's wrong?"

"They just told me at work that they've discontinued the project they hired me for and they're eliminating my job. Then they made me clean out my desk and walked me out of the building," she said, bawling.

I was shocked to hear that. "What? They really just let you go?"

"Yeah," she said, sniffling.

"That's terrible," I said.

"I know. I just can't believe it," she said, sniffling. "I go in to work on a typical Thursday and then in the middle of the afternoon they call me into a conference room and ten minutes later I'm back to being unemployed again."

"Are they at least going to give you some severance pay?"

"No!" she quickly replied. "It was a temporary job, so I don't get any severance and I have no income now."

I tried to calm her down. "It'll be okay," I reassured her. "You'll find another job. This job was temporary anyway. It just ended up being a little more temporary than you thought."

"I guess, but now I'm stuck in my apartment lease," she said. "I just signed another twelve-month lease back in March because this job was supposed to last twelve months."

"Well, just relax," I said, "maybe this is opening a door for you to go back to school to get your Ph.D."

"Honestly Kevin, I don't see how that's going to happen right now," she said argumentatively.

I took a deep breath. I was trying to make her feel better but it didn't seem like I was helping very much.

"Are you at home now?" I asked.

"No, I'm still at work. They just walked me out like five minutes ago and I'm sitting in my car in the parking lot," she said. "I just wanted to tell you right away."

"Are you too upset to drive right now?" I asked.

"No, that's why I stayed here and called you first," she said.

Silence set in for a few seconds before I spoke. "I feel so

bad for you that this happened," I said, "but you have to believe this is all part of God's plan and somehow it'll all work out for the better. In a few months from now I bet you'll be glad this happened."

"I hope so," she said. "I'm sorry to call you like this. I know your family is probably there, so I'll let you get back to them."

"That's okay, I have time," I said. "I can talk for as long as you want."

"Well, thanks but I really should go home now," she said, sniffling.

"I know it's a shock, but it'll all work out," I said. "I'll call you later after my parents leave."

We said goodbye and I stood outside for a minute to gather myself. I felt so bad for her, and I wished I could've been there to comfort her, but I couldn't. As I walked back in to my apartment, I tried to act like I wasn't upset, but I was. However, I was glad to see that Katie's boxes and gym bags were slowly getting unpacked.

I tried to quietly blend back in and didn't offer any explanation as to who was calling. Through these past several weeks, I hadn't told my parents or Katie anything about Megan, other than she was the maid of honor at Scott and Rachel's wedding. I wanted to see if we were going to get back together or not before I told them anything.

But now even after we're back together, I was also hesitating to tell them because they have a way of making a big deal out of things and always seem to ask a million questions. I suppose they have a right to know, though.

It didn't take my mom long to ask, as she was helping Katie unpack a box. "Who was on the phone, Kevin?"

"That was Megan," I said. My response definitely got their

attention because all three of them stopped what they were doing and looked at me.

"Who's Megan?" my mom asked.

"Megan, from college," I said. "She actually lost her job."

"Oh, that's sad," my mom said. "Has she had any interviews yet?"

"No, it just happened like twenty minutes ago."

"Oh! I'm sorry to hear that," she said curiously.

"Yeah, she's pretty upset," I said.

Then Katie quickly jumped into the conversation. "That's sad she lost her job. But why is she calling to tell you that twenty minutes after it happened? Did you two get back together or something after the wedding now?"

"Well...actually, we did," I said.

All three of them looked at me with stunned looks on their faces.

"What?" my mom asked. "This is the same Megan you dated in college?"

"Yep," I said.

"And why didn't you tell us this?" she asked.

"Well, we just got back together last weekend when I was out there," I said, "and I was going to tell you, but with Katie moving and everything, that sort of took the spotlight."

"Out where?" my mom asked.

"Cincinnati, Ohio. That's where she's living now," I said. "We kept in touch after the wedding, and then I went out there this past weekend to visit her. At that point, we decided to get back together." Obviously, I was omitting that she's dealing with an anxiety problem and just had a broken engagement four months ago, but I didn't want to get into those details right now.

Just as I expected, my parents were quick to start firing questions at me about what she's done after college, how we plan on staying together since we live in different states, and if I think this is going to lead to marriage. But after I gave my best answers for those, the flood of questions receded and we got back to unpacking.

~ ~ ~

By the time late afternoon arrived, my apartment surprisingly looked somewhat organized as a lot of Katie's stuff was unpacked and situated—but certainly not all of it yet. It was then when my mom and Katie decided to go to the mall to buy some things for my apartment that Katie wanted that I apparently don't have. So as my dad and I stayed back, we quickly decided to sit down and relax for a while after what had already been a long day.

We both sat down on each end of my couch. He grabbed the TV remote from the coffee table but then hesitated, and ultimately decided not to turn it on. Instead, he looked over at me as the daylight from the patio door illuminated the tiredness on his face—and the slight wrinkles, which seemed a little more noticeable right then.

He sighed before he spoke. "I'll tell you what, this has been quite a week. For the record, your mother and I still don't think Katie is ready for this, because with you hardly being home, she's basically getting her own apartment in this deal."

"Why don't you think she's ready for this?" I asked.

"Well, I love her very much but I know she still has a lot of learning to do because she really hasn't taken on much responsibility since she graduated." He sighed again and shook his head as he stared out the patio door. "I don't know.

When you were her age, you were basically carrying that whole private jet business on your shoulders with everything you did for them. But she...she still has some growing up to do."

Silence took over for a few minutes as the sounds of birds chirping poured in through the patio door. By that point in the late afternoon, it had turned into a sunny, 70-degree day, despite it being overcast for much of the morning.

Finally, I spoke. "Well, she went away to college and didn't do too bad."

"Yeah, that's true," he said. "But it's a good thing she's smart because I know she did her share of partying. But back then, I just didn't have the heart to come down on her for it. I figured it was her way of coping with the tragedy of what happened to her during her freshman year. At that point, I was just glad she wanted to continue with college."

I nodded in agreement, realizing it wasn't often that we spoke of what happened to Katie back then.

My dad then quickly spoke, seeming eager to change the subject. "Well, I really hope this works out with her living here. She'll probably try your patience sometimes, but I'll tell you what your mother would tell you two when you guys were fighting...you need to love each other no matter what."

"I remember that," I said. "But thankfully, we didn't fight too much when we were younger."

"Not too much," he said, "but every so often you two would really get into it with each other."

"I bet that Mom will probably still tell us that before we say goodbye later today," I said.

"You're probably right," he said before pausing with a hint of awkwardness. Eventually, he spoke. "So...I was surprised to hear you're back with Megan now. I think we all were. But

I won't bombard you with any more questions. I just wanted to tell you that I was glad to hear it because she was always a nice girl, and I hope it works out for you two now."

"Thanks."

"And maybe if you could keep us updated a little more with what's happening, that would be nice," he said.

"I will."

"Good, so how about we see what's on TV now?" he asked, raising the remote.

"That sounds good," I said.

He proceeded to flip through the channels for a few minutes before he eventually settled on the news. It didn't matter so much what was on, though, because we both started dozing after a few minutes.

~ ~ ~

"Hello. We're home!" my mom called out, waking up my dad and me after we apparently fell asleep for a while. She and Katie walked into my living room with their hands full of shopping bags.

"Did you find some good stuff?" my dad asked, sounding groggy but still trying to act like he'd been awake the whole time.

"Yep, I think I'm set for a while now," Katie said.

After they showed us everything they bought, it was after 5:30 p.m. already and we decided it was time for dinner. Since this neighborhood is where my family and I lived for the whole time while Katie and I were growing up, we decided to go to our old favorite pizza place. Not only is it still around, but the pizza still tasted exactly the same as when I was a kid.

After dinner, we decided to go see a movie at a nearby theater. By the time the movie was over, it was almost 8:45

p.m. and the nighttime air definitely felt cooler when we walked outside. We then headed over to a hotel in town where my parents would be staying tonight before they fly back to Tallahassee tomorrow morning. They didn't want to stay too long for this trip, probably so Katie and I would have a chance to acclimate to each other on my day off tomorrow. But my dad also mentioned he has a golf outing on Saturday, so that could've played into their decision as well.

After I parked by the front door of the hotel, we all got out to say goodbye. I hugged my mom, and then hugged my dad.

"Hopefully you'll come down soon to visit us," my mom said with tears starting to fill her eyes. "Let us know how it goes with Megan, too. I always thought you two made a good couple."

She then looked at Katie as I could tell my mom's eyes were getting watery. "We'll still see you tomorrow before we leave," my mom said as they embraced.

"Yeah," Katie said. "Don't start crying, Mom."

After that, Katie hugged my dad before we said goodbye and left.

On the drive back to my apartment, Katie was really quiet as she gazed out of the passenger window.

I looked over at her. "Are you okay? You seem sad."

She quickly turned to me. "I'm fine. I'm just thinking about some things," she said, doing her best to force a plain look on her face, even though I could tell she was sad.

"What are you thinking about?" I asked.

"Well, first about how tired I am and how sore I'm probably going to be tomorrow from all of the moving. And then I'm wondering how much of a scene Mom and Dad will make at the airport tomorrow when we say goodbye. Then of course, I'm wondering if I'm ever going to find a job." She paused before her voice got softer. "And I'm still wondering why Todd dumped me, too. And I'm wondering if moving in with you is such a good idea with how opposite you and I have become."

"Well, first of all," I said, "I can assure you that Mom and Dad *will* make a huge scene at the airport tomorrow... especially Mom."

Katie laughed a little as she looked over at me.

"And as far as finding a job goes, I'm sure you'll find something if you devote time and effort to searching," I said. "But before all of that, you need to decide what kind of job you want."

She nodded. "Yeah, I guess I do."

"And about Todd," I continued, "I think you're better off without him, and I'm sure you'll find a much nicer guy at some point."

"Thanks," she said, forcing a small smile.

"And by the way, I think we'll be fine living together," I said, doing my best to hide the concern I felt about that too.

"I hope so," she said softly, staring out of the car window as we both let silence set in for the rest of the drive.

~ ~ ~

When we arrived back at my apartment a few minutes later, it was already 9:15 p.m., so as soon as we got in the door I quickly headed toward my bedroom. "I'm going to call Megan now," I said.

"Yeah, that's fine," Katie said, grabbing the TV remote from the coffee table. "Do you have cable?" she asked.

I stopped and turned back for a second. "No. I'm hardly ever home."

She sighed with disappointment as she plopped down on my couch before I continued back to my bedroom.

Megan's phone barely rang twice before she answered. "Hey," knowing it was me. As we got talking, she seemed a little calmer than she was when she first called me before, but still noticeably upset. She explained a little more how the company abruptly decided to discontinue the software package they were developing because it was costing too much money, and they decided it would be more profitable to focus on other projects.

"I can't believe that I did all of that work for nothing," she said. "With all of the stress they put me through to meet those ridiculous deadlines...and it's all for nothing now."

"Yeah, I'd be discouraged too," I said. "But at least you got paid for it, even if they're not going to use what you did," I said.

"I know," she said. "But this isn't the way I want to spend my days on this earth...writing user guides that'll never even be published and instead be completely thrown out. That's not why I worked so hard through school. And now the worst part is that I'm left without a job, without a paycheck, and of course with no severance pay, all while I'm stuck in an apartment lease wondering how I'm going to come up with rent for the next ten months. Sometimes I just don't understand why all these bad things have happened to me during this year so far...and now *this* happens, and makes things worse."

"Well, back when I was laid off, it didn't make a lot of sense why that happened," I said. "But my pastor reminded me that, often times, good things can come from bad things. Looking back on it now, I know that being laid off taught me to be more thankful for my job when I was called back to it. And then it wasn't much longer after that when I moved into my current job of flying full-size jets, so it all ended well, even though I didn't understand it in the beginning."

"That's nice to hear, but my story is a little different than yours," she said.

"I know it is," I said, "but maybe this is God setting you up somehow to go back to school and get your Ph.D."

She sighed. "I'm sorry, but if I'm sitting here wondering how I'm going to pay rent, I don't see how I'm going to pay for a Ph.D." she said before pausing. "But I know I shouldn't be pessimistic like that."

"That's right," I said. "You just have to stay hopeful and know that however this all works out, you have to believe there'll be better days in your future."

I then heard her take a deep breath on the other side of the phone. "You're right."

"How's your anxiety through all of this?" I asked.

"Well, not very good," she said. "I've already had two panic attacks today."

"Are you eating?" I asked.

"I just ate a few crackers before you called," she said.

"Did you have dinner?" I asked.

"Well, that sort of *was* dinner," she said. "I'm just not hungry right now."

"You have to eat more than that, Megan. A few crackers isn't enough for dinner."

"I know," she said. "But I threw up earlier and I just don't feel like eating right now."

"Do you think you'll be able to eat more tomorrow after you're more settled down?" I asked.

"I don't know," she said. "Maybe. Maybe not. It depends on how I feel."

After hearing that, I became alarmed because she already has stomach problems and from what she told me before, she's already had problems with malnutrition a few months ago. When I was visiting her, I wondered if she had an eating disorder as well, and with what she told me now, I found myself wondering that again. So this time, I had to ask.

"Can you promise me that you'll be honest when I ask you something right now?" I asked.

"Yeah," she said nervously.

"Do you have an eating disorder?" I asked.

She paused for a few seconds. "Well, not really, but I guess you could call the issues I'm having with eating, a 'disorder.' But it's not like anorexia or bulimia. It's just because when I have anxiety, it makes me feel sick every time I eat...so I don't eat."

"So your doctor knows all about how you weren't eating before?" I asked.

"Yes, and that's why they sent me to a therapist to figure out the cause of it," she said. "But my therapist says it's not like a regular eating disorder because I don't have body image issues or anything like that. Instead, it's just from anxiety and the stomach issues that go with that. But even now, my body weight is still in the normal range."

Her response put me a little at ease, but I still couldn't ignore the fact that she doesn't want to eat right now. I then became curious if she'd told her parents that she'd just lost her job and the effect it was having on her.

"So what did your parents say when you told them you lost your job?" I asked.

"Well, I haven't told them yet," she said. "Maybe I will in another week or so, but I just don't need more drama right now. They're going to yell at me for not taking the medication, and having them yell at me is just going to give me more anxiety."

"Have you talked to Rachel about this?" I asked, thinking maybe since they're best friends, she would've at least told her.

"No."

"Have you told *anyone* yet?" I asked.

"Just you," she said.

At that moment, I realized if she's not eating and doesn't want to tell anybody about her problems except for me, then it's up to me to get her the help she needs, even if it means flying out there tomorrow on my day off.

I did my best to hide my panic when I spoke. "Would it make you feel better if I flew out to see you tomorrow?" I asked.

"You don't have to do that, Kevin," she said.

"I know. But I want to," I said, still acting calm. "I still have tomorrow off before I have to go back to flying, and I could fly out there and spend part of the day with you."

"Really, Kevin, you don't have to fly all the way out here just for a day," she said. "By the time you'd get here, you'd have to turn around and go back already."

"Well, okay," I said, realizing she was right.

"I know you're worried about me," she continued, "but I'll be okay. I'll probably be able to eat tomorrow."

"I hope so," I said.

~   ~   ~

As we continued talking for a little while longer, I was able to somewhat convince her that not having that stressful job anymore may actually lessen her anxiety. I also told her that we'll be able to spend more time together now because when I have my random blocks of days off in the middle of the week, I can fly out to see her since she doesn't have to work now. When I told her that, I could tell her mood brightened a little.

Her mood brightened even more when I told her how when I'm done working after my upcoming three-day flying trip, I'll have three days off that we can spend together.

"It'll be really good to see you," she said.

"Yeah, it will. Maybe we can visit all of your duck friends at the lake again," I said. "I'm sure they'll be happy to see you because you seem pretty popular with them."

She laughed a little. "And maybe we can go visit your hippopotamus friend at the mini-golf place too...if they let us back in," she joked.

We said goodbye after that and I told her she could call me any time if she needed to talk—even if it was in the middle of the night. As much as I was glad our conversation turned more lighthearted at the end, it didn't erase my concern for her. If she continues to not eat, I'm afraid it won't be long before her stomach problems get even worse and she begins having big problems with malnutrition as well.

~ ~ ~

But for tonight, there's nothing more I can do for her, and I really hope she's able to settle down. If there's one thing I've realized today through all of this, it's that I still care about her just as much as I ever did. In fact, if I didn't know any better, I'd say that I'm starting to fall in love with her again, which leaves me wondering if she feels the same way about me. But with everything she's dealing with, that's probably not something she's thinking about right now.

Anyway, I know it's getting late as I sit here typing this in my bedroom while Katie is still out in the living room watching TV. So as I bring this entry to a close, I guess I've decided that

I won't be flying out to see Megan tomorrow on my day off. Instead, I'll be spending the day right here at home and probably helping Katie with any unpacking and organizing that still needs to get done.

But I'll definitely be texting Megan quite a bit tomorrow, and I'll probably even call her at least once. Depending on how she sounds, I'll have to decide whether I should go to work the next day to begin my scheduled flying trip, or if I should rather head out to Cincinnati to get her the help she might badly need by that point.

◆ 9 ◆

Thursday, May 27ᵗʰ
Somewhere over Southeast Indiana
6:32 p.m. (Eastern Time)

I'm glad to have this time to catch up with my journal because this past week has brought both challenges and surprises and has given me quite a bit to write about now. This will be the first journal entry I've written from the sky. As I sit back here in coach on my way back to Chicago after visiting Megan, journaling seemed like the best thing to do now.

This flight took off on time from Cincinnati about fifteen minutes ago and I'm somewhere over southeast Indiana right now. This isn't a full flight by any means, since I have this whole row to myself. It's also a pretty quiet one—no screaming babies, no loud conversations, just the soothing purr of the jet engines and the normal airframe noise as we pierce through the air a few miles above land.

Anyway, to pick up where I left off from my last journal entry, I'll go back to six days ago. That was the day I spent at home with Katie after she had moved in the previous day. That was also my last day off before I was scheduled to go back to flying. Whether I would or not, would obviously depend on how Megan was doing, but I'll get to that later.

For that day, it was just Katie and I—brother and sister— spending the day together. It was actually the first time in many years that we'd spent a whole day together like that, and it was...interesting.

After she got back from driving my parents to the airport that morning, we unfortunately had sort of an argument about orange juice, of all things. After I saw her drink straight from the container, I had to say something.

"Could you get a glass next time?" I asked.

She paused and gave me a look like I was out of line by telling her that. Finally, she responded. "I guess...but I only wanted a few sips of it."

"Well, you should still get a glass," I said.

"Just settle down," she said, closing the refrigerator. "Why are you so uptight about everything? What difference does it make if I drink from the container? I'm not sick and I'm not some stranger...I'm your sister."

I resisted the urge to yell back at her for the sake of keeping the peace. But it was a sharp reminder that this living arrangement would require a lot of patience on my part.

Thankfully, we moved past that quickly and I helped her finish unpacking and organizing a few more things around the apartment. Then I took her out shopping and bought her a desk, a chair, a lamp, and a pool towel she happened to see in one of the stores. We also had lunch at one of her favorite burger places in town. After that, we came home and spent some time assembling the desk and chair.

Then just before dinnertime, we went out grocery shopping, since I admittedly didn't have much to eat around my apartment. She picked out everything she wanted, and again, I paid for it all.

After we got home and got all the groceries unpacked, she suggested we make a stir fry for dinner, so we did. I'm not the best cook, simply because I'm usually not home to do it very often. Katie seemed to know a little more of what she was doing, but she still seemed unsure of some things. Nevertheless, it's hard to mess up a stir fry. So before long, we were sitting down at my dining room table to a home-cooked meal that looked pretty good.

Right after we sat down, she turned on the TV. Apparently, she didn't want conversation, but ultimately, we still ended up having a conversation—or more accurately, another argument.

It all started right after we began eating. She turned to me. "You know, you really need to get out of the Stone Age and get cable...or at least get a smart TV and then I could stream the shows I watch."

"I'm not doing that," I said, still chewing. "I'm hardly ever home. And besides, when you're living here now, you really should be looking for a job instead of watching TV."

She sighed. "Well, thanks for making me feel at home," she said spitefully.

I took a quick drink of water and then set down the glass. "You really expect me to dish out more money for a new TV and cable after I just bought you all that stuff today and paid for all the groceries...which, by the way, I never heard a 'thank you' for any of that."

"I thought I said thank you," she said.

"No, you didn't."

"Well, I meant to," she said. "But you have to understand that there's no way I'm going to look for a job every waking hour of the day. TV is the one thing that makes me forget about my situation, and it's the only thing I enjoy right now because I'm not having much fun otherwise these days. But apparently, while I'm living here I'm not even going to have that to enjoy now."

"Well, you can still watch TV, just not cable," I said. "If that's not good enough for you then maybe you could get a part-time job in the meantime and then you could buy a new TV yourself," I said.

She glared at me from across the table for several seconds. At first she looked angry, but then she seemingly realized she had no argument for that. She then continued eating, as did I. Ironically, I was glad the TV was turned on at that point because it drowned out the silence between us.

Thankfully, we both settled down some as the evening continued. After we cleaned up dinner, we watched a movie from my eclectic, yet small collection of DVDs. Then I went to bed around 11:00 p.m. She stayed up for a while after that as she'd apparently found something good enough to watch on regular TV.

~ ~ ~

The next morning came and I needed to finally decide if I should go to work to begin my three-day flying trip, or if I should call in sick and catch a flight out to Cincinnati to be with Megan. Based on what I could glean from the text messages I'd exchanged with her—and a short phone call—during the previous day, it seemed like she was a little better.

She said she was eating some, but I could tell she was still pretty upset and nervous about her situation. Either way, it almost seemed like she would've gotten angry with me if I would've forgone my flying trip and flown out to check on her instead. So I hesitantly made the decision to proceed with going to work that day.

I had a relatively late start time that morning with my first flight not being until 11:45 a.m. As I stood in my kitchen eating a final snack before I left, Katie emerged from her bedroom. Her eyes were still half shut and she was still wearing what she calls her pajamas, consisting of an old pink t-shirt and gray workout shorts.

"Rise and shine," I said, as she walked into the kitchen. I sensed that she probably wasn't accustomed to being up this "early," even though it was already after 9:00 a.m.

She threw a smirk at me as she opened the cabinet and grabbed a cereal bar. As she began unwrapping it, she leaned back on the edge of the counter and looked at me curiously.

"It's been forever since I've seen you in a pilot's uniform," she said.

"Yeah, I guess it has," I said. "Probably the last time was when I worked at the private jet business. That was back before I moved to Atlanta and before you went off to college."

"Yeah, that's been a long time ago," she said, blankly gazing at me as she was still waking up.

A few minutes later, I had to leave.

Just as I stood up from putting on my shoes, she appeared in front of me and wrapped her arms around me. "Be careful flying," she said.

"I will," I said, hugging her back.

Then I headed out to the airport, and about halfway there, my parents called. They wanted to know how it was going with Katie, on what was only the second day of her living with me. I didn't care to tell them about the arguments we'd already had, because I don't think they need to know about every little disagreement. So to put them at ease, I told them it was going fine. They asked if I was planning on calling Katie to check on her each day when I'd be gone, but I didn't see a need for that. I also advised them against doing that too, but I wasn't sure if they'd listen.

In reality, I knew while I was gone, I'd probably be focused much more on monitoring Megan rather than Katie. Given Megan's condition, I still felt more than a twinge of guilt and uncertainty with leaving on a three-day flying trip for work, and I still wasn't fully convinced it was the right choice.

~ ~ ~

Throughout that flying trip, I texted and called Megan a lot and I was pleasantly surprised that she clearly sounded better and better each day. In fact, by the third day of my trip, she sounded completely normal—and even genuinely happy. I later found out why, after I finished my trip and arrived at her apartment that next morning.

Even though it was well before noon, it was already shaping up to be a warm and sunny day as I walked into her building and knocked on her door.

She quickly opened the door and smiled. "Hey Kevin!" She quickly hugged me and her face was gleaming with happiness. She was wearing a bright pink t-shirt and jean shorts and I couldn't tell if the color in her cheeks was from excitement or some light blush she'd put on before I arrived.

"You seem like you're in a good mood," I said as we walked into her living room.

"I am!" she said. "I have some really exciting news! I'm moving to Chicago!"

"Really? That *is* exciting," I said as that was certainly a surprise to me—but a pleasant one. "Did you find a job there?"

"No. Actually the idea just came to me a few days ago," she said. "I was sitting here all worried about not having a job and not knowing what I was going to do. But then it was like a light bulb just went on in my head when I thought about how I have an aunt who lives in the Chicago area. So I called her and she said I was definitely welcome to move in with her, rent-free, until I find a job or whatever I'm going to do. So then the next day I went to the leasing office here at my apartment complex and told them I got laid off and asked if they could let me out of my lease, and they did! The only catch is that I have to be out of here by the end of this month, so that only leaves me less than a week to pack and get out."

"Wow! This definitely isn't what I expected to hear, but I'm really happy," I said as I hugged and gave her a quick kiss. "And you seem really happy, which I'm glad to see."

"I *am* really happy," she said with a smile. "It's like God has just handed me the piece of the puzzle that I need for my life right now. You and I will live close to each other, I'm going to live rent-free with my aunt, and I'll be in a big metro area with lots of jobs and schools around."

"You're right," I said. "But I just have to ask if you're okay with leaving your life in Cincinnati behind...your church, your friends, and any jobs that might come up?" I asked.

She snickered. "There's not much to leave behind. It's been a nice place to live...the people are friendly and the city is safe...but I only moved here for a job. I had no clue that this Cincinnati chapter of my life would include a broken engagement, a layoff, anxiety and stomach problems, and then to top it all off, another layoff. The only thing I'll miss is my church and my small group. They've been great, but I know it's time for me to move on."

"And what about moving further from your parents and brother?" I asked.

"Well, I'll miss them," she said, "but we're already two hours away, as it is. And I'll have you and my aunt around, so I think I'll be fine."

"Okay," I said, "but what about using your mom's tuition discount to get your Ph.D.?"

She frowned a little. "I can't. My mom is retiring after their summer school program finishes this August, and then I won't be eligible for the discount anyway. So there's no decision to even make with that. But it's my own fault...I waited too long."

"Well, you shouldn't feel bad about that," I said. "It's totally understandable that you needed a break after you finished your master's degree. That's a lot of school for anyone."

"Yeah, it is," she said. "What I'm really hoping is that I can find a part-time teaching assistant job at a school somewhere in the Chicago area while I'm enrolled in their Ph.D. program. Then I could get teaching experience and my Ph.D. at the same time. That would be like my dream right now. But I guess I'm still open to taking another technical writer job if I have to. At least it would pay the bills."

"Well, whatever you end up doing, you have a lot of options in a big-city area like Chicago," I said. "And all the while, we'll live close to each other now."

She smiled. "I know. I think that's what I'm most excited about." She then opened her freezer and grabbed two Popsicles and handed me one. "I have to get rid a whole box of these before I move, so eat up."

"Okay then," I said, smiling as we each unwrapped them. "So where exactly does your aunt live?"

"I don't know the Chicago area very well, but I have her address," she said, walking over to her desk and grabbing a piece of paper.

After she handed it to me, I then studied it for a few

seconds. "I think I know this neighborhood. If I remember right, some of my friends from high school lived there." I typed it into my phone with my free hand as she stood next to me watching, also still holding her Popsicle.

"Yeah, this is it," I said. "It's actually pretty close to where I live now, too. It says on here it's twelve minutes from my apartment."

She turned to me and smiled. "Wow, I didn't realize it was that close! I can't believe we're only going to be twelve minutes from each other."

"I know. That's going to be nice," I said. "But you know I'll still be gone quite a few days on flying trips for work, right?"

"I know," she said. "But we'll still see each other a whole lot more than we do now."

"That's definitely true," I said.

After we finished our Popsicles, we walked into her living room and stood next to each other.

She looked at me. "I'm really excited, but I can't believe how much I have to pack before I move next week."

"Well, I suppose I could help a little," I joked.

She smiled and playfully hit my arm. "You better help more than a little, because there's no way I'm getting all of this done by myself."

I smiled. "You know I'll help you. In fact, it'll probably end up being what we do for most of my time here now."

"Probably," she said.

"Are your parents going to help you too?" I asked.

"I don't think so," she said. "They offered to...and they also wanted to help on moving day...but I told them they didn't have to. I've decided I'm just going to hire a moving company. It'll be easier for everyone that way."

"Do they approve of you moving to Chicago?" I asked.

"Well, they have mixed feelings about it," she said. "They initially didn't think it was the best idea, but they're glad that it's making me happy and giving me hope. They're also glad you and I are back together. They always thought you were a nice guy."

"Yeah, I remember they were always nice to me," I said.

She then looked at me, seemingly trying to gather some courage to say something. "Um, I know I'm hiring movers, but I was wondering if you could still fly here on the 31st when I move and drive to Chicago with me. I know that's Memorial Day and everything, but making that road trip by myself still seems pretty daunting."

"Yeah..." I said, "but it might have to be the next day because I'll still be working on the 31st, wrapping up a four-day flying trip."

"That's fine," she said.

"But you have to be out of your apartment on the 31st, so where are you going to stay for that night?"

"I can just stay at a hotel," she said. "It's fine."

"Are you sure?" I asked. "I can see about rearranging my flying schedule."

"No, I don't want you doing that." She then smiled as she turned and faced me. "You know what I love about you?" she asked.

"What?"

"You worry too much about me," she said. "You were the same way in college and that's what I loved about you back then too."

We then embraced tightly and I felt her take a deep breath. As I continued pondering her words, I realized she'd basically just told me she loves me. As that thought resonated in my mind, it brought a smile to my face. Even though we hadn't said that since we've gotten back together now, it seemed clear that we *did* love each other and I was so glad to hear her say that.

I leaned back from our embrace. "So is this the moment when we should officially say 'I love you'?"

She smiled. "I hope so."

"I love you," I said.

"I love you, too, Kevin."

We then stared into each other's eyes for a few seconds before we shared a kiss—and it wasn't just a quick kiss, either.

As much as we both could've stood there all day in each other's arms kissing, we knew we needed to get packing. But before we could do that, we obviously needed boxes. So we embarked on a trip to four grocery stores to gather up as many boxes and as much packing paper as we could fit in her car.

Megan doesn't have a ton of stuff, but enough to make it a challenge to pack everything in the next few days—especially considering the hundreds of books she has. Those are what we started packing first and even though they were easy to pack, they made for an abundance of heavy boxes. Then we moved on to packing anything fragile, which required wrapping those items in ample amounts of packing paper.

After we finished that, it was almost dinnertime, and we were both in full agreement that we'd done enough packing for one day. So we went to dinner at a sandwich place. After that, we came back to her apartment and watched a movie—and caught up with some more kissing too.

By the time I left and made the short drive back to my hotel, the tiredness had definitely caught up with me. I headed straight to bed and fell asleep quickly. But I still managed to say a quick prayer just before that. I thanked God for allowing Megan to move to Chicago and prayed that this will truly be the beginning of a better season in her life.

~   ~   ~

The next morning, I arrived back at her apartment, and we picked up right where we left off with packing. The hours passed quickly as the stacks of boxes in her living room got bigger and bigger. After doing nothing but packing the whole morning, we took what we thought would be a short break and went out and grabbed a quick lunch. But with the sunny and warm weather, we opted to take a longer break and went miniature golfing.

I'm happy to say we didn't lose any clubs or golf balls this time. But Megan still started laughing as soon as we came to the fourteenth hole where the infamous hippopotamus resided. In our minds, he was still solely responsible for the problems we had the last time with losing the ball—and the putter, too.

"Maybe he'll be nicer to you this time," she said, smirking, as I lined up my putt.

"Let's hope," I said, hitting the ball into his mouth. I was relieved when it didn't bounce back out and actually came out of his ear like it should've. Megan then hit her ball and also didn't have any problems.

She then gave me a playful smile. "I think we need a picture with Mr. Hippo," she said. So we both kneeled down next to him as she snapped a picture of us with her phone, laughing the whole time. I realized at that moment that this was the happiest I'd seen her throughout this whole time that we've been back together now, and *this* was the Megan I remembered from college.

It was also encouraging to see her eat almost an entire chicken sandwich at dinner—and we even shared a sundae for dessert. After dinner, we went to the park to watch the ducks, but we mostly took advantage of the peaceful scenery to catch up on some more kissing. Then we came back to her apartment and watched TV for a while before I went back to my hotel for the evening. It's safe to say we had a nice afternoon and evening together, even though we didn't get any more packing done.

But for today, packing was all we did—that is, until I had to leave for the airport later in the afternoon. After this trip, I've definitely seen enough brown boxes for a while. But the good thing is that with all the hours we spent packing during these past three days, there's not much left for her to pack now.

Another good thing is that saying goodbye this afternoon was a lot easier for both of us this time. We both knew this was the last time we'd say goodbye under these circumstances, and that we'll soon only be separated by a twelve-minute drive, instead of hundreds of miles. Not only that, but we'll see each other again in only five days when I'll head out there to make the drive to Chicago with her. But probably the thing I'll remember most about this goodbye was that it included us saying, "I love you."

~   ~   ~

Now, as I'm still in the sky and en route back to Chicago for tonight, the sun is just beginning sink low enough to cast rays through these oval windows. But there's still a while until sunset. In fact, I'll probably arrive in Chicago before it's dark, which actually has me rethinking a few things now. Originally, I was planning on just spending tonight at a hotel near the airport instead of going back to my apartment. It seemed logical since I go back to work tomorrow to begin my next flying trip with an early-morning flight.

But as long as this flight stays on schedule, I'm realizing I'll actually have enough time to head out to the suburbs and spend tonight at home. So I think that's what I'll do. Besides, it'll give me a chance to see Katie and see how she's doing on her own. She hasn't called or texted me, so I assume everything is okay. Admittedly, I haven't seen a reason to be too worried about her during these past six days.

Instead, my thoughts have been much more focused on Megan. But I have to say, I'm still quite amazed at how quickly she bounced back from losing her job—seemingly almost too quickly. I guess since she decided to move to Chicago, she finally feels like this is signaling the end of the tough season she's been through. I really hope that's true.

I certainly did my best to echo the hopeful excitement she was showing when we were together during these past three days. But a part of me is still left wondering if her moving to Chicago is really going to solve her problems.

I worry if she'll be able to find a teaching assistant job, like she's hoping for. If she doesn't, will she be forced to take another technical writer job and be miserable with it again? That could send her anxiety back into full swing too. I also wonder if she'll be okay with living further from her parents and brother. And I especially wonder if she'll be okay with me being gone so much for all the days, nights, and weekends that being a pilot requires.

I don't know the answer to any of those questions, but as I sit here typing, I realize I better stop these thoughts from going any further. Sometimes it's so easy to forget that God has it all figured out already and we simply need to trust in His plan. Like it says in Jeremiah 17:7, "Blessed is the man that [trusts] in the Lord, and whose hope [is in] the Lord..."[1]

Even though it looks like she still might be up against some big challenges—even after she moves—I have to trust that God has a plan for her, whatever that may be. In the meantime, I should just be thankful that the girl I love will only be a twelve-minute drive away...at least for the days when I'm not flying.

◆ 10 ◆

Friday, May 28th
My apartment
10:38 a.m. (Central Time)

Today has been quite a day so far, and even though it's only after 10:30 a.m., I'm sitting here in my apartment, feeling exhausted right now. I was up until 4:00 a.m. last night—or I should say this morning—because I was too upset to sleep. Little did I know after the peaceful flight back to Chicago last night, the rest of the evening would be far from peaceful.

After the flight arrived a few minutes early last night, I made my way through the terminal and after a short shuttle ride, I arrived at my car in the parking lot. As I put my suitcase in the trunk, I still felt the warmth radiating from the pavement from what had presumably been a warm day.

When I got in my car and started it, I saw it was just after 7:00 p.m. It was nice to have gained an hour with coming back into Central time. Clearly, I had enough time to go back to my apartment for the night instead of staying at a hotel near the airport.

That seemed like an even better idea when I realized this would be the last chance I'd have to go home for a while to see how Katie was doing. If I didn't, I'd be gone for work during the next four days, and after that trip was over, I'd immediately be going to Cincinnati to begin a road trip with Megan for her move to Chicago.

So considering all of that, I headed back to my apartment. As I drove west from the airport, I was treated to the tail end of a pretty sunset. Rush hour was long over by then and the traffic was fairly light—at least the Chicago area's version of "light." When I turned down my street, I noticed a lot of cars parked on both sides.

As I got closer to my building, I saw my driveway had two cars parked in it with the last one being Katie's. So with no room left in my narrow driveway to park, I had to drive two buildings down before there was even a place to park on the street.

By this time, it seemed pretty clear Katie had decided to throw a party in my apartment, and I felt my anger beginning to grow by the second. As I walked to my building, I heard some loud music and a lot of laughing and shouting coming from my apartment. My first thought was that someone in this normally quiet and serene neighborhood would call the police—if they hadn't already. My next thought was how I didn't want to deal with this because I needed to get to bed early in order to get up at 5:00 a.m. for my first flight.

I was tempted to just turn around, get in my car, forget I ever saw it, and spend the night at a hotel. As it was virtually a guarantee that someone would call the police, I thought maybe Katie could learn a lesson the hard way for once. But I thought better of it because it's my apartment, and I'm responsible for what happens in it. But more than that, I couldn't stand the thought of letting my little sister get arrested if she and her friends decided to be uncooperative with the police.

"Kevin? What is going on?" Those words startled me from my thoughts as I was still standing in front of my building. I turned around and it was Joyce, my middle-aged next door neighbor, who'd come out of her apartment and looked quite angry.

"Oh," I exhaled, "Hi Joyce." I knew right away this wouldn't be a pleasant conversation.

"You know, all I wanted was a quiet evening at home tonight," she said. "I never thought I'd have to put up with loud partying like this around here...on a Thursday night, no less."

"I'm sorry," I said. "I just got home right now and apparently my sister has decided to throw a party. But don't worry, I'm going to send everyone home. Give it about twenty minutes and everyone will be gone."

"Well, they better be, because I've been putting up with this for hours now. I was almost ready to call the police. And do you know what they're doing on the patio?" she asked.

"No..." I said as I was afraid to even ask.

"They're playing some sort of drinking game where they're throwing ping pong balls into cups," she said. "And they've been constantly trampling across my patio to pick up the balls that get loose."

"I'm sorry," I said again. "I'll take care of it."

I walked up to my door and it was unlocked, so I walked right in. I saw what was once my clean and peaceful apartment now being completely trashed by about twenty people. They were all early twenty-something guys and girls. The guys were wearing bathing suits, t-shirts, and baseball caps—some were wearing flip-flops and others were barefoot. The girls were wearing summer tops, shorts, and flip-flops. Everyone had either a beer bottle or red cup in their hand, and they all seemed well on their way to getting pretty drunk.

I froze in the doorway as I realized that it had instantly become my responsibility to get twenty drunk people home safely. I didn't see Katie right away, so I walked through the crowd of people as my unfamiliar face received some weird looks. Finally, I made my way into my kitchen, which I hardly even recognized, since it was filled with so many people. I quickly spotted Katie standing and talking to a few other girls, and of course, they were all holding red cups.

"Katie," I said sternly. "Let's go outside."

"Kevin? What are you doing here?" she asked argumentatively. "I thought you weren't coming home until like next week sometime."

"Well, I'm home now, and we need to go outside and talk."

She sighed disgustedly as she set down her cup, and then followed me outside.

I made my way out to my front porch and waited a few seconds before she came out and closed the front door behind her.

"What are you thinking?" I asked. "You can't have a party here. These neighbors are going to call the police. In fact, Joyce just told me she was getting ready to do just that."

"Yeah and the police would come out and tell us to quiet down and we'd quiet down," she said. "We're all over twenty-one and besides this is hardly a party. We all gathered at the pool this afternoon after my friends got off from work and then decided to come back here for a little while."

"You took these people to the pool *here*?" I asked, only imagining the chaos they must have unleashed there as it's normally nothing but people sunbathing and floating on rafts.

"Yeah, I did," she said defensively. "It was a hot day."

"And let me guess, you guys got rowdy and the management kicked you out," I said.

"Well..." she hesitated. "After we were there for an hour, they just said we should leave."

I took a deep breath and shook my head. "You know, Katie, I've really tried to help you, and this is what I get?"

"Don't even start with that," she yelled. "I'm not doing anything wrong."

"Yeah, you are," I said. "And you need to get all of these people out of here."

After some more spirited bickering, she then told me they were all planning on spending the night at my apartment so they didn't have to drive home. There was no way I was going to let that happen, but there was no way I was going to let them drive home either. So I agreed I would call a cab for everyone. All of her friends' cars would be left behind at my apartment, but that wasn't my problem. They'd figure something out the next morning.

About twenty minutes after I called, four minivans showed up from the taxi company and I had to prepay the drivers in cash before they'd even let anyone in their vehicles. Despite the widespread confusion and some grumbling I heard from her friends, they all eventually obeyed the order to leave and got in the cabs. It ended up costing me well over a hundred dollars and was yet another time I ended up fixing a problem that Katie had created.

~ ~ ~

After all of the people were gone, I went back into my apartment, which was an absolute mess. Beer bottles and red cups were sitting everywhere. There were a few stains in the carpet, and my kitchen table was still sitting out on the patio from their drinking game. Katie was in the kitchen, waiting for me to come back inside, and she was ready to pounce.

"I can't believe you embarrassed me like that," she shouted.

"I can't believe you're being so irresponsible," I said. "What were you thinking?"

I could see the anger on her face and smell the alcohol on her breath as she spoke. "You're being worse than Mom and Dad," she yelled. "I'm tired of you always acting like my third parent."

"I'm tired of you using me just to get a free place to live and party with your friends," I said. "Who were all those people anyway?"

"People I knew from high school," she yelled back.

"So you just invite them over to trash my apartment?" I asked.

She paused for a few seconds. "You know what? You're not going to have to worry about this anymore. Amy told me tonight I could just move in with her. So that's exactly what I'm doing first thing tomorrow morning."

"Amy was here tonight? That's just wonderful. I should've known she was behind this," I said as I remembered Amy all too well. Thankfully, much of Katie's social life throughout high school was *not* centered around Amy. Instead, it was centered around Beth, a short, skinny, and shy brunette who was Katie's best friend back then—and a much better influence on her than Amy.

Even though it wasn't until college that Katie's partying became much more prominent, there were still times in high school when she wanted to party. In that case, she'd call Amy—not because they were close friends, but rather because Amy always knew who'd be having a party on any given weekend.

Amy was arrested several times for underage drinking before she even graduated from high school. Every time Katie went somewhere with her, it created huge drama with our parents. For a while, they banned Katie from going anywhere with her.

"That'll be real good," I said. "Then you two can throw parties all you want. You think you'll ever have time to look for a job?"

She turned and began walking away. "Just leave me alone."

"You know what? You've lost your chance. I want my keys back right now," I demanded.

She went in her room and came out a few seconds later. She then threw the keys on the kitchen counter so hard that they went sliding off the other end onto the floor. She then stormed off and slammed the door to her room. I didn't hear anything from her room after that, so she presumably had no trouble getting to sleep with all that she drank.

On the other hand, I was way too upset to sleep at that point, so I started cleaning up the mess here in my apartment hoping it would somehow calm me down. I picked up numerous beer bottles and cups, scrubbed beer stains out of the carpet, and dragged my kitchen table back inside from the patio. Even though it put a dent in the cleaning, it still didn't leave me in much of a mood for sleeping.

I tried reading a book for a while, but around 1:30 a.m. the harsh reality set in that there was no way I'd be able to get enough sleep to wake up at 5:00 a.m. for my flight. So I decided to call in "sick" at that point. After I did that, I sat down on my couch, turned on the TV, and started flipping through the channels in an attempt to settle down and get my mind off of this.

~   ~   ~

Eventually, after watching some infomercials—seemingly the only thing on at that hour—I started to relax a little more. As I sat there in my dark living room—illuminated only by the TV—my mind began to wander. I started thinking back to the simpler and better times from when Katie and I were younger. Specifically, I began reminiscing about the long string of summers when we were both on summer vacation from school and our parents were both working.

By my parents' request, I spent every minute of those summers with Katie, since she still needed a babysitter, and since I was almost seven years older than her. But we found a lot of ways to pass the time—and had a lot of fun in the process.

We went to the community pool almost every day for several of the summers, and I taught her how to swim. When I started driving, she was still only nine years old and was surprisingly accepting of when I brought her along to meet up with my friends. I still have images in my mind of her sitting beside the basketball court in the park with a coloring book while I played ball with my friends.

On other days, I remember we'd go get milkshakes and then drive to a strip mall that was next to the municipal airport in town. We'd then walk a good way behind the strip mall and sit down in the grass in front of the tall chain-link fence that surrounded the airport. It was right behind the runway and gave us a great view to watch the small propeller planes take off and land. Even though she doesn't have the same love of flying that I have, she still enjoyed watching the planes buzz over us and then touch down just a few hundred feet in front of us.

And then there were times we'd go hiking at a nearby forest preserve—many times with her best friend, Beth. I remember one day when the two of them took a keen interest in the abundant amount of caterpillars that we kept seeing on the trail. Toward the end of our hike, Katie picked one up and couldn't wait to bring it home and keep as a pet to watch it transform into a butterfly.

When we got home, I found an old shoebox in our basement and punched tiny air holes in the lid. Katie gathered some leaves for it to eat, a paper cup of water, and a small twig for a place to build its cocoon.

When I discovered the next morning that it had somehow escaped from the box, I quickly walked back to the trail, found another one that looked exactly the same, and brought it home before Katie even woke up. Thankfully, I did because after several days of eating leaves, it spun itself into a cocoon. Then a few weeks later, it emerged as a butterfly, and Katie was awestruck by that. I still don't know if she realizes how much I care about her.

As the infomercials were still sporadically lighting up my living room, I eventually came around to thinking that I should probably forgive Katie and try to get her to stay. I thought of James 2:13, which basically says if we don't show mercy to others, then how can we expect God to show mercy to us?[1] I also remembered how my mom would always tell Katie and me to love each other no matter what. She warned us that it wouldn't always be easy, but it would always be necessary.

Even though I was still undoubtedly angry at Katie, I knew I loved her too much to watch her move in with Amy, which would most likely lead her down an even worse path in her life. I really didn't want to see her waste more time in this indecisive, unemployed, and careless state, which has unfortunately been her way of life since she graduated from college last year.

So after I eventually felt settled down enough to go to bed

at about 4:00 a.m., I set my alarm clock for 8:00 a.m. That way, I could most likely wake up before Katie to stop her from leaving and invite her to stay—and just hope that she would.

~ ~ ~

When I woke up to the buzzing of my alarm this morning, I was in disbelief it was already 8:00 a.m. My body wanted to stay in bed, but my mind knew what I had to do. I dragged myself out of bed, half awake, and stumbled across the hall to Katie's room to see if she was still there.

I was afraid she may have woken up before me, packed—at least a bag or two—and had already left to move in with Amy. But when I quietly opened the door a few inches and peeked in, I was relieved to find her still sleeping soundly—not too surprising with all she had to drink last night.

Then I went back to my bedroom and climbed into bed until I felt a little more awake. After about ten minutes, I got up, got dressed, ate breakfast, and started some laundry. It was about 10:00 a.m. when Katie finally emerged from her bedroom wearing shorts and a sweatshirt, along with the remnants of her makeup she had on from yesterday. She had two big gym bags draped over her shoulders and her eyes were puffy and her blonde hair was a mess.

As she was clearly heading for the door, I spoke quickly. "Katie, I've thought about this and I don't want you to move out," I said. "I want you to stay."

"I'm not staying," she said with a surprisingly calm tone, but still refusing to make eye contact.

She then casually—yet decisively—opened the door and closed it behind her as she left. I then ran over to the door and went dashing outside in a desperate attempt to catch her before she left.

When I got outside, there were still an abundance of cars parked on the street from her party yesterday.   But unfortunately, her car was the last car in my driveway, which gave her a clean getaway. She glanced at me as she put her bags in her trunk and then glanced away seeming unfazed by me running out to stop her. Then she walked around to the car door and opened it to get in.

I finally reached her car. "I really don't think you should move out," I said.

"Well, it's too late for that," she said, getting in the car and closing the door. She started it, and I leaned down and tapped on the window.

She put the window down and looked at me waiting for me to speak.

"I'm sorry if I embarrassed you last night," I said, "but it was only because I care about you."

"I don't want to get into it," she said calmly. "It doesn't matter anymore. It'll be better for both of us if I just move in with Amy. I should've just moved in with her to begin with and then you and I wouldn't be having all of this drama right now."

As she said those words, my heart broke as I realized the little sister who I once enjoyed spending time with had grown up and was pushing me out of her life more than ever.

"Let me know when you're home next," she said, putting her hand on the steering wheel. "I'll come by and move out the rest of my stuff."

She shifted the car into reverse to back out and I knew this was the final chance I'd have to try to convince her to stay.

"Is this really the way you want it to be with us?" I asked. "We grew up together, Katie. And now it's come to this?"

She stared down at the dashboard as I talked, but I knew she was listening.

"This is what you want?" I asked, "Where we can't even live together for more than a week?"

She was still unfazed by what I was saying.

"Don't you have anything to say?" I asked.

She quickly turned to me. "What you do want me to say? This isn't working, so I'm moving out. You're not changing my mind."

"Well...okay, but I want you to take these keys," I said as I pulled my spare set of apartment keys out of my pocket and tried to hand them to her. "I want you to know you're welcome to move back any time. The only thing I ask is that you don't have any more parties."

She shook her head and left me holding the keys.

"Just take the keys, Katie," I said sternly.

"Fine!" she said, grabbing them out of my hands. "I'm not coming back, though."

She then backed out of my driveway and drove off leaving me standing there realizing what our relationship had become.

~ ~ ~

I came back inside and sat down and started typing this journal entry because that's all I felt like doing. Now, I'm beginning to wonder when—or if—I'm going to tell my parents about all of this. I know their reaction wouldn't be good if they found out. In fact, I wouldn't put it past my dad to fly up here and make Katie move back to Florida with them if he hears this.

But looking at the clock now, I realize that's something I'll have to deal with at another time. Right now, I need to find a flight to Houston for today. Then, I'll be in position tomorrow morning to go back to work for the remaining three days of what would've been a four-day flying trip. And I suppose another thing that will have to wait is cleaning up this remaining mess from Katie's party.

Speaking of partying, I'm afraid that'll be the only thing she'll be inspired to do living with Amy now. I doubt she'll be looking for a job or trying to figure out her career. Instead, she'll probably continue to live carefree, which has a price much bigger than she may realize. If she goes another year after she's graduated without working, she's only going to have a harder time building a career for herself. But she's the one who will have to come to that realization before she can change. I really hope she does—and soon.

Tuesday, June 1ˢᵗ
My apartment
7:48 p.m. (Central Time)

It's hard to say if this has been a good day or a bad day—it's really had elements of both. However, there's no question it's left me with more than a little unrest as I sit here in my apartment tonight on this first day of June.

But to begin, I'll first go back to Friday of last week—the day Katie hastily moved out. That afternoon, I was able to catch a flight to Houston that still had a few empty seats on it. After I checked in to a hotel there and grabbed a quick dinner, I headed to bed early that night to catch up on my sleep.

By the time I was lining up for takeoff that next morning, thankfully, I felt well-rested and ready to be back at work to begin the remaining three days of my flying trip. With no weather issues or schedule changes, those three days proceeded to be very routine, and just after 8:00 p.m. last night I touched down in Chicago to complete the last flight of that trip.

It was then time to begin a new trip and catch an 8:40 p.m. flight to Cincinnati—as a passenger—so that today I could drive back to Chicago with Megan for the final part of her move. The flight out there went relatively quickly. But with the time change and by the time I caught a shuttle bus to a hotel near the airport, it was almost 11:30 p.m. when I finally walked into my hotel room last night.

I didn't see Megan at that point, because it was obviously too late. However, just as we'd planned, she was staying somewhere in that same hotel since she had to be completely moved out of her apartment yesterday.

The fact that she'd made it to the hotel by herself was actually a big accomplishment for her. It involved her having to drive from her old apartment in the northern suburbs, through downtown Cincinnati, and across the Kentucky state line, since the Cincinnati airport is actually in northern Kentucky. It was only about a forty-five-minute drive but that was obviously something she couldn't do for both of the times I visited her before this. So when she texted me earlier in the day to tell me that she'd made it to the hotel, I was definitely happy for her.

It even brought a smile to my face when I thought about it again as I finally climbed into bed in my hotel room last night. Considering it was after midnight by then and I'd had a full day of flying—on Memorial Day, no less—it took me no time at all to fall asleep. But that was good because I knew I needed the rest since I'd be driving to Chicago with Megan today.

~ ~ ~

This morning, I woke up to the alarm clock at 8:00 a.m.—and to the morning sun shining brightly into my hotel room, since I'd forgotten to close the curtains last night. I then had just enough time to throw on a pair of shorts and a polo shirt, pack up, and make my way down to the lobby to meet Megan at 8:30 a.m.

When I got off the elevator, I quickly spotted her across the lobby, but she didn't see me just yet. She was sitting on a couch waiting for me with a small rolling suitcase standing upright next to her. She looked particularly cute today, dressed in shorts and a purple t-shirt, wearing flip-flops and some subtle makeup. Her hair was tied back in a ponytail with a purple tie matching her shirt.

As I made my way over to her, her face lit up as soon as she noticed me. She quickly stood up. "Hey you!"

"Hey!" I responded as we hugged and shared a quick kiss.

"You made it," she said, smiling at me.

"Yeah, and so did you," I said enthusiastically. "That was a big accomplishment for you to make that drive."

She took a deep breath. "Yeah, it was. But I actually almost got lost two different times and that really triggered my anxiety...but I made it. And after I sat down for an hour in the hotel room, I was able to settle down some."

"Well, it's still progress," I said, looking at her and noticing that she had a slight suntan. "How did you get a suntan?" I asked.

She smiled. "Ironically, I had some spare time a few days ago since I had everything mostly packed already, so I spent a day out at the pool at my apartment complex," she said. "For all the time I'd lived there, I'd never once been to the pool...so I went."

"Well, that's good," I said, realizing she had a healthy and happy glow to her and looked even more vibrant than the last time I saw her. "You look good, and it seems like you're feeling good too."

"Yep, I am," she said brightly. "I'm mostly settled down from yesterday now, and today is the best I've felt for a long time."

"Good, I'm glad to hear that," I said. "How did everything go yesterday with the movers?"

"It went well," she said. "They came and took all the furniture and a lot of boxes too. Then everything else is packed in my car now. I'm hoping that'll be everything I'll need for the next few months, because everything the movers took is going directly into a storage unit by my aunt's house."

"That makes sense," I said.

"Yeah," she said. "And I didn't tell you yet, but my parents and brother actually ended up driving down yesterday to help, even though there wasn't much left for them to help with. But since they all three had the day off from work for Memorial Day, I think they just wanted to say goodbye before I moved."

"Well, that was nice of them," I said.

"Yeah, it was," she said. "They say 'hi,' by the way. They would've stayed longer to see you, but obviously they had to go back to work today."

"Yeah, I understand," I said.

From there, we proceeded to grab a quick continental breakfast right there in the lobby. After that, it was almost 9:00 a.m. and it was time for us to hit the road, and time for Megan to say goodbye to the Cincinnati area...for good.

~   ~   ~

According to the GPS on my phone, it looked like this road trip would be about a 320-mile drive from where we were—near the Cincinnati airport—to Chicago, and would take just under five hours. Megan was certain she wanted me to drive, at least for the beginning of the trip, so I agreed.

After we left, it didn't take long at all to navigate our way onto the interstate from the hotel. As the first few miles passed, the landscape quickly became more open and less-populated. It appeared that Megan probably had a mixture of feelings at that point. She simply sat there quietly in the passenger seat and stared out the window as she held the stuffed raccoon, which she'd just taken out of her backpack.

After about fifteen minutes into the trip, I finally decided to break the silence with an admittedly generic question, but it was all I could think of asking. "So are you going to miss Cincinnati?"

"A little," she said, turning to me. "I mean, I'm still excited about moving, but it'll be different living in the Chicago area. The other day I realized it'll be the furthest I've lived from my parents and brother at any point in my life. Instead of being two hours away, they'll be five hours away now."

"Well, you'll have your aunt around...and me," I said.

"I know," she said. "And that definitely makes this a lot easier. There's no way I'd want to live this far away from my family if I was by myself. I don't know how you do it with your parents and sister living so far away in Florida. But I suppose now that your sister moved in with you, that probably makes things better, right?"

I nervously took a deep breath as I realized I hadn't told her about Katie moving out yet. "Well, actually she's not living with me anymore. She moved out a few days ago."

She quickly turned to me. "Really?"

I nodded and then throughout the next few minutes, I proceeded to explain everything that had happened.

"I'm sorry to hear all of that," she said. "And you haven't heard from her since then?"

"Nope."

"That must be upsetting because I know if I ever had a

falling out like that with my brother, I'd be devastated. Thankfully, we never have. But we're pretty similar, so I guess that helps."

"Yeah, it probably does," I said, staring at the road ahead and realizing how much unrest I still felt about Katie leaving. I think Megan could tell that, so she didn't say any more and consequently, our conversation retreated back to silence.

As some more miles passed, we soon crossed the Ohio River into Indiana. Shortly after that, the interstate took us into Ohio for a brief time before we crossed back into Indiana again. That was when the terrain became very hilly, yet also quite impressive.

For a time, it reminded me of being in the mountains with the way the interstate was built on the side of these surprisingly steep hills. On one side, the terrain sloped sharply upward and was covered by a good amount of deciduous trees that stood mostly vertical. On the other side, there was a steep drop-off that looked like it was a long way down. With a bright blue sky as a backdrop, it certainly made for picturesque scenery and gave me a rare opportunity to see this country up close, as opposed to the view I usually get from 30,000 feet in the sky.

Finally, Megan looked over at me, seeming eager to tell me something. "I didn't tell you yet, but I sat down a few nights ago and updated my resume. After that, I spent some time on the internet looking for teaching assistant jobs at colleges in the Chicago area. I found five jobs that looked good, so I applied to them, hoping at least one of them might work. They all said they'd start in the fall semester and they all preferred a Ph.D. but I applied anyway because you never know."

"That's right," I said encouragingly. "You could be exactly who they're looking for."

She nodded. "I was excited about it, even though it took a lot of time. For some of them I had to write short essays telling why I'd be a good candidate. So hopefully I did a good job on those."

"I'm sure you did," I said. "You've always been a good writer."

She smiled at me. "Thanks."

"Hopefully you'll hear back from them," I said.

She took a deep breath. "I really hope so." She then turned to me. "So I'm curious...what is it like living in the Chicago area?" she asked.

"Well, the area where you'll be—and where I live—is very suburban, so it's a lot different than downtown Chicago, or "the City," as everyone calls it. For one, there obviously aren't any skyscrapers in the suburbs, and there are even some forest preserves. But it's still pretty populated and crowded, which can make traffic bad sometimes, especially during rush hour. But there's every store and restaurant you can ever imagine within a short distance of no matter where you are, so that's convenient. And it's generally a pretty safe area because most of the crime you hear about on the news happens in the city and not so much in the suburbs. Other than that, it usually gets sort of hot in the summer, but probably not as hot as Ohio. And the winters can be pretty cold...and snowy. And almost everyone loves deep dish pizza."

She laughed. "Hmm, I guess that's mostly what I expected." She then reached over and held my hand. "Thanks for driving, by the way," she said, looking over at me. "And for going on this trip with me."

"Sure, it's no problem," I said.

She then smiled at me. "I love you."

I quickly smiled back. "I love you, too."

She then leaned over and gave me a quick kiss on the cheek as I drove.

I quickly glanced over at her. "I have to say, right now I'd never know that you had an anxiety problem because you seem completely normal. So maybe all of that is behind you now...or at least the worst of it is."

She took a deep breath. "I sure hope so," she said, staring out at the rural landscape.

~ ~ ~

Before too long, the landscape became much more urban as we were already entering the Indianapolis area. The interstate curved around the outskirts of the city, but we could still see some of the tall buildings from the downtown area in the distance.

By the time we breezed past most of the city, it was about 11:15 a.m. After flying over this area countless times, I knew the landscape was about to get very rural, very quickly, so we decided to stop for lunch while there was still at least some civilization left.

We soon found an exit that led us onto a two-lane county road that was lined with a few restaurants and gas stations nestled close to the interstate. But beyond that was farmland for as far as we could see. The hills we encountered earlier were nothing but a memory now as everything was completely flat.

We stopped at one of the fast food places and after we got our food, we decided to eat at one of the outdoor tables they had. We found it a little strange that no one else was sitting out there—especially considering how nice of a day it was. But it soon made a lot more sense to us when barely a minute after we sat down some Canadian geese came out of nowhere and began walking over to us.

With their lustrous grayish-brown feathers, long black necks, and robust size, it didn't look like they'd been missing any meals. Based on their bold and incessant honking, they clearly thought our lunch should be their *next* meal. Even though we ignored them and began eating, it didn't take long before eight or ten of them were surrounding us.

As if that wasn't enough, I then noticed a light gray animal in the distance slowly walking across the patio area and heading toward us. With its pointed nose, short legs, and long thin tail dragging behind it, I first thought it was a giant rat, but then I realized it was a possum—which was weird to see in broad daylight.

Even though Megan wasn't too scared of the geese, she quickly pulled her legs up on the bench when the possum came and stood only a few feet from us. Then he simply looked up at us, as if he was saying, "I'm here, feed me," while the geese all continued honking.

Needless to say, we quickly moved inside after that. Neither of us thought it was right that people obviously fed those animals—presumably quite often. But we couldn't deny that it left us with quite a funny story to tell—if anyone would even believe something like that actually happened to us.

As much as I thought that would be what would stand out most in my memories from this day, I was wrong. Little did I know, the events that would soon play out several hours later would unfortunately become what I remember most from this day now.

~   ~   ~

Regardless of what would later occur—and while I was still considering this to be a good day—our road trip continued rather well for the time being. The interstate began to look like nothing more than a long, thin line slicing through a bunch of flat farmland for as far as we could see ahead.

Over the next few hours, we saw some occasional exits for small towns, but for the vast majority of the time, the scenery was still a lot of farmland—mostly corn and soybeans from what I could tell. But eventually, we noticed the scenery beginning to show some signs of civilization. Not much later, the farmland almost entirely disappeared and we found ourselves in the bustling and well-populated region of northwest Indiana, which is basically a far extension of the Chicago suburbs. The interstate became an eight-lane expressway and eventually we headed west and crossed the state line into Illinois.

After another fifty miles—and sharing the road with a lot more cars than before—we finally got off the expressway. We were now in my stomping ground and also not far from Megan's aunt's house. When I glanced down, the clock in Megan's car said 3:12 p.m. but she quickly reset it to 2:12 p.m. for Central time.

When we turned into her aunt's subdivision, it definitely brought back memories from my high school days from when I would pick up or drop off some of my friends who lived there. It was just how I remembered it too. There were an abundance of modestly-sized split-level homes featuring mostly brick and real wood siding. Based on the designs, it was safe to conclude this neighborhood was probably developed sometime in the late 1970's or early 1980's.

Despite their age, the houses were still well-maintained and this neighborhood had a certain old-world charm to it— sort of like the neighborhood where I grew up, which wasn't too far from there. There were many large, mature trees lined up on both sides of the streets that were even larger than I remembered. They'd grown to be towering high above the houses and now provided a canopy of complete shade over the streets.

As I slowly weaved through the narrow streets, I became more eager to meet her aunt Linda. From what Megan had told me about her, she sounded like an interesting person. She's a teacher by day, but likes to paint on the side. Megan said she even has a painting studio set up in her dining room and sells a lot of her paintings, which apparently makes her a decent side income.

But the sad part was to hear that her husband passed away many years ago. He was in the military and was involved in a helicopter crash only a few years after they got married. But according to Megan, Linda has stayed strong in her faith and come to peace with her life the way it is now. Even though they never had any children, Linda apparently has never wanted to remarry because she stands strong in saying that her husband was the only love of her life.

"I think this is her house on the left up here," Megan pointed.

We parked in the driveway and gathered up a few things before we got out of the car. Her house certainly fit in with all the rest, being a split-level with light brown brick and dark brown wood siding. After we walked up the cement steps with wrought iron railings, I noticed her front door had a stained glass design in the top half of it.

Megan noticed me studying it. "She does stained glass too," she said, reaching out to push the doorbell.

"Wow, that's an impressive design," I said.

We waited for a few seconds. "I hope she's home by now," Megan said. "She had to teach today, but she said they're on shortened days this week, since it's the last week of the school year."

A few seconds later, the door opened and her aunt invited us in and gave us each a welcoming hug. Even though Linda is Megan's dad's younger sister—obviously Megan's blood relative—she didn't look much like Megan at all. She was shorter than Megan, had curly dark hair that was about shoulder-length, and her pale complexion indicated she probably spent most of her free time inside working on her paintings.

After Megan formally introduced me to her, we stepped into her living room, which had a very clean look to it but not ultra-modern by any means. There was a beige couch with a floral design in the upholstery, light tan carpeting, and chocolate-colored draperies tied back, letting the light in from the windows.

We shared in some small talk about how the drive went, including how we had lunch with a bunch of geese and a possum. Then Linda told me a little more about her art business before she invited Megan and me upstairs to see the bedroom she'd set up for Megan. We walked in and it had an oak dresser, a double bed, and a nightstand with a lamp sitting on it. Seeing how the bed was perfectly made and the room was spotless, it seemed that Megan would be well-accommodated. That was probably the reason why before we left the room, Megan hugged Linda again.

After we got a quick tour of the rest of her house, we then began the moving-in process by carrying in all the stuff that was in Megan's car. Before too long, her car was emptied out, but that subsequently made her room a cluttered mess. So I helped her unpack and get situated, which took longer than we realized. Eventually, the smell of a home-cooked meal had trailed upstairs, telling us that Linda had an early dinner almost ready for us as it was going on 5:00 p.m.

After I put away some emptied gym bags in her closet, I turned around and Megan was facing me, standing only inches away with an appreciative look.

"After dinner, you don't have to stay here and help," she said. "I'm going to drive you home because you've done more than enough for me today."

"I'm always glad to help you," I said.

"I know. And that's one of many reasons why I love you," she said, coming closer and kissing me. As soon as our lips met, I could tell right away this would be a long kiss, and that was more than fine with me. Looking back now as I type this, I realize those were pretty much the last good moments of this day before things turned bad.

~   ~   ~

When we went downstairs a few minutes later, her aunt had three places set at the kitchen table. After she insisted she didn't need any help, Megan and I sat down. Before we knew it, Linda brought out a big plate of homemade chicken, baked potatoes, and corn on the cob. After Linda sat down, Megan elected me to say a prayer before we ate, so I did.

As we all began eating, her aunt obviously noticed the same thing I did.

"Megan, it's so good to see you eating like this," she said. "I'm so glad you're feeling better now. I just remember those two days I came out to visit you when you'd just gotten out of the hospital and you were still feeling pretty miserable."

In the middle of cutting my chicken, I paused and looked at Megan trying to comprehend what I'd just heard. "You were in the hospital?"

She paused with an awkward look. "Well, yeah. I was going to tell you, but I just haven't found the right time."

I set my knife and fork down and turned to her. "Why were you in the hospital?"

"Well, my stomach problems were worse back then and I was having trouble eating," she said.

"How long were you in there?" I asked.

"Um, well, it ended up being eleven days," she said.

I was shocked to hear that. "Eleven days? That's a long time. When was this?"

"In March. I can tell you about it later," she said, seeming desperate to change the subject.

"Yeah, I think you should," I said, feeling somewhat betrayed that this was the first I was hearing of this.

I glanced over at Linda and she looked very uncomfortable. "I'm sorry, Megan," she said, "I didn't know you hadn't told him about that."

"It's okay," Megan said, looking down at her plate and picking at her baked potato with her fork.

Unfortunately, the rest of the dinner was very awkward and uncomfortable for all of us. Needless to say, when we finally finished eating, we were all eager to stand up from the table. Since I was planning on leaving after dinner, we all quickly migrated to the foyer. After some brief yet courteous small talk with Linda and after thanking her for dinner, I said goodbye to her. Megan and I then left and walked out to her car since Megan still had to drive me home.

But before we got to her car, I backed away from her and looked at her. "Why didn't you tell me you were in the hospital?" I asked with a stern voice. "I mean, we love each other and I didn't think we were keeping secrets like this, but apparently I was wrong. Were you ever going to tell me?"

"You don't have to raise your voice," she said quietly. "People can hear us out here." She paused, seeming to gather

her thoughts. "I'm sorry, but I had my reasons for not telling you," she said.

"Yeah? Well, I'd like to hear them," I said, with some noticeable anger.

She took a deep breath to prepare herself for what she was about to say. "First of all, I didn't want to scare you because while I was in the hospital, it looked pretty likely that I had stomach cancer."

My heart sank in my chest as I felt my head jerk back with shock. "What?" was all I could muster.

"At first, the doctors wouldn't tell me anything. They just kept ordering more tests. But I knew what they were testing for. In my mind, all of the pieces were tragically fitting together. I had all of the symptoms of it, and also my grandmother died of it a few years ago. Since it tends to be hereditary, I really thought it was only a matter of time before they told me I had it too. I thought I was going to die before I was even thirty," she said, breaking down in tears.

I took a step toward her and hugged her.

"I'm sorry I didn't tell you," she said through the tears. "I'm really sorry."

"It's okay," I said, gently patting her back. "But you don't have cancer, right?"

She sniffled. "Well, all of the tests came back negative, but there's still a chance it might be cancer and that it's not being detected on the tests yet. Many times with this, the symptoms can start before there's any detectable tumors. So I have to go every month for CT scans so they can see if there are any masses starting to grow in my stomach. If they find anything, they'll have to remove it right away and test it. So far they haven't found anything, but they still don't know why I had such bad stomach problems."

"So..." I paused, "you might actually have cancer and not know it yet?" After saying that, I realized I repeated what she'd just told me, but somehow saying it was the only way it fully registered in my mind.

She shook her head yes with tears still in her eyes.

"I'm sorry, Megan," I said as I hugged her. "So is your anxiety even causing your stomach problems or is that a completely separate issue now?" I asked.

She drew back a little from our hug. "Well, it's definitely at least part of the cause because the thought of having cancer caused me more anxiety, which then made my stomach problems worse. So it was just this awful cycle I was in. I couldn't eat for a while and that's why they initially admitted me to the hospital—so they could give me an IV and figure out why I wasn't eating. They kept thinking there had to be another cause to all of this besides just anxiety, but they haven't found anything yet."

"You should've just told me all of this," I said, hugging her again.

"Well, like I said, I didn't want to scare you, and when we started communicating again after the wedding, it was like a new beginning to my life. It was the first good thing that happened to me for a long time, and I didn't want this dark cloud hanging over us. I just wanted to escape from the last few months and forget they happened. And now, I've finally started to feel like it was behind me...especially in these last few days when I've been feeling mostly normal. I've been able to almost convince myself that I don't have cancer, even though I still might."

She paused as she looked at me. "But most of all, I knew as soon as I told you, you'd never look at me or our relationship the same way again."

"What do you mean?" I asked.

"Well, you'd treat me different because you'd feel sorry for me. You'd wonder if I'll even be living in a few years. It just changes everything, and all I want is for everyone to treat me normally...because I want so much just to be normal and have a normal life."

I understood what she was saying but I still wish she would've told me about this up front.

"Just promise me that you'll tell me everything going forward," I said.

"Okay, I promise," she said, "Please don't be mad at me."

"I'm not mad," I assured her.

We stood next to her car and held each other for what felt like an eternity. That's really all either of us felt like doing at that point, just holding each other and being close. Eventually, she gave me a ride back to my apartment and after we pulled into my driveway, we sat in her car for a few minutes.

I looked over at her. "I'm sorry you had to go through all of that with being in the hospital and thinking you had stomach cancer. I can't even imagine how tough that was."

"It *was* tough," she said. "It was the most difficult thing I've ever had to go through. But I think it's made me stronger and taught me to have patience. Like James 1:3 says, '...that the trying of your faith [produces] patience.'[1]"

"That's a good way of looking at it," I said. "How about we pray before we say goodnight?"

She nodded as she reached out her hands for me to hold them.

We then joined hands and bowed our heads and said a quick prayer. I asked God to continue to bestow his healing upon Megan and help us through whatever challenges we may be faced with.

Before we said goodbye, we agreed I'll stop by her aunt's house tomorrow morning. We'll finish unpacking some of her things and then—by her request—find something fun to do for the rest of the day. That'll be good since I'll be going back to work for a six-day flying trip the day after that.

We kissed goodnight and we both said "I love you." Then I got out and walked up to my front door as she drove away. When I walked into my dark apartment, it provided a temporary distraction from the situation with Megan, but not a good one. The utter silence was a painful reminder that Katie is still gone, and we're still not on good terms.

The remaining mess from her party several days ago was another reminder I still have some more cleaning to do. But for now, I turned on some lights, got a glass of water, and sat down on the couch with my laptop. I then started typing in my journal with the hopes of decompressing from this long day.

As I reflect on what I just found out about Megan, I realize she was right—knowing this changes everything. It doesn't change my love for her, but it changes what I see when I look at her. I see a girl who's been through a really tough time and is still incredibly scared. But she's trying to not let it get in the way of our love for each other—and hoping more than anything that it won't.

But being that she's feeling completely normal now, I want to believe that she's well on her way to recovery. I don't even want to think that she may be on the verge of a serious, life-threatening illness, but unfortunately, it'll always be in the back of my mind now.

· 12 ·

Thursday, June 3rd
Hotel Room in Seattle, WA
5:49 p.m. (Pacific Time)

Yesterday, Megan and I made the most of her first full day living in the Chicago area, despite there being some tough moments at the end of it. Today, I had to go back to work, which began with me getting up at 3:15 a.m. for my 6:05 a.m. flight this morning. Three flights later, I touched down here in Seattle, which completed my workday—and the first day of this six-day flying trip—even though it was only noon, local time. But I have to say, with having such an early start this morning, noon felt much more like dinnertime, despite the fact that Seattle is two time zones behind Chicago.

Nevertheless, I then rented a car and made the short drive here to my hotel. Luckily they had my room ready early and it quickly became nap time for me. After about an hour nap, I ventured outside and walked around for a little while before I eventually had an early dinner around 3:30 p.m.

Then I came back to the hotel and called Megan and we talked for a while, which will probably become a daily routine for us when I'm away on these trips. And now, while I still have some energy—thanks to my nap earlier—I decided to sit down and catch up with my journal while everything from yesterday is still fresh in my mind.

~   ~   ~

Unfortunately, when I woke up yesterday morning, my concern for Megan—and her health—was still front and center in my mind. It was 6:50 a.m. and I was hoping to sleep much later than that, but it quickly became clear that my unsettling thoughts had me wide awake, so I got up.

After having a quick breakfast and observing, once again, the remaining mess in my apartment from Katie's party—that now felt like it happened ages ago—I figured it would be a good time to clean. After all, I had plenty of time, since I wouldn't be heading over to see Megan until 9:30 a.m. I also thought it would help clear my mind of everything.

It sort of did, in the way that I eventually began thinking less about Megan and her problems...but more about Katie and the disheartening situation that still exists with her. As I was scrubbing my dining room table and realizing some of the beer stains will probably never come off, it felt like I should still be mad at her for throwing the party and for how she treated me—but I wasn't. My anger was long gone, even though I was still far from content with the way things were between us.

So since I still hadn't heard from her since the morning after her party when she hastily moved out, I decided to text her. I at least wanted to know that she was okay...and hopefully begin to get on better terms with her again.

I grabbed my phone and after some brief thought, I decided to keep my message short and simple.

Hey - I haven't heard from you. Are you okay?

After I sent it, I realized it wasn't even 7:30 a.m. and she was most likely still sleeping because she's never been an early-morning person. So the fact that she didn't respond right away didn't panic me.

I got back to cleaning and after vacuuming up the crushed potato chips and pretzels from the carpet and tidying up the kitchen, my apartment was back to a presentable condition again. I checked my phone and there was still no message. By now, I needed to get dressed and ready to head over to see Megan. So I shaved and threw on a pair of shorts and a t-shirt. Then just as I was ready to leave, I looked at my phone and Katie had finally texted me back.

I'm fine.

It wasn't the cordial response I was hoping for, but nevertheless, it was still a relief to hear from her.

Are you still living with Amy? I quickly texted back, while standing in my foyer, ready to leave.

Yeah—why are you asking me that?? I told you that's what I was doing when I moved out.

That angered me—like it's not any of my business to know where she's living or what she's doing after not hearing from her since she moved out.

Sorry for caring about you and wanting to know you're ok!!!

My fingers punched that out and sent it before I even thought about what I was sending. It had a sharp tone to it, and because of that, I was quite certain I wouldn't hear back from her. Sure enough, I was right.

As I still stood there in my foyer, I felt a hint of guilt at that moment. I realized I hadn't talked to my parents in a while; therefore, I hadn't told them about any of this. I knew Katie wouldn't have told them about this either. Knowing my parents, this is something they'd want to know so they could try to correct the problem. But I also knew it would get Katie in a lot of trouble with them...and get her even angrier at me.

So I took a deep breath not knowing what to do, but subsequently choosing not to do anything right then as I left to go see Megan. At least I knew Katie was "fine," even though things between us were obviously still far from fine.

~   ~   ~

During the short drive over to see Megan, my mind was churning with thoughts of how things might be awkward between Megan and I after what transpired the previous day. What if she thought I'm still mad at her for hiding her health problems from me? What if this will change the tone of our relationship like she feared it would?

As I parked in the driveway and got out of the car, it was impossible to ignore the bright sunshine and climbing temperatures that indicated this early-June day would feel much more like the middle of July. That was unfortunately the only calming and pleasant thought in my mind as I walked up the front steps and rang the doorbell.

A few seconds later she opened the door and greeted me with a big smile, then a hug, and a kiss. She was wearing a pastel green t-shirt with jean shorts.

"Thanks for coming over and helping me," she said. "I promise this won't take all day, and we'll get out and do something fun before the day is over."

As I walked in the house, I could immediately sense the happiness radiating from her. She clearly didn't want to revisit our conversation from the previous night and it surprisingly appeared to be the furthest thing from her mind. Whether it was or not, I didn't know. But either way, it was obvious she simply wanted to enjoy this summer day and not dwell on something out of her control. At that moment, I figured it was time I did the same.

As she led me through the living room to go upstairs to finish unpacking her room, it took me a minute to realize this was a weekday, and therefore, her aunt was gone all day teaching.

As soon we got upstairs into her room, Megan kissed me.

"I love you," she said, smiling at me.

"I love you, too," I said.

She then went back to rearranging some of her clothes in her closet, presumably picking up where she'd left off before I arrived. But with all the unpacking we did yesterday, there wasn't a lot left to do today. When she left for a few seconds to take an empty box downstairs, I had just the right opportunity to take the stuffed raccoon and hide it in one of her empty dresser drawers. Little did I know just minutes later she'd decide to take some of her clothes from her closet, fold them, and put them in that very drawer.

I watched her unknowingly open the drawer as I tried my hardest not to laugh. She gasped and jumped back a little as she was startled by it.

"Kevin!" she shouted, as I began laughing.

She shook her head as she also began laughing. Then she sighed. "I can't believe you got me that easily. All I have to say is that I'm going to get you good when you least expect it," she said, throwing the raccoon at me.

"Uh-oh. He doesn't like to be thrown like that. Now he's mad and going to attack all of your stuffed animals."

She had several other stuffed animals sitting on her bed, so I rushed over and plopped myself on her bed and pretended the raccoon was biting all of them.

"No!" she shouted playfully as she hurried over to stop me. She jumped on her bed with me and grabbed the raccoon out of my hands as we both began laughing hysterically.

Before I knew it, we were kissing. It was spontaneous, yet felt very passionate as we were lying very close to each other on her bed in a completely quiet and empty house. After several minutes, it was clear that this could easily advance to something more, which I knew both of us would deeply regret, since we've both committed to saving ourselves for marriage.

So I stopped kissing her and sat up. She then also sat up and looked at me showing concern at first, but then seemingly realizing why I'd stopped.

"I'm sorry," I said. "I just don't want us to do something we'll regret."

"No, you're fine," she said, putting her arm around me. "I'm glad we stopped."

She then held my hand and turned to me and whispered. "I'm still going to scare you really good with that raccoon. And you're going to scream like a girl."

I laughed. "Somehow, I doubt that."

We then both got up off of her bed and she'd mostly finished unpacking in her room by that point, so we went downstairs. In the living room, there were quite a few boxes of her books still taped up and stacked against the wall. These were obviously the books that we took with us in the car—the ones too special for the movers take.

I began to appreciate why after we both sat down on the floor and she showed me some of them. Many of them were signed by the authors and she told me how when she was younger, her parents would take her to quite a few book-signing events so she could meet the authors who wrote the books that she enjoyed reading so much. She also showed me some books that her late grandmother had bought for her as gifts throughout the years.

But it wasn't just books that were in these boxes. She also had several spiral notebooks of handwritten short stories and poems she had written through the years. She said some of the poems she had written as recently as a few months ago. I could see the excitement in her eyes and hear the passion in her voice as she showed them to me. It's nothing I already didn't know, but this made me realize even more that literature is a huge part of her life—just as much as flying is a part of mine.

I looked at her. "I think if anyone should teach literature, it's you."

She gave me a half-smile but I couldn't help but notice how her bright mood seemed to dampen right then. "Let's just hope I can find a school who also thinks that," she said.

"I'm sure you will," I said encouragingly.

She lightly nodded but didn't seem too convinced of that as she grabbed a few more notebooks out of the box to show me.

~ ~ ~

Noon came rather quickly, and after Megan had finished showing me all of her books and writings, lunch was definitely on our minds. So I took her to a deli that's a well-known favorite in the area for their amazingly good sandwiches and for their fresh-squeezed lemonade.

Being in the heart of the lunch hour, the line was almost out the door. But it moved quickly—as it always does—and before we knew it, we had our sandwiches and two large cups of their lemonade. When we turned around from the cashier to find a place to sit, we quickly realized every table was taken, so we decided to eat back at my place. After all, it would give her a chance to see my apartment for the first time.

When we arrived, I unlocked the door and let her go in first.

"Wow," she said, standing in my foyer as she looked around. "I didn't realize you live in such a nice place." She began laughing. "You must've thought my apartment in Cincinnati was a dump."

"No, I didn't," I quickly replied.

She walked into the dining room and peered into the kitchen. "Fancy," she said enthusiastically. "I love the cabinets and the granite countertop. I love how it all contrasts with the stainless steel appliances."

"Thanks," I said.

We then sat down across from each other at my dining room table, said a quick prayer, and began eating. After having a few minutes of comfortable silence as we both ate, she finally spoke.

"I got my first rejection email this morning for one of the teaching assistant jobs I applied to before I moved," she said.

"I'm sorry to hear that," I said, realizing that explained why she didn't seem very hopeful about finding a teaching job when I mentioned it earlier.

"It's okay...I guess," she said. "That school wasn't on the top of my list anyway."

I took a drink of lemonade before I spoke. "I haven't had to do a ton of job searching in my career, but I'd imagine getting rejected for jobs is all part of the process. Not every job you apply to will lead to an offer."

"Yeah, I know," she said. "I just really hope that I can get a teaching job. It would be so good because I could get teaching experience and a tuition discount so I could start my Ph.D. And from what I've heard, the people who have those jobs walk right into a professor job after they finish their Ph.D."

"Well, I'm sure if it's meant to be, you'll find one," I said. "But even if you don't, you always have the option to go back to school full time this fall on your own, right?" I asked.

She snickered. "I can tell you don't work in the education field. I wouldn't expect that you'd know this, but typically you need to apply by December or January to get accepted for the fall semester."

As she spoke, I began to remember that from many years ago when I was applying to colleges during my senior year of high school.

She continued. "But if a school is running low on enrollment, they might extend the deadline. Although being early June now, I don't think any school would extend their deadline *this* far."

"So they don't have those same deadlines for teaching assistant jobs?" I asked.

"Not really," she said. "I've seen them fill those jobs right up until the beginning of the school year in August sometimes, if people get another offer and back out at the last minute. And if I get one of those jobs, since I'd be working on campus, they might let me enroll in a few classes for my Ph.D., even though it would be well past the deadline."

"It sounds like that could work out perfectly for you," I said.

"It would, if I could just find one," she said, "because if I don't, then I'll probably have to look for another technical writer job."

"Couldn't you go back to school for the spring semester?"

"I guess," she said. "But going to school on my own like

that isn't really the way I want to get my Ph.D. because I'd have to take out some big student loans to pay for it, and since I wouldn't be get teaching experience, it would probably be harder to find a professor job when I was done."

I noticed her face showing more concern and discontent as this conversation progressed.

"Let's not think about that," I said. "It's still early in your job search, and I think you still have a good chance at finding a teaching job. But ultimately you have to believe that if God wants this to happen, it'll happen."

"I know," she said looking down, stirring the ice around in her lemonade. "It's such a weird feeling to want something so much but not know if it's God's plan for me."

"Yeah, I'd imagine it is," I said.

After she stared down at her glass of lemonade for a few more seconds, she went back to eating her sandwich, as did I.

After a few quiet moments passed, she spoke again, clearly wanting to change the subject.

"You were right, this sandwich is amazingly good...and huge," she said. "But I think I might actually finish the whole thing."

"That's good," I said.

"It's still seems weird and a little scary to feel so normal like this, considering how bad I've felt through these past several months."

"Well, maybe this is it, and you're finally better now," I said. "It seems like now that you've gotten out of that job, your anxiety has gone away, and maybe that's given your stomach a chance to heal now."

"You don't know how much I hope this is the end of all of that," she said. "I'm hoping pretty soon they'll tell me I can stop going for the CT scans every month, but who knows how long they'll keep making me do that."

"Well, you seem to be feeling normal now, so that's got to mean something," I said.

She nodded. "Yeah, it seems like it should."

~   ~   ~

After we finished our sandwiches, we were eager to get outside and enjoy the picture-perfect sunny day. When we discussed what we should do, we actually both had the same idea—go to the pool at my apartment complex.

Obviously, it had been since college since Megan and I had been to a pool together. For a while back then, we went every week to the indoor pool on campus—sometimes with our mutual friends, and sometimes just the two of us. We'd swim a few laps at first, but usually we'd end up just playing around in the water and acting like kids. Either way, I remember we always had fun, which is probably why we were both so eager to go to the pool today.

After we made a quick stop back at her aunt's house for her to change into her pool attire, we came back to my place and made the short walk over to the pool. As we got closer, it appeared we'd be the only ones there. That wasn't too surprising since it was in the middle of the day on a Wednesday when most people were at work, and school was still in session—at least for this week.

When we walked through the decorative black gate, it was just as impressive as the first time I saw it during my apartment-hunting days. The sprawling bright blue oval-shaped pool was surrounded by a large sundeck with lounge chairs lined up in perfect rows. As I looked across the pool, there were several patio tables, each with royal blue umbrellas raised over them. That scenery reminded me very much of the public pool where my sister and I spent so many of our summer days when we were younger.

"Wow, it's like having our own private pool," Megan said as we began walking over to the lounge chairs.

We picked two chairs in the sun and sat down. We slathered on some sun block and decided to sunbathe for a little while so we weren't swimming right after we ate lunch. After about a half hour, we decided to get in the water. I jumped right in and it was just the right temperature—cool enough to be refreshing from the hot sun, but not so cold you get uncomfortable. Nevertheless, Megan decided to inch her way in using the steps in the shallow end.

After she finally got in all the way, we decided to play catch with a sponge ball I brought. After a few normal exchanges, she thought it would be funny to throw it so it landed right in front my face and splashed me. She giggled and I quickly returned the favor.

After she did it a few more times, I decided I'd had enough of that. "You're in trouble now," I said playfully.

I quickly pushed off the bottom and started swimming toward her. She playfully screamed and tried to swim away from me, but I caught her and pulled her under. As soon as we came up to the surface, she started splashing me. That began a long-lived cycle of splashing, chasing, and dunking. We were just like two kids playing in the pool together without a care in the world.

There's something about being in the water on a bright sunny day that makes you forget about all of your problems. I can assure you that finding a job or wondering if her stomach problems are finally over was the furthest thing on her mind at that point. She was simply enjoying the moment and having fun, as was I.

After we eventually became tired from chasing each other, we decided to get out and sunbathe some more. I quickly dried off and sat down in the lounge chair. But she stood beside me and leaned her head to the side and purposely squeezed the water out of her ponytail right onto me.

"What are you doing?" I asked, laughing.

"It's payback for scaring me with the raccoon earlier," she said casually.

She then pushed her chair next to mine as close as it would go and sat down. We held hands and then I leaned over and gave her a quick kiss.

She then took a deep breath. "I'm tired now. I'm not used to swimming around like that."

"Yeah, we're getting old," I joked.

"Promise me we'll come out here as much as we can this summer," she said.

"Absolutely."

She looked over at me and smiled. "I love you."

"I love you, too," I said.

We drifted into comfortable silence as we were lying there hand-in-hand with our sunglasses on as the warm sunshine radiated down from the cloudless sky. As my mind drifted, Psalm 118:24 came to mind, "This is the day which the Lord [has] made; we will rejoice and be glad in it."[1] It's one of my favorite verses because it reminds us to be thankful for every day we have. Whether it's a good day or a bad day, it's the day the Lord has made for a purpose.

In this case, it was certainly a *good* day as Megan and I were enjoying this seemingly perfect day at the pool. As we continued lying there in the hot sunshine, I realized just how much God had done for us lately and recited all of the reasons we had to rejoice. Arranging for us to cross paths again after so many years was a miracle of its own. But now, instead of us having to carry on a long-distance relationship, we were now only separated by a twelve-minute drive.

Even more, our love for each other had grown even stronger within these past few weeks, and it now felt very reminiscent of the fairy-tale romance we had in college. But most importantly, Megan seemed mostly back to normal from her anxiety and stomach problems, which I was very glad to see.

Even though the looming uncertainties regarding her health and if she'd be able to find a teaching assistant job began to eventually drift into my mind, I pushed those thoughts away. This picture-perfect day at the pool seemed like neither the time nor place to be preoccupied with those things that ultimately neither of us can control. Instead, it was a time to be thankful for all of what God had done, and wait with patience for the things He will do for us in the future.

~   ~   ~

After we spent the rest of the afternoon relaxing at the pool—in and out of the water—we decided to cook dinner together at my apartment. Since there wasn't much food at my place, we made a quick stop at the grocery store and then started cooking. Thankfully, Megan is much better at cooking than me, and together, we made some pretty good spaghetti.

We spent the rest of the evening relaxing and watching some TV. But soon enough, it came time for me to take her home—and after that, for me to head to bed, since my six-day flying trip for work would begin with an early-morning flight.

So we made the short drive to her aunt's house and all too

soon we found ourselves standing next to each other in her aunt's driveway trying to say goodbye. Even though the sun had already set by that point, I still felt the residual warmth radiating up from the driveway from what had been a hot summer day...and a very good one, too.

She reached out and held both of my hands. "Do you really have to go on this trip? Can't you just call in sick for the next six days?" she joked.

I laughed. "I don't think that would go over too well. But it'll go fast and then I'll be back home for a few days."

I could see sadness growing on her face and tears welling in her eyes. "Be safe," she said. "It still terrifies me that you're 30,000 feet up in the sky every day."

"Don't worry, I'll be careful," I said. "I'm always careful."

"Let's say a quick prayer," I said.

Still holding hands, we bowed our heads and we prayed asking God to watch over both of us and keep us safe. We then thanked Him for the great day we'd just spent together and asked Him to continue to guide us in our relationship.

We said Amen and lifted our heads. She kissed me, then wrapped her arms around me and rested her head against my chest. We stood there holding each other tightly for at least a whole minute. It felt so good to have her in my arms and I really didn't want to let go—nor did she.

But eventually she drew back. "Okay, we should say goodbye now before I start crying even more," she said.

"I'm sure it'll get easier after we both adjust to this," I said.

"Maybe," she said, rather doubtfully.

She gave me one last glance before I got in my car. She didn't need to say anything for me to know exactly what she was thinking—saying goodbye was the hardest thing for her to do and she wished it wasn't this way. She stood there as I started my car, backed out of the driveway, and drove away.

During the short drive back to my apartment, the sadness resonated with me. At that moment, it didn't seem to matter that we lived just twelve minutes from each other. No matter how close we live, and no matter how great of a time we have together when I'm home, there will always be another goodbye looming around the corner. Sadly, this was only the first one in a long series to follow, with no end in sight.

· 13 ·

Tuesday, June 8th
My apartment
8:14 p.m. (Central Time)

I touched down this afternoon here in Chicago to complete my workday—and my six-day flying trip—and little did I know that a series of surprises would soon follow. But before all of that, I woke up this morning in Phoenix, completely unaware of what I'd be facing later in the day and more than a little eager to complete the two remaining flights of this trip today.

As I was getting dressed in my hotel room, an undeniable happiness came over me because I knew I'd be seeing Megan in only a matter of hours. It had been a long six days on this trip without seeing her, but soon I'd be home and we'd have the next three days to spend together. I grabbed a quick breakfast in the lobby of the hotel and headed to the airport. Even though it was a Tuesday, it sure felt like a Friday to me.

After a smooth flight to Dallas, and a brief stopover there, we were soon airborne again for another smooth flight to Chicago where it was 87 degrees with clear skies when we touched down. We arrived at the gate just before 3:15 p.m.— several minutes early. As soon as I got off the plane, I texted

Megan while I was walking through the airport, making my
way downstairs to catch the parking shuttle.

*Hey! I just got off the plane and I should be home in less
than an hour. I'm so glad to have 3 days off now! Since it's
such a nice day, I'm thinking we could head to my pool as soon
as I get home. Sound good?*

By the time I got on the shuttle bus to the parking lot she
had texted me back. *No, I don't feel like doing that. It's been
a rough day.*

I quickly texted her back. *Why? What's wrong?*

*I don't want to get into it now. You can stop by when you
get back and we'll talk.*

Okay, I'll be there in about forty minutes then.

That obviously left me concerned. I became even more
concerned when I remembered how she didn't want to talk on
the phone last night. It was the only night of this trip we hadn't
talked, but I didn't suspect anything right then because her
excuse of being tired and wanting to go to bed seemed viable.
After all, I didn't get done with my last flight until after 9:30
p.m. last night, which was actually 10:30 p.m. for her, being on
Central time.

But that wasn't all. As my concern and curiosity got the
best of me while I was still sitting on the shuttle to the parking
lot, I began looking through her text messages on my phone
and realized they'd become a little sparse starting from about
yesterday afternoon. The few I received from her since then
were a far cry from the countless messages we'd been
exchanging for the first four days of this trip. I became mad at
myself for not noticing this sooner, but I suppose it's a
testament of how, as a pilot, you become so temporarily
detached from your normal life during a flying trip.

By the time I arrived at the parking lot, I felt a twinge of panic run through my body as it was now crystal clear that something was wrong with Megan, but I had no idea what. I made the short walk to my car, which was one row over from the shuttle stop. I then loaded my suitcase in the trunk and headed out. The radio came on when I started the engine, but I quickly turned it off. I wasn't in the mood for music, and I just wanted to get back and see Megan and find out what was wrong.

~   ~   ~

After a relatively quick forty-minute drive, beating the worst of the rush hour traffic, I arrived at Megan's aunt's house around 4:15 p.m.

Still in my uniform, I walked up the cement steps on the front porch and rang the doorbell.

A few seconds later, I saw Megan approaching the door through the stained glass window. When she opened it, I could immediately tell she looked upset—and tired. She was wearing black shorts and an old gray t-shirt.

"I've missed you so much," she said, walking out on the porch in her bare feet to hug me.

Her tight and long embrace was proof of that, and it felt good to hold her as I'd certainly missed her as well.

"I've missed you, too," I said. After our long hug, we shared a quick kiss.

"So what's wrong?" I asked.

"We'll talk in a minute," she said as she stepped inside and walked back toward the kitchen as I closed the front door and followed her.

Her aunt was standing at the counter pouring some iced tea for herself. She wore a navy blue, scoop-neck shirt and dark tan shorts. She was on summer break now from teaching, so I wasn't surprised to see her home.

She glanced over at me. "Hi Kevin." I could tell by her demeanor something wasn't right.

"Hi Linda, how are you?"

"I'm hanging in there," she said as she put the pitcher of iced tea back in the refrigerator. "I was just grabbing some iced tea before I head out on the back patio to read."

Then with a book tucked under her arm and a glass of iced tea in her hand, she walked over to the patio door.

"Well, it was good to see you, Kevin," she said.

"Yeah, same here," I said, fully aware of how awkward it felt to say hello and goodbye to her all within fifteen seconds. But it seemed she was giving Megan and me some privacy for whatever Megan was about to tell me.

She went outside and closed the sliding glass door behind her. She sat down on a chair on her patio facing away from us, set her glass down on the ground, and opened her book.

I leaned back on the kitchen counter and then turned to Megan. "So what's going on?

She took a deep breath before she began speaking. "I got a call yesterday afternoon from one of the schools around here that I applied to before I moved," she said. "It was for a teaching assistant job in their Literature Department. They did a quick phone interview with me right then, and then they said they wanted to meet me for an in-person interview. They said they want to have the position filled as soon as possible, even though it doesn't start until late August. So we set up the interview for Wednesday at 2:00 p.m., which is tomorrow already."

I was partially relieved to hear this because it appeared her strife was somehow due to this phone call about the job, instead of due to something much worse like a death in the family. From the way she and her aunt were acting before, I couldn't tell *what* had happened.

"Okay, that's good news so far," I said. "What happened next?"

"Well, at first I was really glad that at least one school is interested in me and that maybe I'd have a chance at getting a teaching assistant job after all. But then I started getting really nervous about the interview. Dinnertime came and went yesterday and I didn't eat anything. This morning, I woke up and had a panic attack and threw up and now my stomach feels just as bad as it did during the worst of all of this a few months ago."

"Have you eaten at all?" I asked.

"Some," she said. "My aunt told me she'd take me to the emergency room if I didn't eat today, so thankfully, I was able to eat half of a bagel earlier and some plain pasta for lunch."

She looked at me, ready to cry, and I reached my arms out and hugged her and she comfortably rested her head against my chest.

"I love you," she said softly.

"I love you, too."

"I'm so glad you're here right now," she said. "It's so hard to deal with all of this to begin with, and then having you gone for so many days like that makes it even harder."

"I know," I said, still embracing her. I knew that my being gone so much was still an issue—a big issue—but I also knew the more immediate issue was dealing with her anxiety about the interview tomorrow.

"You just need to relax," I said, letting go of her and looking her in the eyes. "I'm home for three days now. And you should be glad you have this interview because it could be a really good opportunity for you."

"I know," she said, looking down trying to hold back tears. "I just don't think I can go."

"You have to go, Megan. You're going to really regret this if you don't go," I said.

"I don't think I can," she said. "Even if I can somehow get the courage to go, all I'm going to do is make a fool of myself. They said the interview is with five people, which includes the department chairman and several professors. Right away, they'll see me be a nervous wreck and wonder how I'll ever be able to teach a class of thirty people if I can't even do an interview with five people."

She brought about a valid point and I began to wonder that myself. At that point, I started thinking she should seriously consider getting some help.

"Have you found a doctor around here yet?" I asked.

"No, I still need to do that because they still want me to do CT scans every month," she said.

"Well, you should definitely find a doctor soon and have that done," I said. "But before this interview tomorrow, maybe you could go to a walk-in clinic and they could prescribe you something that'll help you get you through the interview."

As soon as I said that, I could see the anger and opposition quickly grow on her face. "I know I've told you this before, but I guess I have to tell you again...I really don't want to take medication." she said.

"Do you still have health insurance now?" I asked.

"Yeah, I'm still on the COBRA plan from when I was laid off the first time," she said.

"Well, if you're not going to take any medication and forfeit this interview then I really think you should find a psychologist to help you with all of this," I said.

"I was actually seeing one when I lived in Cincinnati, and she was really good, but then I reached the maximum number of sessions that insurance would cover so I had to stop going."

"If you find one here, I'll pay for all of it," I said. "I don't care how much it costs. I just want you to get better."

"You don't have to do that," she said quietly, still staring downward.

I continued. "But before any of that, I really think you should go to a walk-in clinic tomorrow morning and they could write you a prescription. Then you could take one of the pills before the interview, and you'd probably be fine."

"I think you need to stop telling me what to do," she said sternly but calmly. "I'm not going to this interview. There's no way I can handle it."

I shook my head, getting more fervent. "I can't believe you're not going, Megan," I said, noticing my voice getting louder. "This job is what you've wanted all along, but you're just giving up before you even try." I think her aunt must have heard me through the patio door because I saw her quickly glance back from outside.

"Why doesn't anyone believe that I can get through this on my own?" she said loudly. "Everyone thinks I should just shove pills down my throat. I don't want that. I just need to learn how to deal with life's difficulties on my own. Taking pills isn't going to let me do that."

"Megan, this is interfering with your life," I said. "You can't even do the things you want to do right now." I leaned down to make eye contact with her. "You need to get help."

She took a few steps away from me, covered her face with her hands, and began to cry.

With more than a hint of frustration, I spoke. "I'm only telling you this because I love you, Megan."

Then silence set in, except for Megan sniffling and the hum of refrigerator. I had no idea what else to say to her, so I didn't say anything and simply let her cry.

~ ~ ~

After a few moments, the sliding glass door opened and her aunt walked in. I don't think it was any coincidence she came inside at that moment.

"How's everything?" she said, trying hard to portray a positive tone.

Megan walked out to the living room and sat down on the couch, still crying with her hands to her face.

"Well, it looks like she's decided she's not going to the interview," I said, "and she doesn't want to get any help, so that's where we stand right now."

Linda sighed. "I had the same argument with her this morning when she wanted to call and cancel the interview. Somehow I convinced her not to do that, but later I almost took her to the emergency room to force her to get help and hopefully start eating more."

"That might not have been a bad idea," I said. "I really don't know what else to do for her right now."

"Well, I think she just needs to settle down," Linda said. "Let's hope she'll be better tomorrow."

Megan quickly came into the kitchen and grabbed several tissues from the box on the counter. "I'm going to my room now, and then you guys can talk about me all you want."

"Megan, can't we just talk?" I called out.

"There's nothing else to talk about," she yelled as she was already halfway up the stairs. A few seconds her bedroom door slammed shut.

I turned to Linda and she shook her head.

"I've never seen her like this," I said.

"Well, this is pretty much how the whole day has been," she said. "She doesn't want to go to the interview, doesn't want to go to the doctor, doesn't want to take any medication, and doesn't even want to eat. But I can tell you right now, if she doesn't eat a decent dinner, I'm taking her to the emergency room."

"Well, let me give you my cell number so you can let me know if that happens," I said.

After we exchanged phone numbers, Linda put her phone back in her purse on the counter and took a deep breath. "I guess I'm going to have to call her parents at some point and tell them what's going on. I think they should know all of this."

"Yeah, you're right," I said.

She looked up at me. "I know this is tough to deal with right now, but just remember that Megan is a really great person...as I'm sure you already know that by now. You shouldn't think any less of her because of this. We all have tough times and things that we struggle with."

"I know," I said. "Don't worry, I don't think any less of her."

"She'll get better," Linda said. "I don't know how or when, but we just have to trust God with that."

"Yeah, you're right," I said. "I don't know what to do now. Should I stay here and try to talk to her or should I leave to give her a chance to settle down?"

"Well, I think she just needs to settle down," Linda said. "You're welcome to stay, but I don't know if it'll do any good right now."

"Yeah, I guess you're right. But definitely let me know how it goes with her tonight," I said, reaching in my pocket to get my keys.

"I will," she said.

So I said goodbye to Linda and started out back to my apartment. It was a bad feeling seeing the girl I love struggling so much with these issues. I felt completely helpless like I couldn't do anything for her—mostly because she wasn't letting me.

I figured I'd probably spend the evening on the couch watching TV or maybe reading to try to calm down from all of this. Either way, I hoped I wouldn't be spending it in the emergency room with Megan if she refuses to eat dinner. But then I realized if that's the thing that will force her to get the help she needs, then maybe that *was* how I wanted to spend the evening.

~ ~ ~

When I drove up to my apartment, it was just about 5:15 p.m. and I was startled to see a car parked in my driveway. As I got closer, I realized it was Katie's car. I didn't know why she was there, and my mind quickly came up with a few options. *Maybe she's just now moving the rest of her stuff out. Or maybe she's getting ready to have another party.* I parked out in the street and walked up to the door and hoped it wasn't the latter because I really didn't want any more drama after what had just happened with Megan.

I tried the front door but it was locked, so I used my key to open it and stepped inside.

"Hello? Katie?" I called out.

She came around the corner from the living room and was startled to see me. "Oh, hey. I'm baby-sitting today, and I was just getting the kids ready to take them home for the night." I caught a glimpse of two kids—one boy and one girl—standing in my living room curiously peering around the corner at me. The boy looked to be about six years old and the girl was probably around four. With them both having bright blonde hair, along with having an obvious resemblance to each other, there was no question they were brother and sister.

"So did you decide to move back in, or are you just using this as a place to baby-sit?" I asked.

"Um, well, I decided to move back in a few days ago," she said. "I was going to let you know at some point." She paused and looked straight at me. "I'm sorry...for everything." She kept looking at me, desperately wanting me to say something.

For a second, it felt like I should still be mad at her, but I was dumbfounded how she wasn't still mad at *me*. "It's okay," I finally said. "I'm glad you're back."

She took a sigh of relief and gave me quick hug, then went back in the living room and finished packing some dolls in the girl's backpack.

This certainly wasn't what I was expecting considering just six days ago when I texted her to see if she was okay, she snapped back at me, said she's still living with Amy, and seemed angrier than ever at me. But now she's moved back in and she just apologized for everything?

"Who's that man, Katie?" the boy asked.

"That's Mr. Kevin," she said. "He's my brother."

"Is he a pilot?" he asked, looking up to Katie.

"Yeah, he is," she said with excitement.

I decided I should meet these kids so I walked in the living room where they were.

The girl was shy and hid behind Katie while clenching her stuffed dog. But the boy, wearing a bright red shirt, was staring up at me, probably quite taken with my pilot's uniform.

I kneeled down. "What's your name?"

"Jacob," he said.

"I'm Kevin, nice to meet you," I said as I shook his hand.

"So when you're flying, how high does the plane go?"

"Usually around 35,000 feet."

His face lit up. "Wow, that's high! How fast does it go?"

"Well, at cruising speed, we can go over 500 miles per hour."

His eyes got big. "Whoa, that's fast," he said. He looked over at Katie, "That's really fast."

"Yeah, I know. It's *really* fast," she said, leading the girl over to me. "Madeline is going to say hi to Mr. Kevin now."

"Hi Madeline, it's nice meet you," I said, holding out my hand for her to shake it.

Eventually she shook my hand, but she was still too shy to say anything.

"Okay, guys," Katie summoned them, "go in the kitchen and make sure you didn't leave any dominos on the floor."

The kids obeyed and hurried off into the kitchen and then Katie looked at me. "We were doing domino races on the kitchen floor earlier."

"Oh, I bet they had fun with that," I said.

"Yeah, they did."

"They seem like good kids," I said. "Whose are they?"

"Do you remember my friend, Stacy, from high school?"

"Vaguely," I said. "She would sometimes hang out with you and Beth, right?"

"Right," she said. "Well, I met up with her for lunch last week just to catch up and she told me that she's a nanny for this family in town here, but she was going on vacation this week and they still hadn't found someone to take over while she's gone. So I decided I'd meet with the family and see if they liked me…and if I liked the kids. Thankfully, we all did so I have them every day this week from 8:00 a.m. to 5:30 p.m."

"Good," I said. "I'm glad you're doing this."

She then looked at me sheepishly. "And since they're having their house painted this week, I have to baby-sit them here in your apartment, if that's okay with you."

"Yeah, I don't mind," I said.

Jacob came running up to us holding a domino in his hand. "I found one. It was in the corner by the dishwasher."

"Okay, good job," she said.

She walked over and put the domino in the box sitting on the dining room table with some other games they had there. Then she went over and put Madeline's backpack on her and stood up and looked at me. "Well, I have to take them home now. They live pretty close, so I'll be back in like fifteen minutes," she said.

Then they left, but not before Jacob said goodbye to me and Madeline gave me a small wave. I knew I'd be seeing more of these kids around my apartment for the next three days while I was home, and that wasn't a bad thing because they seemed like really good kids.

~   ~   ~

After the door closed, I walked in the kitchen to find something to eat because I was starving by this point. I opened my refrigerator and I was surprised to see Katie must have gone to the grocery store because there was deli meat, cheese slices, lettuce, fruit cups, pudding cups, and countless other snacks for the kids. I saw a loaf of bread sitting on the counter, so I quickly made myself a sandwich and quickly began eating.

I felt a certain happiness as I stood there in my kitchen devouring my sandwich. Katie had come back—and even apologized—and that was good news at a time that I needed some good news after what had just happened earlier with Megan.

Not only was I glad to see Katie back, but I was glad to see her taking some responsibility—a lot of responsibility—with caring for two young kids like that for nine and a half hours of the day. But she's always enjoyed being around kids and they seem to enjoy being around her as well, which would explain why she did her share of baby-sitting when she was younger. For as much partying as she's done throughout her life, it's weird that the minute kids come into the picture, she suddenly transforms into a responsible adult.

Just as I was almost done with my sandwich, Katie got back. She took a deep breath when she got in the door. "Are you eating?"

"Yeah, it looks like you went to the grocery store," I said.

"Yeah I needed food for the kids," she said. "Speaking of food, I'm starving right now. Running around with them all day makes me hungry...and tired."

I laughed. "You want a sandwich?"

"Yeah, anything at this point."

She quickly slapped together a sandwich and stood next to me at the counter and started eating.

It didn't take me long to finish the rest of my sandwich. "Can I have one of those pudding cups in the refrigerator?"

She laughed. "Go ahead. I got them for the kids, but there's plenty in there."

I quickly grabbed one out of the refrigerator but then realized she was standing in front of the silverware drawer. "I need a spoon."

"No, you have to eat it with your finger," she said, smiling at me.

I laughed and gently pushed her out of the way and got a spoon and began eating the pudding.

"So what made you move back here?"

She paused while she finished chewing. "Well, Amy kicked me out a few days ago. We had a big fight and she told me to gather up all of my stuff and leave. She called me a freeloader and an immature brat who doesn't want to take responsibility for herself."

"Ouch," I said.

"Yeah, it was harsh," she said, "but I realized she was right. I know Mom and Dad hated it when I hung out with Amy in high school because they thought she was a bad influence on me with all the partying she did. She probably was. But she's way more responsible now and has a real job, and to hear someone like her tell me that just...it really got me thinking."

She took a deep breath and continued talking. "And then when I had to leave and realized if you wouldn't have made me take the keys back I wouldn't have had anywhere to go that night, it just made me realize what a great brother you are to put up with me. Even after I screamed in your face that night of the party you still were going to let me keep living here and I really don't know why."

"Well, the Bible says love should never give up," I said. "So considering we're blood relatives, we should love each other no matter what, even if one of us is hard to love. And you were definitely hard to love that night."

She laughed. "I know." She put her arm around me. "I appreciate you letting me live here. I don't know if I ever thanked you for this." She turned and looked straight at me. "So thank you, you're a good brother." I hugged her back.

"I don't know if I ever officially apologized either," she said. "So I'm sorry for throwing the party and for moving out and not being very nice to you and for snapping back at you when you texted me to check on me last week. You're not still mad about any of that, are you?"

"No, I'm not," I said.

"And you don't mind me moving back in, do you?"

"No, I'm glad you came back, but just so we're clear, I don't want you having anymore parties here," I said.

"Okay, that's fair," she said, "but you're not going to get mad if I go out with my friends occasionally, are you?"

"No," I said, "just be responsible."

"I will," she said. "You won't have to bail me out of jail," she joked.

"I better not," I said with some seriousness.

"You won't. I promise," she said, hugging me again.

After a few seconds, she let go of me. "I'm glad Mom and Dad never found out about me moving out. At least, I'm assuming they never did because they never called to yell at me about it."

"No, I never told them," I said. "They would've freaked out."

"If they only knew all the things we've hidden from them through the years..." she said.

"Let's be glad they don't," I said as we both laughed.

"By the way, I'm giving you the money I'm making from baby-sitting this week for rent," she said, just before taking another bite of her sandwich.

"I told you when you moved in that you don't have to pay rent," I said.

"I know. But I want to," she said with her mouth full.

"Okay, I hope they're paying you decently because that's a big job to watch two kids for the whole day, even if they're good kids."

"Yeah, they're paying me very well," she said. "They live in one of those huge houses in that subdivision off of Lincoln Street."

"Oh, wow," I said.

"Yeah, the father is a doctor and the mother is a pharmacist, so they're loaded," she said.

Katie then finished her sandwich then went to the refrigerator to get a pudding cup also. "So do you want to tell me what's bothering you now?" she said, peeling open her pudding.

"What do you mean?" I asked.

"Well, I saw how you looked when you walked in and I know you were surprised to see me here, but I could tell something else was bothering you."

I took a deep breath. "Well, you're right," I said. "It's about Megan."

I proceeded to tell her a condensed version of what was happening. But I didn't tell her that Megan was in the hospital for eleven days back in March and that there's still a chance she could have stomach cancer.

Because of some things Katie unfortunately had to go through in her past, I knew that if she discovered the somewhat scary reality of Megan's condition, it would get her even more concerned and upset. So in order to protect her from knowing that, I did the typical big brother thing and only told her about the struggles Megan is having with anxiety.

"That's sad to see someone be so consumed by anxiety like that," she said. "Do you think she'll be able to go tomorrow?"

"Honestly, I don't see how she will," I said. "It's really a shame because this teaching job is exactly what she's wanted all along."

"But if she can't even go to the interview, then how is she going to teach classes?" Katie asked.

"I don't know," I said, shaking my head.

~   ~   ~

Not long after Katie and I finished the impromptu dinner we had standing at the kitchen counter, I retreated back to my room to start journaling after this long and eventful day.

I checked my phone and I had a text message from Linda.

Megan just ate a bowl of plain pasta and an apple for dinner, so at least she's eating. She's still very nervous, though. Let's pray she feels better tomorrow and can go to the interview.

Speaking of text messages, when I just checked my phone right now, I had another one, but this one is from Megan.

Hey, I appreciate what you're trying to do, however I think you should also respect my decision about not wanting to take medication. But even though I got mad at you today, I never want you to think I don't love you. I DO love you SOOOO much, and I hope you still love me after today.

I just replied. *Hey, of course I still love you. That's why I got upset today—because I love you so much and I hate seeing you like this and I want so much for you to get better. But I know I didn't go about things in the right way today. I'm sorry for that. Get a good night of sleep tonight, and I'm sure you'll feel better. I'll say a prayer for you tonight. See you tomorrow.*

I have no idea what will happen tomorrow. It remains to be seen whether this interview will end up being a huge accomplishment for Megan if she's able to go, or a huge wake-up call for her to get help if she *can't* go. If it's the latter, it seems Megan, and all of us who are close to her, may have some difficult days ahead of us—including tomorrow.

◆ 14 ◆

Wednesday, June 9th
My apartment
11:37 p.m. (Central Time)

As I expected, today was a challenging day for all of us, and unfortunately it ended up with Megan in the emergency room. It's just past 11:30 p.m. now and I'm sitting at my dining room table typing while Katie is sound asleep in her room preparing for another day of baby-sitting tomorrow. I should also be sound asleep, but despite my tiredness, I don't feel like sleeping right now.

Going back to this morning, the day began with me waking up at 7:00 a.m. after hearing Katie's alarm clock go off. Despite both of our doors being shut, I guess the sound still travels quite well because a few minutes later I heard her get up from the air mattress I've given her to sleep on. She then opened her door and walked to the kitchen, presumably to have breakfast. In less than an hour from that point, she'd have to be at the kids' house to pick them up for another full day of baby-sitting. It was good to see that she was taking this responsibility seriously, even if it meant getting up "insanely early" as she'd probably describe it.

I lingered in bed for a few minutes and grabbed my phone and texted Megan to see how she was doing. *Hey, how are you feeling today?*

She was awake already because she texted right back before I even got out of bed. *I'm really nervous. I already had a panic attack and threw up about an hour ago and now my stomach feels awful. There's no way I can go to this interview today.*

I honestly had no idea how to respond to that or what to do for her, but I knew one thing was certain—this day was already shaping up to be a challenging one for all of us, and I hadn't even gotten out of bed yet.

A few minutes later, I got up and walked to the kitchen to have some breakfast. Katie was standing at the counter, still wearing the old pink t-shirt and gray workout shorts she sleeps in. I then noticed she was eating several slices of deli turkey with her hands.

I laughed. "Turkey for breakfast?"

She smirked. "It's the only thing that fills me up," she said with her mouth full. "And it gives me energy, and you know I'm going to need it running after two kids all day."

"Whatever floats your boat," I said, opening the cabinet to get a cereal bar.

"You don't look very happy," she said. "Are you still upset about Megan?"

"Yeah, I am," I said and proceeded to tell her about the text messages Megan and I had just exchanged a few minutes earlier.

"That's hard when she just refuses to go like that," she said. "And it's even harder when she refuses to get help and refuses medication."

"Yep," I said, looking down, unwrapping my cereal bar.

"What time is her interview supposed to be?" she asked.

"Two o'clock," I said before taking a bite.

"Well then you need to get her out this morning to get her mind off of everything," she said. "You should take her shopping or go to a movie or something."

I liked Katie's train of thought and it made me think of something. "I could actually take her to the pool," I said. "Every time we've gone swimming together, she's loved it and had a great time. And it's going to be another hot and sunny day, so that would be perfect...if she'll agree to go."

"Well, don't ask her, just tell her that you're taking her to the pool this morning," Katie said.

"It's worth a try," I said.

"I have to get dressed. Text her now and don't let her tell you she can't go to the pool," she said as she headed back to her bedroom.

Right after that, I followed Katie's advice and texted Megan. *Since it's going to be hot today, we should go to the pool this morning. How about you come by here at 9:00?*

A few minutes later, she texted back and surprisingly agreed to it—at least mostly. *Okay, I can sit out by the pool with you, but I doubt I'm going to swim.*

~ ~ ~

By the time 9:00 a.m. came, Katie had picked up the kids and they were already back at my apartment and well into building a castle with toy blocks on my living room floor. As I sat behind them on my couch—wearing my bathing suit and an old t-shirt, waiting for Megan—I realized Katie was probably having just as much fun as the kids were.

The doorbell rang and I jumped up and headed to the door.

"Someone's here," Jacob said with excitement.

"I know, it's Miss Megan," Katie said. "Just stay here and you'll get to meet her in a few minutes."

I opened the door and Megan forced a small smile, then stepped inside and we both hugged and shared a quick kiss. She had her sunglasses on and her hair was tied back in a ponytail. She wore a black tank top and tan shorts, presumably with her bathing suit on underneath. Given that she hadn't said a word to me yet, it certainly didn't seem like she was in a talking mood.

"Katie is here baby-sitting two kids today," I said.

"Oh, she moved back in?"

"Yep, she did," I said.

When Megan took off her sunglasses it looked as though she'd been crying earlier. She didn't have any makeup on and the uncharacteristic dark circles under her eyes indicated she probably didn't sleep well last night.

I figured it would probably be best not to dwell on what was wrong, which would probably get her more upset. So I didn't ask her how she was feeling. I already had a good idea just by looking at her.

She walked over to the dining room table and set her purse down.

"Hi Megan," Katie said getting up from the floor and walking over to hug her. "It's been forever since we've seen each other."

"I know," Megan said as they embraced for a few seconds. "It's good to see you again."

The last time they saw each other must have been at some point during my senior year of college and Katie was probably about fifteen or sixteen years old at that point.

By this time, Jacob had walked over and wanted to meet Megan. After Megan kneeled down and introduced herself to Jacob—and later to Madeline—Megan and I headed out to the pool.

~ ~ ~

It was barely 9:30 a.m. as we walked over and the air still had a thick and damp feel to it—typical of a summer morning in the Midwest. But the sun was shining and I knew it wouldn't take long before it turned into another hot day—one of many that this area has had lately.

Megan continued to be pretty quiet on the walk over. When we arrived at the pool, I wasn't at all surprised we were the only ones out there, given that it was a weekday morning. Half of the pool was sparkling in the sunshine while the other half was still in the shade because of the low angle of the morning sun. We picked two chairs in the sun and Megan spread her towel over the chair and sat down.

I took off my t-shirt and decided to jump in the water right away, even though Megan didn't want to join me. I quickly regretted it because being so early in the day, it felt downright cold. After I swam around for barely two minutes, I got out, dried off, and sat down next to Megan.

We put some sun block on and decided to lie out in the sun for a while. She actually fell asleep for over an hour, which I was happy to see because I'm sure she needed the rest. After she woke up, we sat on the edge of the pool for a while, not saying much, just sitting close to each other and swinging our feet around in the water.

After that, we left and she seemed to be in a slightly better mood than when we came. But for the entire morning—other than the two text messages we exchanged right after I woke up—there wasn't any mention of her interview. It was probably for the best, but it clearly created an elephant in the room, so to speak.

When we got back to my apartment, it was just past 11:15 a.m. and the two kids were sitting at my dining room table eagerly waiting for Katie to finish making their lunch.

"Oh hey, guys," Katie said, peering out of the kitchen. "You're welcome to join us for lunch. I'm making sandwiches."

"Okay, but we just need to change out of our bathing suits first," I said. Megan went in the bathroom and I went into my bedroom and a few minutes later we came out and sat down with the kids at the table. Katie gave us both a glass of lemonade and made me a sandwich and gave Megan a piece of plain bread because that's all she wanted. Then Katie finished making herself a sandwich and came over and sat down at the table, and the five of us had lunch together.

After we finished eating and after I got done telling Jacob more about what I do as a pilot, his intrigue seemed stronger than ever.

"How do planes fly?" he asked.

"Well, I'll show you," I said, getting up from the table to get some pieces of paper. I proceeded to spend the next twenty minutes showing him how to fold a paper airplane and then showing him how to fly it. I'm not sure he fully understood the principle of lift, but he's only six years old. What mattered most is to see the astonishment and enjoyment on his face as he watched the very paper airplane that he folded gracefully glide through the air.

After that, Katie was going to play another game with the kids, so Megan and I decided to go down by the pond that my patio overlooks. We walked down through the grass and sat on the bench beside the water, which gave us a good view of the fountain along with a few geese contently floating. She rested her head on my shoulder and I held her hand.

After we sat there silently for several minutes, I finally decided it was time to address the issue at hand. "So what are you thinking about the interview?"

"I'm actually feeling better right now," she said. "It seems like I've settled down, even though my stomach is still bothering me some."

"So are you thinking you'll be able to go?"

She nodded. "I think so...believe it or not. I'm still terrified but somehow I feel peace at the same time. I guess that means God wants me to go."

I nodded in agreement. "The fact that you've settled down enough now to go to the interview could mean He really wants you to have this job," I said.

"Let's hope," she said. "Can you imagine how great it would be if I actually get this job?"

"You could be a professor in a few years," I said, "and then I'd have to call you 'Doctor' all the time."

She laughed and then kissed me. "I'm sorry for putting you through all of that yesterday. I just get so nervous about things still. And I'm sorry I got mad and yelled at you."

"It's okay," I said. "I'm sorry too for trying to force you to go to a walk-in clinic and take medication."

"It's okay," she said. "I know it was just because you love me, and I love you too," she said, before kissing me again. We then held hands and prayed together, thanking God for giving Megan the peace she needs to go to the interview and asking God to do His will, whether that be allowing Megan to get this job or opening some different doors for her in the future.

After we prayed, we realized she should probably head back to her aunt's house to get ready for the interview since it was 12:15 p.m. already and her interview was at 2:00 p.m. As we walked through the grass back to my patio, all I could think about was how happy and relieved I was that she'd finally settled down enough to go to this interview. And not only that, but for the first time, she was seeing this interview as something good and something to be excited about.

We decided I'd follow her over to her aunt's house so I could be there when she left for the interview. Regardless of whether she gets the job or not, this was still a big moment for her and a huge personal achievement that she was even able to go and I wanted to be a part of it.

~   ~   ~

When I arrived at her aunt's house, Megan had already headed upstairs to get ready, which left Linda and me downstairs while we waited for her. So we decided to go outside and she gave me a tour of her yard and showed me all of the flowers she'd planted, which were held in ceramic pots displaying intricate designs she'd painted on them. We then had a seat on her patio and shared in some casual conversation.

After a while, we went back inside and she showed me the painting she referred to as her "current project." It was an ocean scene before sunset with some dark clouds over the water and the sun's rays leaking out from behind the clouds.

"I'm painting this for Megan," she said. "But she doesn't know it's for her yet. I wanted to encompass the fact that even when there are clouds, we know the sun is still there."

"It looks good," I said as we both stepped back and studied it for a few moments.

"How do I look?" we heard Megan say behind us. We both quickly turned around and saw her standing at the top of the stairs, fully dressed for her interview.

"Good," we both said enthusiastically. She looked stunning. She was wearing a navy blue suit, which fit her perfectly. She'd curled her hair, which made for light brown wavy curls elegantly draping down over the collar of her suit. She'd put on some makeup, which looked meticulously done, and wore some subtle earrings. It was a complete transformation from how she looked earlier. Whether it was because of her makeup or her nap at the pool earlier, there were no more dark circles under her eyes and she looked quite refreshed.

"I didn't think I'd ever be able to go, but here I am and I'm not even that nervous or tired right now," she said, carefully stepping down the stairs in her high heels.

My aunt quickly grabbed her phone to take pictures. She asked the two of us to pose together.

"I don't think we match very well," I said because I was wearing shorts and an old t-shirt.

"It doesn't matter," Linda said, taking several different poses of us standing together.

Then she took a few of Megan by herself and then I took a few of Megan and Linda together. After that, Megan and I kissed goodbye.

"Good luck. But I don't think you'll need it," I said.

She smiled. "Thanks."

Then she left and after all of what took place in the days leading up to today, a part of me still couldn't believe she was actually able to go.

~ ~ ~

I came back to my apartment and Jacob and Madeline were on the couch watching some sort of kids' show on DVD while Katie was cleaning up the kitchen.

"Hey," Katie said. "I need to tell you something," signaling me to come into the kitchen. I walked over to her and she came close and began whispering. "Just so you know, I found some anxiety pills in Megan's purse this morning and I crushed one up and put it in her lemonade at lunch."

"What? I exclaimed. "You drugged her?"

"Shh. Don't get the kids stirred up," she said. "They're being really good right now."

"Why did you go through her purse?" I whispered, shaking my head in disbelief.

"Well, when you two were at the pool and the kids were playing on their own, I just thought I'd look through it, thinking she'd probably have some sort of medication in there. And sure enough, I was right."

"But she's been so adamant about not wanting to take anything," I said. "It doesn't make any sense why she'd have that in her purse."

"Well, I know her type," she said. "In her mind she was probably keeping it in there in case she has a huge nervous breakdown or something, even though she'll most likely never touch it, no matter what happens. It looked like a free sample she probably got from her doctor. It was in a small plastic bottle and it said it was antianxiety medication on the label. It said it had ten pills in it, and all ten were still in there."

I took a deep breath. "I can't believe you did this. She's going to be really upset when she finds out about this."

"Kevin," she said before quickly lowering her voice again, "there was no way she would've gone to this interview otherwise. She looked terrible when she showed up here this morning. And besides, now we can tell her we did this, and she'll realize the medication actually works and maybe she'll start using it."

I shook my head. "It's not going to go like that. She's going to refuse it even more now and get really mad at us for doing this. But why am I saying *us*?" I asked with my voice raised. "It was *you* who did this, but now I'm right in the middle of it."

"You can be mad at me if you want," she said, "but it got her to the interview, didn't it?"

Jacob walked into the kitchen. "Katie, our DVD show is over now."

She looked at me. "Their parents gave me some books they want me to read to them, so I think I'm going to do that now."

"Fine, I'm going for a walk," I said.

I grabbed my sunglasses off the counter and left. I headed over to the neighborhood across the street from my apartment complex, hoping to calm down. I was sort of mad at Katie, even though I know she was trying to help Megan—albeit in a forceful and deceptive way. But mostly I was disappointed and let down that Megan's ability to go to the interview wasn't because she's getting her anxiety under control; instead it was simply because Katie drugged her. But there wasn't anything I could do at the moment except wait for Megan to text me when her interview was over and hope the medication didn't wear off before that.

~ ~ ~

After a long walk through the neighborhood I made another trip to the pool—partially to stay out of the way of Katie and the kids and partially to cool off after my walk during the hottest part of this 91-degree day.

Finally, Megan texted me around 4:30 p.m. *I just got out*

of the interview and I'm heading home now. It took longer than I thought.

As we planned earlier, I then headed over to her aunt's house so I could hear all about how her interview went. When I arrived, Linda answered the door and I could tell by the look on her face something was wrong. I walked in and looked down into the den and saw Megan lying on the couch.

"Hey Megan," I said.

"Hey," she said softly.

The curtains over the windows were pulled shut making the room fairly dark. She'd already changed out of her suit and into shorts and t-shirt, but I noticed her makeup was still on and her hair was still curled.

"She's not doing well," Linda said. "She threw up when she got home, but it was really more like dry heaving, because she's hardly eaten anything all day."

I walked down the four stairs into the den and kneeled down next to the couch. "Hey, so how did it go?"

She turned to me, still lying down. "Luckily I felt better than this for most of the time there, and they said they want to meet me for a second interview," she said. "I think they're going to offer me the job after that, but I don't see how I'll be able to do it."

She continued. "I just started panicking toward the end of the interview and it was like all of my anxiety just came flooding back. But luckily, I was able to hide it pretty well until I got out of there."

It was clear the medication had worn off, but this hardly seemed like the right time to tell her that Katie had secretly put the pill in her lemonade earlier.

"How do you feel otherwise?" I asked.

"I'm exhausted and my stomach is really upset," she said.

"Do you think it would help to eat something now?" I asked.

"I can't," she said. "I don't think I can keep anything down," she said.

I turned to Linda and she nodded, knowing exactly what I was thinking. Linda then went upstairs and packed a bag for her, and I stayed downstairs at her side. As she continued lying on the couch, she closed her eyes periodically as I held her hand. Not only was she overcome with anxiety, but I could tell she was exhausted from the interview and weak from not eating anything—except a slice of bread—all day.

"Are you in any pain?" I asked.

She opened her eyes. "Not really. My stomach just feels really upset right now and I can't settle down."

Linda came down a few minutes later with Megan's backpack.

I stood up next to Megan. "We're taking you to the emergency room now," I said decisively.

She gently shook her head in disagreement and some tears came to her eyes, but beyond that, she didn't put up much of a protest. I helped her up from the couch and walked her to my car and helped her into the back seat. Then Linda got in and sat next to her and we left.

~   ~   ~

After walking into a surprisingly crowded emergency room for a Wednesday evening approaching 6:00 p.m., we checked in at the desk and took a seat among the many rows of dark tan, upholstered chairs lined up in several rows, most occupied with people. Linda filled out an abundance of paperwork for

Megan and then turned it in, and we proceeded to wait some more. Megan rested her head on my shoulder and occasionally glanced up at the flat panel TV hanging from the ceiling, which was broadcasting an all-news channel.

By 7:00 p.m. they finally called us back. After a brief visit from a nurse, and after we left the room for a minute while Megan changed into a hospital gown, it was back to waiting. I sat with Megan on the exam table, and she eventually decided to lie down and rest her head on my lap. After almost another hour, the doctor finally came in.

He sat down in front of the computer in the room and asked Megan about her symptoms and quickly typed in what she was saying.

"Do you have any pain in your stomach?" he asked.

"No," she said. "It's just upset."

"Do you have any lightheadedness or faint feeling?"

"No."

"Do you have any shortness of breath or feelings of irregular heartbeats?"

"No."

He listened to her heart for several seconds and then had her take some deep breaths. "Sounds okay there," he said, backing away and putting his stethoscope around his neck.

"So we're going to give you an IV to get you hydrated and we'll also give you something to settle you down a little. Then after an hour or so, you're going to try to eat. If you can't eat, we're going to have to keep you overnight and run some tests, because looking at your history, I'm a little concerned about your stomach. But if you're able to eat a decent meal and your stomach feels better, we can send you home tonight and I'll write you a prescription for some antianxiety medication. But you really need to see your regular doctor sooner rather than later so you can have your next set of CT scans for your stomach...and to put together a treatment plan for your anxiety."

After spending barely ten minutes with her, he was gone and probably on to the next patient.

The next hour went pretty slowly, but I guess it went about as well as it could have. They put her in a temporary out-patient room and gave her an IV and some pills, which she surprisingly didn't resist taking. It seemed like they gave her a high dosage because she drifted off several times after that.

Then they brought a tray of food for her with a sandwich, a bag of snack crackers, and a fruit cup, and she surprisingly ate all of it. She then said her stomach felt a little better after eating. So given that she still didn't have any pain and she didn't vomit, they discharged her and we brought her back.

By the time we got back to her aunt's house, it was nearly impossible for her to stay awake for more than two minutes at a time. So she went to bed, but not before we hugged and said 'I love you' to each other.

Then I came back to my apartment and Katie had already gone to bed to recover from this day she spent with the kids, and to prepare for another day with them tomorrow—and another day after that.

~   ~   ~

As difficult as this day has been, I'm glad Megan was able to go to the interview and I'm glad she might be coming around to realizing she needs help. She might even be willing to take medication now considering she willingly took it tonight in the emergency room. Speaking of that, I still feel obligated to tell her about Katie drugging her, but I'm going to wait for the right time. I can imagine that she won't be very happy to find that out.

But for now, all I can do is pray that she'll be able to go to the second interview and get the job, if that's what God wants for her. But most importantly, I pray for her recovery because even if she gets the job, it's clear she's still in no condition to be working right now.

· 15 ·

Tuesday, June 15th
My apartment
7:26 p.m. (Central Time)

Today, my day of flying began much like any other and I had no reason to believe it would end much differently—but it did. As I'm sitting here in my quiet apartment tonight and starting to decompress from this difficult day, I'm realizing this will end up being a day I remember for a long time, whether I want to or not.

It's certainly taken its toll on me because it's not even 7:30 p.m. yet, but I'm absolutely exhausted. That may explain why it's taken me the last five minutes to figure out where I should begin with this journal entry. So much has happened today, but to keep everything in chronological order, I suppose I should start from where I last left off—six days ago.

That was the day of Megan's interview and her subsequent trip to the emergency room that night. I had the next two days off after that and I'm happy to say she got a little better through that time. Her stomach was still bothering her and she still wasn't eating normally, but she *did* eat. She also seemed a little calmer at times, but still not her normal self.

I took her to my pool on Thursday and she enjoyed being outside in the nice summer weather and swimming around in the water a little. But she wasn't in the mood for our typical splashing, chasing, and dunking routine.

Then on Friday, which was my last day off, I took her hiking at a nearby forest preserve and she seemed to enjoy that more than I thought she would. But shortly after we got back to her aunt's house, she got a phone call around 3:30 p.m. from the school she interviewed with two days earlier. They were calling to officially set up a time for her second interview, and they agreed on Wednesday at 10:00 a.m., which is now tomorrow already. From the time she hung up the phone, I could tell her anxiety had already taken a full grip on her again. For the rest of that afternoon, all she did was lie on the couch at her aunt's house—not sleeping, not watching TV, not reading—just stressing about the interview.

Linda and I tried our best to calm her down. As dinnertime approached, we strongly suggested that she take the medication. Surprisingly, she did, and she was able to eat a reasonable dinner and was noticeably calmer after that. Later that evening, it became time for me to say goodbye to her because I'd be going back to work the next day to begin this four-day flying trip.

We ended up standing outside next to my car in her aunt's driveway and after a really long hug, several kisses, and her shedding some tears, I left. She still seemed reasonably calm, but definitely sad I was leaving, as was I.

~   ~   ~

Throughout the trip, we texted a lot and talked on the phone every day, as we normally do when I'm gone. She didn't seem any worse throughout that time—if anything, a little better—but she said she was still dealing with some anxiety and her stomach still didn't feel right.

My flying trip didn't necessarily go fast, but this last day seemed to arrive quicker than I thought it would. I had to wake up early this morning for my first flight and despite it still being completely dark outside, the fact that I'd be seeing Megan later in the day gave me all the energy I needed. After flying two uneventful and on-time flights, before I knew it, we were pushing back from the gate in Nashville to begin the last flight of the day, which was scheduled to put me back in Chicago at 2:35 p.m.—thanks to the early-morning start I had.

We took off on time, and I had the honor of flying this one because the captain had flown our previous flight. As we got closer to Chicago, it looked like we'd have about a twenty-minute delay before we could land. From what we heard, some rain showers had moved through earlier and now thick clouds and a low ceiling were what remained, causing reduced visibility for the arriving flights.

As we continued our descent, we said one last goodbye to the sunshine just before the plane submerged into the thick cloud cover that overspread the entire Chicago area. We then began a holding pattern where we circled for about twenty minutes. Finally we landed, and were greeted by a gloomy, 71-degree day—quite disappointing for mid-June in Chicago.

~ ~ ~

After I got off the plane, it was just after 3:00 p.m. and I made the relatively short walk to the pilots' lounge to sign out and was surprised to see my boss, Tom, standing near the door just as I walked in. He was wearing his typical white dress shirt, fancy tie—today it happened to be light blue—with black dress pants, and freshly-shined black dress shoes.

"Hi Kevin," he said.

"Hey boss," I said, walking over to the water cooler.

After I grabbed a paper cup and filled it up with water, I stood up and realized he had followed me over.

"Are you here to see me?" I asked.

"Actually, I am," he said.

"So what's up?" I asked before taking a sip of water.

"Well, actually we should go into my office," he said.

That didn't sound good and I wondered if I was in trouble for something, but there was nothing I could think of that I'd done that was against policy or procedure.

"Is everything okay?" I asked.

He hesitated for a second. "We'll talk in my office," he said, signaling me to follow him.

I quickly threw out the mostly full cup of water and quickly followed him carting my rolling suitcase behind me. I said a quick, silent prayer asking God to help me through whatever was about to happen.

We finally arrived at his office and he let me enter first. I set up my rolling suitcase in the corner and I noticed my hands were shaking when I retracted the handle down. He walked behind his desk, sat down, and immediately picked up his phone and dialed a number.

"Hi Joanne, we're ready now," he said.

I nervously sat down in one of the two chairs facing his desk. I had no idea what was going on and I had no idea who Joanne was, but I knew this didn't look good.

He stared down at papers on his desk, and then looked up briefly. "We just need to wait for Joanne, and then we'll get started." He immediately buried his face back down in the papers creating an incredibly awkward situation.

Thoughts kept racing through my mind. *Are they going to fire me? What could I have possibly done wrong? I'm so meticulous about following procedure with everything I do.* In an attempt to shift my focus, I quickly took a glance around his undeniably large office and it reminded me of the day of my interview, which was almost a year ago now. It looked mostly the same—the large dark wooden desk with some ornate trim, two bookcases on either side of his desk holding more plastic replicas of airplanes than books, navy blue carpeting, and a thriving, five-foot, fig tree sitting in the corner.

Finally, I heard someone enter and assumed it was Joanne.

She closed the door behind her and walked up to me and shook my hand. "Hi Kevin, my name is Joanne, I'm from the Human Resources Department."

She was middle-aged with dark hair and wore a pale blue blouse and black pants. She had a notebook and some folders tucked in her arm. The sympathetic half-smile she gave me and her somber and restrained tone confirmed even more that something bad was about to happen and my heart was racing as she sat down in the chair next to me.

Tom began speaking. "So you're probably wondering what this is all about."

"Yeah," I said.

"So unfortunately, Corporate has made some decisions to eliminate some flights from our schedule, and we're also eliminating service to a few cities altogether. Some of the flights we're eliminating will take months to decommission from our schedule. But for others that have been running at about sixty percent capacity, we've already reassigned them to smaller planes, which will be operated by our regional jet partner companies, not us. So obviously, with fewer flights, we need fewer pilots. As a result we have to put some pilots on furlough. Unfortunately, you're one of those pilots, and we're eliminating your position for the time being."

When he spoke those words, my heart started beating very hard in my chest, panic shot through my body, and I felt myself tense up.

"As you probably know, this is all determined by seniority," he said, "and the pilots with the least amount of seniority are the first to be put on furlough. Since you've been here about a year, you don't have a lot of seniority built up because, as you know, we have pilots who've been flying with us for several decades. And then, of course, in the event of a recall, the pilots will be called back in order of their seniority."

I inhaled quickly and I felt like I was going to hyperventilate. I looked down and I couldn't believe this was happening as my mind began to primitively piece together what my life will look like without flying—and without working.

"I'm sorry, Kevin," he said. "It's not personal, it's all based on seniority."

"So how long is this going to last?" I finally asked.

"Um...I'll let Joanne answer that," he said.

She looked at me. "Well, we really can't give an answer on that at this point because we don't know. It depends on market conditions, like if we add any new flights or destinations in the future, how many pilots retire in the coming months or years, and how many pilots ahead of you in seniority decide to return in the event of a recall. There are a lot of factors and there's no way to give a time estimate at this point."

"Well, are we talking months or are we talking years?" I quickly asked.

She shook her head. "I really can't give you any time estimate at this point. I'm sorry."

It was so frustrating they couldn't even answer that question. It could be as little as my previous furlough of five months, or it could be many years. I've even heard of some pilots not getting recalled until after eight years. But since they couldn't give me an estimate, I have no clue what to plan for.

"I'm just shocked," I said. "I had no clue that there was any reason for a furlough right now." It didn't make a lot of sense because just a few years ago most of the big airlines recalled all of their pilots who were put on furlough from the really ugly times the airlines went through several years before that.

"Well, these decisions were made to increase our profitability," Tom said. "It's not that the airline is trying to avoid bankruptcy like it was years ago. It's just attempting to be more efficient. We don't want to have flights in our schedule that are only sixty percent full. And we don't want to fly to cities where customer demand is shrinking."

I shook my head, still in disbelief.

"So right now, you'll need to start thinking about when you want your last day to be. Basically you have two options. The first is taking the thirty-day notice, where you would work through the next thirty days, making your regular salary. The second option is something that the pilots' union has just approved where you can make today your last day, but still collect pay for the next fifteen days. So we'll need an answer on that before you leave today. You'll have a chance later to make a brief call to your family if want to discuss it with them first. But right now, Joanne will go through the paperwork with you."

She opened up a thick folder in front of me and began going

through a bunch of details. At that point, I couldn't concentrate on anything. I was still in shock, because essentially, I'd just lost my job. But I did my best to try to pay attention to what she was saying.

After at least ten minutes of that, it came time to decide on my last day. All I needed to do was think of Megan and the tough time she's been having lately. I figured if being home with her during these next thirty days will help her in any way, then I'll gladly do it. So I opted to make today my last day.

~   ~   ~

When the meeting ended, an airline employee who I'd never met or seen before was waiting outside of Tom's office and walked me to the pilots' lounge. I then proceeded to empty my locker into a brown box while he watched me and then I said goodbye to the few other pilots who were in the lounge at that time.

Then he walked to the parking shuttle with me and he even rode with me to the parking lot. Neither of us spoke a word to each other, probably from the awkwardness of the situation. Nevertheless, I was glad he stayed with me, since it would've been nearly impossible to carry a big box while also carting my suitcase.

We arrived at my car and he set the box in my trunk. "Take care. Hopefully you'll be back flying soon."

"Thanks," I said halfway waving at him as he turned and walked away.

I closed my trunk and came around and got in my car, which wasn't hot at all because of this gloomy and cool day. When I shut the door, everything got silent and it was such an awful feeling as I began to feel the full weight of what had just happened and how different my life will look now. As I stared down at the steering wheel, the feelings reminded me somewhat of my first furlough, but this seemed worse. This time, instead of a challenging, low-paying regional jet job, this was truly my dream job that I had just lost.

I took a deep breath trying to settle down and then started my car. The clock read 4:17 p.m. and I realized Megan and I agreed earlier in the day that I'd text her when I was done flying and we'd get together tonight. In that case, I'd be facing her in as soon as an hour and have to tell her what happened. And not to forget Katie, who said she'd be home just after 5:30 p.m. from baby-sitting Jacob and Madeline, as her one-week stint has now turned into two weeks.

I really didn't feel like reciting the painful details to anyone, yet I knew I'd have to because I couldn't abandon Megan and Katie for the evening and leave them wondering what was wrong. But in an attempt to make things easier, I decided to text Megan to tell her right away—and then worry about telling Katie later. So I pulled my phone out of my pocket and began punching out a text message.

Hey, I'm back from my trip and going to head home from the airport now. I just got laid off from my job, believe it or not.

She texted back right away. *WHAT?!?!?!?! I'm so sorry to hear that. Are you okay?*

Well, as okay as I'll be for now.

She texted back. *How about I stop by your place when you get back? Then you can tell me all about it.*

That'll work. I'll text you in about forty minutes to let you know I'm home.

Okay. It breaks my heart that you have to go through this, but we can talk more when you get home. I love you :)

I love you, too. Thanks.

I took a deep breath, feeling some slight relief that I'd just told her, and then I began my drive home.

~   ~   ~

After dealing with the beginning of rush hour traffic, I made it home by about 5:15 p.m. I carried the box inside and set it in the corner of my living room, knowing it'll probably sit there for several days before I'm ready to begin going through everything. When I took my phone out of my pocket to text Megan, I noticed Katie had texted me.

Hey, just letting you know I'm going to be home late tonight. Their father is working the late shift at the hospital, and their mother had to unexpectedly work a twelve-hour day at the pharmacy. So I'll probably be home by about 8:30.

Okay, thanks for letting me know. Are you okay with having the kids for all that time?

Yeah, at least they're good kids, and I get another two and a half hours of pay! :)

I figured it probably wasn't the most opportune time to tell her that I was laid off, so I didn't. Instead, I texted Megan letting her know I was home and hardly fifteen minutes later, I heard my doorbell ring. When I opened the door, she was standing there wearing tan shorts and a bright blue long-sleeve t-shirt and looked up at me sympathetically.

I quickly invited her inside and she then hugged me.

"I'm so sorry," she said. "I know what that job means to you, and I hate that you lost it. But it's all going to be okay. It's all in God's hands."

They were simple words, but it brought me relief to hear them spoken. During those painful moments from when they first told me I'd lost my job, it sure felt like my world had crumbled, but in reality, it hadn't.

As Megan and I stood there in my foyer, still tightly hugging each other, I remembered 2 Corinthians 4:8, "We are troubled on every side, yet not distressed; we are perplexed, but not in despair..."[1] Despite this being a tough thing to deal with, it reminded me that God had a plan to get me through this.

We finally let go of each other, and she quickly kissed me. We then walked into my living room and sat down facing each other on my couch. I took a deep breath and began telling her how it all happened and explained how there's a fair chance I could get recalled back to work, but I had no idea when. Reciting all of the details wasn't as painful as I thought it would be, and it even felt slightly therapeutic.

When I finished telling her everything, she put her hand on mine.

"We'll get through this," she said.

"Yeah, I know. I just need to figure out what I'm going to do during this time, however long it ends up being," I said.

"Well, like you told me when I got laid off back in May, God will see to it that one way or another you'll end up being better off after it. I know that turned out to be true for me," she said. "And in the meantime, you get some time off right during the summer, which I'm sure we'll enjoy together. And you'll have some severance pay, if they're paying you that."

"No, they're not," I quickly said. "It's a furlough, so they don't pay severance because they're technically not severing me from the company. But it looks like I'll be able to collect unemployment, and I have some money saved up to hold me over, too."

"So can you look for another job during this time?" she asked.

"Well, yeah, and I'll probably have to," I said. "But if I go to work at another airline, I'd lose my seniority, which means I'd have to start back at the bottom of the pay scale. But I guess I don't have too much to lose since I've only been at this airline for a year."

"Do you think you'd ever want to work at a different type of job?" she asked.

"Well…I was thinking about that on my drive home," I said. "If I don't get recalled back to work very soon and if I can't find another flying job, then unfortunately, I might have no choice than to do something different because I'll have to pay my bills somehow. But I really don't want to think about that right now."

She looked at me with her face still showing sympathy, and as I looked at her, I realized we hadn't even talked about her interview yet.

"I'm sorry," I confessed. "I haven't even asked you about your interview tomorrow."

"No, you're fine," she said. "You're situation is a bigger deal right now than mine."

"Well, I don't know about that," I said. "How are you feeling now?"

"Okay, but not great," she said. "I'm still feeling nervous, and my stomach still doesn't feel right. But I've been eating, but still not normal amounts yet."

"Do you think you'll be able to go tomorrow?" I asked.

"I think so," she said, "but I might have to take some medication beforehand."

I was glad to hear her say that she's at least open to the idea of taking the medication. That felt like progress, since that was such a big issue before her last interview. It also reminded me that I still needed to tell her about Katie sneaking the pill into her lemonade before, but this definitely didn't seem like the right time.

"Are you excited?" I asked.

"A little more than last time," she said, "but if they offer me this job I'm either going to have to find a way to settle myself down or be taking a lot of pills in order to do the job."

"Well, if this job is what God wants you to do, then He's already got a way figured out for you to do it without being overcome with anxiety," I said.

"I know," she said, looking at me with a small smile.

I then hugged her and she heard my stomach growling.

She chuckled. "It sounds like you're hungry."

"Yeah, I guess I am," I said. "With everything going on this afternoon, eating has been the last thing on my mind. But now that I think about it, I haven't eaten since 10:30 this morning."

~ ~ ~

We then went out to grab a quick dinner. It was approaching 6:15 p.m. when we left, and it almost felt like an autumn night with the cool temperatures and the gloomy skies making it appear to get dark much earlier than normal. We made the short drive over to the popular deli—the same place we went on her first day after she moved here. It wasn't quite as crowded, but we still decided to eat back at my place.

Megan ate about half of her sandwich, but considering they're big sandwiches, I'd still call that a reasonable meal. Either way, after I finished my sandwich, I gladly ate the rest of hers because I was hungry. When we were done eating, it was about 7:15 p.m. and Megan said she still wanted to read through some manuals about teaching methods to prepare for whatever questions they might ask her during her interview tomorrow.

So we agreed I'll stop by her aunt's house tomorrow morning, so I can see her off to the interview. Then we kissed goodnight, and she left.

As soon as she left, I was briefly tempted to go to bed, but it wasn't even 7:30 p.m. yet, and it just didn't seem right, regardless of how tired I was. So I grabbed my laptop, plopped down on my couch, and now an hour later I'm sitting here finishing up this journal entry. Katie should be home very soon and I know I'll need to tell her that I was laid off today. She still has no clue, given that she's been babysitting all day.

I was a little surprised when she told me a few days ago that she'd be baby-sitting Jacob and Madeline for another week. But after she told me Stacy came down with a cold at the end of her vacation last week, it made sense. I think Katie enjoys being with the kids, but for her sake, I hope the rest of this week won't include a lot of days like today where she's working twelve hours. That has to be exhausting to look after two kids for twelve hours straight.

She might even be as tired as I am by the time she gets home tonight. But either way, I'll still need to tell her the news. I know she'll be shocked, just as I was. But as the shock is beginning to subside, I know every bit of what happened today was God's plan and I know I'll get through this in whatever way that may be. Maybe I'll be recalled back to work pretty quickly or I'll find another job with another airline. But maybe I won't.

I know it terrified Megan every time I'd fly, and I know we both hated saying goodbye to each other every time I'd leave for a trip. I can't help but wonder if this is God's answer to those problems, and if He doesn't want me to be a pilot anymore.

Even though that thought is very unsettling to me right now, my desire to live out God's will for my life along with my deep love for Megan obviously exceed my love for flying. So if it turns out that I'm not meant to be a pilot anymore, I'll have to accept it. But there's no question it'll take me some time to come to terms with the possibility that my last flight today may have been the last time I fly a plane for quite a while—possibly forever.

◆ 16 ◆

Thursday, June 24th
My apartment swimming pool
5:20 p.m. (Central Time)

I decided to come out to the pool now and do some journaling because these past nine days have given me lot to write about...and think about. With dinnertime approaching and the sun taking its late-afternoon position in the sky, there are only a few people here right now, even though it's still 82 degrees. Despite today starting out as a good day for all of us, it certainly took a turn for the worse this afternoon and has left me questioning a lot of things right now.

But up until this afternoon, I can't forget these past nine days have given me plenty of good things to write about. Wednesday of last week was the first of those nine days and was also the day of Megan's second interview. As we planned, I went over to her aunt's house that morning around 8:30 a.m. to see her before she left. She'd already had a mild panic attack before I arrived, but then she took some medication, and thankfully, she seemed fine by the time she left.

I headed back to my apartment and Katie had already left to baby-sit Jacob and Madeline at their house for the day. I came inside, closed the door, set my keys down on the table and it was almost 10:00 a.m. It was the first day of this "unemployed" season of my life and as I stood in my living room, my apartment had never seemed so quiet. I realized I had nowhere to be and I had no job to do, nor would I, for the foreseeable future. It was a stark contrast to a typical day of flying, when I'd usually be more than halfway through my first flight by 10:00 a.m.

I don't know if I've ever felt so antsy and had such a desire to find something productive to do. Thankfully, I found some things to do that needed to be done anyway. I first filed for unemployment, which I was glad to find was as simple as logging on to a website and answering some questions. Then I went through the huge packet of information my airline gave me when I was laid off. I then called my parents to let them know the news. They were obviously upset, but they seemed confident that, in one way or another, things will work out for the better.

After that, I decided to text Scott to tell him the news. I knew it was a weekday and he was at work, but barely two minutes after I texted him, he called me. He was obviously sorry to hear I was laid off, but offered some good words of encouragement for me.

Then I began organizing my kitchen cabinets. But before I could get too far with that, Megan texted me around 12:30 p.m.

Hey, I just got out of the interview now. I think it went well and I think they're going to offer me the job.

I texted back. *That's great! I hope you're excited.*

She replied just seconds later. *Sort of.*

I headed over to her aunt's house after that, and we all sat down and had a late lunch. Megan was clearly relieved that all of the interviews were over, but she wasn't as excited as I hoped

she'd be. Even though she didn't mention it, I think she was
still concerned if she'd be able to do the job with her anxiety.
Also, the fact remained that she still didn't have an official
offer. Even though it looked likely she'd be getting one, there
was still no guarantee.

~   ~   ~

During the next two days, which were Thursday and
Friday, Megan and I spent a lot of time together—much of it at
my pool enjoying the great weather we had. Linda was busy
with her paintings, and Katie was hardly around because she
was baby-sitting Jacob and Madeline.

Finally on Friday afternoon, just after Megan and I got
back from the pool, we were standing in my kitchen eating
Popsicles, and Megan's phone rang. She quickly handed me
her Popsicle and rushed over to the dining room table to dig
her phone out of her bag.

"Hello?" she answered. "Yeah. I'm fine, how are you?"

It was the school calling to tell her they were officially
offering her the job. When she got off the phone, she said she'd
have to go through a week-long orientation program starting
on August 16th, and then she'd officially start the job on August
23rd. In addition, they'd let her enroll in some classes to start
on her Ph.D. while she taught.

"They want a final decision by Monday," she said to me,
setting down her phone on the table.

I smiled. "Well, that'll be an easy decision."

After she looked away and didn't answer, my smile quickly
faded.

"They think I'm fine," she said, turning back to me. "I
never told them I have an anxiety problem and stomach

problems to go with it. And if I can't even get through the first week of the job, I'll really be letting them down because they'll be without a teacher and have classes that aren't covered."

"Well, you can't worry about that," I said. "They'll never have a full guarantee with anyone. Someone else they would've hired, could find a different job and back out at the last minute, or start the job and decide they don't want it. They're an organization, and they have to adapt to things like that. But ultimately, I think once you start this job, you'll get into a familiar routine each day and your anxiety won't be a problem."

"That's what my therapist back in Cincinnati would always tell me," she said. "Routine is key."

"You owe it to yourself to take this job," I said. "If you don't, you're giving up before you even try."

Shortly after that, we headed over to Linda's house for dinner. Even though it was Katie's last day of baby-sitting, she had to work late, so she couldn't join us. After enjoying a home-cooked meal that Linda made for us, Megan and I spent some time watching TV in the den while Linda worked on a painting.

Eventually, Megan and I said goodnight and I left. I came back to my apartment to find Katie asleep on the couch with the TV on—not surprising, considering that she just finished a full five-day week of baby-sitting. She woke up a few minutes after I got home and went to bed shortly after that.

Right before I went to bed that night, I saw Megan had texted me.

I just sent an email tonight to officially accept the job, so they'll get it first thing Monday morning and then I'll enroll in a few classes for my Ph.D. after that. I love you so much and

I'm sorry I was such a nervous wreck and put you through all of the drama with the interviews. You've really helped me through this and I'm so thankful for your love...I love you :)

I replied back. *I love you, too, and I'm so happy you got this job and I'm even happier you accepted it now. I'm glad I could be there for you and I know you would've done the same for me. Good night :)*

After I punched out the message, I set my phone down on my nightstand, turned out the light, and got into bed. I knew I'd sleep well knowing she'd accepted the offer.

~   ~   ~

The next day was Saturday and Megan and I decided to go to the pool again. From the time she arrived at my apartment that morning, I could immediately tell she was much more relaxed and happy—and she should've been. Her interviews were over, she got the job, she still had eight weeks before she'd start orientation, and in the meantime, she had most of the summer to enjoy without working and taking classes.

Since Katie's two-week baby-sitting stint was over, she agreed to come with us to the pool. When we got there, it was just past 11:00 a.m. and about ten people were already there sunbathing. Even though the heat and humidity were building and the pool looked as inviting as ever with the way it sparkled in the sunshine, not a single person was swimming, and it couldn't have been quieter.

We picked three lounge chairs and I set down my towel, took my shirt off, and jumped in right away. Katie soon followed, but Megan stood at the edge.

"Is it cold?" she asked.

"Well, you can see for yourself," I said, as I began splashing her. After a few seconds, Katie joined in. Megan backed away and giggled, and we kept splashing her even more. By the time she finally jumped she was soaked anyway from all of our splashing. It's no wonder why she immediately chased after me in the water and tried to dunk me—but I ended up dunking her instead.

In return, she stood right in front of me and wouldn't stop splashing me. Before I knew it, Katie joined in and there wasn't much I could do except keep my eyes closed and try to splash them back. By this time, some of the sunbathers were lifting their heads and giving us curious looks because we were clearly acting like kids.

After spending several hours at the pool, the three of us agreed we'd go to dinner later at an arcade/sports bar, which was Katie's suggestion. It turned out they had very good food, and they even had four pool tables off to the side complete with stained glass light fixtures hanging over each one. So after we ate, the three of us played several games of pool before moving to the arcade area.

When we walked through the doors separating it from the pool tables, the numerous-pitched dings and video game music filled the room along with many people much younger than us. We proceeded to spend the next hour playing games, which continued our trend for the day of acting like kids. After we dropped off Megan at her aunt's house that night, Katie and I started the short drive back to my apartment.

Katie turned to me in the car. "You know, I like Megan. I never noticed this until now, but her personality really reminds me of Beth."

"Now that I think about it, you're right," I said, realizing the significance of what she'd just said because Beth and Katie were best friends starting in fourth grade going all the way through high school.

Before long, we got back to my apartment and shortly after that, I headed back to my bedroom, even though Katie stayed up for a little while watching TV. Before I went to sleep, a smile came to my face as I realized what a great day it had been.

~   ~   ~

The next four days looked much the same as that one and began with the three of us going to my church on Sunday. Afterwards, it was so good to hear Katie say that she liked the sermon because when she was in college, she definitely strayed away from church, and more recently when she lived with our parents, she went only because they made her. I'm happy to say Megan also liked the sermon—and my church—and we all agreed that we'd go every week.

Those four days continued with all of us making many more trips to the pool, doing some hiking at some local forest preserves, and eating virtually every lunch and dinner together. We all enjoyed each other's company, and I was glad to see Megan relaxed and feeling quite good throughout this time.

Even yesterday when she had to go for her monthly CT scan, she was surprisingly calm about it and by the time she got home in the mid-morning, we all proceeded to have another good day at the pool, followed by another trip to the arcade/sports bar where we've spent more money on games recently than I care to think about.

So far, these summer days have been a rare opportunity to have a "summer vacation" of sorts where none of us have to work. I hadn't spent this much time with Megan since college, and it had been since high school that Katie and I had spent this much time together. In addition to that, it was clear Megan and Katie were building a bond that would last far beyond this "summer vacation," despite them being almost seven years apart and having clearly different personalities.

All of this certainly helped me to settle in to this "unemployed" season of my life. But there were times, when something would remind me of flying and I felt a twinge of alarm run through my mind as I knew I didn't have a job and I'd need to do something about that soon.

~   ~   ~

By the time this morning arrived, I found myself standing in my dining room, waiting for Katie who was still in her bedroom packing for our trip.

"We're supposed to pick up Megan in ten minutes," I called out to her.

"Okay, I'm almost ready," she yelled from her bedroom, sounding a little annoyed with me.

How much stuff can she possibly need to pack for a day-trip? I thought to myself. I stood there waiting as the sun from this Thursday morning still poured into my dining room and I stared down at three plastic water bottles sitting on the table watching more condensation build on them with each passing second. I looked at the clock on my wall once again, and it read 8:51 a.m. I figured it would probably be at least another ten minutes before she'd be ready to go. That would put us at Megan's house about fifteen minutes late.

But I tried to remind myself that unlike every flight I've ever flown, this mere road trip had no expected arrival time that needed to be met. We were going purely for fun and we all hoped this hiking trip would live up to that expectation.

Since we enjoyed hiking in the local forest preserves we

visited through this past week, it was a unanimous decision among the three of us to take a day-trip "up north" to a huge state park that's still in Illinois but sits only a few miles from the Wisconsin border. We would, of course, be doing our easy version of "hiking," which involves walking on some well-maintained paths, enjoying the natural scenery, and hopefully taking some good pictures of it all.

As I still stood in my dining room, I heard what sounded like my phone ringing, but it was muffled because it was in my backpack sitting next to the front door. I quickly ran over to get it. I thought it could be Megan, which was concerning to me since there aren't many good reasons someone would be calling just moments before you're supposed to pick them up to go on a trip. I un-zipped my bag, and quickly saw it was Tyler, a pilot I worked with during my days of flying regional jets in Atlanta. We became friends back then, but I hadn't talked to him in months because neither of us did a great job of keeping in touch after I took the job in Chicago.

I quickly answered. "Hey Tyler."

"Hey Kevin, long time no talk, huh?"

"Yeah," I said curiously, wondering why he was calling me out of the blue.

"So listen, I heard you're on furlough now."

"Yeah, I am. Word travels fast, I guess."

"Yep, faster than the planes we fly," he joked. "Actually, Rob told me because we still keep in touch, even though he deserted me for another airline, just like you did."

I laughed. "I can't believe you're still there. Are you like number one in seniority yet?"

"You're funny," he chuckled. "But I'm actually not there anymore. I found this corporate gig with this company here in

Atlanta. You know, a lot of these big companies have their own private jets so they can fly around their CEO and all their big-wigs. And guess what? They need pilots! This company I work at now just bought two brand new private jets and they hired me in as a captain and I hardly have to work any weekends. It's a sweet deal."

"Well, that's good."

"Yeah, and they're looking for another captain too," he said. "So since you flew around CEO's in your first job, I thought of you right away."

He told me a little more about the job as I walked back and forth in my living room listening to him. He said he thought they'd probably pay me about the same as I was making before I was put on furlough, but he said I'd have to move to Atlanta because they don't want any of their pilots to commute. He seemed convinced that I had a good shot at getting an offer because of my experience and because I knew him.

"So what do you think?" he finally asked.

"Well, I don't know about moving," I said. "My girlfriend just got a job up here now."

"Whoa, since when do you have a girlfriend?"

After I briefly told him about Megan, he continued. "Well, whatever you want to do is fine with me, but if you're at all interested I pretty much need to know right now. They're setting up interviews for the week after next and I need to give them your name to reserve an interview slot."

"Well, I guess I could come down for an interview…"

"Good," he said. "I'll let the recruiter know and they'll call you to set up a specific day and time for you to come down."

"Okay," I told him as I turned around and saw Katie had come out of her bedroom. She appeared ready to go as she stood next to the couch, holding her backpack. Apparently, she had overheard my conversation because she was giving me a very confused look.

After I hung up with Tyler, Katie still stood in the same spot, looking at me. "Did you just get an interview?" she asked.

"Well, sort of, but I'd have to move to Atlanta, so I'm going to have to talk to Megan about it."

"Oh," she said with a hint of concern. "Would that be permanent or just during your furlough?"

"It would be permanent," I said, putting my phone back in my backpack. "It's a corporate pilot job."

"So if you move to Atlanta, where does that leave me?" she asked.

"Well, you could move with me, if you want."

"Why would I want to move to Atlanta?" she quickly asked. "I don't know anyone there."

I sensed her concern building but I tried to diffuse it. "Well, it just sounded like a good opportunity because I'd hardly ever have to work weekends. But I'm going to talk to Megan about it, and I might not even go to the interview."

"Were you going to talk to *me* about it?" she asked.

"Well, yeah, of course," I said. "Just don't get upset about something that hasn't happened yet," I said, zipping up my backpack. "It might not happen at all."

"When would the interview be?" she asked.

"The week after next," I said.

I could see the disappointment on her face as she walked over to the foyer carrying her backpack in her hand. When she got to the front door, she looked back at me. "I'm ready to go now."

"Okay." I said. "And one more thing, let's not mention this to Megan yet. This trip is supposed to be for fun and I don't want her getting upset. After we get back today, I'll talk to her about it."

"Fine," she said.

We then put our gym shoes on, slung our backpacks over our shoulders, grabbed our water bottles, and headed out.

~ ~ ~

The drive up there took about an hour and ten minutes with minimal traffic. As we got closer, the feel of densely populated suburbia was traded for a more rural setting including numerous farm fields and even a few gentle hills. By the time we got close to the park, we were on a winding, two-lane road, which provided alternating scenery from untouched prairie land to dense trees forming tunnels around the road. Before long, we turned in to the park entrance and continued on a winding narrow road for almost a mile before we came to the trailhead. We parked in the parking lot where there were only two other cars.

It was just after 10:30 a.m. and when we got out of the car, the bright blue sky seemed more expansive and the temperature felt a few degrees cooler—no surprise being about fifty miles north of where I live. But my car still read 77 degrees and the sun was bright, when it wasn't blocked by a passing cumulus cloud. The three of us stood at the back of the car and strapped our backpacks on, which mainly contained snacks and our water bottles and then we began hiking.

At times, the trail went through deep forest with tall and thick trees filtering the sun, allowing only small patches of sunshine to reach the ground. At other times, it was completely open with brown prairie grass on both sides and distant clusters of bright green trees providing a picturesque back-drop. In the latter part of our hike, the trail wound around a lake that was like a sheet of glass perfectly reflecting the tree line that surrounded it along with the blue sky—cumulus clouds and all.

After several hours, and after each of us took a lot of pictures and enjoyed a few breaks where we sat down and had snacks, we arrived back at the trailhead where we started. According to the park map, we had hiked over six miles and even though none of us were exhausted, it was safe to say we'd hiked enough, so we headed out. It was also safe to say it had been a good day for all of us so far, but unfortunately, that would soon change.

~ ~ ~

On the drive back, initially there wasn't much conversation. We were all content listening to music because we were a little tired after hiking. But about halfway home Katie decided to get more talkative.

She leaned forward from the backseat. "So Megan, I know we've been spending a lot time together lately, and I feel bad that I haven't told you about something."

I cringed, fairly certain what she was about to say.

"Okay, what is it?" Megan asked.

"Remember the morning of your first interview, when you were so nervous?"

"Yeah."

"Well, I found some anxiety medication in your purse and crushed up one of the pills and mixed it in your lemonade that day."

"What?" she exclaimed turning around to face her.

"I'm sorry," she said. "I was only trying to help you."

Megan turned back around and stared ahead. "So that explains why I felt so calm before the interview. It wasn't that

I was learning to control my anxiety, it was because you drugged me. Why would you do that to me?" she said with her voice getting louder.

"I just really wanted you to go to the interview and so I took matters into my own hands," Katie said. "Maybe it wasn't the right way of going about it, but it got you to the interview and you ultimately got the job."

Megan turned to me. "Did you know about this?"

"Well...yeah, she told me after she did it," I said.

She shook her head and quickly looked away from me and stared out the side window.

"This really isn't Kevin's fault," Katie said. "It wasn't his idea and he had nothing to do with this. If you're mad, you should be mad at me."

"I *am* mad...at both of you," she said. "I can't believe with all the time we've spent together lately that neither one of you told me about this."

She was clearly upset, and I felt terrible about that. I began wondering if telling her about my interview as soon as we got back was still a good idea, given that she was so upset. Yet if I didn't tell her, then I'd be keeping another secret from her. I had no idea what I should do, but I knew I'd have to decide soon.

~   ~   ~

As the miles passed, none of us spoke a single word. Megan stared out the side window, Katie did much of the same with occasionally looking down at her phone, and I just focused on driving. Finally, after a very long and awkward thirty minutes, we got off of the expressway and were only about ten minutes from dropping off Megan at her aunt's house. Katie then began looking down at her phone again.

"Oh wow," she said, breaking the silence. "There's a headline that says, 'Airliner Catches Fire in Mid-Air Over Atlanta.'"

"Really?" I asked.

"Yeah, I'm going to it right now," she paused for a few seconds as she read. "It's says the plane took off early this afternoon from Atlanta and then one of its engines caught on fire, and they had to circle back and do an emergency landing. Wow. They have pictures of all these fire trucks surrounding the plane on the runway."

"Was everyone okay?" Megan asked.

"Yeah, it says they landed safely and there were no injuries."

I looked at Megan and I could see the fear on her face as she closed her eyes and shook her head.

"Well, luckily they landed safely," I said.

Katie was still staring down at her phone apparently still browsing through the article. "Yeah, hopefully there won't be any planes that catch fire when you're down there in a few weeks," Katie said to me.

The instant she said that, panic shot through me and our eyes met in the rear-view mirror.

It didn't take her more than a second to realize what she'd said and she quickly gasped and covered her mouth. "I'm sorry," she said through her hand.

Megan turned to me, looking just as angry as earlier. "Why are going to Atlanta?"

"It's for an interview, but I don't even know if I'm going. And I was going to tell you."

"When?" she demanded.

"As soon as we got back from this trip," I said. "I just found out about it this morning. Right before we left to pick you up, my friend Tyler called and he said the company where he works is looking for another pilot and asked if I'd be interested."

"So what did you tell him?" she asked with a heated tone.

"Well, I told him I might come down for an interview, but I'd have to talk to you about it first."

"And by 'talk to me about it' what you really mean is hide it from me until you get around to telling me that you've decided to go?"

"No, I honestly was going to talk to you about it as soon as we got back today," I said.

She shook her head and took a deep breath and turned away and blankly stared out the window.

"I don't have to go," I said. "It was just a thought because the pay would be good, I'd have most of the weekends off, and I thought they have a lot of schools in Atlanta where you might be able to find another teaching job."

"So I guess I should be happy with that," she said sarcastically. "I'd start my job search from scratch again and be able to see you for two out of the seven days each week."

"I can tell you don't like this idea, so I'm not going," I said. "It's as simple as that."

She looked away and didn't say anything.

Just a few minutes later, we pulled into Linda's driveway and it was almost 4:00 p.m. I barely had the car in park, before Megan had her door open and began hastily gathering her things.

"Megan, wait," I pleaded.

She got out anyway, and I quickly got out and followed her up to the porch. She stopped and turned around just before she opened the door. "What do you want to say?" she said with a stern look, still holding her backpack.

"I'm not going to the interview," I said. "And I'm really

sorry for not telling you about it as soon as I got the call this morning...and for not telling you about the pill."

She exhaled. "I'm mad that you didn't tell me about those things, but I'll probably get over that. But what really hurts me is that you'd consider a job in Atlanta. I moved to Chicago to be close to you and now I finally found a good job that's actually something I want to do where maybe I won't dread going to work every day. And now, you're going after some job in Atlanta behind my back and expect me to give up my job and move again. And it'll all end up with you being gone on flying trips for work and me being home by myself."

"No..." I began.

Before I could say any more she spoke. "Is this really how it's going to be with us?"

"What do you mean?" I asked.

"Where you make all of the decisions and I just have to deal with whatever you decide?"

"No," I said.

She opened the screen door. "I have a lot to think about."

When she said those words my heart sank and an awful feeling came over me because that sure sounded like she was considering breaking up. I didn't know quite what to say so I walked toward her and reached my arms out to hug her. She hugged me with one arm as she held her backpack with her other arm.

"I know you're upset right now, and you have every reason to be, but let's talk tomorrow, okay?" I asked.

"Fine," she said before walking inside and letting the screen door shut behind her.

It was clear she didn't want me to stay, and I knew if I did, it wouldn't make this problem any better right then, so I left.

~   ~   ~

I walked back out to the car and got in. Katie had moved to the front seat and the look on her face left no question that she felt very bad about what had just happened.

I shut the door and started the car and shook my head in disbelief. "Well, that went about as bad as it could've gone," I said. "And now she told me she has a lot to think about. That's never a good thing to hear in a relationship."

"I'm really sorry," Katie said. "I just totally wasn't thinking when I said you'd be in Atlanta in a few weeks. I feel awful about that."

"Well, I would've told her as soon as we got back anyway," I said, turning around to back up. "It's just unfortunate it had to be right after you told her about hiding the pill." I put the car in drive and spun the steering wheel around and headed out. "I probably should've just told Tyler no when he called this morning. I should've known Megan doesn't want to move to Atlanta."

"Well, I'll be the first to admit I also wouldn't be thrilled if you moved to Atlanta because I don't know where I'd live then," she said. "But if it's truly what you want to do, I'd never want to stop you because I know what flying means to you. But I'm getting the feeling Megan might have different thoughts because it seems pretty obvious she doesn't want you to be a pilot anymore."

"I know. I've already thought about that," I said, staring ahead at the road.

She turned to me. "So what are you going to do? Give up flying?"

"I guess," I said, resting my hand on top of the steering wheel.

"Are you okay with that?"

"Well, it seems like it's what God wants me to do," I said.

"How do know you that?" she asked.

"Well, I don't know for sure, but being that Megan and I are in love, it just seems like the right thing to do."

Katie then looked over at me. "I've known you longer than Megan has, and I know flying is a huge part of your life...and to give up that part of your life for someone is a big deal. Do you really think that's what God wants you to do?"

"I think so."

"What's that Bible verse that Mom would always recite to us from the King James Version about how God will give us the desires of our heart?" she asked. "I know it's in the book of Psalms."

"Do you mean Psalm 37:4? 'Delight thyself also in the Lord: and he shall give thee the desires of thine heart.'"

"Yep, that's the one," she said.

"What's your point?" I asked.

"Well, you should think about if being with Megan will truly give you the desires of your heart, and also if it'll give *her* the desires of *her* heart."

"What are you saying? Megan and I love each other," I said defensively.

"I know," she said. "But have you ever wondered if maybe God has someone else out there for you who might not get terrified every time you fly? Who might not mind spending time by herself when you're away on flying trips for work? And who might actually enjoy traveling with you?"

I shook my head trying to deny what she was saying.

She continued. "And that maybe God has someone else out there for Megan whose heart isn't set on being a pilot and someone who doesn't have to give up a huge part of his life to make the relationship work?"

I shook my head again to imply she was wrong, but I could see her point, whether I wanted to or not. I kept driving and didn't say anything until we got closer to my apartment. After a few minutes, I turned to her. "Are you hungry?"

"I'm starved," she said.

So we stopped at a drive-through and grabbed a quick meal. It wasn't even 4:30 p.m. but after eating only a few small snacks all day and hiking over six miles, it was no secret why we were so hungry. We then came back my apartment and ate in front of the TV. After we were done, I got up. "I'm heading out to the pool right now to do some journaling...and some thinking."

She looked up at me from the couch. "Are you mad at me?"

I hesitated for a second. "Not really," I said, knowing that deep down she had good intentions with everything she'd done.

She then stood up and hugged me. "Think about what I said. I just want you to be happy. And if you and Megan will be happy together, that's great because I think she's a really great person. But don't just deny the problems just to stay together and avoid the heartbreak. That's not fair to you...or to her."

Her words were insightful and caring and closely resembled what my mom would probably tell me. Despite the differences Katie and I have had in the past, I've never doubted that we both deeply care about each other, and this was proof of that.

Now, I'm sitting at a table by the pool, typing in my journal as I try to make sense of all of this. There's no question it was deeply unnerving when Megan told me earlier that she has a lot to think about. The very thought that we could be breaking up puts tears in my eyes and a sick feeling in my stomach right now. But the insightful words of my sister continue to resonate in my mind now. I realize—just like Megan—I also have a lot to think about, because I have no idea right now if God wants Megan and me to stay together or go our separate ways.

· 17 ·

Friday, June 25th
My apartment swimming pool
3:51 p.m. (Central Time)

Not knowing if the girl I love is going to be a part of my life anymore took its toll on me last night, and needless to say, I didn't sleep much. As I sit here once again at my pool on this Friday afternoon typing in my journal, I definitely feel the tiredness catching up with me now.

Last night, after I got back to my apartment from doing just this—journaling at the pool—Katie was watching TV, so I sat down and watched with her. That ended up being how both of us spent the rest of the evening, but it helped take my mind off of things temporarily.

I finally decided to head to bed around 10:30 p.m. After peeling the covers back and fluffing my pillow, I climbed in and turned off the lamp on my nightstand and the room went dark. Before getting comfortable, I said a prayer—a pretty long one—asking God to give Megan and me clarity with this situation and asking Him to do His will, whatever that may be.

I then rolled over and tried to go to sleep. I had my window open, which let in the fresh and comfortably cool air of a summer night along with the soft sounds of crickets and a mild fragrance from a blooming tree outside. It all seemed ideal for sleeping, but as I was lying on my back with my eyes wide open, I realized I had way too much on my mind to sleep.

After reflecting on what Katie said earlier about how I might meet a girl who'd be fine with me being a pilot and who'd enjoy traveling with me, I realized it's never bothered me that Megan doesn't like to fly. I've accepted that difference between us, but obviously the same can't be said about Megan's feelings toward this matter.

I think Katie was right when she said Megan probably doesn't want me to be a pilot anymore. Giving that up would clearly be a big deal because obviously flying has been a huge part of my life for a long time. But I can't forget I have a degree in Aeronautical Engineering, which could provide some alternatives for me. I could sort of see myself helping to design planes, but a job like that would probably be hard to find and it would definitely feel much more like work with sitting at a desk all day.

But I stopped my thoughts right there and had to remind myself that whatever I do for a living ultimately comes down to the fact that it's only a job. If being a pilot is going to cause this much of a problem for Megan, it really doesn't seem worth it to continue. So after reflecting on it for several more quiet minutes, I finally came to peace with giving up flying for the one I love.

I hoped that would keep Megan and me together but as my mind continued to churn, I began to have doubts. I feared that the minute I'd offer to give up flying, Megan would feel like she's holding me back from doing what I love. Given that she seems increasingly convinced that she doesn't want the one she loves to be a pilot, breaking up would be the only option left.

My dark and quiet bedroom felt a little darker and lonelier when those thoughts came over me and I hoped so much that wouldn't be the way this would turn out.

After lying in bed for several more sleepless hours and after a rather robust early-morning thunderstorm rolled through, I finally got out of bed around 7:15 a.m. The first thing I did was pick up my phone and text Megan. *Hey, what time do you want to meet up to talk today?*

I walked to the kitchen and grabbed a cereal bar and a glass of water and by the time I was done, she'd texted back. *I can meet anytime.*

Okay, how about I stop by at 9:00 this morning? I asked. *That works.*

I then threw on a pair of shorts and a t-shirt and sat down on my couch and watched part of a nature show that seemed somewhat interesting and sort of kept me calm. When it was time to leave, Katie still hadn't gotten up yet, so I wrote her a note letting her know where I was going. I set the pen down on the counter, grabbed my keys, and headed out, not knowing what this day would bring.

~ ~ ~

On the drive over, the morning sun was bright, and the early-morning thunderstorm was long gone. When I pulled into the driveway at her aunt's house, I really got nervous. The clock in my car said 8:56 a.m. and as I sat there for a few seconds, I realized Megan and I could be just minutes away from going our separate ways.

As I walked up the cement steps to the porch, I tried to convince myself that it was still possible we'd stay together. I rang the doorbell and began staring at the stained glass design in the front door, while my heart was pounding in my chest.

After waiting several long seconds, my mind began racing. *Did I push the doorbell hard enough? We said 9:00, right? Maybe they're both out on the back porch.*

Finally, after a few more seconds, the door abruptly opened and it was Linda. Despite not knowing her very well, the expression on her face clearly told me something was wrong.

"Hi Linda," I said.

"Hi Kevin, come on in," she said.

I stepped inside and closed the door behind me. "Is Megan around?"

"She's upstairs right now packing a bag..." she said tentatively.

"Why is she packing a bag?" I quickly asked.

"The hospital called about fifteen minutes ago and said they found a small growth in her stomach from the CT scan she had two days ago. So they need to do a procedure so they can take a biopsy and also so they can closely check the inside of her stomach for any more growths. They had an opening in their schedule this morning, and I guess the doctor recommended she get this done as soon as possible. So since she hasn't eaten yet today, I'm taking her in right now."

I froze, realizing this didn't sound good at all. Suddenly my concern of whether Megan and I were on the verge of breaking up was over-ridden by the question of whether Megan was on the verge of a serious illness.

I looked up. "Is this like full surgery or just an out-patient thing?"

"They called it an upper endoscopy and it's an out-patient procedure. Basically, they'll put a scope down her throat, into her stomach, so she'll have to be sedated, but she won't be under full anesthesia. They said from the time she walks in until the time she walks out, it should take two to three hours. I think she actually had this...or at least something similar to this...done back in March when she was in the hospital."

I took a deep breath trying to calm myself down.

"I'm sure she wouldn't mind if you went up and talked to her right now," Linda said.

"Okay." I started up the stairs. "Megan?" I called out as I got close to her room.

"I'm in here," she said softly from her bedroom.

I walked in and she was leaning over her bed, stuffing a shirt into her backpack. She looked up at me and the fear on her face was as obvious as the tears running down her cheeks. "Did Linda tell you?"

"Yeah, she told me," I said, walking up to her and wrapping my arms around her.

As soon as we embraced, she began crying harder than I'd seen her cry in a long time—probably since we broke up in college—and I felt her tears falling down on my shirt as we embraced.

She sniffled several times before speaking in a broken voice. "This is really bad, and I'm really scared right now."

"They just have to take a biopsy to be on the safe side," I said, trying to reassure her, still holding her in my arms. "It doesn't mean it's cancer."

"But they didn't see this growth a month ago when they did the scan," she said, "so that means it's probably growing really quickly."

"Let's not jump to conclusions right now," I said. "Why are you packing a bag?"

She let go from our embrace and wiped the tears from her cheeks with both hands. "Depending on what they find, they might want to do major surgery right away and who knows how many days I'll be there then," she said. "I learned my lesson back in March when a trip to the emergency room turned into an eleven-day stay in the hospital."

"I don't think that's going to happen this time," I said.

"We can't be so sure," she said, sniffling.

She continued packing a few more things in her backpack, including her Bible. She tried to zip it up, but she struggled because her hands were shaking so much from being nervous. So I helped her zip it, and then we headed downstairs into the foyer where Linda was waiting.

"Are you all set?" Linda asked her.

"I think so," Megan said.

We all paused for a second. "I can come with, if you'd like," I said.

She turned to me. "Thanks but it's going to be a long time to sit there and I feel bad enough Linda has to go."

It was clear she didn't want me going and I knew she'd feel bad making me sit there for several hours. But I wondered if the bigger reason was that she simply didn't want me around after what transpired yesterday.

"Okay, then I guess this is goodbye," I said trying to hold back some tears. I hugged her tightly and I hoped more than anything she'd be back home in a few hours. "Let's say a quick prayer before you leave."

The three of us stood close with our hands joined and I prayed asking for her procedure to go well, and for the growth to be benign.

After we all raised our heads, she nervously took a deep breath. "Well, this is it," she said, picking up her backpack.

We all proceeded out the front door and they both headed

to Linda's car in the garage and I headed to mine parked in the driveway.

"Text me to let me know how it's going and when it's done," I called out to Linda.

"I will," she said, before getting into her car.

We all left and I knew the next several hours would be tough for all of us, but especially for Megan.

On the way home, I still had no clue what the status of our relationship was, but at that point, it didn't matter. The only thing that did was for her procedure to go well and for the growth to be benign.

~ ~ ~

I arrived back at my apartment shortly after that. "I'm home," I called out as I walked in, figuring Katie must be out of bed, since it was almost 9:30 a.m.

"You're back already?" she said, stepping out the kitchen, holding a half-eaten bagel with peanut butter on it. "What's the matter? Did she break up with you?"

I shook my head no. "We didn't even talk about that. She's on her way to the hospital with Linda for a procedure right now."

"What?" Katie said with a confused look.

I began telling her how they found a growth in her stomach when they did the CT scan two days ago. I could see the concern grow on her face with each word I spoke.

"So why did she have to go for that scan in the first place? She's been having problems, I take it?"

"Well, sort of." Katie obviously knew Megan was dealing with anxiety, but I'd never told her how she was in the hospital for eleven days back in March and how she—and the doctors—

were thinking she had stomach cancer at that time. So I told Katie all of that and I knew by the tears beginning to stream down her face that she was very concerned about Megan, as was I.

After that conversation, I knew the last thing I wanted to do was pace around in my apartment while I nervously waited to hear from Linda. So I grabbed my phone and decided to go for a walk around the neighborhood. I asked Katie if she wanted to come with, but she declined, knowing I needed some time alone.

As I walked, I realized it's not often I see tears come from Katie's eyes. It was proof of how close she and Megan have become now. But I think this also reminded her all too much of something she had to deal with during her freshman year of college. But it actually began many years before that when she was in fourth grade.

Pretty early in that school year, her class was out on the school playground for recess one day and she noticed some of the other girls picking on one of her classmates named Beth. Even though Katie didn't know Beth very well at that point, she didn't think it was right so she took matters into her own hands...quite literally. She gathered handfuls of gravel from under the swing set and threw them at the girls to get them to stop. The result was a trip to the principal's office, a week-long detention, a stern phone call to my parents from the principal, but also the beginning of a great friendship between Katie and Beth.

On the surface they didn't seem much alike. Beth was a short, skinny brunette with pale skin, and dark brown eyes. Of course, that was a stark contrast to Katie's blonde hair, blue eyes, and ability to tan quite easily. But there weren't just physical differences. Beth had a pretty shy and soft-spoken demeanor while Katie—even back then—was very vocal and never afraid to speak her mind.

Despite all of that, they still connected on a deep level because their family situations were nearly identical. They each had a significantly older brother who was their only sibling, and they both had parents who were still married and more than a little protective at times. So in that regard, it made sense they were friends and it wasn't too surprising that they became almost like sisters to each other.

We all liked Beth. She was polite, respectful, quite smart, and a good influence on Katie who was notorious for finding her way into trouble at times. Through the years, they went to all of the same schools and by high school their group of mutual friends had grown to four or five, and Katie even had a few guys who she dated along the way too. But it was clear Katie and Beth's friendship was still as strong as ever because during their senior year, they both decided to go to the same college in downstate Illinois and be roommates.

Unfortunately, only a few months into their freshman year, out of nowhere, Beth started to feel sick. After several trips to the doctor and tentative diagnoses of the flu or a virus of some sort, further tests finally showed she had an aggressive cancer and her prognosis wasn't good. Katie spent more time in the hospital visiting Beth than anywhere else that semester. Sadly, Beth's short battle with cancer ended, and she passed away a few days before Christmas that year.

Barely a week after Beth's funeral, Katie went back to college for the second semester of her freshman year, but this time without a roommate and without her best friend. Her way of coping with the loss was simply to party the pain away. She started going to parties and drinking quite a lot and obviously with her being a freshman, she wasn't even twenty-one yet. My parents sort of knew this was going on, but her grades somehow didn't suffer and they knew this was her way of coping, so they came down on her pretty lightly, and many times, not at all.

We all hoped this phase would pass, but it never really did. It ultimately ended up defining the majority of Katie's time in college, but fortunately, she still managed to graduate with a 3.2 GPA. If she would've studied more, she probably would've been closer to a 4.0 because she was always really smart, and definitely smarter than me.

Even though it's already been four and a half years since Beth passed away, it still brought tears to my eyes as I thought about it during my walk through the neighborhood this morning. So I can only imagine what Katie is still feeling.

~   ~   ~

When I got home from my walk, it was approaching 11:00 a.m. and I found a note on the counter from Katie.

Went to the grocery store. Be back before lunch.

I still had no text message from Linda, so I assumed no news meant everything was going as planned. Desperate to turn my attention to something, I decided to organize my dresser drawers in my bedroom. For weeks, it had been driving me crazy to have winter clothes jammed tightly in with summer clothes and I figured there were probably things I could get rid of and donate to free up some space.

I sat down on the floor in front of my dresser and started with the bottom drawer because I knew that one needed the most work. I took the first t-shirt out and suddenly a furry face was staring at me—that of the stuffed raccoon. It startled me for a second, but then I smiled and figured Megan must have somehow snuck him in there at some point during the past week. I picked him up out of the drawer and my smile quickly turned to tears. As I sat there holding him close, all of the memories began flashing through my mind.

Little did I know when I bought this twelve-dollar stuffed animal for her during our freshman year of college that it would later become a treasured symbol of many fond memories we'd shared together. Also, little did I know that more than eleven and a half years after I bought him, I'd be sitting here wondering if Megan is at the beginning of a battle for her life, when she's not even thirty years old.

After everything that had happened up to that point today, I guess I'd just reached my limit and as I sat there on the floor with the drawer still open in front of me—still holding the raccoon—I completely broke down and cried. I can't remember the last time I cried that hard. I'm thinking it may have been since Megan and I broke up in college.

I just kept thinking how I wished these past two days were simply a bad dream and I'd soon wake up to another summer day where we'd happily continue with our summer. But I knew this was real—too real.

After a few more minutes of sniffling with tears flowing down my face, Katie got back from the store.

"I'm home," she shouted from the foyer. "Kevin?"

I really didn't want her to see me crying, but there was nothing I could do to hide it. By the time I gathered myself to call out to her, she must have heard me sniffling because she quickly appeared in the doorway to my bedroom. She looked down at me and then paused as I could see her sympathy for me growing by the second.

I don't think she knew the significance of the stuffed raccoon but I'm sure she figured it related back to Megan somehow. With her clearly seeing the tears in my eyes, she didn't say anything—she didn't need to. Instead, she sat down next to me on the floor and put her arm around me. She probably knew exactly what I was feeling, considering that she went through a similar situation with Beth.

Just as there were very few instances in Katie's adult life that I'd seen her cry, I'm not sure if she'd ever seen me cry in my adult life and I couldn't help but feel a twinge of embarrassment.

I sniffled a few times and held up the raccoon. "This was a gift I got for Megan in college," I began saying, wiping tears from my eyes, trying to get my composure back.

By the time I finished explaining it to her, she hugged me with both of her arms, still sitting next to me. "It's okay to be upset."

"It's just so hard," I said. "I just...I don't know what's going to happen and I love her so much."

"I know. It's an awful feeling," she said. "It took me a while to come to peace with Beth passing away. But what finally gave me that peace was when I realized there wasn't anything to be devastated about. She went to heaven...and that's what we all long for when God determines that it's our time to go. Yet everybody's so afraid to die...and it's like they've never read the first part of John 14...or they've forgotten about it. But it says right there in that chapter that we shouldn't be troubled because there's a place prepared for us in heaven."[1]

She took a deep breath and I could see some tears in her eyes. "When I found that verse, it got a lot easier for me to handle everything, but I still miss her...even now. I knew I would because we grew up together and we were like sisters, and now she's gone. But I know I'll see her again someday."

I nodded as I was trying my hardest not to break down and cry again.

She continued. "She must've accomplished everything she needed to because otherwise He wouldn't have taken her to heaven," she said, wiping tears from her eyes. "I know she had a good effect on a lot of people's lives...including mine.   I haven't told anyone this before, but she's the main reason I even went to college. And then after she passed away, I felt like I had to finish college for her, even though that was the last thing I wanted to do at that point."

She sniffled as she wiped some more tears from her eyes. "But this isn't about me, or about Beth. I'm sorry I went on about that."

"That's fine," I said, so glad that we were opening up to each other like this.

She then spoke again. "But just know that if this is Megan's time to go, then you can be assured that she must've fulfilled her assignment here on earth."

"Yeah," I said, as I hugged her. We sat there on the floor for several minutes simply hugging while we both occasionally sniffled. Even though it was a sad moment, I couldn't deny how good it felt to be close to her again. It was the closest I'd felt to her probably since we were kids. It was also good to see her have the courage to talk about her faith. I always knew, deep down, she was strong in her faith but it was rare when she talked about it.

After a few minutes, we both got up from the floor and walked out to the kitchen. We then had a quick lunch together as I tried my best to carry on with this difficult day.

~ ~ ~

Before long, it was approaching 1:00 p.m. and I found myself walking briskly and nervously up to the main entrance of the hospital after Linda had texted me a few minutes earlier.

Hi Kevin, Megan's procedure is finished now and it basically went well, but they decided to keep her a little longer because her blood pressure spiked afterwards. But they said this happens sometimes as the sedative begins to wear off. She's still a little dazed, but she's awake and talking. It's your choice if you want to visit her now or wait until she gets home. I think we'll be here at least another few hours.

I texted back right away. *I'm on my way.*

When I approached the entrance, the glass doors slid open and I walked in to the expansive lobby noticing the stylish furniture and the shiny floor. I texted Linda again because I had no idea where to go. She came down a few minutes later and as we walked, she updated me on everything.

"The procedure went well," she said, as we stepped into the elevator and she pushed the button. "The doctor said they found a second growth during the procedure that didn't show up on the CT scan. It was smaller than the initial one and they were both still small enough to remove right then. He said the two places inside her stomach where they removed them should heal within a few days. Now, she's in the recovery room but her blood pressure is running high, so just a few minutes ago they gave her some different medicine hoping it'll relax her and bring her blood pressure down."

"So the only reason it's high is because she's nervous?" I asked as the elevator doors closed.

"They think so," she said. "Did they say anything else about what they found during the procedure?"

"Yeah, the doctor said she has a few small ulcers but they're not very advanced, so he said he wants to keep an eye on them for now. He said those might be partially causing the symptoms she's been having. But obviously the bigger concern right now is the growths they removed. He said they'll send the samples to the lab to test them and we should hear back in a few days about that."

"Did he give any indication if they looked like they were cancerous?" I asked.

She frowned and shook her head. "Not really. Technically they can't say anything until the results come back. But by the doctor's demeanor and the way he seemed really sympathetic, it seemed that he probably thought it was cancer. Unfortunately, Megan sensed that too, even though she's still really groggy from the sedative. But I've been trying to act positive around her."

I looked down and closed my eyes for a few seconds, before the elevator dinged and the doors opened.

As we began walking down the hallway, Linda turned to me. "Oh and while I was waiting, I called her parents and they seemed pretty concerned, so they, and her brother, are driving here tonight from Ohio and they'll be staying at least for the weekend."

Hearing that didn't sit well with me as this was starting to feel like it was a very serious situation. A few seconds later, seeing Megan reclined a hospital bed as we entered the recovery room also didn't sit well with me...and downright startled me for the first few seconds. She was wearing a hospital gown, had a thick white bracelet around her wrist, a blood pressure cuff around her arm, and a monitor on her index finger.

She lifted her head a little after we walked in and gave me a small smile. "Hey," she said softly with a hint of surprise.

"Hey, how are you feeling?" I asked, as Linda and I sat down in the chairs next to her bed.

"Okay, I guess" she said.

"It sounds like everything went okay," I said.

"I guess," she said, resting her head back on the pillow, "but I could tell by the way the doctor looked at me that he thinks it's cancer."

I shook my head. "He doesn't know that. Nobody will know until the results come back."

"Yeah, but I could tell," she said with a groggy voice. "I could tell."

She then closed her eyes to rest for a few minutes. Linda and I stayed in the room with her throughout the next hour. Eventually, the nurse came in, and thankfully, Megan's blood pressure had come down to the normal range, so they released her.

At that point, she was pretty tired from the medication they gave her to relax and also from the sedative they initially gave her for the procedure itself. So I decided the best thing I could do was to say goodbye to her for the day and let her go home and rest. So after we made our way down to the front entrance, and after Linda pulled the car around, Megan and I turned to each other to say goodbye.

She looked at me with her tired brown eyes and at that moment I wanted to tell her I still loved her, but I knew this wasn't the right time to start that conversation.

"It was really nice of you to come here today," she said.

"Yeah, I'm glad I could be here with you," I said. "I'll talk to you tomorrow, and in the meantime, I hope you feel better."

"Thanks."

I gave her a quick hug before she got in the car and then they left.

I got back to my apartment just after 3:00 p.m. and Katie was anxious to hear how everything went with Megan. After I told her everything, I decided to come out here to my pool to catch up with my journal. My hope was that being out here might somehow make me feel better. I don't know if it has, but I can't deny that it's gotten me out of my apartment and under the warm sunshine where I'm surrounded by quite a few people enjoying this sunny and pleasant Friday afternoon at the pool.

Many of them are kids playing and laughing, enjoying their summer in the most carefree way. As I watch them now, it brings tears to my eyes because just a few days ago Katie, Megan, and I were doing the same. But right now, it feels like this summer—and my world—has come to a sudden stop as we all nervously wait for Megan's biopsy results.

◆ **18** ◆

Monday, June 28th
My apartment
7:24 p.m. (Central Time)

As I sit here on the eve of a trip I never thought I'd be taking, I've decided to use this remaining spare time to catch up with my journal. I'm sitting out on my patio right now and as I look out across the pond, the spray from the fountain is still glistening in the sun that's about an hour away from setting on what's been a pleasant 83-degree day.

As I reflect on these past few days, I realize quite a bit has happened since the last time I wrote, which was on the day of Megan's procedure. Later that same day, her parents and brother arrived in town shortly after she got home from the hospital, but as I figured, we didn't see each other the rest of the day because I wanted to give her time to rest. That night, I had another nearly sleepless night as my concern for her ran very deep.

~ ~ ~

The next morning, I finally got out of bed around 8:00 a.m. and after I had a quick breakfast, Scott called me. He'd heard through Rachel about the situation with Megan, and wanted to call to see how I was handling it all. As we began talking, I realized how much it really helped to have someone to talk to at a time like this. Scott and I don't talk as often as we did years ago but there's no question that he's still my best friend. We talked for almost a half hour and he offered some words of encouragement and said that he will keep praying for Megan...and for me.

After Scott's phone call, I texted Megan.

Hey, how are you feeling today?

She texted back about ten minutes later. *A little better, but my stomach is still bothering me some. Do you want to come over sometime this morning so we can talk? My parents and brother are here but we can go somewhere for a little while to talk.*

Okay, what time? I quickly responded.

Like around 10:00? Or whenever you have time.

Okay, I'll be there at 10:00.

The fact that she wanted to talk indicated she'd probably done some thinking and had come a decision of some sort about our relationship. I had no idea what she'd decided but I'd soon find out.

~ ~ ~

When I arrived at 10:00 a.m. she answered the door and invited me inside. Unlike every other time, there was no hug and no kiss as we greeted each other. She was dressed up a little more than I thought she'd be, wearing a stylish turquoise t-shirt and light gray shorts and even some subtle makeup. She didn't look quite as tired as she did yesterday either.

"You look better," I said as I stood before her.

"Thanks, but like I said in my text message, my stomach

isn't normal and I'm still pretty tired," she said. "But at least I'm coherent today."

As we walked toward the living room, I first saw Linda around the corner, sitting in a chair, and then as we entered the room, I saw her parents and brother sitting on the couch as they all quickly looked over at me. I sported a small smile and a wave.

It had been many years since I'd seen the three of them. Her parents—now in their mid-50's—looked mostly the same as I remembered, but they'd certainly aged some. Her dad's hairline had receded and he looked a bit stockier than before. Her mom was still as thin as she'd always been but having a shorter hairstyle and glasses now was a noticeable difference for her.

As for her brother, Matt, he definitely looked more grown up now, but given that he's twenty-six, that shouldn't be a surprise. His short dark hair, stylish glasses, and his rather formal-looking white polo shirt gave him a more refined look, compared to the high school kid with scruffy hair that I remembered him to be.

Her dad quickly stood up from the couch. "Hi Kevin, it's good to see you again," he said, reaching his hand out. We shook hands and then her mom and brother stood up to give me a warm greeting as well. At that moment, I wondered if they had any idea what had unfolded between Megan and me a few days earlier.

After that, Megan looked at them. "We're going for a walk now, and we'll be back in a little while."

"Okay," her mom said, with her look revealing that she probably *did* know what had transpired between Megan and me, and also knew why we were going for a walk.

"Well, it was good to see all of you," I said, acknowledging them. They reciprocated some pleasantries before I turned away and followed Megan to the foyer. She put on her shoes and then we headed out the front door.

~ ~ ~

As we walked down the driveway, neither of us said anything and this all felt very weird. I'd just seen her family after all these years but barely for two minutes, and now I didn't know if I'd ever see them again. Obviously, if Megan was going to break up with me, I probably wouldn't go back into the house after our walk—I'd probably just get in my car and leave. In that case, I realized that might have just been the last time I'd ever see Linda too. But what scared me the most was that this might be the last time I see Megan.

"There's a park down the street and they have benches where we can sit down and talk," she finally said.

"Okay," I said, looking over at her trying to gauge her mood as we walked on the sidewalk next to each other.

It wasn't long before we came up to the park. It was an expansive oasis of green grass in the middle of an otherwise densely populated neighborhood. Beyond the large area of grass, it had a playground area and a swing set off to one side, and a few benches surrounding them. It was deserted, even though school had been out for a few weeks already, and it was a fairly mild morning with the temperature somewhere in the mid-70's, even though it was completely overcast with gray clouds hanging pretty low in the sky.

We both sat down sideways on the bench, so we were facing each other. I looked at her. "Before you say anything, I just want to say I'm sorry that I didn't tell you about the interview...and about the pill."

"I know," she said as her eyes met mine. "When it all came

out the way it did, I just felt like you'd already decided that you were going without even talking to me."

"I honestly was going to talk to you about it after we got back that day..."

"I know," she said before I could say any more. "It's okay. I forgive you for that."

I was so glad to hear her say that. "And I want to say that I've thought a lot about this and I know how it scares you every time I fly and I know you don't like me being gone so much, so I've decided I'm fine with not being a pilot anymore."

She shook her head. "No, I know how much you love flying and I don't want you to give that up. I'm so sorry if I implied that the other day. I did a lot of thinking that night before all of this drama came up with the growths in my stomach. Then this morning before you got here I talked to my parents and basically I've concluded that it's not fair to make you stop flying. Even if you're willing to give it up now, my parents said it would cause resentment over time and especially if you have trouble finding another job or end up in a job you don't like. The fact would always be that I was the reason you're not flying anymore. So basically they told me I have two choices—and I agree with them, by the way. I can either stay with you and come to terms with you being a pilot, or if I can't handle you flying and being gone on trips, then I should break up with you."

I felt a bunch of butterflies rush into my stomach. "So what did you decide?"

"Well, it didn't take me long to conclude that I'd much rather have you in my life, and if that means having you flying and being gone sometimes, then I can deal with that."

As she spoke those words, I felt relief rush through me and I reached out and hugged her. But just as quickly, some concern came over me as my mind continued to process what she'd just said.

"You're really going to be fine with me going back to flying? I mean, I know it still terrifies you when I fly and I'd still be gone a lot, even if I was able to have more weekends off."

"Well, I love you...a lot. And I want you to be happy," she said. "When you're flying, I know you're happy. And as for me, I'm going to get used to it," she said, nodding her head confidently. "And I've decided that you should go to this interview in Atlanta," she continued, "and if they offer you the job, we can determine which of our job offers sound better, and if it's the job in Atlanta, I'll move there with you and look for another teaching job down there. But I don't mean I'd move in with you, though—we'd still have our separate places."

"Yeah, I agree with the separate places," I said. "But I don't want you giving up your job here. If I'm going to continue flying, it shouldn't be that hard to find a job based out of Chicago...at least I hope."

"Well, I guess that's your decision, but I'm fine if you want to go," she said.

"I'll think about it," I said. "I probably have a few days before they'll be calling to set up an interview." I paused for a few seconds as I looked at her and smiled. "It's funny, most couples argue over who will get to take the job they want, but we're arguing over who will get to give up their job."

She looked at me with a tender look in her eyes. "I don't think there's much question how much we love each other," she said. "It really says something that we're both willing to make these big sacrifices for each other."

"That's what love is about," I said, leaning over to kiss her, which then turned into a much longer kiss.

After that, we bowed our heads and I said a quick prayer

thanking God for letting our love for each other overcome these challenges and asked that He continue to bless our relationship.

We raised our heads and smiled at each other. "Well, is there anything else we need to talk about?" I asked.

She shook her head no, still smiling at me.

"Okay, then do you want to head back?" I asked.

"Sure," she said, getting up.

I stood up and held her hand as we began the short walk back to Linda's house.

"So all we need now is to hear that your biopsy results are negative and then we can pick up where we left off with this summer," I said.

I could see the fear grow on her face after I said that. For this entire conversation, we hadn't mentioned anything about her health, and I wished I would've kept it that way.

"I'm sorry," I said, looking over at her as we walked. "I didn't mean to remind you of that."

"It's okay," she said, appearing to hold back tears. "It's weird because a part of me wants to know the results right away, but another part of me doesn't because this might be the last few days that my life will look anything close to normal."

I put my arm around her as we continued walking. I wanted to say something to comfort her, but the words just didn't come to me.

A few minutes later, we arrived back at Linda's house and when we walked in, everyone was still in the living room. After Megan's mom asked how everything went, we both said we had a good talk. The fact that we were holding hands as we stood before them left no question that we'd decided to stay together.

~ ~ ~

Shortly after that, the six of us decided to head out to go mini-golfing. We split up into two groups, and I played with Megan and her brother, Matt. I was glad to have the chance to catch up with him because we always got along quite well.

By the time we reached the seventeenth hole, the overcast skies finally gave way to a few raindrops, but we were still able to finish. After we grabbed a quick lunch, and after I texted Katie to make sure it was okay, I decided to bring them back my apartment so they could see her. It was the first time in many years since she'd seen Megan's parents and brother, and actually the first time she'd ever met Linda.

After we spent a good hour sitting in my living room talking, Megan looked more tired as each minute passed—not surprising considering it was only one day after she'd had the procedure. So before long, they all headed back to Linda's house, but not before we agreed we'd all go to my church the next morning.

After getting somewhat of a decent night of sleep, I woke up the next morning to another overcast day with no sight of the sun. As I got dressed, I realized it was the first time in a quite a while where I was actually able to go to my own church for two Sundays in a row. It was a good service and they all seemed to like it.

Afterwards, we all dodged some raindrops and went out to a small café in town for a late breakfast. By the time we were done eating, I could tell a debate was brewing between Megan and her parents. Simply put, her parents wanted to stay for several more days until the biopsy results came back, but Megan insisted that wasn't necessary. From what I could gather, Megan felt like if they left, things would return to some sort of normalcy during this time as she waits for the results, which definitely made sense to me.

Eventually, her parents agreed that they'd head back to Ohio, and in the early afternoon they left. After that, I decided to give Megan time to rest, because like the day before, she kept looking more tired as the day progressed. So we said goodbye and agreed that we'd see each other the next day. As the weekend came to a close, I was so glad she was still my girlfriend.

~   ~   ~

And that brings me to today. Right after I woke up this morning, I was glad to see the sun peeking through my curtains in my bedroom. It provided a welcome change from the overcast skies and rain showers we've had during the past few days. I stayed in bed for a few minutes after I woke up and did some quick figuring in my head. Megan had her procedure done on Friday and the doctor said the results of the biopsy would take a "few days." It was now Monday—the third day— yet two of those days were weekend days and I don't think the labs work on weekends. So as I got out of bed, I concluded this probably wouldn't be the day she'd receive the results, and we'd probably have a few more days to wait.

I walked out to my living room and even before I ate breakfast, I texted Megan. *How are you feeling today?*

Better. I'm not as tired as I was the past two days, but my stomach still doesn't feel normal.

Do you want to get out and do something today? I texted back.

Not really, I'm trying to educate myself a little more about what I might be facing. She texted back.

After we exchanged a few more text messages, she eventually agreed that I could come over after lunch to spend some time with her. After Katie woke up a little later and found out I was going, she was eager to come with because this would be the first time she'd see Megan since the day of our hiking trip, when all of the drama unfolded between all of us.

We arrived just after 1:00 p.m. and Linda answered the door expecting it would just be me, but then saw Katie.

"Hey guys," she said. "This is good you both came because Megan has been at her computer all morning, so maybe two is better than one to convince her that she needs to get out and do something this afternoon."

"Yeah, let's hope," I said.

Katie and I walked through the living room and into the kitchen where we found Megan sitting at the table leaning in close to her laptop screen with her hand on the mouse. She had a look of sheer devastation on her face as she looked up to greet us.

"Hi," she said quickly.

I wanted to ask her what was wrong, but Katie spoke before I could.

"I know you weren't expecting me to come here today," she said, "but I really wanted to see you because the last time we saw each other was the day of all of that drama and I hope you're still not mad at me about the pill."

Megan looked up at her and gave her a small smile. "I'm not mad anymore. I know you were just trying to help and I forgive you," she said before her eyes drifted back to her computer screen.

"What are you doing on the computer?" I asked.

"I'm doing some research," she said, "and I'm realizing that I've had almost every symptom of stomach cancer in these past few months. And I've found some medical forum websites and

I've read postings from people who said they had the same symptoms as I did and then after a few months they went in for a CT scan and they discovered a growth—just like they did with me—and it was the beginning of stomach cancer. It just breaks my heart to read all of these people's stories, and it terrifies me that I might be one of them."

I walked behind her and looked at the screen and in addition to the page she had up, I saw at least seven or eight windows minimized at the bottom.

"And even though it's rare in the U.S. it's says your chances increase significantly if you have a family member who had it." She looked up as us. "Remember I told you, my grandmother had it?" She then picked up a notepad with the first page almost completely full of writing. "I've found different numbers on this, but if these growths they found are in fact tumors, then there's a good chance they're malignant. If they're cysts or polyps, they might be benign but depending on what type they are, this still could be the very beginning of stomach cancer. And then I found that the 5-year survival rate for it in the U.S. is only 29 percent, and from some of these stories it sounds like many people die well before 5 years. It's no wonder the doctor looked at me so sympathetically after the procedure. Just by the look on his face, I could tell that he knew it was cancer but he couldn't say anything yet."

I gently took the notebook from her and examined it for a few seconds. "We don't know if that's true. He doesn't know for sure either. And how do you know these statistics that you're finding are correct?" I asked.

"These are from legitimate studies they've done," she said.

"Well, whether these numbers are accurate or not, you can't be doing this. It's not helping you at all. None of this is going to change the results of your biopsy."

"It's really not," Katie said. "All it's doing is scaring you. I can see the fear in your eyes and you look miserable right now."

Megan didn't say anything, she just stared down, studying the wood-grain in the kitchen table and looked like she was trying to hold back tears.

Then Katie spoke again. "I haven't memorized a lot of Bible verses like Kevin has but I know a few, and Psalm 23:4 has helped me through some tough times especially when I was in college. It says something to the effect that even though you '...walk through the valley of the shadow of death...fear no evil...' because God doesn't leave your side."[1]

"I know," Megan said looking up. "Even if I'm dying I know I shouldn't be afraid...but I am. Maybe it just needs to sink in and then I won't feel so afraid...I don't know." She finally sat back from her computer and she stared out the patio door.

Before much silence set in, I spoke. "I think you need to get out of the house this afternoon and get your mind off of this for a while."

"Yeah," Katie said. "We could go to the pool or go hiking, if you feel like it. We'll do anything you want."

Megan gave us a blank look and I couldn't tell if she was agreeing or disagreeing.

"I don't know," she finally said.

"Or maybe we could do something different," I said. "Is there anything you wanted to see since you moved here, like go to downtown Chicago or something? It's only about a forty-minute drive."

"Not really," she said.

Then Katie looked like she had an idea. "It'll still probably be a few more days until you get the results, so maybe this would be a good time for you and Kevin to take a vacation somewhere."

"I'd be up for that," I said.

Katie looked at Megan. "Can you think of somewhere you've always wanted to go in your life, but never have?"

Megan quickly looked up at Katie. "You mean so I can cross off one more thing from my bucket list because you think I'm dying?" she asked, starting to hold back tears.

"No, I didn't mean it like that," Katie said, leaning down and wrapping her arms around her as Megan still sat at the table. "I just meant this would be a good time to do something neat to get your mind off of everything. And besides, this a great time to take a trip anyway. You don't have to start your job until August and Kevin doesn't have to work now either. But there's nowhere you want to go, even in the whole country?"

Megan sat there staring down at the table not saying anything, lightly shaking her head no.

"How about the Grand Canyon?" I asked.

Megan quickly looked up at me and as our eyes met, it was clear my question stirred up a memory that was familiar to both of us. She and I almost took a road trip out there during the summer after our sophomore year of college. She'd never seen the Grand Canyon before, but wanted to very much. Not long into our planning, her parents decided they didn't like the idea of the two of us going on that type of trip together, even though we would've stayed in separate hotel rooms.

That was actually the second time she'd been denied a trip to the Grand Canyon, with the first being when she was twelve years old. Her family was all set to drive out there during the summer that year, but two days before they would've left, her brother fell off of his bike and broke his arm and had a mild concussion, so the trip was off. Luckily, he recovered pretty quickly, but they never rescheduled the trip. Still to this day, Megan has never seen the Grand Canyon.

Our eyes were still locked and I was expecting she would've quickly said no, but she hadn't yet. "I know you've always wanted to go," I said. "So what do you say?"

"Well, I guess we could," she said.

"We might want to consider flying, because that's a really long drive out there," I said, realizing we may not have the luxury of taking a leisurely ten to twelve day road trip, since her doctor would probably want to start treatment right away— that is, if the results are positive.

She looked away from me and stared blankly across the room, probably coming to that same realization right then. She finally turned back to me after several seconds. "Yeah, I guess we could fly."

"Really?" I asked. I was absolutely shocked to hear her say that.

"Why not? If I take some medication before we leave, I'd probably be okay...I hope." She then turned to Katie. "You're welcome to come with us."

Katie shook her head no. "It should just be the two of you. You'll finally get to take the trip you both wanted to take in college," she said, obviously remembering that situation from years ago.

In the minutes that followed, Megan and I sat down at her laptop right there at the kitchen table and began looking for flights and hotels. Megan was very adamant that we'd split the cost of everything halfway. Either way, I knew it would be a tall order to find anything even close to affordable considering we were hoping to leave possibly as soon as tomorrow. But I also knew with all of the layovers, schedule changes, cancellations, and diversions I've encountered as a pilot, it's given me years of experience with exactly that type of thing.

So with some targeted searching on the internet we were able to find flights and a hotel room that ended up being fairly affordable. We'll actually be leaving tomorrow (Tuesday) and coming back on Friday. We looked into staying out there longer, since that would lead into the Fourth of July weekend, but the hotel and airfare prices were almost double the price for those extra days. With neither of us working right now, we couldn't justify spending that much extra money. I'm certain, though, that in our four-day trip we'll have enough time to see everything while we're out there.

From the times I've been to the Grand Canyon, I'm also certain that Megan will be quite taken with it. I'm really glad Katie gave us this idea to go. I have to say, with how easily all of this planning came together, it seems clear that God must want us to go on this trip. I don't know what that says about Megan's fate, but I'm trying not to think about that right now.

Megan also made it clear she doesn't want to think about that now because she's already decided that she'll be turning her phone off for the entire trip. She said this trip isn't the time or place she wants to be getting a call regarding her biopsy results, which is certainly understandable.

~ ~ ~

For the rest of the day, we *did* end up getting Megan out of the house when the three of us went for a short hike in a local forest preserve down the street. After that, Megan and I said goodbye for the day knowing we both had some packing to do.

Now that I've finished that and I'm sitting here on my patio, a part of me is still baffled how she agreed to this trip. But obviously, I'm very glad she did because it'll be so neat to travel with her and we couldn't be going to a more awe-inspiring place. I think it's been about two years since I've been to the Grand Canyon, so it'll definitely be neat to see it again.

I know she'll probably have to take a high dosage of her anxiety medication, and I hope that'll be enough for her to get on a plane for the very first time in her life. But more than any of that, I hope this won't be the last chance she has to see the Grand Canyon. But honestly, I think that possibility is probably the very reason she made this surprising decision to go.

◆ 19 ◆

Friday, July 2ⁿᵈ
My apartment
8:36 p.m. (Central Time)

Megan and I just returned from our trip to the Grand Canyon a few hours ago and there's no question this trip made for a very eventful four days. Now, I'm sitting here at my dining room table catching up with my journal as it's now only two days away from the Fourth of July. Thanks to these long summer days, it's not quite dark outside yet, despite it being after 8:30 p.m.

For a Friday night, it's certainly quiet around here too. Katie texted me earlier just after I got off the plane saying she'd be baby-sitting Jacob and Madeline tonight because their parents had last-minute plans. So I have the apartment to myself now, which gives me an opportunity to reflect on these past four days, which I'm certain I'll remember for the rest of my life.

~ ~ ~

On the morning Megan and I left, we had a 10:15 a.m. flight to Phoenix. As I got dressed and finished packing a few final things, I tried to be quiet so I wouldn't wake up Katie. I knew how much she likes to sleep late, and I knew it was only about 7:15 a.m.

I finally headed out the door carrying my suitcase into the garage. Just after I loaded it in my trunk, I looked up and saw Katie wandering out in her bare feet to see me, wearing the pink t-shirt and gray shorts she sleeps in. With her eyes half open and her long blonde hair spilling everywhere, she walked over to me and gave me a long hug.

She spoke softly. "The garage door woke me up and I wanted to say goodbye to you before you left. I hope you have a good trip and tell Megan I'm praying for her."

"I will," I said.

She smiled at me and then turned and went back inside—probably to go back to bed. I then started the short drive over to pick up Megan on what was an overcast and cool Tuesday morning. When I arrived, it was just past 7:30 a.m. and she was ready to go. After a quick hug and a kiss, I loaded her suitcase in the trunk and we started out for the airport.

As we drove, she sat very quietly in the passenger seat, and I could only imagine how nervous she must have been at that point. Eventually, out of the corner of my eye, I saw her take out her phone from her pocket.

A few seconds later, she looked over at me. "Okay, my phone is officially turned off now," she said.

"Okay, good," I said, quickly glancing over at her as I drove. That brought me a hint of relief knowing—just as we'd planned—we'd at least have the next four days free from any potentially bad news regarding her biopsy results.

As we got closer to the airport, the morning rush-hour traffic got heavier. But after we arrived, parked, took a shuttle bus to the terminal, and got through security, we still had some time to spare. That gave me a chance to show her around since it was the first time she'd ever been inside of an airport.

But before too long, it was time to board. She was very quiet as we made our way down the jet bridge and onto the aircraft. As we then walked down the narrow aisle toward our seats, I noticed her looking around curiously—similar to what I remember doing the first time I set foot on an airplane many years ago.

When we arrived at our seats, I gladly took the middle seat and let her have the window because I wanted her to see every square mile beneath us from this view she'd never seen. After we got settled, I looked over and smiled at her. A part of me still couldn't believe she was actually sitting on a plane with me. However, it was impossible to ignore how incredibly nervous she looked by that point.

So I leaned down in front of me and pulled the stuffed raccoon out of my backpack and set him on her lap. She immediately turned to me and smiled as she affectionately took him in her arms. "So you must've found him in your drawer...and I bet he scared you, but you'll never admit it."

I smiled. "Well, he startled me for a second," I said, omitting the fact that it actually brought me to tears that day. But we certainly didn't need anything bringing down our mood at that moment as we sat on the plane.

After a few more minutes, we pushed back from the gate and the clouds outside seemed even thicker and lower than before. We taxied for a short time and then turned onto the runway and the engines began to roar. The plane went faster with each second and Megan clenched my hand and braced herself in her seat as we felt every bump in the runway—just as you always do at that point. Then just when we lifted off of the ground, the ride became smooth and she looked over at me and her face obviously showed fear, but I also saw a hint of excitement—something I hadn't seen in her for a while.

I also felt my own version of excitement because I was so glad to see her flying for the first time. This was also the first time I'd flown since I was put on furlough over two weeks ago. So it felt like a part of me came alive again as we made our steep ascent through the clouds.

About five minutes into the flight, we were already breaking through the top of the cloud cover and quickly made our way up into the sunshine.

She leaned forward and peered out the oval window and then turned to me. "The sun is coming out."

I smiled. "It's always been out. It was just blocked by the clouds before...but now we're above them," I said.

"That's neat," she said, turning back to look out the window again. "So this is what the top of the clouds look like, huh? It's like this wispy, three-dimensional dream world. It looks like you could step right out and walk on them."

I laughed. "Yeah, it looks like you could, but don't try it."

She smiled. "Don't worry." She continued peering out the window taking in this scenery she'd never seen before. "I have to say, it's pretty neat up here. The sun is shining, the clouds are pretty, and you feel like you're completely away from the world."

"Yep, this was a typical work day for me," I said.

She turned to me. "I can see why you like this so much." Her eyes then studied me in a way like she suddenly understood a part of me she never had before.

~ ~ ~

As the miles passed below, Megan had stayed glued to the window for much of the time as she stared down at the landscape below. By the time we got into the latter part of the flight, the clouds below had dissipated, which gave us a great view of the terrain out west. It became very mountainous for a time, but as we got closer to Phoenix, the topography changed to the expected tan, dry-looking soil indicating it was, after all, a desert.

It had been a smooth flight up until our approach when a few more noticeable bumps caused Megan to grab my hand and brace herself in her seat.

I turned to her. "Is your stomach upset?"

"Not any more than it has been, but it hasn't felt normal the last few days," she said, still clenching my hand. "But if you're asking if I'm going to throw up because of the turbulence, I'm not."

"So I guess you'll miss out on the experience of using a barf bag on this flight," I joked.

She smiled nervously. "I will...and that's a good thing."

Just before we touched down, she squeezed my hand hard probably expecting our landing to be much rougher than it was.

After we landed and turned off the runway, I hugged her and gave her a quick kiss. "I'm proud of you."

"It wasn't as bad as I thought it would be," she said, "and it was prettier than I ever imagined."

We pulled into the gate mostly on time, just before 12:05 p.m. local time in Phoenix. They announced that the temperature was 98 degrees with fair skies right then, and it was expected to climb to a seasonable high of 106 later in the day. After we made our way off the plane, we had a quick lunch at an airport café and then picked up our rental car and headed out. As we began the three-and-a-half-hour drive north to get to the Grand Canyon, I was still somewhat in disbelief that Megan had actually flown, but obviously very happy about it.

~ ~ ~

The next morning, it was barely 8:00 a.m. but Megan and I had already taken a bus ride down deep into the Canyon—essentially to the very bottom. After treading through some wet sand, we stepped up on a fairly large motorized pontoon raft to take a half-day trip along the Colorado River with a tour guide and eighteen other passengers.

We found a good seat on one of the pontoons and I looked over at her after we sat down. She smiled at me and looked particularly cute wearing her sunglasses and baseball cap with her ponytail threaded through the back of it. We were both dressed for what would be a hot, sunny day, even though the morning air felt comfortable right then as the sun was still at a low angle.

Believe it or not, this rafting trip was Megan's idea, which originated from her seeing a brochure for it in the lobby of our hotel just after we checked in the previous night. We knew this trip would give us great views of the Canyon from a perspective not everyone sees—from the bottom looking up. Beyond that, we—especially Megan—hoped that "smooth-water" would actually turn out to be just as it sounded, despite the repeated warnings to carry our valuables in waterproof cases and the suggestion of wearing our bathing suits under our clothes.

After the last of the people boarded the raft, we set sail. We were immediately treated to some spectacular views of textured walls of rock towering high on each side of the river. It was neat how one side of them was partially illuminated by the morning sun, which brought out their natural orange and red colors.

Closer down by the river, the landscape consisted of some rocky and sandy areas sloped down toward the water with loose rocks and boulders sitting there looking like they could roll down at any second. There were also some thick green bushes growing near the edge of the water in some places, which provided a nice accent color to this picturesque, "postcard-like" scenery.

As the trip progressed, the sun was getting higher in the desert sky—and hotter—as each minute passed. About halfway through, we docked on a "beach," which was essentially a small sandy area along the river, which gave everyone a chance to walk around and actually swim in the Colorado River, if we wanted. However, our tour guide said the water was a constant 47 degrees all the time.

After we stepped down from the raft, Megan and I both looked down at the water, which was crystal clear and then Megan looked up at me.

"What do you think? You want to swim?" she asked.

I laughed, dismissing the idea and assuming she was joking.

"I'm serious," she said.

"You really want to do this?" I asked.

She eagerly nodded. "How many chances do we have to swim in the Colorado River?"

I looked at her and smiled. "Okay, let's do it," I said, starting to take off my shoes.

After a few seconds we'd shed our clothes down to our bathing suits and began wading into the water, holding hands.

"Oh, this is really cold," she said.

I laughed. "You can't complain. This was your idea. I think it'll be better if we just jump in all at once," I said, as we stood almost waist-high in the water. "On three...one, two, three."

We both pushed off the bottom and jumped all the way in. The cold water took my breath away for a few seconds, but after a few minutes it became tolerable and even borderline comfortable—possibly because our skin was starting to go numb and we just couldn't feel the cold anymore. We swam around for a few minutes and shared a quick kiss before we came up to the shore to get out. We ended up being the only ones in our group that swam and the rest of the people looked at us like we were crazy.

As we dried off with an extra towel that the tour guide let us borrow, Megan looked over at me. "That was even colder than I thought it would be, but, I have to say, I'm glad I wasn't a chicken like all the rest of these people," she said with a small, almost devious grin I'd never seen before.

It didn't take long to warm up on what had become a characteristically hot day, nor did it take long to dry off in the typically dry air of the Southwest.

Shortly after that, we boarded the raft again and set off for the remainder of our trip, which ended up being a truly smooth-water ride all the way through. After taking in more of the picturesque scenery and even seeing a blue heron gliding between the towering walls of rock, we docked and boarded the bus to head back up to the rim. It was then when I realized that I'd just seen an adventurous side of Megan that I never knew existed—and probably didn't exist—before this trip.

~ ~ ~

When we arrived back at the top of the Canyon, we grabbed a quick lunch, where Megan ate a fair amount but still said her stomach didn't feel normal. After that, we made the drive back to our hotel to make a quick stop in our rooms to clean up. Needless to say, we both felt it was appropriate to stay in separate rooms for this trip simply to avoid putting ourselves in a situation that could be full of temptation.

After the quick stop in our rooms, we still had a good part of the afternoon and the whole evening to explore and sightsee—this time from the top of the Canyon. So we took our rental car and drove to several of the scenic overlook points on the South Rim. The first one we stopped at, we got out of the car and only had to take a few steps before we found a rock to sit down on to take in a wonderful view.

The horizon was mostly flat in every direction you looked, except for some mountains off in the far distance that looked miniature, even though they obviously weren't. The expansive blue sky held a few stray cumulus clouds and the bright mid-afternoon summer sun illuminated the Canyon and all of its rich colors perfectly.

As we stared ahead, what caught my eye next were the countless rock formations within the Canyon that looked like they were carefully-sculpted works of art. They were all unique in their own way—some looked like rounded hills made of solid stone, some were wide with a flat top, and others looked almost like pyramids. When I looked all the way down into the Canyon, the winding Colorado River provided beauty of its own.

"This is even more amazing than I thought it would be," Megan said. "But amazing doesn't even begin to describe it."

"I guess it's okay," I joked.

She playfully hit my arm and smiled. We then held hands and shared a kiss.

"So you finally got your trip to the Grand Canyon," I said.

"I know and I'm so glad I came," she said, smiling at me.

She wrapped her arm around me as we both continued gazing into the distance. It was great to take in this beautiful place that felt almost like it was in a different world...or at least *across* the world from where we live. But it was even greater to see Megan experience it for the first time.

~   ~   ~

As the day pressed forward, we drove to several more of the overlook points to see the Canyon from different angles. But before long, it was approaching dinner time, so we headed back toward the hotel and ate at a nice restaurant. After that, we had just enough time to head back to one of the overlook points to watch the sunset. We were surprisingly the only two people at that particular overlook. So we sat down on a nice flat rock and I wrapped my arm around Megan as she leaned up against me.

As the sun sank lower, the sky became prettier and radiated some impressive shades of deep orange and red. But what was most breathtaking was how the Canyon reflected those colors. The light illuminated the rock formations within the Canyon making them appear almost as if they were glowing from within.

As we sat there watching all of this, I heard Megan sniffle a few times. I looked over at her and she was looking down and I could see tears flowing down her cheeks.

"Are you crying?" I asked.

She sniffled. "A little bit."

"What's the matter?" I asked.

"I feel like this is the first time in my life where I've actually *lived my life* and didn't let my fear and anxiety control what I do...or more likely, what I *don't* do."

"Well, that's good," I said. "Maybe you're finally putting your anxiety behind you."

"Maybe I am, but the only reason I got on that plane yesterday and the only reason I had the courage to do the rafting today is because for once, I wasn't afraid of dying...mostly because I think that I already might be."

Before I could offer her any words, she continued. "I mean...what if this is the end of my life, where I have stomach cancer and after they try to treat it, they eventually tell me that I only have a few months to live?"

"Well, let's hope that's not the case," I said. "But if it is, you can be assured that none of us are meant to stay on this earth forever and we're all going to die at some point. I'm sure you know it says that in many different places in the Bible that our lives on this earth are short. James 4:14 is the one that comes to my mind first. It says our life is like '...a [vapor], that [appears] for a little time, and then [vanishes] away.'[1] So whether we live to be thirty or eighty, it's a really short amount of time in the grand scheme of things."

I paused and took a deep breath before I continued. "But if this turns out to be your time to go, at least you can know that you've lived a good life and you'll be going to a better place." As I spoke those words, I tried my hardest not to begin crying myself.

She sighed, not seeming very content.

I turned to her. "Are you afraid you won't go to heaven?" I asked.

"No, it's not that," she said. "I know we, as believers, have eternal life through Jesus...I've known that since I committed my life to Christ when I was twelve years old. It's just that sometimes I think I could've done more with my days on this earth. I just think of someone like Rachel who's traveled the world to spread Christianity and changed a bunch of lives, and I haven't done anything like that."

"Well, first of all, not everyone is meant to travel the world to spread His word, and that's okay, because God gives each of us different gifts. And second, you can't possibly have forgotten what happened during our freshman year of college?"

She gave me a confused look. "What do you mean?" she asked.

"It was the first week of classes, right after we met, and you told me how you weren't sure how it would work out with you and Rachel being roommates. You said how you were surprised the college had paired you up with her because you two had nothing in common. I remember you telling me how she and a bunch of girls from her soccer team wandered down to the frat houses to party the first few nights and stayed out really late. And then I remember how it made you sad when you found out she hadn't been to church for years and didn't own a Bible."

She stared ahead and lightly nodded, as I clearly was stirring up this memory for her.

"Who was it who convinced her to come to church? Who was it who went out and bought her a Bible? Who was it who invited her to a small group?"

She nodded.

"Just think," I continued, "all of those lives she touched on her mission trips...she would've never touched any of them if it wasn't for you. And not to mention there's no way she would've been interested in dating Scott, who was really strong in his faith, if it wasn't for you who'd already started opening her heart to Christ before we introduced them."

She turned to me and gave me a small smile.

"I don't ever want you to feel like your life was a waste," I said. "You've done so many great things. Anyone who's been close to you, I'm sure would say that you've made their life better in some way. For me, it was only after seeing the way you loved me in the first few months after we met when I finally I realized what true love is all about. Sometimes it can be a fairy-tale romance, but many times it isn't. But either way, it's caring about someone else more than yourself and loving someone no matter what, the same way God loves us— unconditionally. And you taught me all of that."

She turned to me, smiling with tears welling in her eyes and then wrapped both of her arms around me. "Through all these years, you've always known what to say to make me feel better."

After a really long hug, she rested her head on my shoulder as we both stared forward and watched the sun continue to set. I felt good that I was able to convince her that she'd done some great things in her life, but that conversation got me wondering how many great things I could say I've done in *my* life. It made me feel a little better when my sister came to mind and all the things I've done for her through the years. But I realized I could—and should—do more as I sat there watching the sunset.

As the sun got lower, darkness crept upward on the rock formations—eventually to where only the tops of them were illuminated. After a few minutes, the sun sunk below the horizon and it was like a light switch had been turned off and the Canyon became completely dark. The only remaining light was from the sky still softly radiating hues of orange and yellow. Just like that, the sun had set on this day that I'm certain neither of us will ever forget.

~   ~   ~

The next morning we planned on meeting in the lobby at 8:30 a.m. to take advantage of the free continental breakfast. I arrived only a few seconds before she did. She was wearing shorts, a t-shirt, flip-flops, and a big smile as she walked toward me.

"Hey you," I said, smiling at her.

"Hey," she said, hugging me and then quickly kissing me. She eagerly handed me a brochure with her eyebrows raised seemingly waiting for my reaction.

I quickly looked at it and then looked up at her. "Helicopter tours? You want to do this today?"

"If *you* do," she said.

"Sure, I'll do it. It sounds like fun," I said. "I'm surprised you want to do it, though."

"Well, this is the new me," she said.

"You still might want to take some extra anxiety pills," I said, "because helicopters can be sort of a rough ride."

"I think I'll be okay," she said confidently.

"Why, what do you mean?"

"I haven't taken a single pill on this whole trip, and I don't plan to either," she said.

"Really?" I was shocked. "Not even for the flight out here?"

She shook her head, smiling. "Not even for that."

I looked at her and smiled contently as I never thought I'd see the day where she'd actually be excited to go up in a helicopter.

We then had a quick breakfast and headed over to take the helicopter tour. I knew Megan was a changed person after we lifted off the ground and she looked over at me wearing the mandated headphones and a big smile on her face with not a hint of fear.

This tour gave us some great views of the Canyon that are simply impossible to get from land. While we were suspended in the air above this incredible natural landscape, it really gave me a sense of how big and vast it really is. On the tour they said it's up to 18 miles wide at its widest spot and over 250 miles long. That's truly mind-boggling, considering that's about the distance from Chicago to Green Bay, Wisconsin.

After we landed, we continued our sightseeing from the ground and went to several more scenic overlook points around the South Rim. Before we knew it, the day was coming to a close, so we had dinner and then saw another great sunset from a different overlook point this time. That marked the end of the third day of our four-day trip already, which meant this would be our last night at the Grand Canyon, and in less than 24 hours we'd be back in Chicago.

~ ~ ~

The next morning, we had a somewhat leisurely breakfast in the lobby of the hotel and then we headed out to begin our trip home. Even though it was very sad to see this remarkable trip end, all of our traveling went smoothly and Megan seemed to enjoy the flight back just as much as the first one.

By the time we arrived back and pulled into her aunt's driveway, it was already mid-afternoon. I turned off the car, and was ready to get out and walk her up to the door, but I looked over at her and she wasn't ready to get out yet.

She was staring down at her phone, which was still turned off, as it had been for the entire trip. Panic shot through me as soon as I realized this could be the moment she turns it on and we'd find out the results of her biopsy. I reached over and held her hand as she still stared down at her phone, seemingly contemplating whether she should turn it on or not.

She finally spoke quietly. "I don't think I want to know the results just yet," she said. She then looked over at me with a surprisingly content look on her face. "Today's Friday and if it's cancer, they're not going to start treatment over a holiday weekend, so why should I ruin the Fourth of July?"

"I guess you're right," I said. "Whatever you want to do."

She took a deep breath and stared out the car window. "You know, a part of me just wants to throw my phone away in a pond and pretend nothing's wrong with me right now. You and I could travel the world for the next few months and hope I don't fall ill in the process. But I know I can't do that. If this turns out to be cancer, my best chance of surviving is to get treatment early instead of waiting until I might be really, really sick."

She then stared straight ahead as we sat there inside the completely silent car. "I think that's what scares me the most right now...if I end up having cancer and I have to go through a long treatment process where I feel miserable, all just for a chance to survive."

After some silence, she spoke again. "Another thing that really scares me is if I die, what's going to happen to you and my parents and brother...and everyone else who's close to me. I really want you...and everyone...to know that I'll be in a better place and I want you to pick up your lives and still be happy even after I'm gone. And I really don't want anyone to go through years of grieving."

I took a deep breath before I spoke as I held back some tears. "Well, *if* you won't be with us anymore, and that's still a big *if* at this point...then I'd imagine we'd all go through a grieving process, but ultimately we'd be comforted by knowing that you're in heaven...the best place you could possibly be."

I reached over and held both of her hands and we bowed

our heads and prayed, simply asking God to do His will, whatever that may be, and to give all of us strength in the process.

After she took a deep breath. "Well, even though my stomach still doesn't feel right and hasn't for this whole trip, it's not bad enough to stop me from doing things for now, so we might as well enjoy this weekend."

She then started naming off everything she wanted to do including going to the pool, going to some festivals, possibly riding in a hot air balloon at one of the festivals, and of course, seeing fireworks on the night of the Fourth.

We eventually got out of the car and I got her suitcase out of the trunk and carried up to the porch. When we arrived in front of the door, I set it down and then we shared a long hug.

After that, she stared deep into my eyes. "I can honestly say this was the best trip of my life," she said.

"Me too." With all of the trips I've taken and all of the awe-inspiring places I've seen, none of them compared to this one because of one simple fact—Megan wasn't with me on any of those trips.

"I love you so much," she said.

"I love you more," I said.

She cracked a small smile before we kissed and eventually said goodbye...until tomorrow.

I then came back to my apartment and now, of course, I'm sitting here at my dining room table journaling. I'm still trying to grasp how much Megan has changed in these last four days. Even though she understandably still has some fears, it was good to see her overcome some of her fears on this trip.

The thought that this may have just been the last trip she's able to take in her life still causes me great sadness. But if it turns out that these are, in fact, her final days on this earth, maybe I should be joyful instead of being devastated. After all, she'll be going to a place that the rest of us will have to wait to experience—a majestic place that all Christians agree is our ultimate home. But even though that brings me comfort, I still can't even fathom how much I'll miss her if she's gone.

◆ 20 ◆

3 ½ months later...

Saturday, October 23rd
My apartment
11:54 p.m. (Central Time)

As I sit here on this October night beginning to type this journal entry, I've decided this will be the last of these I write for a while. Thinking back to the last time I wrote, it was two days before the Fourth of July. Now after several months have passed, the long and hot summer days have been traded for cooler and shorter days, colorful trees, and plenty of autumn leaves covering the ground.

To say there's a lot to catch up on would be an understatement. But there's probably no better place to begin than where I last left off—July 2nd, which is hard to believe that's been more than three and a half months ago already.

~ ~ ~

As Megan planned, she kept her phone turned off that whole Fourth of July weekend because she didn't want to know her biopsy results yet. We tried our best to not think about any of that by keeping busy over the course of that three-day weekend. The weather included a lot of sunshine and temperatures in the upper 80's. It allowed for Katie, Megan, and me to spend the first day of the weekend at a festival in town, later followed by some time at the pool.

On the second day, which was the Fourth, Katie spent time with some of her friends from high school, probably because she sensed I wanted some time alone with Megan. So Megan and I took a hot air balloon ride at one of the festivals, which gave us some amazing views of the sun coming up and of the town below. Megan loved it, which was proof that the adventurous spirit she'd adopted during our Grand Canyon trip was here to stay.

Later that night, we went to a very crowded park and spread out a blanket on the grass—among hundreds of other people—to watch the fireworks. With the humid nighttime air, the familiar smell of bug spray, and the fireworks bursting in the sky above, it couldn't have felt more like summer. There was no place I would've rather been than right there with Megan.

The following day, we spent some more time at the pool and checked out another festival. Before long, the weekend was coming to a close and we knew these were the final hours before we'd be finding out the results of Megan's biopsy the very next day.

~   ~   ~

We planned that Katie and I would go over to Linda's house around 9:00 a.m. that morning to be with Megan when she'd turn on her phone and called the hospital to get the results. But Megan adopted a different plan because around 8:30 a.m. she texted me.

I just called to get the results and they said I have to schedule an appointment with the doctor to review them, which doesn't sound good. Their next available appointment isn't until tomorrow at 10:00 a.m., so unfortunately, we have another day of waiting.

Katie and I ended up spending most of that day with her as we all waited and wondered. Megan was fairly convinced the results were likely positive since they wanted to see her in person. Deep down, I sort of thought the same. But I obviously didn't say that, and I really tried my hardest to think positively.

Finally, the next day arrived and even though Megan told us we didn't have to go with her, we did anyway—Linda, Katie, and myself—and I know Megan was glad we were there. But strangely, Megan was probably the calmest of all of us that morning. I remember as we all sat there in the waiting room, I nervously kept taking deep breaths trying to calm myself. Finally, Megan looked over and put her arm around me.

"It's okay," she said calmly. "Whatever the results are, I can handle it. If it's my time to go, I'm not afraid of dying anymore and it's amazing how much that's changed my view on life."

I quickly glanced over at her and gave her a small smile but quickly looked away as I was honestly trying my hardest not to cry at that point.

Before too long, they called her name, and we all went with her into the exam room. By this point, I felt my heart racing as I knew I was just moments away from learning the fate of the girl I loved very deeply. After the nurse did the typical things of taking Megan's temperature and blood pressure, she left, and it was back to waiting.

After about five minutes, the door opened abruptly and it startled all of us. As the doctor came in, my heart began racing even faster and I don't think I've ever been so nervous in my life.

He wore the traditional white coat with a stethoscope around his neck and held her chart in his hand as he closed the door behind him. He quickly glanced at all of us and most likely saw the concern on our faces.

"I'm not sure what they told you when you scheduled the appointment, but it's standard procedure for our practice to only disclose test results in person. It doesn't matter whether it's good news or bad news, we do this the same way. In your case," he said with a hint of surprise in his voice as he sat down, "it's mostly good news. You'll be happy to know the two growths that we removed were benign."

Megan immediately folded her hands, bowed her head, and closed her eyes for a few seconds, apparently saying a quick prayer. I know we all felt a huge relief at that moment. There was also a feeling of surprise, since we'd all been preparing ourselves for some bad news.

The doctor continued. "After they did some further tests on them, they found them to be the most common form of stomach polyp and it's the least likely form to develop into cancer. But going forward, I suggest we continue the CT scans every month for now, just so we catch any new growths before they get too big. It's very possible, you'll have more of these throughout your life, and if you do, we're going to want to remove them and test them. Even though these types of polyps usually aren't cancerous, sometimes they *can* be, and we don't want to take any chances."

Megan nodded her head as the doctor continued.

"So regarding the symptoms you've been having with your stomach, it's possible the two polyps may have been causing some mild symptoms of an upset stomach, but usually they aren't very symptomatic. And like I mentioned after the procedure, we found some mild ulcers, which aren't advanced enough to require treatment, but that may be part of the reason for your symptoms as well."

He paused for a minute as he thumbed through her chart. "I see on your chart you've dealt with some anxiety and that could be part of the cause as well. Beyond those things, there could be other causes and it becomes sort of a guessing game at that point. But right now we don't believe it's anything serious or life-threatening. It could even be an allergy you've developed to a specific type of food, which might explain why the symptoms seem to come and go. We can test for allergies if you want, but that's your choice."

After the doctor eventually left, we all stood up and hugged Megan.

"Thank you guys for coming with," she said. "I'm sorry for everything you've had to put up with during these past few months. But those days are over now. I promise this is a new beginning for me. I feel like God has given me this second chance at life and I'm never going to forget that."

~   ~   ~

As the month of July was still rather young at that point, we all finally felt like we could start enjoying our summer. For Megan, it truly *was* a new beginning. Much like on our Grand Canyon trip, her anxiety was virtually non-existent. But her stomach still bothered her some, so she decided to get some allergy tests done. In turn, they revealed nothing, except for some minor seasonal allergies that would have no effect on her stomach. But as each day passed, it seemed her stomach bothered her less and less, which could've been because the ulcers that she had were healing.

Those summer days allowed Katie, Megan, and me to spend a lot of time together, since none of us were working at that point. Obviously, I still didn't have a job—although I was definitely looking. Katie's temporary babysitting gig with Jacob and Madeline had ended a while ago when Stacy got back from vacation. And, of course, Megan's teaching job didn't start until mid-August.

So when my pastor hinted that the three of us should consider teaching a mid-summer Vacation Bible School class, we did. It was a week-long class, in the middle of July and the twenty-two kids in our group kept all three of us on our toes. But it seemed Megan and Katie had more of a natural ability to deal with kids than I did. Even though it was exhausting at times, it was really neat to be able to teach the kids about Jesus and it was amazing to see how quickly they learn.

Just a few days after that class ended, my birthday arrived. That day officially marked the beginning of my thirties...and, somewhat sadly, the end of my twenties. But it was a good day and it meant a lot to me that Megan and Katie went out of their way to make a nice birthday for me. Just as they'd planned, we went on a local hiking trip and then went to the pool afterwards. Then the rest of the day included presents, cake, and dinner at my favorite pizza place.

Since Megan's birthday is just a mere four days after mine, we all celebrated her birthday in much the same way. Needless to say, she was very glad that she lived to see this birthday.

A few days after that, I got a call from Tyler one morning to let me know the pilot job in Atlanta that he'd recommended me for had been filled. Basically, he said they didn't want to interview someone from out of state, and with over 120 applicants they obviously didn't have to. It was fine because I wouldn't have moved to Atlanta anyway, knowing that Megan would soon be starting her new teaching job in the Chicago area.

But it didn't leave me feeling very hopeful as there was no sign that I'd get called back to my job from the furlough anytime soon. Additionally, I'd already applied to a lot of pilot jobs throughout the month and hadn't heard back from any of them. I even contacted the owner at the private jet business where I began my career, but he didn't have openings. So as July came to a close, I began to seriously wonder if God still wanted me to be a pilot—and if not, what in the world did He want me to do with my life?

~   ~   ~

The month of August began with Katie getting a phone call she certainly wasn't expecting. It was from her friend, Stacy, who'd just received an offer for an accounting job in Portland, Oregon. That was Stacy's major in college and I guess it wasn't until this point when she was finally able to find a job in that field, so she'd been babysitting in the meantime. Anyway, she asked Katie if she'd be interested in taking over babysitting Jacob and Madeline. But this was a much bigger opportunity than just a simple babysitting job.

It was a full-time nanny job that paid surprisingly well. It would entail Katie taking the kids to school each day, and then running errands, doing grocery shopping, and doing some cleaning around their house before picking up the kids from school. Then she'd watch them until their parents came home around 5:30 or 6:00 each night. Given that Katie enjoyed babysitting them before, she was very excited about this. So after she met with their parents, she was offered the job and she accepted it.

After she started the job, I continued looking for a job of my own...and also spent a lot of time with Megan, enjoying the summer days. But before we knew it, we were at the point where Megan had only one week left until she'd start orientation for her new teaching job. So we decided—rather spontaneously—to take a road trip during that week.

We headed out to Ohio so Megan could see her parents and brother one more time before her busy school schedule started. It was good to see her family and they were really nice to me— as they've always been. After we stayed four nights, we headed back, which was good because I can't say her parents' couch made for a comfortable place for me to sleep.

When we got back, it was obviously down to just one weekend before Megan would start her orientation. She and I spent most of that weekend at the pool, and it felt sort of like our last real weekend of summer, even though it was still only mid-August.

~ ~ ~

Before we knew it, Monday morning arrived and from the tone of her text messages that morning, she was pretty excited about her first day. Going to work was something she hadn't done for almost three months, and considering everything she'd been through during those months, this was a big milestone for her.

After her week of orientation went well, she officially began her teaching assistant job the very next week—along with her two classes. All of that promised to be a busy schedule for her, and it's safe to say by the end of that week she was sufficiently tired. But she was still very happy to have this opportunity.

By then, Katie was also working some long days with her nanny job. With all of her responsibilities, she was also tired by the time she'd get home in the evenings. Before long, a new routine seemed to emerge for the weeknights. It involved me cooking dinner and having it ready each night by the time

Megan would come over after work and by the time Katie would get home from babysitting. We'd then all three sit down and eat together.

Later in the evening, we'd sometimes do a short Bible study. But for many evenings, the two of them would be falling asleep on my couch in front of the TV before I was even done cleaning up the kitchen from dinner. Either way, it was those evenings when my apartment felt more like a home to me than it ever had before.

A lot of that was because Megan was over so much, but having Katie living there definitely contributed to that as well. Even though there had still been times when Katie and I got on each other's nerves and tested each other's patience, the majority of time we got along well—the best we had since we were kids.

She even volunteered to split the rent and utility bills shortly after she started her job, since they were paying her what most would consider a "living." She said she'd continue living with me for as long I needed to split the rent, even though her eventual plan was to find a place of her own.

Her staying with me actually helped me a lot, since I was obviously still not working and coming to realize the savings and unemployment checks I'd been living off of since I was laid off wouldn't last forever. I also realized it was probably time to start seriously exploring other (non-pilot) career options. It didn't make me happy to think that way, but I tried to remember that God had a plan—even though I didn't see it yet.

~ ~ ~

By the time September arrived, Labor Day weekend came and went very quickly. Just a few days after that, a powerful cold front moved through, which yielded several cloudy days with highs only in the 60's and a brisk north wind.

I remember how I spent those gloomy days inside, sitting at the computer, looking for a job. I came across a few flight instructor jobs, which I applied for, even though they were part-time and didn't pay well. I also applied to some retail store management training jobs and even some sales trainee jobs—having no clue what kind of salesman I'd make. Even though none of those garnered much excitement for me, I knew I might have to settle upon one of those paths—provided an out-of-work airline pilot would be qualified for any of those.

On a brighter note, after only a few days of cooler and dreary weather, it warmed back up into the low 80's again. That allowed me to get back out to the pool for quite a few days, which they surprisingly kept open, despite it already approaching mid-September by that point. In fact, that's where I was when I got a phone call, which turned out to be one I wouldn't soon forget. When it rang, I thought I recognized the number, but I wasn't sure.

"Hello?" I answered.

"Hi Kevin, this is Jim."

"Oh, hi!" I said, sitting up in my lounge chair. It was the owner of the private jet business and I felt some brief butterflies in my stomach as I was eager to hear what he had to say.

"Well, listen," he began, "I think I might have some good news for you. I have a pilot who just told me he's leaving in two weeks to go to a regional airline. So if you're still looking for a job, this might be a good thing for you. But I have to warn you, it's not a captain job, so you might be over-qualified, and it's not going to be a big salary."

"That's fine," I said, as I knew I didn't have any other leads, and wanted very much to get back to flying.

"Okay, we'll still have to interview you just so we follow procedure," he said.

So the very next day, I went for an interview and the day after that, they offered me the job. The salary was a little higher than what they were paying me back when I started my career there because I have more experience now. It would certainly provide a modest living for me, but it was still a significant pay cut from what I was making at my most recent airline job. Nevertheless, I decided to accept the job. Megan and Katie were very supportive of my decision, and they were happy that I finally found something.

After I passed the re-certification to fly small commuter jets again, my first day of work arrived very quickly. My excitement was undeniable as I left my apartment that morning wearing a pilot's uniform. That was something I hadn't done in more than three months. I remember lining up for takeoff that morning for my first flight and feeling so glad I was able to get back to flying. God really came through for me, even though there was a time before this when it looked like my pilot career was over.

As I settled into the job, it didn't take me long to realize it was pretty similar to when I worked there at the beginning of my career—and that was a good thing. Surprisingly, many of the same pilots I worked with before were still there and eagerly welcomed me back. Even some of the passengers—the CEO's and corporate executives—were the same and they also welcomed me back. I also appreciated being home for most weekends...and many of the evenings as well. In fact, one of those evenings—just a few weeks ago—has actually left me with a lot to write about now.

~   ~   ~

It was the last day of September and I'd gotten home from work around 6:00 p.m.   Katie was already home from babysitting, but Megan had a department meeting at her school that she was expecting would go pretty late.   Her school's accreditation review was coming up, so they were preparing for that.

I'd barely been in the door for ten seconds—still wearing my full pilot's uniform—before Katie turned off the TV, stood up from the couch, and walked over to me as I was taking off my leather jacket in the foyer.

She was still wearing jeans, which was odd because she usually changes into sweatpants the minute she gets home from work.   She looked straight at me as she stood in front of me.   "I have to ask you something…"

"What?" I quickly asked, not having any idea what this was about.

She continued.   "Where do you see yourself in, let's say, a year from now?"

With a curious look, I answered quickly.   "Well, I guess wherever God wants me," I said as I hung up my jacket in the closet.

"I know," she said.   "But you probably have some thoughts on where you'd want to be in your life then, right?"

"Well…" I said, pondering her question for a few seconds, all while she was standing just inches in front of me, eagerly waiting for my response.   "Hopefully Megan and I will at least be engaged by that point, and maybe even married.   And hopefully I'll still be at my job, flying."

"So when you say you want to be engaged to Megan…when were you thinking of proposing to her?" she asked.

"I don't know," I said, untying my black dress shoes.   "I

don't want to rush anything, and I want to make sure she's ready."

"Are *you* ready?" she quickly asked.

"Yeah, I'm ready," I said confidently as I slipped off my shoes. "I've been ready for the past few months."

"What if I told you she was ready too, and she's been waiting for you to ask her?"

"Really?" I asked as I felt a smile come to my face. "She told you that?"

"Yep," Katie said eagerly. "She actually said the exact same thing you just said...she's ready to get engaged but wasn't sure if you were ready yet."

"Wow," I said, still smiling. "When did you guys talk about all of this?"

"We met for lunch today," she said. "Megan wanted to go to lunch because she'd have to stay late tonight...but I'm guessing the main reason was because she wanted to talk about this. And, of course, I had time because Jacob and Madeline were at school."

"Well then, I guess it's time for me to ask her," I said with excitement.

Katie then hugged me. "I think it is. I'm so happy for you two."

After that, we took a few steps into the living room as I began eagerly pondering the details of all of this. After a few seconds, I spoke. "I should call her father in the next few days to get his blessing and then I guess it'll be time to start looking for a ring. And after that, I'll need to figure out all the details of how I'm going to propose."

Katie then looked at me eagerly. "So since I'm sure her dad will say yes, I think it's safe to buy a ring before you talk to him," she said. "Speaking of which, I think tonight would be a good night to go...and I can come along, if you want."

"Like right now?" I asked, realizing this was probably why she hadn't changed clothes after work.

"Well, think about it..." she said. "What other time are we going to have where we can sneak out like this? I mean, since the three of us spend so much time together now, we always know where we all are and what we're all doing.

I nodded. "That's a good point. And yeah, you should probably come with me so I don't end up getting her something that looks like a Super Bowl ring."

Katie laughed. "Well, then let's go, so we're back before she gets home."

So after I changed out of my pilot's uniform, we headed out and grabbed a quick dinner, then went to a jewelry store. After we were showered with congratulations and called a "cute couple" by the associate, we quickly explained it wasn't us getting engaged. We proceeded to look at several rings there, and then went to two more stores and looked at quite a few more.

After that, I finally made a decision...of course, with Katie's approval. I actually decided on the first one we saw at the first store we visited. From the moment I saw it, it stuck in my mind and when we went back there and saw it again, I knew it was the one. Katie admitted that was her favorite one as well. It certainly wasn't the cheapest one, but it also wasn't the most expensive either. The store said it would be ready in a few days, so then the only things left were to call her father and then figure out when, where, and how I was going to propose.

~　~　~

I actually called her father the very next day after I bought the ring. As I expected, he gave me his blessing and was very happy to hear that I'd be proposing. A few days after that, I picked up the ring and Katie agreed that it looked very nice. I then decided that I'd propose on October 23rd. I wanted to keep the "23" in the picture, considering that August 23rd was the fateful day when we first met in the campus bookstore over twelve years ago now.

So that meant I had the next two weeks to figure out where and how I was going to propose. After I gave it some thought, I decided that I'd take her on a day trip out to Indiana. The fact that the 23rd fell on a Saturday, thankfully made that possible. It would first involve going hiking at a state park not too far from the campus where we went to college. My hope was that the weather would be good and the autumn leaves would be in full color.

After hiking, we'd go out to dinner, followed by a casual walk around campus. Then hopefully, we'd end up at the place we called "our spot" behind the science building, and that's where I'd propose. But since I hadn't been back to the campus for many years, I had no clue if that spot still existed or if a new building would be standing on top of it by now. Nevertheless, I figured if it was gone, we'd settle upon some other spot on campus that would still be familiar to us.

After I decided all of that, it was simply waiting for today to arrive—Saturday, October 23rd. I'm happy to say that I mostly got the weather I was hoping for today. It was a sunny and clear day—and evening—with not even a single cloud in the sky. But it was chilly—low 50's—after a cold front moved through last night, which left us with some noticeable wind as well. But it *did* feel very autumn-like...I'll give it that. And it was still worlds better than rain.

When I arrived at Megan's aunt's house this morning to pick up Megan for this trip, it was just before 10:00 a.m. She was certainly dressed for the chilly day, wearing jeans and her navy blue fleece jacket over a heavy sweatshirt. I was hoping she wouldn't read too much into all of this and simply assume this was a hiking trip, and nothing more. But I sensed her subtle curiosity very quickly.

After we made the drive out to Indiana, we had a quick lunch at a local restaurant there, and then we made our way to the park. Thankfully, it wasn't as windy in the woods. Also, we couldn't have picked a better time to go in terms of the fall foliage. The towering trees were very colorful, and in many spots, an abundance of bright yellow and orange leaves covered the trail.

After a fairly long hike, we made the thirty-minute drive to campus and had dinner at a restaurant that had been one of our favorites throughout our time in college. Not only was the restaurant still there and open, it looked virtually the same on the inside, except for some minor updates they'd done. It was the only "sit-down" type of restaurant within walking distance from campus. Rather fittingly, back when we were in college, most of the times we went there were on Saturday nights, just like tonight was.

After we finished dinner, I looked at her and tried to act as casual and relaxed as I possibly could. "You want to go for a walk around campus...for old-time's sake?"

She smiled. "I'd like that."

From that point forward, my heart was racing, even though I tried my hardest to appear calm on the outside. I suppose my nervousness was justified, being that we were quickly approaching a moment we'd both remember for the rest of our lives.

~   ~   ~

As we walked through the campus, the sun had set, but it wasn't quite dark yet. It gave us a chance to see some of the new buildings they'd built—and realize which of the familiar buildings were now missing from the landscape. But before long, we came up to the science building, which I was glad to see was still standing as strong as ever. But the very sight of it unleashed a ton of butterflies in my stomach as I knew I'd soon be proposing in just a few minutes now.

We then instinctively went around to the side and stepped over the short concrete wall to get to our spot behind the building. When we got there, it was thankfully, one of a few spots on campus that looked exactly the same as it did when we were in college. Surreal would probably be the best word to describe how it felt standing there after all these years. Yet in some ways, it felt like we'd just traveled back in time and this was simply another Saturday night while we were in college.

We held hands as we both stood there smiling at each other with undoubtedly a lot of emotions running through our minds at that point. For me, it was mostly nervousness, but that still didn't stop me from making her laugh.

I turned to her. "So I assume our raccoon friend has probably moved on to bigger and better things than eating banana peels out here."

"You think he graduated?" she asked jokingly.

"I'm sure he did," I said. "He's probably a CEO by now."

"CEO of what?" she inquired with a smile.

"Probably of a waste disposal company," I said. "He obviously had a lot of experience with that."

She giggled. "You're funny," she said as she slowly looked up and shifted her attention to the sky as it was mostly dark by now.

The chilly weather not only made for a clear day, but also a clear night because we could see a lot of stars.

She then spoke softly. "Even though it's not a full moon tonight, the crescent moon is pretty in its own way."

"Yeah, it is. And it lets you see more stars too," I said, as my heart was practically beating out of my chest by this point. I finally decided right then that this would be the moment, so I grabbed the ring out of my pocket and then got down on one knee beside her as she kept staring up at the sky.

After a few seconds, she turned toward me and quickly realized what was happening. She gasped with joy—maybe some surprise too—and covered her mouth with her hands as tears began filling her eyes.

"Megan, I'm so glad God brought us back together after all these years and I can't imagine my life without you now. Will you marry me?"

"Yes, Kevin. I'll marry you," she said, smiling at me with tears running down her face before she quickly wrapped her arms around me.

After a few seconds, we let go and she held her hand out. I then put the ring on her finger. I knew right then this was a moment we'll cherish forever.

"I know you can't see it very well in the dark," I said, "but hopefully you'll like it."

"I'm sure it's beautiful," she said, before giving me a kiss and wrapping her arms around me again.

"I love you so much," she said.

"I love you, too."

We then stood there holding each other tightly. I can honestly say that was the best moment of my life so far, and I'm sure she'd say the same. After a few minutes, we said a quick prayer together thanking God for the great love we'd found in each other and asking Him to continue to guide us in every part of our relationship with each other.

~   ~   ~

Before long, we decided to lie down in the grass right there in our spot. We then held hands and stared up at the star-filled sky together. We were both ecstatic about what had just happened and we eagerly began discussing the details of our wedding. We decided quite effortlessly that we wanted a late-spring wedding and decided on May 23rd, to keep the "23" in the picture. So obviously that means we have exactly seven months to plan a wedding.

We then talked about what kind of wedding we want— probably not a huge one, but big enough for all of our family and close friends to attend. We also decided that Scott and Rachel will serve as our best man and matron of honor. Megan was also very certain she wanted Katie to be one of the bridesmaids.

After we made those decisions, we drifted into comfortable silence, both of us filled with joy, and me still trying to wrap my mind around the wonderful reality that Megan is no longer just my girlfriend, but rather my fiancé.

After several peaceful minutes, she took a deep breath and then spoke. "Life sure has had some twists and turns for us since the last time we were here in this spot."

"Yeah, especially for you," I said. "But I'm so glad you've come through all of that now."

"Yeah, me too," she said. "But I've definitely learned a lot from it."

"So what would you say the biggest thing is that you've learned?" I asked.

"How to trust God," she said. "And not just say I trust Him, but actually fully trust Him and surrender everything to Him.

It's been amazing how much better my life has been since I've done that. I remember right before we left for the Grand Canyon trip, the 'old' me would've been fearful of every bad thing that could've possibly happened on a trip like that. But I finally realized as clear as ever that everything is in God's hands. As it says in Ephesians 4:6, He is 'One God and Father of all, who is above all...'[1] So if I worry that God—who is above everything—isn't in control of my life, then it's like saying I don't trust that He's God."

"That's a good point," I said, as I realized that I've probably learned just as much as she has from being by her side during all of her adversities.

She then continued talking. "I also realized that there's never been a time that God has ultimately failed me. Even though I've had a lot of hardships to deal with, ultimately, He's rescued me from all of them. Just like it promises in Psalm 9:10, He has '...not forsaken [those] that seek [Him].'[2] And even if I die, He still wouldn't be forsaking me because He'd be taking me to heaven."

She then put her hands in the pockets of her fleece jacket as she continued staring up at the nighttime sky. "That was a big thing for me...overcoming my fear of dying. Before all of this, death was my worst nightmare. It made me literally sick to even think that one day I'm going to die. But once again, trust comes into play and I'm able to trust that God has already determined how long we will live...specifically even the number of months, as it says in Job 14:5.[3] But even more than that, if we're believers, then Jesus has a place prepared for us in heaven, as it says in John 14:2.[4] And in the very next verse in 14:3 it says, '...[He] will come again, and receive [us]...' so that we can be with Him.[5] So now, instead of feeling dread and fear about dying, I'm comforted knowing that I'll be going 'home.' And from every description of heaven in the Bible, it should be much better than this earth. But we should still be thankful for every day that God has given us to live on this earth."

"You're right," I said. "I'm impressed with all the Bible verses you've memorized."

"Thanks," she said. "Those were the verses I clung to during the really tough times when it looked like I might die."

"I'm really glad it wasn't your time to go," I said.

"Me too," she said. "I think there's still a lot that God wants me to do on this earth."

After some silence set in as we calmly stared up at the sky, she spoke again. "Isn't it funny that after all these years, we come out here again and still have deep conversations like this?"

"Yeah, I think it's something about the stars and the quietness," I said. "Just think, we might be still coming out to this spot when we're 80."

"I hope so," she said as she turned to me and smiled.

Then I turned toward her and we began kissing. As we kissed under the stars in this familiar spot we called our own, it felt like we were back in college, but of course with one big difference now—we're engaged.

~ ~ ~

We eventually got up and left our spot. Then after one more leisurely walk through campus, holding hands, we made the drive back to Illinois. During that drive, Megan eagerly called her parents, then her brother, and then Rachel to tell them the good news. She also called Katie, even though we both decided we'd stop by my apartment to see her before I took Megan home for the night.

When we got back to my apartment, it was no surprise that Katie had waited up. She quickly stood up from the couch and turned around. "Oh, it's *both* of you! So how does it feel to be engaged?" she asked, quickly walking toward us.

"Good!" we both said almost simultaneously.

Katie then wrapped her arms around both of us. "I'm so happy for you two."

Megan then officially asked Katie to be one of her bridesmaids, and Katie enthusiastically said yes. As the two of them stood there beginning to talk about what type of wedding dress Megan will want, I realized more than ever that the two of them had become sort of like best friends. That was something Katie hadn't had since Beth passed away years ago. And it was something Megan hadn't had for a while either, since Rachel lived in a different part of the country now.

As I stood there smiling at the sight of them talking, I realized how glad I was that my sister has become a part of my life again during these past several months...and a part of Megan's life, too. After all, Megan probably wouldn't be where she is right now if it wasn't for Katie and some of her bold, yet thoughtful actions. I doubt Megan would've ever been able to go to the interview for her job if Katie hadn't secretly given her the medication that day. And obviously, if Megan wouldn't have gone, she wouldn't have gotten the job.

Then, of course, there was the Grand Canyon trip, which was Katie's idea. I know neither Megan nor I ever would've thought to take a trip during that tumultuous time, but it actually was the best thing we could've done. Either way, if we wouldn't have gone, Megan obviously wouldn't have had the opportunity to fly for the first time, which was an important step for her in overcoming her anxiety...and more importantly, trusting God with her life. And of course, this very night wouldn't have happened—at least not this soon—if it wasn't for Katie telling me that Megan was ready to get engaged.

Before too long, I took Megan back home for the night to her aunt's house. But just after we pulled into her driveway and I turned off the engine, she leaned over and kissed me. I could tell by her kiss she was in no hurry to go inside—or to see this great, once-in-a-lifetime evening come to an end. So we spent the next few minutes kissing before I walked her up to the door, where we proceeded to kiss some more. Eventually, we said goodnight and I left.

~   ~   ~

And now, I'm sitting here at my dining room table as I finish typing what I've already decided will be the final entry in this journal for a while. With Megan's good health, along with us getting engaged tonight, it somehow feels like this past six-month segment of my life has concluded tonight—on a very good note. So it only seems appropriate to conclude this journal now.

Even though I'm ending this journal on what I'd consider the best day of my life so far, it's also seen me through some of the most difficult days of my life during these past six months. But as difficult as some of those days were—especially recently when it looked as though Megan may be leaving this earth—God rescued us from all of that, which I'm so grateful for.

But even before He rescued us, it was amazing to see how different Megan's life had become after she stepped "into the sunshine" and began trusting God completely with her life, rather than living under the dark clouds of fear. After all, God wants us all to take rest in the peace that comes from trusting Him with our lives and knowing He will always be with us during our stay on this earth...and beyond.

But it's naïve to think we won't still encounter some tough times before leaving this earth.   In fact, realistically, our departure from this earth may be preceded by illness and temporary suffering.   But as it says in John 3:16, anyone who believes in Jesus will "...not perish, but have everlasting life."[6] And in the last part of 1 Corinthians 15:54, it ends by simply saying that "...Death is swallowed up in victory."[7]

Through all of this, Megan and I have come to learn even more that death shouldn't be feared. When God calls us—or any believer—home, then death is merely a passageway to a place where there's even greater sunshine...if there's sunshine in heaven. But whatever there is, I'm sure it'll be unfathomably great.

But before we get there to find out—and despite whatever tough times we encounter—I'm betting that God still has quite a few sunny days planned for us during our stay on this earth. And I know for sure that Megan and I will cherish those days more than ever now.

◆ THE END ◆

A Message from the Author:

Once again, I want to express just how much it means to me that you devoted your time to reading this book. I hope you enjoyed the positive message it brought and I also hope you were entertained at the same time.

The reason I write books is to bring God's message of hope to as many people as I can. So as I continue to build my writing career, I would greatly appreciate if you could spread the word about this book. That is, if you enjoyed reading it and liked its positive message, then feel free to tell your family and friends about it. Even in this increasingly digital world, I still believe good old-fashioned word-of-mouth is the best way for a book to gain widespread awareness based on its own merit.

In the meantime, this book isn't quite over. I hope you enjoy the special features that I've put together on the following pages.

God Bless!
-Mark

Connect With the Author

To stay updated on the status of my upcoming books, to read insightful posts, or to simply see pictures from whatever hiking trip I've recently taken...follow me on Twitter at:
www.twitter.com/MarkRitterBooks
Or search for my Twitter username: **@MarkRitterBooks**

After arriving on my Twitter page, click the "Follow" button to be sure to see all of my posts!

Contact for Fundraiser Opportunities

If you'd like to learn more on how this book could potentially be used as a fundraiser at the church you lead or attend, please email the publisher to find out if there are currently any promotions running: **gmhpublishing@outlook.com**

◆ Special Features ◆

– Reading Group Guide –

Including...

1. Discussion Questions for Book Clubs

2. Thinking Points (Answers) for Book Club Discussion Questions

3. Discussion Questions for Small Groups and Personal Reflection

– The Making of the Book –

The inspiring story behind how this book became a book.

– The Lost Chapter –

The captivating and suspenseful chapter that didn't quite make it into the story.

◆ Reading Group Guide ◆

Discussion Questions For Book Clubs

Spoiler Alert - Some of these questions give away some storylines that occur in the book. You may want to wait to read these questions until after you've read the book.

These questions are designed for book clubs since they focus on the story and the characters, which make them great for initiating interpretative discussions about the book.

1. Do you think Kevin made the right decision to break up with Megan at the end of their senior year?

2. It wasn't easy for Megan to attend Scott and Rachel's wedding, since she still wasn't feeling well from the many months of health problems she'd been having. How much do you think her motivation to attend was because she might have been eager to cross paths with Kevin again?

3. Do you think Katie's reason for moving in with Kevin was because she wanted to restore their sibling relationship, or do you think it was simply that she wanted a free place to live (away from her parents) where she could have parties?

4. Despite being brother and sister, Kevin and Katie clearly had different personalities. However, in what ways do you think they were similar to each other?

5. Do you think Megan did the right thing by hiding the severity of her health problems from Kevin...that is, until Kevin later found out?

6. Do you think Kevin should've quit being a pilot when Megan moved to Chicago, since Megan clearly didn't like him flying?

7. Do you agree with Megan's beliefs on not wanting to take any medication that would've obviously helped her situation?

8. Do you think Kevin & Megan's love story was an example of "opposites attract," or do you think they were actually more similar to each other than different?

9. What are some of the different meanings you think the title, "Into the Sunshine" has throughout the different stages of the book?

10. Were you surprised at how the story ended?

◆ Reading Group Guide ◆

Thinking Points (Answers)
For Discussion Questions

Spoiler Alert - Once again, some of these thinking points give away some storylines that occur in the book. You may want to wait to read this portion until after you've read the book.

Below are some thinking points for the discussion questions designed to provide some insight into the topics that the questions covered. These could be especially helpful for those leading a discussion in a book club.

1. **Do you think Kevin made the right decision to break up with Megan at the end of their senior year?**

    Kevin tried very hard to do what he thought God wanted him to do, which was break up with Megan. Ultimately, you could argue that is what God wanted because they both later admitted that they weren't ready to get married just after college. On the other hand, you could argue that they could have stayed together, postponed their plans of marriage, and tried to deal with a long-distance relationship instead of completely breaking up. But neither of them seemed to want that at the time.

2. **It wasn't easy for Megan to attend Scott and Rachel's wedding, since she still wasn't feeling well from the many months of health problems she'd been having. How much do you think her motivation to attend was because she might have been eager to cross paths with Kevin again?**

   Obviously, one of the big reasons that Megan wanted to attend the wedding was to see Rachel get married and be able to serve as her maid of honor. But since Megan had recently become single again, it's possible that just as much of her motivation to bring herself to the wedding was to see Kevin. She probably heard—through Rachel— that Kevin was also single, and she seemed quite content spending time with him outside on the terrace during the reception.

3. **Do you think Katie's reason for moving in with Kevin was because she wanted to restore their sibling relationship, or do you think it was simply that she wanted a free place to live (away from her parents) where she could have parties?**

   On the surface it appears, Katie's intentions were only to use the situation to her advantage. But early on, when Katie calls Kevin and asks to move in with him, there's a hint she may have deeper intentions. When Kevin tells her that he's not home very often, she sort of gets offended by that, since he's implying that he's glad he won't have to be around her very much. Also, she'd just broken up with her boyfriend at that point, so maybe this was her way of turning to her big brother for comfort, just like she did when they were kids.

4. Despite being brother and sister, Kevin and Katie clearly had different personalities. However, in what ways do you think they were similar to each other?

The biggest way Kevin and Katie are similar to each other is that they both show empathy for other people. Kevin is clearly an empathetic person as he cares very deeply for Megan, regardless of the status of their relationship. But, as we get to know Katie better, she also cares very deeply for Megan as she tries some bold, yet well-intentioned tactics to get her better. Also, it's clear early on that Katie cares about Kevin, despite their differences because she tells him to "be careful flying," at the end of each of their phone calls.

Another similarity they have is that they're both strong in their faith. Kevin is clearly strong in his faith throughout the whole story. For Katie, as the story progresses, her strong faith becomes more prevalent as it's shown how she's dealt with a tragic loss in her past by showing unwavering trust in God. Additionally, what she faced in her past is quite similar to what Kevin faces in the latter part of this story, so that's also something they end up having in common.

5. Do you think Megan did the right thing by hiding the severity of her health problems from Kevin...that is, until Kevin later found out?

It's easy to understand why Megan hid her problems. At the point in the story when she and Kevin got back together, she simply wanted to have a normal life, have a normal relationship, and be treated like a normal person. She didn't want to be viewed or treated as "special" due to the fact that she might be dying. Whether or not that excused her from essentially "lying by omission" is a judgment call. But it's a strong argument to make to say there should be honesty and transparency in all relationships, and that Kevin had a right to know the full situation.

6. **Do you think Kevin should've quit being a pilot when Megan moved to Chicago, since Megan clearly didn't like him flying?**

   It clearly terrified Megan that Kevin would fly so much. But it doesn't seem she wanted to stand in the way of his dream job either. On one hand, a person shouldn't dictate to their spouse or significant other what career path they should or should not follow. On the other hand, part of being in a relationship is making sacrifices for the other person. This question is certainly one that's open for debate.

7. **Do you agree with Megan's thoughts on not wanting to take any medication that would've obviously helped her situation?**

   You could see Megan's point that she didn't want to be dependent on taking medication in order to live a life that was within the realm of "normal." On the other hand, you could see Katie's point that the medication clearly helped Megan. This is yet another question that's open for debate.

8. **Do you think Kevin & Megan's love story was an example of "opposites attract," or do you think they were actually more similar to each other than different?**

    It's easy to observe throughout the story that Kevin was much more adventurous and much less fearful than Megan. Additionally, given that he recently attained his dream job of becoming a pilot of full-size jets, he seemed to have a brighter outlook on life while the hardships that Megan faced seemed to make her a more fearful person who didn't have the most positive outlook.

    However, taking a closer look, there were some definite similarities between them. First, they were both strong in their faith. Second, they both enjoyed some of the same things...hiking, observing the stars at night, etc. Third, they both had similar senses of humor. Fourth, they both seemed to genuinely care about other people, not just each other. So maybe they actually had more similarities than differences.

9. **What are some of the different meanings you think the title, "Into the Sunshine" has throughout the different stages of the book?**

    The first mention of it is when Kevin states that one of the big reasons he fell in love with flying as a kid was the ability to climb above the clouds and get "into the sunshine" when he would fly. Another mention that comes later in the book is Megan's ability to overcome her fear and anxiety by getting "into the sunshine"—quite literally, when she flies for the first time and breaks free from the anxiety that had been keeping her "under the clouds" for all of that time. And finally, it's referred to in the last part of the final chapter, which describes going to heaven as going "into the sunshine," that is, if there's sunshine in heaven.   In all of these instances, the theme centers around getting to a better place.

10. Were you surprised at how the story ended?

My goal with writing this book—especially the chapters leading up to the end of the book—was to make it anything but predictable. I wanted each and every reader to finish reading Chapter 19 (the second to the last chapter) and genuinely not know how this story will end. Part of what made that easier to do was because I, myself, didn't know how the story would end as I wrote this book. I had two very solid—yet vastly different—ideas for the ending, but I didn't choose which one to use until late in the writing process. I even had written primitive drafts of the alternate ending before deciding upon the ending I used.

◆ Reading Group Guide ◆

Discussion Questions for Small Groups and Personal Reflection

Spoiler Alert - Some of these questions give away some storylines that occur in the book. You may want to wait to read these questions until after you've read the book.

These questions are designed for small groups and/or personal reflection, since they focus on a variety of deep, thought-provoking topics brought up in the story.

1. In the beginning of the book, Kevin had to make a difficult decision to break up with Megan, and later wondered if he'd made the right decision. In your life, have you ever been faced with a big decision that you honestly didn't know which way to decide? How did you ultimately decide? How did your faith and prayer factor into that decision?

2. Megan clearly hid the severity of her health problems from Kevin until he eventually found out. Have you ever hid some big things from family members or people close to you because you felt it would be better for you (or for them) if they didn't know? In what circumstances (if any) do you think that's acceptable?

3. Kevin and Megan's personalities were different in some ways, but similar in other ways. Thinking of your friends or spouse, do you think they are fairly similar to you, or do you think they're actually more different from you...or even opposite? In what ways do you see them to be similar or different from you? How does your faith compare to theirs?

4. From the time that Kevin and Megan broke up at the end of college to the time they reunited at the wedding, it's safe to say that Megan had changed some. Her attitude and viewpoint didn't seem as bright or hopeful as it was in college (at least at the time in the story when she and Kevin reunited at the wedding). That was most likely because of the hardships she faced during those years after college.

    Think back to an earlier time in your life when you were in a different situation than you are now...maybe back when you were in high school or college, or back when you were living in a different place, or back when you were working at a different job or company. In what ways (if any) was the "past you" different from the "present you"? Has your faith grown or waned since then? Do you strive to be more like the "past you" or the "present you"?

5. Many people say that "everything happens for a reason." With all of the hardships that Megan faced throughout this story, you could say the reason behind them was to help her trust God much more with her life, which then made her a happier and more relaxed person later in the story. When you think back to some hardships that you've faced in your life, do you see any good that came from them? Do you think they brought you closer to God?

◆ The Making of the Book ◆

The Inspiring Story Behind How This Book Became A Book...

I think the story behind how this book became a book is one that's worth telling. This isn't a story about how this book is based on true events of my life, because it's not. Rather, this is a story about what was going on in my life while I was writing this book. But before I get too far ahead of myself, I should first share some background.

Long before the idea for this book even entered my mind, I graduated from college with a Business degree and began my corporate career in the Business Analytics field. That's basically a fancy term for developing sales reports and crunching numbers to provide insight on business trends and company performance. It was what I wanted to do with my Business degree and I felt blessed to have found a job like that not too long after I graduated.

Just a few years into that career, I decided to devote some of my weekends to begin writing my first novel. Up until that point, I'd written some short stories—some even dating back to college—because I always enjoyed writing, especially fiction. Given that my faith plays a big role in my life, I decided the novel would be Christian-themed.

So during the next six months of weekends, I wrote a novel, which is actually NOT this novel. When I finished it, I was proud of my accomplishment, but I knew what I'd written was very primitive and nowhere near the caliber it needed to be in order to be marketable. So I chose not to publish it, and over time, I didn't think about it much at all anymore.

After a few more years of continuing to build my Business Analytics career, I had an idea for a second novel, which has now become this book. So I decided to begin writing it, but doing so by focusing very strongly on making it a marketable book, while not compromising one bit on the Christian theme. It was my hope that a well-written book could bring a positive, Christian message to a lot of people.

But the problem quickly became time. As with pretty much anything, good results require a good amount of time. In this case, writing a good novel was taking a lot more time and focus than writing a primitive, unstructured novel like my first one. I also had more responsibility at my business job than before, which didn't leave me with much energy or enthusiasm to write on the weekends.

Not surprisingly, after only writing about the first 15 percent of this book, I eventually put it on the back burner and it became the furthest thing on my mind. That is, until one day when the company I worked for announced it was being bought by a competitor. Ultimately, I was laid off as a result of that...along with many other people as well. Losing my job was an awful feeling of uncertainty and doom, and my heart goes out to anyone who's going through that now...or has had to go through that in the past.

In my first week of unemployment, I felt God calling me to start writing again, so I began to pick up where I left off with this book. Little did I know that within only a few days, my enthusiasm, energy, and motivation for writing would be stronger than it had ever been. As a result, I was able to

complete the first 40 percent of this book before I found
another business job after having 11 weeks off.

After I began the new job, I was back to the same problem
of time. There just wasn't enough of it, and it broke my heart
that I had this great story to write, but not enough time or
energy to do it. But after only a year at the new job, I was called
into a conference room one day and was told my position was
being eliminated as part of a massive cost-cutting endeavor.
After the initial shock wore off, happiness is what I mostly felt
for this second layoff. It sure felt like an answered prayer
because now I had time once again to write! I also had
severance pay to hold me over so I wouldn't starve.

The result was a summer—and autumn—that provided me
with some of the best months of my life...and a huge amount of
time to almost finish writing this book. It also included a lot of
time at the pool, which provided some inspiration for the pool
scenes in this book. After having five months off, I found
another job and was able to finish the remaining parts of this
book in my not-so-abundant free time. After that, the rest is
history, as they say.

So I hope the story behind this book gives you hope that
God can use bad things in our lives to create good things. After
all, if I never would've been laid off (twice, no less), I highly
doubt you'd be reading this book right now, because I likely
would've never had the time to finish it!

✦ The Lost Chapter ✦

The Captivating and Suspenseful Chapter That Didn't Quite Make it Into the Story…

First, some notes about this chapter…

This chapter features Kevin recalling how one of his "routine" flights turned into a harrowing and downright scary situation. If it would've been included in the book, it would've happened several months before the story of this book began. Then, with it still being somewhat fresh in Kevin's mind, he would've recalled this by way of having a "flashback" somewhere around Chapter 5.

If I would've included this chapter, it would've introduced a "sub-story" of sorts. I liked how Kevin would've still had flashbacks of this fateful night, and the effects it had on him would still be apparent months later. I thought it created an interesting feature because flying was something he loved so much, but for the first time in his life, he saw the real—yet very rare—dangers of it. I also liked that it provided some validation for Megan's fear of flying because Kevin could no longer say that nothing bad ever happens while flying.

But ultimately, I decided to cut this chapter from the book—rather early on—because the sub-story that it introduced simply wasn't what I wanted this book to be about. It didn't advance the main stories (Kevin and Megan's romance, Megan's health problems, and Kevin reuniting with his sister). So basically, I was left with a very well-written chapter that simply didn't belong in this book.

Writing this chapter was a challenge, but also a lot of fun for me. When I was a kid, I wanted to be an airline pilot when I grew up, which is the very reason the main character in this book is a pilot. But I never became a pilot. However, I've certainly spent many hours piloting a virtual aircraft in the form of a flight simulator computer game. I've also educated myself quite well on the principles of flight. Despite all of that, I still had to do a lot of research to write this chapter to create a believable and accurate account of what would actually happen during a situation like this.

Given my level of satisfaction with how it turned out, I decided to give this chapter its "moment in the sun" by including it as a special feature in this book. So I hope you enjoy reading it, but be sure to stay in your seat with your seat belt fastened! Sorry...I just had to say that!

Sunday, May 9th
Hotel room in Minneapolis, MN
8:54 p.m. (Central Time)

Touching down here in Minneapolis earlier tonight marked the end of my flying shift for the day, but also stirred up some memories I wish I could forget. As a pilot, my schedule seems to bring me here to Minneapolis quite often, even though I'm based in Chicago. Today was no exception. After starting out in Chicago, I flew to Atlanta, and then had a quick stop in Jacksonville, and then my final flight of the day brought me right here to Minneapolis, where I'll be spending the night.

It's a pretty nice city...but I suppose it should be referred to as "cities" not to leave out its "twin" city, St. Paul. But I confess I'm not the biggest fan of flying here in the winter because they get a lot of snow up here and I've certainly spent many long hours stuck in the airport during snowstorms waiting for the snow to stop and the runways to be cleared.

However, when I landed here tonight, snow wasn't the problem. As I expected, the biggest issue was the wind. A cold front moved through Minneapolis a few hours before I landed here and it ushered in plenty of wind, along with some chilly temperatures. In fact, it was only in the upper 30's when I landed, despite it being early May.

I was the pilot flying for that leg of the trip and the northwest winds proved to be quite substantial coming in for our approach. With each gust, I had to quickly counter steer to re-align for the runway. It was a bit of a rough ride with some rocking back and forth, but nothing too much out of the ordinary for landing in windy conditions. Thankfully, it ended up being a pretty smooth landing. But it's times like those when memories from December 17th come flooding back into my mind.

For any aviation enthusiast, like myself, December 17th is a very significant day in history. In 1903, it was the day of the Wright Brothers' first successful human flight. That day didn't *change* aviation, it *began* aviation. But after this most recent December 17th, that day is unfortunately etched into my memory for another reason.

As much as I would love to completely forget the most recent December 17th, and pretend it never happened, I know I never will. Just a mere four months ago, that day is when a very difficult season in my life began, and I found myself having to deal with something I never thought I'd encounter in my flying career. Even now, memories of that day quickly flash through my mind every time I'm cleared to land.

I remember it very clearly. I had one final flight to fly that evening from Minneapolis to Chicago. In Minneapolis, it was a cold and windy night—colder than tonight because I remember there were a few passing snow flurries. In Chicago, the weather forecast looked much worse. There was a Winter Storm Warning already posted and they were calling for snow to develop later in the evening. The snow would also be accompanied by strong winds—with gusts over fifty miles per hour—which were sure to create blizzard conditions.

Despite the approaching winter storm in Chicago, my flight still departed mostly on time because air traffic control calculated that we should arrive in Chicago before any of the precipitation would start...and before the winds would get too strong, even though they'd still be gusty.

Since the captain flew the previous leg of the trip, this one was mine to fly while he'd handle the radio communications. After they sprayed the wings with de-icing fluid before we left the gate, we taxied to the runway, and before we knew it, we were cleared for takeoff and had a smooth ascent out of Minneapolis. Little did we know that a series of events would unfold during the latter part of this flight that would quickly turn this routine flight into the most harrowing—and scariest—flying experience I've ever encountered.

~   ~   ~

After the majority of the flight went very routinely, I remember it was just as we entered the Chicago airspace that I began to realize this flight may not end normally. A good way into our descent, I tried to extend the wing flaps to prepare for landing, but the on-board monitoring system quickly threw a fault message back at me saying the right flaps were unable to extend. Obviously, it didn't let me extend the left ones either—not that I'd ever want to—because that would quickly send the aircraft into a continuous roll, like in an air show.

The captain immediately contacted air traffic control and told them the situation. Then he took control of the aircraft from me, since procedure states that in any situation like this, the captain should be the one flying the plane, since usually they're more experienced than the First Officer. That was certainly true in this case because he was in his late 50's and had been flying since before I was born.

To continue to follow procedure, we began to carry out the steps on the on-board monitoring system to attempt to fix the problem. Just as it said to do, the captain pulled then pushed the yoke to test the tail-wing elevator, then slightly wiggled the rudder, and tapped the spoilers. Thankfully, there were no fault messages after any of that, so at least those crucial parts of the aircraft were still working. But when he tried to deploy the flaps again, the same fault message reappeared. It was at that point, I remember feeling the stress and adrenaline beginning to build.

It's safe to say the captain and I were very surprised by all of this—shocked, actually. I'd never had anything like this happen during my flying career, and as he admitted, he hadn't either. Mechanical failures of this sort are extremely rare. The only explanation we could garner was that maybe there was ice accumulation on the wings, which could've frozen the flaps in place. But that still made no sense because even after the de-icing fluid wears off during flight, these planes have anti-icing systems that usually do a good job of preventing ice from forming on the wings. And we didn't get any fault message indicating *that* wasn't working.

Either way, trying to figure out how or why this happened was irrelevant right then. The reality remained that we had a tricky landing ahead of us. Thankfully, it's still possible to land an aircraft without deploying the flaps, but it has to be carried out differently than a normal landing. Since the flaps give you more lift at low speeds, without them extended, you have to approach and land at a higher speed to maintain good control of the aircraft and to prevent a mid-air stall, which happens if the aircraft loses lift and it basically falls from the sky.

Since we had this mechanical trouble and we'd be landing at higher than normal speeds, air traffic control classified this landing that we'd soon be making as a precautionary emergency landing. But after what happened next, it would soon be upgraded to a full emergency landing.

~   ~   ~

As our descent continued, the winds were getting worse. The flight went from being relatively smooth to being noticeably turbulent. But it was probably perceived as nothing more than a "bumpy flight" to the passengers...at least for now.

Not much later, air traffic control notified us that the Chicago airport had gone on ground stop because of snow affecting the visibility. So they were temporarily suspending all departures and arrivals, which definitely made things more complicated and stressful for us. By the way, the snow wasn't supposed to start until later in the evening, but apparently it had already begun falling. It was at that point I saw the captain getting noticeably stressed as he kept taking deep breaths, trying to calm himself.

Air traffic control gave us options to circle for a few minutes to see if the ground stop was lifted, divert to the other

Chicago airport that had notoriously short runways, divert to Milwaukee, or divert to Indianapolis. None of those were ideal options, but they were our *only* options, and the captain needed to make a decision quickly.

After a full minute of silence as he kept his hands on the yoke continuing on the flight path to land, I finally turned to him.

"So what do you want to do?" I asked. "We can't land here and they need a decision pretty quickly."

It was then when I noticed his breathing sounded irregular and labored. I took a closer look at him and I realized he'd become sweaty and pale and didn't look well. It seemed each one of his breaths was requiring great effort.

"What's wrong?" I asked.

He glanced over at me with a panicked look on his face. "I think it's my heart."

At that moment, it suddenly became clear to me that he was most likely having a heart attack. Even though all of us pilots undergo regular physicals, it's true that some heart attacks can come without warning, at any time—in this case, at a very inopportune time for the captain, and for everyone on board. But I stayed calm—at least on the outside—because I knew if showed too much concern, it would probably panic him even more. I knew I was no doctor but it didn't seem like a severe heart attack because he was still conscious, even though his breathing was definitely labored.

I immediately took control of the aircraft, since he was no longer in any condition to fly the plane. Then I got on the intercom and asked if there was a doctor or nurse on board. Unfortunately, no one came forward. So I called the flight attendants and one of them came into the cockpit to assess him. She took his pulse and gave him some aspirin. She asked him if he wanted to go back in the cabin to be more comfortable but he shook his head no.

His speech was interrupted by heavy breaths. "I'll be more help to Kevin...staying here...rather than...back in the cabin."

There wasn't much else we could do for him, since he was conscious and breathing. But before the flight attendant left to go back into the cabin, I told her to strap down in the jump seat just outside the cockpit. That way, if the captain lost consciousness, she'd be right there to perform CPR on him, since they're trained in that. So am I, but I needed to focus on flying and saving everyone else on board.

After she left and closed the door I looked over at him. "You're going to be just fine," I said, trying to portray a calm demeanor.

He looked back at me as he was now halfway lying in his seat. "I'm glad it's you...that's my copilot right now."

I nodded as that was certainly a compliment.

After that, I contacted air traffic control and let them know our captain was having a medical emergency. That was when the first good news of this situation came when they told me the snow squall that briefly plagued the airport had passed and they were opening the airport again. That's also when they upgraded this to a full emergency landing and cleared us to land by letting us "cut in line" ahead of all the other planes that were circling and waiting to land.

I told them we'd need an ambulance waiting at the gate when we arrived. After that, I refocused on the night sky in front of me and took a deep breath. At that point, I knew it was entirely my responsibility now to get all of the passengers and flight crew on the ground safely, despite the mechanical failure, adverse weather, and the captain's heart attack.

~ ~ ~

As I continued the latter part of our descent into Chicago, I knew it would only get bumpier as we got lower—especially now that I'd deployed the landing gear, which thankfully, deployed with no faults. I said a quick, silent prayer at that moment and asked God to protect everyone on the plane, to give me the ability to land the plane safely, and to be with captain until he gets the help he needs.

I then went on the intercom to notify the passengers that due to a mechanical issue we'd be approaching and landing at a higher speed and it could be a moderately rough landing. I then urged and insisted that they stay in their seats with their seat belts fastened. I didn't mention that the captain was having a heart attack because that would've sent widespread panic throughout the cabin.

I turned the plane to line up for the runway, and just moments later I pierced through the lowest layer of the clouds, which always creates turbulence. When we finally got below the clouds, I quickly realized snow was filling the air, but it wasn't too heavy because the visibility was still reasonable.

What I remember most from that point were the erratic and powerful wind gusts that made it a difficult job just to continue on course. My hands were tightly clenching the yoke and my heart was racing. Each gust blew the plane off course and I had to quickly jerk the yoke to re-align with the runway. That was causing the plane to rock from side to side and creating a pretty rough ride for the passengers—all while we were speeding through the sky at much higher than normal speeds to account for the flaps that didn't extend. Luckily the spoilers still worked because I certainly used them several times through this tricky descent.

Before long, we were on final approach and the runway lights were coming into view through the dark, snow-filled sky. I'd been going through this touch down in my head several times during the previous minutes. I knew I had to touch down as early as I could on the runway to have enough distance to stop, since I had to approach with such a high rate of speed— about 25 knots faster than a normal landing.

As I finally approached the runway, I felt the tenseness building even more in my whole body. I gently pulled back on the yoke to raise the nose, reduced the thrust, and tapped the spoilers. Before I knew it, the rear wheels set down hard on the runway. I made it a hard landing on purpose so I could touch down earlier on the runway, and also so the rear wheels could get some good initial grip in the wintry conditions. I then set down the front wheels, reversed the engines, threw the spoilers up all the way, and began applying the brakes.

With the engines roaring and plane slowing some, I remember seeing the low traction warning light flashing back at me. There only appeared to be a dusting of snow on the runway, but there must have been some ice underneath it, so the brakes weren't going to be much help.

Barely a few seconds later, I quickly realized the end of the runway was approaching and we might not stop in time. We were still going about 50 knots, which was scary with that being about 58 miles per hour.

In those crucial seconds, it briefly crossed my mind to hit the manual over-ride and intentionally lock the brakes in order to skid the aircraft to a stop. But that's usually a last resort maneuver because when you're on ice, the aircraft can skid anywhere and in any direction, and sometimes that can result in it rolling over.

Besides, I learned long ago it's always better to continue

controlling the aircraft's direction and heading no matter what, if it's at all possible. So I decided to be gentle with the brakes, keep the wheels straight and let the plane overshoot the runway and head into the overrun area.

I quickly came on the intercom. "Hold the seat in front of you and keep your heads down."

Ultimately, we ran a few hundred feet beyond the overrun area into the "grass," which at that point, was barren grass partially covered with snow. After a bumpy ride through the grass, the plane finally came to rest.

I contacted the tower but they said they already had fire trucks and ambulances on their way. They instructed me to shut down the engines and lock the brakes and then not touch anything else on the instrument panel after that.

I looked over at the captain. "Help is coming," I said.

He was still out of breath, but said. "I don't know if most copilots...could've done what you just did."

"I don't know," I said as I quickly unstrapped my harness and got up. I knew he was in no condition to help evacuate the passengers from the aircraft, so I went alone. When I emerged from the cockpit, many of the passengers applauded me. But for others, I saw the panic on their faces, heard kids crying and screaming, saw some adults crying, and saw some people praying.

"We're going to need everyone to go to the closest emergency exit," I yelled. Then I heard the inflatable exit slides inflating and people frantically began exiting. It was at that moment that I realized the severity of situation that had just occurred. After it sank into my mind for a few minutes I also began realizing how much worse it actually could've been. What if I would've locked the brakes in a desperate attempt to stop and the plane rolled over and this whole ordeal turned into a fiery crash? What if literally any other equipment would've failed on the aircraft that night and a controlled landing was no longer an option?

~   ~   ~

Before I knew it, there were more than a dozen fire trucks and ambulances surrounding the plane. The EMT's quickly climbed up the inflatable exit slide to tend to the captain. Otherwise, it didn't seem like anyone was injured. They closed the airport almost immediately after this happened and it remained closed for the rest of the night because of the blizzard. They also left the plane right where it came to a stop to investigate this incident.

They took the captain to the hospital and took me into a room for interviewing and wanted me to provide a full account of everything that had happened. After that, they gave me a drug and alcohol test, which I knew I had nothing to worry about with that, at least. We were both put on an indefinite leave of absence until they finished the investigation, even though the captain would be out on medical leave anyway because of his heart attack.

Not only was this incident scary because of the safety aspect and the fact that it could've had a very tragic ending, but it was also scary because there was a chance I might lose my pilot's license and I'd never be able to fly again. That thought was devastating to me. But I kept having to remind myself that I didn't do anything wrong. I did everything in my ability to get that plane full of passengers on the ground safely.

During the time I was waiting for them to finish their investigation, I spent a lot of that time at home. It was appearing on the local news channels and was all over the internet, which didn't make me feel any better. I visited the captain several times in the hospital in those days as well. Thankfully, it was a mild heart attack and his prognosis looked good.

When they finally finished the investigation, they first found that the cover that goes over the mechanical gears that control the movements for the flaps on the right wing, was damaged—possibly by a fuel truck or baggage truck on the ground. It caused one of the seams of the sheet metal to separate a little bit and when we took off in Minneapolis some moisture must have leaked through that separation and froze as we ascended into the frigid air aloft. The result was wing flaps with frozen gears that couldn't move.

They said the gap in the seam was quite small and there's no way we could've seen that during the pre-flight inspection. They called this a "very rare occurrence" as they had no record of this ever happening before.

As for my landing, they concluded that my approach speed was appropriate, given the fact that there were no working flaps. They also concluded my touch down point on the runway was not late—rather, it was advantageously early. Most of all, they concluded that stopping the plane before the end of the runway that night would've been impossible for any pilot because of the icy runway and higher landing speed. So they said all of my actions were within proper procedure and I was cleared to begin flying again, so that was a huge relief. The captain also returned to flying a few months later, but this time with a better diet and more exercise.

But an incident like that doesn't just disappear from your mind the next day. It truly changed me as a pilot...and as a person. As a pilot, it made me realize how much every passenger's life is in my hands each time I fly—even on the flights that feel like they're nothing but routine. Also, no matter how competent of a pilot I am, I'll never be fully safeguarded from something like that happening, even though it's rare for most pilots to encounter anything like this throughout their entire flying career.

As a person, it made me realize more than ever that my life is in God's hands and I need to fully trust Him. I realized if that night was the time, the place, and the way God had planned for me to leave this earth, there wasn't anything I could do to change that. But it obviously wasn't my time to go that night, so God must have "...[given] his angels charge over [me]..." as it says He can do in Psalm 91:11.[1] There are times I'm still amazed how I landed that plane in those conditions with no one getting injured and not even putting a scratch on the plane. But I really believe it was because of God's divine protection.

Anyway, I think it's time to bring this entry to a close on this windy and unseasonably cold night here in Minneapolis. After I've spent the last forty-five minutes typing this, it's times like these when I realize that I'll probably never be able to fully forget what happened on that fateful night. I really hope it's the only "incident" I'll have in my career, because I'd hate to think I'd have to go through something like that again. But if I do, I at least know that God is always with me.

♦ Notes/Footnotes ♦

CHAPTER 1

1. "To every thing there is a season, and a time to every purpose under the heaven:"

    —Ecclesiastes 3:1, King James Version (KJV)

CHAPTER 4

1. "Trust in the Lord with all thine heart; and lean not unto thine own understanding."

    —Proverbs 3:5, KJV

CHAPTER 5

1. "Rejoicing in hope; patient in tribulation; continuing instant in prayer;"

    —Romans 12:12 KJV

CHAPTER 6

1. "Behold the fowls of the air: for they sow not, neither do they reap, nor gather into barns; yet your heavenly Father feedeth them. Are ye not much better than they?"

    —Matthew 6:26 KJV

CHAPTER 7

1. "(For we walk by faith, not by sight:)"

    —2 Corinthians 5:7 KJV

CHAPTER 9

1. "Blessed is the man that trusteth in the Lord, and whose hope the Lord is."

    —Jeremiah 17:7 KJV

CHAPTER 10

1. "For he shall have judgment without mercy, that hath shewed no mercy; and mercy rejoiceth against judgment."

    —James 2:13, KJV

CHAPTER 11

1. "Knowing this, that the trying of your faith worketh patience."
   —James 1:3, KJV

CHAPTER 12

1. "This is the day which the Lord hath made; we will rejoice and be glad in it."
   —Psalm 118:24, KJV

CHAPTER 15

1. "We are troubled on every side, yet not distressed; we are perplexed, but not in despair;"
   —2 Corinthians 4:8, KJV

CHAPTER 17

1. "Let not your heart be troubled: ye believe in God, believe also in me. In my Father's house are many mansions: if it were not so, I would have told you. I go to prepare a place for you. And if I go and prepare a place for you, I will come again, and receive you unto myself; that where I am, there ye may be also."
   —John 14:1-3, KJV

CHAPTER 18

1. "Yea, though I walk through the valley of the shadow of death, I will fear no evil: for thou art with me; thy rod and thy staff they comfort me."
   —Psalm 23:4, KJV

CHAPTER 19

1. "Whereas ye know not what shall be on the morrow. For what is your life? It is even a vapour, that appeareth for a little time, and then vanisheth away."
   —James 4:14 KJV

CHAPTER 20

1. "One God and Father of all, who is above all, and through all, and in you all."
   —Ephesians 4:6, KJV

CHAPTER 20 (continued)

2. "And they that know thy name will put their trust in thee: for thou, Lord, hast not forsaken them that seek thee."
   —Psalm 9:10, KJV

3. "Seeing his days are determined, the number of his months are with thee, thou hast appointed his bounds that he cannot pass;"
   —Job 14:5, KJV

4. "In my Father's house are many mansions: if it were not so, I would have told you. I go to prepare a place for you."
   —John 14:2, KJV

5. "And if I go and prepare a place for you, I will come again, and receive you unto myself; that where I am, there ye may be also."
   —John 14:3, KJV

6. "For God so loved the world, that he gave his only begotten Son, that whosoever believeth in him should not perish, but have everlasting life."
   —John 3:16, KJV

7. "So when this corruptible shall have put on incorruption, and this mortal shall have put on immortality, then shall be brought to pass the saying that is written, Death is swallowed up in victory."
   —1 Corinthians 15:54, KJV

LOST CHAPTER

1. "For he shall give his angels charge over thee, to keep thee in all thy ways."
   —Psalm 91:11 KJV

✦ About the Author ✦

MARK RITTER lives in the Chicago suburbs and enjoys swimming and hiking in his free time. After building a career for himself in the corporate world, he then decided to put his long-time love for writing to work, and began crafting novels. His main goal with writing is to bring God's message of hope to anyone who reads his books.

Made in the USA
Columbia, SC
31 August 2020